Praise

Would I write an endorsement? The answer was no – endorsements aren't my thing – but then I read Daniel Myers' *Corporate Blue* and my mind was changed. The cocktail of clichés blended into every other endorsement you see are no good here – page turner, pushes the limits, can't put it down – these don't do it justice. It's all that and more, it's full of three dimensional characters who are his best to date, they pull you into a corporate world filled with humour and pain and make you seriously wonder who in the hell is manning those control towers!
– Paul Cleave, author of *The Cleaner* and *The Killing Hour*

Fasten your safety belts for a wild ride. In this sharp, mordant, persistently funny, outrageous and scary book, Myers has kicked the chocks out from under air traffic control and the corporate world. Myers writes straight out of today's headlines. After reading *Corporate Blue* you'll never want to fly again.
– Mike Johnson, author of *Counterpart* and *Stench*

It was Horace who wrote that 'poetry should delight and instruct.' This admonition should apply to all writing, and we certainly find it in Daniel Myers' second novel *Corporate Blue*. While one could easily be caught up in the page turning speed of the novel, it would be a disservice to the author to neglect its bombastic, comedic properties. *Corporate Blue* is very funny. So flip the pages, enter the world of air traffic control, and laugh out loud.
– Ben Greer, author of *Murder in the Holy City* and *Slammer*

Also by Daniel Myers

The Second Favorite Son

DANIEL MYERS

CORPORATE BLUE

A NOVEL

REED

For two men of true quality, and whom I admired very much
They were good controllers, good friends and are gone too soon

For Horse and Wingnut

Wayne McMillan
(1947 — 2001)

Kerry Campbell
(1947 — 2004)

This is a work of fiction. Some of the airports and locations really exist, while others such as Milton Gorge do not; however, all are used fictitiously. All the characters in this book are products of the author's imagination – any names or personality traits associated with these characters are not meant to represent any real person whether living, dead, or currently on the run from law enforcement. Any such resemblance would certainly be pure coincidence.

Established in 1907, Reed is New Zealand's largest book publisher, with over 600 titles in print.
www.reed.co.nz

Published by Reed Books, a division of Reed Publishing (NZ) Ltd, 39 Rawene Road, Birkenhead, Auckland 0626. Associated companies, branches and representatives throughout the world.

This book is copyright. Except for the purposes of fair reviewing, no part of this publication may be reproduced or transmitted in any form or by any means, electronic or mechanical, including photocopying, recording, or any information storage and retrieval system, without permission in writing from the publisher. Infringers of copyright render themselves liable to prosecution.

© 2007 Daniel Myers
The author asserts his moral rights in the work.

ISBN-13: 978 07900 1173 8
First published 2007

National Library of New Zealand Cataloguing-in-Publication Data
Myers, Daniel, 1958-
Corporate blue : a novel / Daniel Myers.
ISBN 978-07900-1174-5
I. Title.
NZ823.3—dc 22

Design by Suzanne Wesley

Printed in China

Acknowledgements

I once tried to explain to my brother-in-law what the writer's life was like: the many long, lonely hours typing away, foregoing real human contact in favour of a different world that existed only in my mind. Then the many months or years trying to find a publisher, all the while being rebuffed with letters and cards that have grown shorter and colder with the years. My brother-in-law nodded thoughtfully and was quiet for a moment before he summed up my life in a line; 'so, basically, writing is years of isolation followed by years of rejection.' He continued to nod thoughtfully as if this now fully explained my personality to him and, being a social worker, I'm sure he had a programme in mind for me.

My brother-in-law still looks at me and nods with sympathy to this day, even after letters of rejection turned into acceptance and the book I toiled over has brought together a group of very fine and talented people, too numerous to mention here even if I did remember all their names. They know who they are (and if you don't, my brother-in-law can get you into a programme). They are the team at Reed Publishing led by Sam Hill, and I am deeply grateful for their enthusiastic support and expert handling of my manuscript from its first draft to what you now hold in your hands. And a special thanks to my very good friend and long-time ally in writing, tramping, and tipping the odd pint back, Sean Cardell-Ryan who first brought it to Sam's attention.

All that I write is consistently made better by the feedback of those fellow writers willing to read and comment on early drafts. Dean Krystek, Wade Tabor, and Paul Cleave — who now must take the time out of his own rising literary career to give me his expert advice. Once again, guys, I owe you.

The technical advisors are also some of my closest friends and I am grateful for their assistance: in matters concerning air traffic control Grant Edge and Greg Kingery were of great help as was Captain John Dore for his extensive knowledge on airline procedures and operations of both B737s and B747s.

As always, I will be eternally thankful for the unwavering love and support of my Mom, my Dad and my whole family, none of whom have once brought up the suggestion of 'a real job' and have, at the very most, only offered an occasional shrug and a 'it could be worse, he could be writing for television.'

And finally, a special thanks to my many friends and colleagues in the air traffic control profession both past and present who steadfastly, and against overwhelming odds, manage to hold the safety margin strong against the onslaught of the profit margin.

Part One: The Good Ol' Days

One

My first day on the job with those nutcases, I was greeted by the loser's end of a very large handgun. A more intuitive man would have taken that as a sign to turn around and just walk away, to leave that place and never think of it again. It would have been the wise thing to do.

In my own defence, however, I could point out that I didn't have a lot of options as to where I could turn. The President of the United States, and what I imagine were his Homeland Security Goon Squad, among others, were pissed off with me and I didn't think I would be welcome back there any time soon. The best thing to do, I figured, was to lie low and make the best of a new situation in a new country. In time — a year max I figured — it would certainly all have blown over. Forgiven and forgotten. They would let me back in. They would let me come home.

The 'new country' was New Zealand. My 'new situation' right now was me looking into the gaping barrel of a particularly unforgiving looking weapon. Attached to the opposite end of the gun — the end with the trigger — was a gentleman who looked every bit the battle-scarred veteran gone off the deep end. It was not so much the hunting jacket, the military fatigue pants, the week of untrimmed beard, or the unkempt collar-length hair that gave that impression as the feral, hunted look in his eyes.

'This is about to be your worst day ever, flyboy,' he said through clenched teeth.

Raising my hands slowly, without making any sudden movements, I took a step back. 'Maybe I should go check in with security first,'

I said, though I had no idea where security was. Indeed, even by American standards, security here seemed a bit lax for an airport. The door at the base of the control tower was unlocked and I had just walked in.

There didn't seem to be much of a threat when I arrived. At barely 8.30 on a Monday morning the airport appeared lifeless. No wind, no airplanes taxiing, not a soul to be seen. The lingering patches of ground fog accentuated the stillness and, like the tumbleweed rolling through a ghost town, added that final touch of emptiness, of a place once filled with life now hollowed out and long forgotten by time.

I had considered the possibility that I was in the wrong place, that maybe this was just an abandoned airfield and the Milton Gorge Aerodrome I was looking for was farther down the road. This place looked like a throwback to the Second World War. Large Quonset hangars and wood-frame buildings, all weather-beaten from the years, lined the perimeter on three sides. The control tower, a sad looking structure from a bygone time, stood between the two huge runways that crossed in a lopsided X. Its wooden walls showed the marks of many years of neglect. A tattered, chequered flag hung limply from the pole on one corner of the roof.

The door was open, so I had walked in and, seeing nobody in the office downstairs, I had climbed the stairs to the next floor. The tower was not tall as far as control towers go. On the second floor were the ladies and gents toilets, and another room, a general-purpose area with a refrigerator, sink and cupboards to one side. On the opposite side was a table and some bookshelves filled with ancient, rotting binders, and an assortment of cheap looking paperbacks and magazines, the only cover of which I could read from my vantage point was for *New Zealand Pig Hunter*. I had continued up the stairs to the top floor — the tower cab. Except for the creak of the floorboards, there was not a sound — no hushed voices coming from the top of the stairs, no radio chatter. Again, I was convinced the place was deserted. A few steps from the top, just as I had peeked over the railing to get my first view inside

Milton Gorge Tower, I had found myself attracting the unwanted and sudden attention of a guy who looked like he wasn't interested in taking any hostages.

'Are you one of them?' the gunman asked me.

'No,' I said, not really sure to whom his 'they' referred, but reasoned that a psychopath would probably never consider 'them' as allies. 'I'm one of you, I think — possibly less violent, but definitely unarmed.' I glanced at his trigger finger, which I thought I had just seen twitch.

He narrowed his eyes and studied me as he held his aim for several long, disturbing moments. His eyes darted quickly to his right towards the door to the catwalk, and then back to me. The tension in his face relaxed slightly as he studied me for a moment longer. Then he made a sudden move to his right, kicked the door open, levelled the pistol at a building on the far side of the taxiway and fired.

The gun was a signal pistol used for firing flares and, in this case, bird-scaring cartridges that make a whirring noise until they explode with a loud bang at the end of their trajectory. The trajectory, again in this case, ended about fifty feet before the door to the building.

I eased myself down to a lower step, so I was just high enough to see the building through the window without making myself an exposed target of retaliation.

'I need to wake these bastards up in the morning,' he said, staring at the building, then turning his attention back to me, with a crooked smile and leaning back against the doorframe, pistol hanging loosely at his side.

'Who? Who do you need to wake up?' I asked in my calmest, most patronising impression of a hostage negotiator, as I stole a glance across the wide expanse of grass and tarmac. Through the thin puff of smoke that briefly hung in the air in the spot where the cartridge had exploded, a couple of men dressed in the blue uniform of flight instructors emerged from the front door of what I now decided was a flying school and began waving their arms, gesturing rudely and yelling something in the direction of the tower. Although distance made their words indistinct, even in the silent, still morning air, their meaning was obvious. I ducked down so they could not see me and inched my way down yet another step.

'I don't think those guys liked your wake-up call.'

'They never do,' he said. 'Never mind. By tonight I'll have bought them a round at The Tie Down and they'll have forgotten all about it.' He glanced back at the gathering mob of instructors and grinned. 'Until tomorrow morning, that is.'

'You do that often?'

'Sometimes,' he said. 'After all, we are supposed to test the signal pistol on a regular basis.'

'I see,' I said, nodding as I glanced down the stairs, wondering whether I should just leave before I became any more involved.

'He's still mad about his car,' the gunman added without encouragement.

'What car?'

'Brandon, the short guy on the left,' he pointed out one of the five or six people still making rude gestures towards the tower. 'I set his car on fire a few months ago,' he explained, shaking his head. 'It was an honest mistake, if you know what I mean.' He winked at me as if I knew what he meant. 'You're tired after a ragged night and you reach for the wrong cartridge. You load a flare instead of a bird cartridge. Next thing you know … kaboom!'

'Kaboom?'

'Haven't you ever made that mistake?'

'Well, no, I haven't, but we never used …'

'Well, that's what makes you a better controller than me, mate. You would probably have known the flares have a longer trajectory. Anyway,' he glanced down, looking almost melancholy for a moment, then shrugged, 'Christ, it was only a Corolla. And he had to go and have it painted that awful pea-green colour. God, what an eyesore! So,' he turned his attention back to me and, still holding the pistol, folded his arms across his chest, 'I can see by your outfit that you are a cowboy,' he said in a poor mimic of my

American accent and in reference to a song I wouldn't expect any New Zealander to know, 'which means you must be our cowboy.'

'My name's Tom Hardy,' I took a step up and leaned over, cautiously offering him my hand, unsure if that was a good idea.

'I'm Flynn.' He switched the pistol to his left hand and gave my hand a quick shake.

'I'm a controller, I was supposed to —'

'I know who you are. We were expecting you months ago.'

'There was red tape — getting a visa and all that. I came as fast as I could.'

'So the only question left is: Are you in or are you out?'

'I beg your pardon?'

'Were you hired before or after the big change? The big "switcheroo" as you would say.'

'I don't think I've ever said "switcheroo".'

'It makes a difference, you see. I mean, we were expecting you a while back.'

I had no idea what this guy was talking about. Without having to overtax my ability at logic, I could have told him without looking that it was his own Civil Aviation Authority that had hired me — it wasn't like there was going to be more than one government agency hiring controllers. Maybe he wanted to know the name of the person who signed the letter, but even that seemed a trivial matter. I patted myself down until I located the letter in my back pocket, extracted it and held it out to him. As I guessed, it was from the Civil Aviation Authority offering me a position at Milton Gorge Aerodrome.

'Hmmm, CAA.' Flynn shook his head. 'That's not good.'

'Why not?'

'It was before the New World Order.'

'The New World what?'

He handed the letter back to me and grinned. 'Ah well, no worries, mate. She'll be right.'

'Who will? Do you know something I don't know?'

Flynn shrugged. 'Not me. They never tell me anything around

here. Anyway, welcome to the end of the line. Welcome to Exile Tower.'

'Is this Milton Gorge Tower? Maybe I misread the directions.'

'It's Milton Gorge, mate,' he said, but his attention was distracted elsewhere. Something had caught his attention, something like a voice inside his head that no one else could hear. It was the way he cocked his ear up towards the open door — the flight instructors had all wandered back into their building, so it wasn't them. Then he slowly turned his attention to the sky and squinted.

'No fucking way,' he said. 'Not today, you old son-of-bitch.'

I looked at the spot that had drawn his attention and then I saw it too — an elongated spot on the sky, hard to see in the glare of the sun, but I had spent enough years of my life looking for tiny specks in the sky to take notice. I couldn't make it out. It had to be an airplane, perhaps just passing by, en route elsewhere. But there was something wrong. It did not appear to be moving, but growing. Then I squinted into the glare. Not one airplane, but two, three, maybe more.

Aside from being an air traffic controller, I had once been a pilot and flight instructor. In the cockpit, there is a moment — the briefest of all moments — for which the pilot must always be ready. If an observed target appears to move forward through the pilot's field of vision, the observer will pass behind the target. If the target appears to move backwards, the observer will pass ahead. The target that appears stationary is on a collision course, and that sort of target is the most difficult to spot because of its lack of motion. In that brief moment of realisation that the spot in the sky is not a speck on the windscreen but another aircraft on a collision course, there is often only that single moment in which to make a decision and take evasive action.

Fortunately, control towers do not travel through space and, thus, the rate of closure is fully dependent on the airspeed of one object and not two. Unfortunately, a control tower cannot take evasive action. My attention was fully focused on the ever-increasing target and not on Flynn, who had yanked open a desk drawer and was fumbling with more cartridges — bird or flare I had no idea.

One, two, three, four — four aircraft descending steeply out of the early morning, and they were closing rapidly in on the control tower.

I took a step closer to the window with my eyes fixed on the target. 'Are we under attack?'

'Battle stations!' Flynn said as he slammed the cartridge home and headed out to the catwalk. Apparently controllers here, however, can take defensive action.

I do not consider myself a coward by any means. However, I am not an idiot either. Whatever those aircraft had in mind, the exposed tower cab was not the place to be. I decided it was more prudent to make my exit from Exile Tower with the utmost of haste, and leave these guys to fight their own fights. As the thunder of the aircraft engines grew louder, I left Nutcase number one to deal with them his own way — out on the catwalk with a flare gun — and I was halfway down the stairs when I ran into Nutcase number two.

'What?' I paused. I could see his eyebrow twitch. Somehow I got the feeling this guy sitting across the glass-topped desk didn't believe me.

'I didn't say anything,' he said and gave me a smug smile, which I took to mean that if he didn't say something, then I was too stupid to pick up on the nuances of a raised eyebrow.

'Well, what then? You told me to start at the beginning.'

'Yes, I guess I did — but, well, what you're talking about happened a long time ago — almost two years, if I'm not mistaken. We're here to discuss the more recent events of the night of 17 February.'

'Too early then?'

'Maybe — but then again, maybe not. Maybe you could tell me more about your life before New Zealand. Before you left America. Why was the President angry with you?'

'Forget it.'

'Do you feel persecuted by people in power?'

'It wasn't the President personally, okay? I got in trouble with his plane, Air Force One, and the people who had entrusted me with its safety. Forget it.'

'Okay,' he shrugged. 'So where were we? You were running away.'

'Yeah, I was running away. And it was a habit I was trying to break.'

Two

Freddie Moore stepped into the elevator and pushed the button for the eighth floor, glad he was alone and glad there was a mirror — it gave him the opportunity to do a quick check on his appearance. The all-important first self-impression was good. He made a minor adjustment to the expensive silk tie he had grabbed off the rack in haste only ten minutes earlier. The tie was a good match to his dark blue suit and gave him a solidly conservative look. Despite being rushed, he still had enough taste to steal the right tie. He practised his 'confident-but-not-too-cocky' smile and checked his teeth for remnants of the Egg McMuffin. He didn't really have to steal ties from menswear stores any more. He just liked keeping in practice — it was like a game, and he liked playing.

In his youth, Frederick Templeton Moore III hated his name as much as he hated his poverty. But he learned to tolerate the former when he discovered how it could be used to alleviate the latter. It was all about having the right attitude. At the time he was living outside Toronto at the Scarborough Home for Youthful Offenders — better known to the local citizens as 'Scarberia', and to the teenage inmates as the SHITs — an acronym that was supposed to stand for the Scarborough Home for Incorrigible Teens, but the management of the facility refused to cooperate on the renaming issue. He was still embarrassed that he had been sent to that bleak place for the most blue-collar of all teenage crimes — stealing cars. The very thought of sinking so low brought a momentary twinge and a flicker to his otherwise easy smile. But that was the end of his days as a lowly car thief. Leave the petty stuff to the deadbeats, the punks, the losers and the blue-collar schmucks, as his old man used to call them. Of course his old man was one of the biggest losers around, a petty criminal whose greatest talent was for getting caught. Indeed, the mere fact that he 'emigrated' to Canada from his native Detroit was the only time he ever really got away. What his old man was running from Freddie never knew. Their relationship was not exactly the kind you see in real estate adverts on the suburban idyll. Most of his conversations with his father were limited to visiting hours, and the only three pieces of wisdom he could remember his father passing on to him were: 'The world's full of chumps — don't be another,' and, 'Listen up, kid — whatever you do, don't ever get caught.' That last one said with a glass partition between them.

The third, Freddie had to figure out for himself.

Alfie Moore was wise enough to advise Freddie never to get caught — it was just a shame he wasn't smart enough to know how to avoid getting caught himself. Fortunately, Freddie was smarter than his old man and, while Alfie fulfilled his station in life, Freddie decided on his. His station, his destiny, was among a much higher class of people.

While at Scarberia, he got an education and began a transformation that would take him from Fast Freddie the teenage car thief to his proper and full potential. He learned everything he could from every inmate there. He learned to talk fast and to talk smooth and he never once had to use his fists to prove himself. It was around that time that he first understood why a petty crook by the name of Alfie Moore could label a scrawny little kid with as outlandish a handle as 'Frederick Templeton Moore III'. But the old man had a bit of sense after all, if only a bit. He made up the 'Templeton' and tacked on the 'III' because he thought it made him sound classy. And what Freddie finally came to understand to be the most valuable piece of unspoken wisdom from his old man was to become Freddie's motto for life: 'It's not who you are that counts, but who they *think* you are.'

Freddie brushed his fingers lightly across his hair to tidy it up. Should have got a haircut, he thought. He was just glad he still had his hair past forty. He stepped back and took one last glance over his whole presentation before the doors opened. It was still good — he was tall, but not imposing, his dark hair was flecked with the right amount of grey to offset his boyish good looks, and his thickening middle made him look successful.

The elevator doors opened and revealed the reception desk with an attractive woman sitting behind it. Freddie liked beautiful women well enough, but what immediately caught his eye was the stainless steel corporate logo that adorned the wall behind her. 'ControlCorp' it said. Both the Cs dipped and swooped down under the other letters, suggesting a pair of jets tracing contrails in the sky, the polished silver letters on a field of blue. To Freddie Moore, that was beauty, and he had no doubt that it would soon be his logo, his company. When that day came, he would have the receptionist as his mistress, just because she looked so good under the corporate logo.

'Hello, sweetheart,' he said to her with a warm smile that would disarm any offence she might take to his greeting, as it always did. 'I'm Frederick Templeton Moore.' He leaned in close to her. 'The third,' he added with a wink, as if it meant they had finally perfected Frederick Templeton Moores.

'Yes, Mr Moore,' she responded with her own smile that contained the faintest suggestion of an extracurricular interest and wonderment at what the first two Frederick Moores must have been like. 'We've been expecting you. Welcome to ControlCorp. I'll let them know you're here.' She picked up the phone.

Freddie stepped into the warm sunlight flooding through the tinted window and looked at the view from the eighth floor lobby. The sun shone on Wellington like a jewel waiting to be uplifted from its lonely place in the jeweller's case and wrapped warmly and lovingly in his fist. It would be his city, his company, his mistress. There was so much opportunity here he could taste it. This was a new beginning for him. He had finally found his place. To hell with practising law. This, the corporate world, was his destiny.

He didn't regret putting himself through law school. Most of it was just a lot of work doctoring the necessary records. Forgery had been one of the many 'unofficial' night classes he had excelled in back in Scarberia. He knew the law well enough to sail through with no problems and, although he wasn't too thrilled about being disbarred last year, he could see now that it was all for the better. At least he was able to deal himself out of doing time.

He smiled to himself, a cell door closes and a window opens. To hell with the law. All he had to do with ControlCorp was play his cards right, be patient, keep a high profile at the right time, a low profile at other times, and always know what time it was. It was going to be a breeze getting in good with these poor stupid, civil-service-trained chumps.

'Hello, Freddie.'

Freddie turned to the sound of the familiar voice.

Speak of the devil, hello chump. He smiled and reached out his hand, 'Why, hello, Carlton. It's so good to see you again.'

Carlton Woodcock was a short, mousy-faced guy with big glasses hanging on his mousy little nose and a disproportionately large, square forehead. He looked at Freddie's outstretched hand and reluctantly gave it a quick, limp shake.

Woodcock was several years younger than Freddie and his past was uninspiring. He went to school and studied hard — had a BSc in chemistry of all things, then switched to business and worked even harder for an MBA. He had a disturbing mean streak in him — the kind that liked frying bugs with magnifying glasses on summer days — but lacked the spine, cunning and charm to be a really good confidence man.

He should have stuck with the chemistry, Freddie thought. Only chumps sat around and waited to get what they deserved, which invariably they did, and it was squat. You had to take what you deserved. Freddie was clever enough to do that, but someone like Woodcock was only smart enough to attach himself like a leech to more talented men. He was the good ol' reliable 'Number 2', the guy who did the dirty work, a professional sidekick.

Freddie had no doubt why Woodcock had brought him into

ControlCorp, and why Woodcock had encouraged the Board to support and swallow whole Freddie's curriculum vitae. Woodcock knew what the score was: regardless of their job titles, there was a pecking order, a 'master–disciple' relationship to be honoured.

Woodcock was used to it; they had worked together before. When Freddie first arrived here in this new land of opportunity several years earlier, Woodcock had been a steerer for him, directing pigeons towards Freddie's real estate investment venture. At least it had paid off his student loans from business school. Of course, when it all turned to shit, Woodcock did a bloody good disappearing act. Freddie himself was struck off, but it was a small price to pay. They made some money, had a good time. To hell with the law.

'I'll show you to your new office,' Woodcock nodded down the hall, carpeted in thick, blue plush. 'They've given you a better office than mine.'

'Just a humble little cubicle will do,' Freddie said with smile.

'The Board was impressed, Freddie,' Woodcock said as they started to walk. 'You must be especially proud of that little piece of fiction you call a CV.'

'Fiction is only a more potent truth, Carlton. I'm sure the Board just recognised talent.'

'Yeah, I'll put your name in for the Montana Book Awards. You really played up the overseas experience.'

'Hey, I've been to nearly all those places.'

'That, and an MBA since last year?'

'You want to see it?'

'But don't you think "Corporate Reformer" might have been pushing it a bit? And how the hell did you manage the article in *The Business Times?*'

'I didn't say it was from *The Business Times*? I think I said it *should have* been run there.'

'I see — another fabrication to add to your portfolio,' Woodcock huffed.

'Don't know what you're talking about.' Freddie put his hand on Woodcock's shoulder and patted it gently. 'Remember what I taught you, Carlton.'

Woodcock twitched at Freddie's touch and shook him off. 'Let's see now: "Never admit to anything; leave someone else's fingerprints — oh, and call your mum once a week."'

'No, no, Carlton — "Know your audience."'

'You mean, know that they are either too busy, too old or too close to being indicted themselves to worry about background checking?'

'Oh, don't make it sound so cynical, Carlton. I was only highlighting my strengths. You know, sarcasm doesn't suit you. If I didn't know better I could get the impression you were not completely thrilled to see me here.'

'Well, I'm responsible for bringing you here, aren't I?' Woodcock paused, looked up at Freddie, then let out a snort through his little mousy nose — a habit, Freddie was reminded, that was especially irritating and betrayed the kid's vulgar origins. 'I guess I'm just a little worried, Freddie. Yes, we need you here to do your thing, exploring the commercial opportunities side. But this is also the best break I've ever had. This is legit, and the best chance to make a mark in the business world. I want you to promise you won't get carried away. This is a business with huge potential, and all legally exploitable.'

'Which is why you brought me in as your Manager of Commercial Operations.' Freddie gave Woodcock's shoulder a gentle squeeze. 'And don't think I'll forget you for opening the door for me.'

'All I'm saying is don't get —'

'Carlton, please. You insult me. You brought me in because I'm the best man for the job. And, like you said, there's so much potential. What do you think I'm going to do — steal pens from the stationery cupboard?'

'If that's all you do …' Woodcock paused, stared at Freddie for a moment, then let out another little snort in resignation.

'That's my boy.' Freddie smiled.

'Here's your office.'

Freddie entered slowly, savouring the moment of crossing the threshold into his new office, his new world, and the lair from which to rule it — a corner office no less.

He suppressed a smile, simply nodding his approval instead. To one side there was a sofa, chairs and wet bar for entertaining important visitors and 'relaxing' with the secretary, to the other, the business end. He walked behind the desk and admired the view from his eighth floor office, again nodding his approval of the diamond-like sparkle Wellington had on a sunny day. He could see the waterfront which, unlike the smelly port back home, was an ocean port with the clean, sticky smell of salt air and water a person could swim in without having to worry about dead fish or toxic waste.

'It'll do,' Freddie said, finally turning back to Woodcock.

'Corner office,' Woodcock grunted. 'I wanted this office.'

'Commercial opportunities, Carlton my boy. That's why they put me here. My job will be to impress big shots from the outside. Besides,' he sank into the smooth leather chair and had to resist the urge to let out a sigh of orgasmic satisfaction with its gentle caress, 'you're always welcome in here.' He motioned Woodcock to the seat opposite. 'This is where you and I will spend many long hours turning this two-bit operation into a formidable corporate power.'

Woodcock flopped into the chair. 'Yeah, well, before you start restructuring your kingdom, keep in mind they're waiting for us in the boardroom. They've laid out a little spread for morning tea in there.'

'Good, I'm starving.' Freddie clasped his fingers behind his head, leaned back and gazed into the soft, fluorescent lighting. 'Just a couple things I thought we could go over before we meet everyone else.'

'Yeah?' Woodcock glanced at his watch.

'Well, just one thing really. You know, it's all been such a whirlwind: the headhunting, preparing the CV, the interviewing, flying here, flying there, meeting the Board. There are a few things I haven't had a chance to get caught up on.' He glanced at Woodcock. 'You know, just some background business info.'

'Well, they'll catch you up on the details over the next few days,' Woodcock shrugged.

'Yeah, the details.' Freddie leaned forward and bent across his desk, lowering his voice. 'But generally speaking ... what is it ControlCorp actually does?'

When Woodcock squinted, it made him look like a near-sighted mouse and was just as unbecoming as his little snort. 'You're kidding?'

'I mean, just out of general interest,' Freddie shrugged nonchalantly. 'Ultimately, business is business — it doesn't matter what they actually do. They hired me for my business expertise. I don't care if we make airplanes or garbage can lids.'

'We don't make anything. We're the sole provider of air traffic control to the entire country and a sizeable chunk of the Pacific — a service that was previously provided by a government department.'

'Oh, a service industry! That's even better — no suppliers to deal with. And the traffic controller is the guy with the orange torches?' He motioned his hands in a backward wave of his fists.

'No, not the guys on the tarmac. These are the guys on the radio, in the tower, behind the radar screens — you know, air traffic controllers. They're professionals, they're well paid, they're arrogant and they're unionised.'

'All minor points to be dealt with, one at a time. Okay, I'm ready.' Freddie slapped his leather armrests. 'Let's get to that little reception, Carlton.' He stood up and paused as he took a deep breath and put his hand on his heart. 'Yes, sir, aviation's been a secret passion of mine since my childhood. Oh, no, I don't regret having to give up those dreams of pursuing a career as an air controller for one moment when my father was killed. My mother and my little sister needed me to be working.'

'Christ,' Woodcock snorted as he pushed himself upright and followed Freddie out the door, 'I think my ulcer is flaring up again.'

Three

The roar of the engines of four T6s and a DC3 cranking up so early in the morning might have bothered a neighbour or two, but it was not an unusual sound coming from this airport. In a semi-rural area like this, the noise seldom drew any complaints from those who had already been hard at work since daybreak. It was only unusual in the fact that it was occurring on a Monday morning instead of a Saturday or Sunday, when all those old Warbirds got together for a play for old times' sake. And the noise was earlier than normal, as the Warbirds usually gathered later in the afternoon, so they could finish up in time to head for The Tie Down to relive that flight and a thousand others.

They had lifted off at 0750 that morning — ten minutes prior to the tower opening, so they were reasonably certain there would be nobody in the tower cab to notice their departure. Even if the controller was in the tower, he or she was probably downstairs in the equipment room setting up the tape machine that would record the frequencies and all that would be said that day. The great roar of the formation flight departure would have been out of the ordinary, but not so much as to cause concern.

The four T6s took off in a staggered formation first, and as they stirred up the thin patches of ground fog and rose into the crisp, clean blue sky of the new day, the DC3 with its special cargo took up the rear. They climbed out steep and high and were soon too distant to be seen or heard as the ground fog settled back into stillness.

They called themselves the Wild Blue Squadron and had a long roster of ageing pilots who would sign up for the weekend formation training. Only the best of them would actually get to perform at air shows, but they all got a chance at the practice flights and the formation training every Saturday or Sunday afternoon, weather permitting.

Today was not a practice run, however. Today they were going into a battle that had been planned to the last detail. It involved an early morning departure, then forming up over the harbour and doing a little precision work until the allotted time arrived: 0845 hours. It was the exact time at which, after cutting a wide circle around to the east, they would approach the airport from directly out of the rising sun. A surprise attack.

Blue Leader circled far to the east to position the squadron between the target and the sun so the unsuspecting enemy would not see them until it was too late. Their mission: neutralise the enemy airfield at Milton Gorge, and take out the enemy control tower, with minimum casualties. Many of their friends were being held captive on the ground — held captive by landing fees, fuel taxes and, now, new charges for air traffic services being provided by an enemy that had taken over the airfield in a brutal and unwarranted assault on their peaceful home.

The Squadron Leader pressed the little red button on his stick with his thumb. 'Okay men, tighten up,' he said to the other three aircraft that were inching their way into position. 'Blue two, bring it in closer.'

'Roger, Blue Leader.'

'Blue Leader to Dakota Blue. Are you in position?' the Squadron Leader asked the fifth member of the strike force, the DC3 flying somewhat lower and closer in. If all went as planned, the second the four T6s of Blue Squadron crossed the control tower on their strafing run at eight hundred feet, the DC3 would be arriving from east-northeast, and crossing their flight paths just behind at one thousand five hundred to deposit its payload. The T6s would break left, over the DC3, which would then position itself number five and depart the area until a damage assessment could be made.

Their objective was simple: strike hard, strike fast and be

gone before the enemy had a chance to know what hit them. It was routine. Most of them had been doing this for many years, although these days it was more difficult to tell the enemy apart. Friend looked like foe. Except for the uniform, the enemy dressed in blue suits. But that was enough to the old men of the Wild Blue Squadron. Their eyes may not have been as sharp, their senses not as keen, but their trigger fingers were just as quick.

They pulled into formation and from then on moved as one aircraft. Only Blue Leader had the target airfield in sight. Each man to his right kept his eyes glued to the wing of the man to his left. The fourth plane in line was Blue 4, Amos Scuffield. There was something he had not told his comrades in the briefing room that morning — this was to be his last flight. Even this flight was illegal. The doctor had pulled his medical the day before; he was grounded permanently. Amos Scuffield had been diagnosed with cancer of the liver. After this flight, he would no longer fly with the men of Wild Blue Squadron. His flying days were forever over.

He had been flying since he hit puberty sixty years ago. He didn't know how not to fly. It was in his blood; it permeated his very soul. When he rested on the front porch of his house in the afternoon, he never watched the passers-by on the road; his eyes and thoughts were on the sky. That's where he lived and without it he would die for sure. That's why he decided not to mention it to the boys in Wild Blue Squadron. He didn't want their pitying eyes glancing at him sideways, and he didn't want to hear about the passing of an era and the fact that he was the last pilot in the squadron who had been in the war — the big one — and got in on the tail end of the action in the Pacific theatre. He could still keep his plane tucked in close behind Blue 3; his hand was still as steady. By right of seniority, he could have been Blue Leader. But he opted for the fourth position, as it suited his plan better. He was not ready to give up what meant everything to him, and he was damned sure he was not going to spend the next year or so rotting away on the ground, in a hospital ward smelling of antiseptic and remembering what used to be. Wild Blue Squadron's plan was simple. His was more so.

'All right, men,' Blue Leader announced. 'We're going in.' He nudged the nose of his aircraft over, keeping his target centred right above the nose.

Wild Blue Squadron approached the field boundary at eight hundred feet. They levelled off for their fly-by. That went exactly according to plan, but then Blue 4 commenced his own 'Plan B'. He keyed his mike and transmitted a message. 'Blue four dropping out. I'm going in alone.' And without waiting for a reply, he pushed his nose down and dipped out of the formation. There was a jumble of confused transmissions. Blue Leader thought at first Blue 4 had had engine failure and was making an emergency landing, but in a millisecond it sank in — Blue 4 was Amos Scuffield. He had long been concerned about Amos's mental capacity. It was time for the man to retire, but he had not had the heart to do it. Flying was everything to Amos.

'Blue Four! No!' Blue Leader yelled into his mike, but there was so little time. He did not know in the split second that remained what could be said to make Amos Scuffield divert from whatever he was intending to do. He pulled back on his stick and brought the remainder of his squadron up to two thousand feet, and held his breath.

Amos had only one objective — he was going to destroy the control tower by flying right through it. Maybe it was not the most efficient way to remove the building, but it would certainly make his point. Sure, there would be fatalities — his was already sealed in a lab report at his doctor's office. And the others that were doomed to die that day worked for the same government that was taking his wings away. All these old windbags at Wild Blue Squadron thought they would make a difference by pulling off this silly little stunt, an unapproved fly-by, a buzz and break, the DC3 dumping a couple of hundred pounds of flour on the tower — all in protest against the privatisation of their airfield and the proposed new charges that were to be levelled at the flying public.

Silly old men, Amos had thought, pretending to be fighter

pilots. No one would take notice of their flaccid complaint. It was like spitting on the beach to protest the ocean. If they wanted to make a difference they needed to leave a gaping, bleeding, open wound, a scar that would last. And who better for the job? He had reasons to be rid of that building, reasons that went back to a time when most of these old blowhards were waiting for their testicles to drop. He dropped his plane down almost to the deck and pulled it level with the tower cab. They were a bunch of old men full of hot air. Only he was willing to take the action that would get someone to take notice. His hands tightened on the stick; he did not breathe; his eyes were locked on the target.

Amos Scuffield was the last remaining active pilot who had been with the squadron in Bougainville. Of the rest of the active roster, most of them spent their weekdays sitting in the cockpits of 747s pushing the autopilot button and the flight attendant call button for coffee refills. None of them had known what he had known tangling with the Japs in the skies over New Guinea. On the ground, it was like living in hell, with the heat, the malaria and the misery. The only place to escape it was the air, where the Japs fought with a fierceness he had never expected. They were relentless, never letting up. And, for all that misery, they were the best days of his life. He was where he was supposed to be for the only time in his life. He was an airborne warrior tasting the total freedom of flight, the pure adrenaline of the fight, the camaraderie. The best friend he ever had in his life, the only friend, was a wild young man named Arthur Capstone. Together, Cappy and he ruled the skies; no one dared challenge their authority. They were young and insanely brave. They were invincible — or so they thought. Then, in an instant, Cappy disintegrated in a ball of flame off Amos's wing one day, hit by enemy fire. None of these button-pushing old farts had seen their best friends disappear in fire off their wing.

His eyes were totally focused on the target. He did not blink. Estimated time of impact, about two seconds. 'It's taps for you ol' Rumbold,' he whispered.

On the catwalk that ran along the outside of the tower cab,

he could see someone standing there defiantly, holding … what was that he had in his hand? A gun? A flare pistol? Good Lord, what was the man thinking? That he could put a nasty scorch in the plane as it obliterated the building? Was he so foolish as to think that thing would do anything but bounce off his plane at this speed? Was he such a fool? Or was he insanely brave enough to know he had no time left and no other choice but to stand and fight with whatever he had?

Then there was that moment. He locked eyes with the madman on the catwalk with the flare pistol. He knew that boy. It was Flynn. He didn't like him much; he was rude, wild, unpredictable and foolishly unflappable enough to try to stare down a T6 at full throttle. He was Cappy. He wasn't Amos's enemy, merely a foot soldier caught on the wrong side. If only it had been Rumbold out there, it would be easy. But that traitorous pencil-pusher probably wasn't even in the building at this hour of the morning.

Amos jerked his hand back and flicked the nose just high enough to clear the roof of the tower, his wingtip clipping the limp chequered flag off, then banked hard to the left as he flew into the cloud of flour being dropped from the DC3 only a couple hundred feet above him. With another flick of his wrist, he banked it hard right to avoid the other T6s reforming to the south of the airfield for their landing and flew off into the morning sky, destination unknown. He needed some time to think about things, to reflect on life, death, war and courage and the willingness to die for causes.

No one in Wild Blue Squadron tried to persuade Amos to come back in as he flew off into the morning light, barely clearing the tops of the green hills and then disappearing beyond.

'Chicken shit! Chicken shit! Come back and try that again!' was all the flight instructors and students could make out as they ran out on to the lawn as the booming noise of the high-speed fly-by receded. 'Scuffield, you chicken shit! Come back and try me again,' was what they all agreed they thought they heard, but the sound was slightly muffled by the swirling cloud of what at first looked to be smoke, but, judging by the rate it was settling, could only have been flour. The shadowy figure of Flynn continued yelling 'chicken shit' and waving his flare pistol long after Amos Scuffield's plane had disappeared from sight.

Fearing that Flynn's gun might still be loaded, and considering the remaining cloud of flour dust that was slowly drifting in their direction, the group decided to retreat to the safety of the indoors. Brandon stayed behind, and with his hands pushed deep into his pockets he began to laugh. 'Burn, baby, burn.'

FOUR

'Amanda and I were literally thrown into each other's arms from the very beginning.'

'How's that?'

'It was like an earthquake. She was just starting up the stairs from the second floor with an armful of books, and I was coming down. This plane came so close to hitting the tower it shook the whole building like an earthquake. She dropped her books and I tripped over the last step and ended up in her arms. It was like the earth had thrust us together.'

'You liked her?'

'Yeah, for the first week. But she had that dangerous quality of appearing utterly normal on first meeting, yet being completely insane. A first impression would only tell you that she was an astonishingly attractive, intelligent, confident woman.' I glanced across at the guy. He seemed only mildly interested, with his heavily lidded eyes and emotionless expression. He looked like he could doze off at any minute. 'It was all part of her deception, you see; she was attractive in the same way a black widow spider must look to her doomed mate. She was a dominatrix in civilian clothes.'

'You were attracted to her?'

'At first, maybe. Sure, why not? She had all the right parts in the right places. And there was something magnetic about her. Seductive. In any case, I seem to go for strong women. Janey, my ex-wife, was like that.'

His eyebrow twitched again. 'So, you were married in the States?'

'Yeah.'

'And now?'

'Divorced.'

He nodded thoughtfully, then asked, 'And how would you have described your marriage?'

'It was like a fairy tale,' I said.

'Good?'

'Grimm.'

✈

'I'm Amanda Sheppard,' she said, still in my arms and looking straight into my eyes. She had long, blonde hair, clear, blue eyes and graceful, if not slightly sharp, features.

'Tom Hardy,' I said, then suddenly realising we were still embracing I decided to do the gentlemanly thing and release her instead of doing the instinctive thing and kissing her beautiful mouth.

'Oh yes, you're our cowboy.'

'I'm a controller.'

'So I heard.' She offered her hand, which was warm, soft, and, though gentle, quite firm. 'It's good to meet you at long last. We've heard so much about you.' Then she bent down and started gathering up her books and I followed her down into a squatting position to lend a hand.

'*Business Administration*?' I asked, looking at the title I picked up.

'Yes, I'm doing a business degree at university. I have no intention of being left behind.' She started up the stairs and I could not help but notice her beautifully sculpted and expertly manoeuvred legs. I was thoroughly impressed. Amanda Sheppard knew the power of presentation.

'Left behind by what?' I asked, my eyes fixated on her own behind so gently shifting back and forth under her skirt like the ebb and flow of a gentle surf as she led me by the eyeballs back up the stairs into the tower cab.

Flynn was just coming in from the catwalk, a walking cloud of flour mumbling something about chicken shit without taking the least notice of Amanda. He stopped and looked at me. 'Oh good, you're back. Did you bring the cavalry?'

'Don't take any notice of him,' Amanda said, her words taking on a sudden harshness, 'and whatever first impression he gave you, ignore it. He's hardly our best ambassador.'

I decided not to tell her about my first impression of Flynn.

'Ambassador?' Flynn grunted, then glanced up at me and grinned, his teeth appearing yellow in his flour-covered faced. 'Amanda, on the other hand, will be glad to do what she can to change your impressions.'

Amanda ignored Flynn. 'Well, first we'll start with a cup of tea.'

'No thanks, I'm not a tea drinker.'

'No, don't worry.' She shook her head in disgust at the mess Flynn had made around the sink. 'It's no trouble.'

'I'll have mine black, thanks,' Flynn said.

'Make it yourself,' she said to him with a coolness that brought the temperature down a full two degrees. 'So how was your flight?' she asked me with a warm smile. She took her time to clean out the teapot carefully and scrub two cups clean as the electric jug began to boil.

'Long,' I said. I was about to tell her about the talkative 280-pound Australian rugby fan who sat next to me for eleven and a half hours, but then figured she probably was not interested.

She was making the tea in a pot, rather than in cups, and preheating the now clean cups.

'And how do you find New Zealand?'

'It's fine, I guess. I only arrived this morning. Haven't seen much …' I let my sentence trail off, assuming she wasn't really listening. Flynn, seemingly unconcerned that he was still covered head to toe in flour, which made him look like a living, talking Michelangelo reject, had sat down and opened the drawer in which he had grabbed the signal pistol cartridges. I was somehow relieved when he opened the signal pistol up and let the unspent cartridge drop out into the drawer; somehow relieved that he hadn't fired it at the aircraft; somehow relieved that he was, just maybe, not so much dangerous as simply insane.

As Amanda was carefully doling out milk in each cup with a

certain exactitude, Flynn propped his heavy work boots up on the work desk and became deeply engrossed in cleaning the signal pistol.

'So,' she said, 'welcome to Milton Gorge.' She pronounced it as if it was a joke name. 'And to the end of an era.'

'The end of what era?'

'The end of the old days,' Amanda said smiling, her eyes were alive with the optimism of someone whose favourite political candidate had just been elected. She handed me the cup of tea. 'The end of an outdated, outmoded bureaucracy. The end of the prodigal system.'

'Oh,' was all I could think to say as I looked past Amanda at Flynn, who rolled his eyes, suggesting Amanda was a loonier tune than he was. 'The prodigal system, you say? Is there something I'm missing?'

'Not at all,' Amanda said, almost laughing. 'You're just in time for it. And don't worry, I know there will be room in the new system for you.' She briefly tilted her head venomously in Flynn's direction.

'That would be the New World Order. Could you elaborate on that for me?' I said, even though I wasn't sure I wanted to know any more.

'I don't have time myself,' she said as she tucked her books under one arm and held her cup of tea in the other hand. 'I have to get some studying done.'

'Gee,' Flynn piped in loudly, 'and here I thought you might have come here to do some controlling.'

'Oh yes, of course. It is busy, isn't it?' she said, calmly sarcastic. 'But, a great controller like you shouldn't be too overworked by, let me see, zero airplanes? So just call me if you need me, Owen.' She nearly spat his name.

'I told you not to call me that!' Flynn's upper lip twitched.

'See you later, Cowboy,' Amanda said, returning her attention to me with a seductive smile. I was impressed at how easily, and how completely, she could toggle between charm and spite. 'Thornie should be in any time now,' she said as she disappeared down the stairs. 'I'll catch up with you later.'

'Thornie?'

'Believe me,' Flynn said, his attention still fully focused on the pistol. 'You don't want to know until you absolutely have to.'

I slumped down in the chair next to him and looked into my cup of tea. 'Is everybody around here ...?' But didn't know how to finish.

'Some of them are worse,' Flynn said. 'Wait till you meet the guy with the rat. Now, if you don't mind.' Flynn stood up and started for the stairs. 'Since Princess isn't going to give me a break, I have some important business to attend to. Watch that for me, will ya?'

'Watch what?'

'Well, what do you think?' Flynn asked. 'You can either watch me take a dump, or you can watch that.' He waved his hand at the chair where he had been sitting — the tower controller's position. 'You *are* a controller, aren't you?'

'Well, yes, but ...' I didn't know where to begin. Even an experienced controller needed training at a new airport. Besides, I hadn't done it for months, and never in this country.

'But, what?' Flynn shrugged. 'Thornie said you were the best cowboy in town.'

'Who's Thornie?'

But Flynn had already disappeared down the stairs. I looked around the tower cab. Was this just a weird dream I was having, I wondered, brought on by some indigestible additive in the in-flight meal? Still, it was quiet here. And that's what I was looking for. I did a quick scan of the airfield. The ground fog had pretty much dissipated. There were traces of movement here and there. I saw a car pull into the parking lot of a building on the far side of the runway, but still there was only silence blanketing the whole scene.

'Milton Gorge Tower,' the radio at the tower controller's position crackled with a suddenness that made me jump and splash hot tea across the back of my hand. 'Echo delta mike is ready to taxi for the circuit at the flying school.'

I stared at the radio. This was not a dream.

'Tower?' the radio crackled again. 'You there, tower? Hellooo tower, come in,' the pilot said impatiently.

'*An' let poor damned bodies be*,' I whispered, reaching for the microphone. My hand, red from the tea burn, was shaking as I keyed the switch. 'Ah, calling the tower, say again?'

'Echo delta mike,' the pilot started again slowly. 'At the school, taxi for circuits.'

'Echo delta mike,' I responded with as much authority as I could muster without knowing what the hell I was talking about. 'Taxi approved.'

'Thank you, tower.' The pilot sounded suspicious: 'Which runway you using?'

Yes, of course. Which runway, indeed. If only I knew what runway numbers they used at this airport. But a good controller has to be able to think on his feet, even if he doesn't know where he is, or why he is there — and the only thing I knew about where I was, was that it was on thin ice, so I may as well dance.

I put the mike up to my mouth and glanced at the anemometer on the control panel. 'Echo delta mike, the wind is three five zero degrees at five knots. Runway's your choice.'

'Roger that. We'll take three-zero.'

Great. Three-zero. That meant the other end was one-two. Just avoid using the crossing runway, and we should not have to suffer any public embarrassment.

When I spotted the Cessna 172 taxiing from the area Flynn had recently fired upon, I was already well on my way to figuring this place out and feeling the old confidence returning, so I decided to push it. 'Echo delta mike, advise your direction of flight.'

'We're remaining in the circuit.'

The what?

'Roger,' I said to the plane, 'And what will you be doing there?'

'Touch and go's, what else?' the pilot spoke hesitantly as if he were talking to an idiot.

Okay, making a mental note: they call it the 'circuit'. In America we call it the 'pattern', the traffic pattern. 'Roger,' I said authoritatively. 'That's approved.'

'You're new here, aren't you?' the pilot asked.

'Does it show?'

'Only a little.'

'Just started today.'

'Today?' There was a momentary silence, then, for the second time already that day I was asked, 'Are you one of them?'

I keyed the mike and applied the same philosophy I had with Flynn. 'No, I'm one of us.'

Perhaps I was in the wrong place. It crossed my mind again that maybe this sad place was just an unused airfield, fenced in, and where the authorities let the lunatics roam free. But at the moment I was considering the possibility that maybe this dilapidated relic of an airport could be just what I needed — a quiet place where nothing happened, where nothing ever went wrong, and Air Force One was never ever going to come. Besides, air traffic control is like riding a bike and a few months away from it was hardly going to make me rusty. By the time that plane made two trips around the traffic pattern — the circuit — I was already feeling fairly comfortable at the old job, at least, with one airplane at a time.

'Milton Gorge Tower,' a new voice showed up on the radio. 'Wild Blue Squadron minus one over Mokarangi, inbound for landing.'

'Mocha-what?' I said aloud to myself.

'Southwest, seven miles,' came the answer from behind. It was Flynn standing at the top of the stairs.

'Good, you're back.' I stood up.

'What are you doing?' Flynn asked as he went to pour himself a cup of tea from the pot Amanda had prepared. He drank his straight black. 'You're doing fine. Just give them left base joining, tell him they'll be following the guy on downwind, the T6s will land first, then the Dakota, and everything will fall right into place. Then tell them they can all come over and wash the flour off all our cars.'

I issued the instructions to the lead pilot of the flight of four aircraft, picked up the binoculars and scanned the horizon for the incoming traffic. Here I was talking to airplanes, working again, only hours after setting foot in this country. This was nuts.

Flynn settled down in the seat next to me with his cup of tea. 'Thornie's here. You might as well go down and get it over with.'

'Go down where? Get what over with? And who is Thornie?'

Five

'Thornie?'

'Number three. He was sort of King of the Nutcases.'

A cold southerly was kicking up outside and tapping at the window.

'Well,' I said, turning towards the window, 'he was actually a pretty good guy, a kind of sweet old harmless guy. At least he was the most …' I paused but could think of no better word, 'harmless.'

'Was?'

'Yeah. He's dead now. Murdered.'

'Murdered? That's terrible. What happened?'

I looked across the glass desk between us — it was too big, like a barrier, like an impassable gulf between us. He was leaning back in his leather and chrome chair, staring at me with his half-open eyes, his arched fingers just touching in a carefully struck pose, possibly to suggest a Zen-like wisdom to his judgement. For a moment, I hated him. I did not ask to come here and have him dig into my life. He was supposed to be questioning me on the events of one single night when a lot of people got very close to getting killed. He was going to write a report that would probably decide my future — something my paranoia assumed had already been decided. That's why I hated him at that moment. Perhaps he was going to exonerate me because this was supposed to be just a formality. But why did I also want to tell him about my past? He didn't know Thornie. He didn't know or really care about me, or where I came from, or my dad or Sarah, or whatever it was that was haunting me enough to make most nights a hell of sleeplessness. He only knows what the Corporation told him about me.

So why was I compelled to tell him anything more than I needed to answer his standardised questions? Was it merely keeping a promise to a friend?

Perhaps I thought to gain an insight I have not already gained in the last few days. Did I think he could somehow help me put some order back in my life? Or solve an unsolved murder?

'I'm not a cop. I don't know.' I narrowed my eyes and stared back at him. 'And they never solved the crime.'

'Okay. So who was Thornie?'

'Thorndike Rumbold,' the old man sitting behind the desk said in a soft voice. He was dressed in a grey tweed suit, white shirt and red bow tie, much as one would expect a high school science teacher to be dressed in the 1960s. Despite his obvious age, his eyes were clear behind the wire-rimmed glasses, his round cheeks glowed with colour and his bald head shone like polished marble. 'Perfectly dreadful name, don't you think? And I won't even tell you what all my middle names are. 'Tis a simply appalling name, I tell you.'

'I'm sure it's not that bad,' I reassured him and glanced across the room to Amanda, who was collecting her books again from a small table against the wall behind Thornie's desk and preparing to depart upstairs. She offered little more than a smile and a wink for support.

'I should know.' He held his hands in the air. 'I've had to live with that dreadful moniker for many, many years.'

'Well, it is a mouthful.' I looked around the dusty old office. It probably hadn't changed since the Second World War. The solid wooden desk sat in the centre of the office; Thornie sat in a leather-bound swivel chair that could easily have dated back to the 1940s; two wooden chairs were arranged neatly facing his desk and a more comfortable leather wingback was to the side. One wall had windows offering an excellent view of the airfield, and the other had a couple of steel filing cabinets and bookshelves packed to the ceiling with ancient looking books, yellowed manuals, and dusty old binders that looked like they hadn't been opened in decades. I drew in a slow lungful of the musty air. The place smelled like the basement floor in a library, like a museum exhibit that was lovingly cared for by its lifelong curator. It reminded me of my dad's office when I was a kid.

'Now, who might you be, young man?' he smiled warmly.

'Thomas Hardy,' I said, though Amanda had already introduced me only seconds before.

'How wonderfully literary!'

'Don't you remember, Thornie?' Amanda said in a gentle, reassuring tone. 'This is the cowboy from America.'

'No,' I protested, 'I'm a controller. I've never even been near a —'

'Oh yes indeed!' Thornie said and half stood as he offered me his hand again. 'Please, sit down.'

I sat down across the desk from him in one of the wooden chairs.

'Well, we're so glad you could come and — oh, damnation.' Thornie abruptly cut himself off and pressed his lips together so tightly they disappeared. 'We haven't had our morning tea yet.'

'I'm fine, I've already had —'

'Don't you worry, Thornie,' Amanda cut in, 'I'll go fix it. You just relax and have a nice chat to Thomas.'

'Who?'

'Thomas,' she said, indicating me. 'The cowboy.'

'Oh yes, of course. Silly me.' He returned his attention to me and smiled again. 'You know, when I was a child, I wanted to be a cowboy.'

'I'm not a cowboy. I'm an air traffic controller.'

'You're a controller, too? Well, you are something then.'

Amanda leaned over me as she started out. 'I'll put in a good word for you,' she whispered to me. 'And we'll catch up later.'

'Thank you, my dear,' Thornie said to Amanda as he watched her depart. Then he turned to me, his eyes shining eagerly. 'So, how do you find Milton Gorge?'

'It's fine. Maybe a little —'

'Good!' He seemed truly delighted. 'I'm so glad you like it here at our little provincial aerodrome. I must confess, though, I do take it rather personally.'

'Take what personally?'

'Milton Gorge. You see …' He leaned forward and lowered his voice as if he was about to divulge a military secret. 'I'm the original.'

I leaned forward and asked in a respectful whisper. 'The original what?'

Thornie leaned back and laughed. 'My dear boy, I'm the original controller.'

'You're a controller?' I had assumed he was a civil service clerk who had been assigned to take care of the administrative functions at Milton Gorge. He certainly didn't project the image of the controller with his soft voice, gentle, slightly effeminate mannerisms as he waved his hand rhythmically — not to mention the fact that his mind appeared to wander aimlessly, far from reality.

'Not *a* controller, my boy, but *the* controller.' He paused to let that sink in. 'You see, I was the first civilian controller here at Milton Gorge.'

'Really?'

'Yes, indeed. In 1962, the Civil Aviation Authority decided it was time to introduce air traffic control here at Milton Gorge and, for the first three months, I was the only controller here. I worked Monday to Friday, from eight in the morning until three every afternoon. After the first three months, they hired a second controller and … let me see, that was Norwynne Skidmore — long since dead, I'm afraid. Nonetheless, he was very much alive in those days, and the two of us alone were air traffic control at Milton Gorge for nearly two years.' Thornie leaned back, looked up at the ceiling and let out a satisfied sigh as he appeared to lose himself in memories of his youth. 'Oh yes, those were the days. What rapscallions we were, old Wynnie and me.'

Thornie sat, entranced in the ceiling for a good thirty seconds. I was unsure if it would be safe to wake him from the trance, but, fortunately, he jolted himself out of it.

'Oh dear,' he said. 'I'm getting ahead of myself. Milton Gorge had been around since long before 1962.' He rose from his chair, walked to the bookcase and stretched to reach the upper shelf and retrieve a photo album. Then he took the chair beside me, placed the album in my lap and reached across to open it. The photos were of the Second World War era and accompanied by brittle old newspaper clippings. ''Twas you Yanks we have to thank for building our little aerodrome. They were frightfully worried about the advancement of the Japanese in this part of the world and so thought to make this a major base. Of course, the Japanese never got close enough to pose any real threat, so as soon as they were finished building, all the Yanks were shipped off, just like that. But, look what they left us.' Thornie turned the pages and pointed at photographs, yellowed with age, of Milton Gorge Aerodrome in its early years. I was impressed at the size of the runways, far bigger than necessary for a small general aviation airport.

'Why did they build it so big?'

'To be prepared, of course. A very American attitude, don't you think?' He let out a quiet giggle at his little joke. 'They wanted to be able to accommodate virtually anything that would come along, and you must remember, in those days, labour and materials were practically free for the taking — at least, you Yanks seemed to think so. They started building those runways and had little better to do for two years but to continue building. Do you know, those runways are twelve feet thick.'

'Really?' I didn't know how thick runways normally were, but it sounded impressive.

Thornie now seemed to be in full use of his senses, able to recount the smallest detail and was obviously relishing the audience. He gave me a step-by-step walk through history, gently touching the newspaper clipping or photograph as he explained each. 'The Aeroworks Maintenance hangar.' He pointed to a 1956 photo of the hangar that still occupied the northeast side. 'The Milton Gorge Flying School opened in 1960,' he said, caressing another. 'And here,' he pointed to a photo from 1964 that showed three middle-aged or older men in clerical garb, two younger ones in leather flying jackets and one in a suit and tie, standing in front of a twin Beechcraft. 'The inauguration of Holy Air.'

'Holy Air?'

'I believe their motto was "Flying for God",' Thornie said, suppressing a grin. 'They're still in operation, though their mission may have changed somewhat. Started as a group of religious zealots wanting to spread the word of the Lord. But I'm afraid the Lord's word didn't pay for aviation fuel and so they got into charter work.' He looked at the photo for a moment in silence. 'They're mostly all dead now, too. This one was killed in 1968.' He pointed to one of the younger men, 'And this one in 1975,' he said pointing to the other.

'And who's that cheerful looking guy?' I pointed to a barely discernible face that was scowling at the camera from inside the cockpit of the plane.

'Oh, I say, what remarkable eyesight.' He leaned forward and squinted. 'Oh yes, of course, that would be the Holy Terror himself.' He leaned back, gave his head a brief, serious jerk as if to shake loose an unpleasant thought. 'Amos Scuffield — bit of bad news if ever there was one. He wanted this job, but I got it, and I'm afraid he's held quite the grudge ever since.'

We reached the end of the first photo album and Thornie gently closed the cover, brushed off some dust with his palm and returned it to its place on the shelf. 'I have three more albums,' he said as he reached for the second. But, thankfully, Amanda returned with a tray of tea.

'Oh my dear, you are a lifesaver.' Thornie restored the second album to its place on the shelf, returned to his seat behind the desk and began serving the tea. He hesitated, counting only two cups. 'My dear, won't you be joining us? I've been having the most delightful conversation with this young man.'

'I'd love to, Thornie,' Amanda said, 'but I'm afraid our Mr Flynn is throwing a fit. So I'd better give him a break before he hurts someone.'

'Oh, yes,' Thornie said, letting another brief giggle slip out. 'Mustn't keep your comrades waiting. Duty calls.'

Amanda touched my shoulder as she departed.

'Yes, this is much better.' Thornie offered me another cup of tea and a shortbread biscuit. I reluctantly accepted it and set it down without taking a sip. 'Now then ... Thomas was it? Tell me what brings you here to Milton Gorge?'

'What do you mean?'

'Well, I'm sure you didn't come all the way from your ranch in America just to hear the history of Milton Gorge.'

'I came to work, don't you remember?'

Thornie rubbed his chin and contemplated this seriously. 'Well now, I don't know too many people in the cattle industry, but I suppose I can make some enquiries.'

'I'm not a cowboy. I'm a controller. Look ...' I dug the letter from the CAA out of my pocket and put it in front of Thornie. 'Don't you know anything about this? They offered me a job here, said I would be stationed at Milton Gorge Tower. Wasn't anybody expecting me?'

Thornie took his glasses off, carefully polished them with his handkerchief, then picked up the letter and studied it for a full two minutes.

'I see,' he said as he put the letter down in front of him. 'This is a dilemma.'

'Why is it a dilemma?'

'You see, things have changed.'

'I know, I know, a New World Order or something.'

'It's the Corporation!'

'What Corporation?'

'ControlCorp,' Thornie huffed. 'We've been privatised, my boy.'

'Who's been privatised?'

'We have — air traffic control. The CAA has gone and flogged us off. They say it's going to make us more "efficient" or some such nonsense. Mind you, I don't approve. I think they just wanted to make a "quick buck" as you Yanks like to say. I say we've been quite happily going on about our business for nearly four decades now and why mess with it?'

'So, you're saying, the CAA hired me but the Corporation's not interested in employing me?'

'Yes, I'm afraid that's it in a nutshell.' He looked truly apologetic. 'At least, that's the way it will be in a few days.'

'What happens in a few days?'

'Friday, at the close of business. That's when the changeover takes place. That's when we become ControlCorp.' He screwed his face as if the name left a bad taste in his mouth. 'And they informed us that only air traffic control staff who are fully licensed by the CAA at the time of the changeover will be employed by the Corporation.'

I opened my mouth but could think of nothing further to say, so just left it open for a few seconds, should a thought occur. Were they kidding me? They offered me a job. I flew all the way from the USA only to be told they couldn't employ me after all? Lacking any intelligent response, I stood up to leave. When I turned, I saw Flynn leaning against the doorframe. He had managed to brush much of the flour off, but still presented a ghostly appearance.

'Good morning, boss,' Flynn said cheerfully.

'Well, good morning, Flynn, and how are you today? Look's like you've taken a bit of a dusting.' Thornie sounded cheerful and fully recovered from the problem that had weighed heavily on his mind only five seconds earlier.

'Yes, sir. Had a clear shot at Scuffield, too. Probably could have got him between the eyes.' He plopped himself into the leather wingback.

'Oh dear, what an awful mess that would have been.'

'His fly-bys are getting lower, Thornie.'

'Oh well,' Thornie shrugged. 'Let the boys have their fun.'

Flynn shook his head and obviously decided not to pursue the subject.

'So have you met Mr Hardy?' Thornie asked Flynn. 'He's a cowboy *and* a controller.'

'Of course, I met him, and he's not *a* cowboy, Thornie, he's *the* cowboy. And I've got to tell you, it was one of the best decisions you made to get him on board so quickly.'

'Oh, I'm afraid it's a very unfortunate turn of events for our young friend. He's arrived a bit late to make the transition.'

'What do you mean?' Flynn slid further into a slouching position. 'You can't cut him loose now, he's halfway through training.'

'But how can that be?' Thornie asked. I, too, was interested in the answer.

'Well, he's been here all weekend.'

'I don't remember seeing him here yesterday.'

'You weren't here yesterday, were you? You don't work on the weekends. Don't you remember?' Flynn leaned forward. 'You told me to keep an eye out for the new guy if he showed up over the weekend and to get him started right away. Remember?'

'Well, not —' Thornie scratched his bald head.

'Sure you do,' Flynn countered in a gentle, reassuring tone.

'Well, now that you mention it, I do seem to remember saying *something*.' He stopped scratching. 'But, still, how could he be halfway through the training programme if he only just started this weekend? Training should take at least four weeks.'

'Not with this guy — he's *that* good!' Flynn pointed at me, but I could think of nothing to say, so I stood with my mouth hanging open again. 'You remember when you told us about him a couple of months ago? You showed us his file and told us how he worked at a busy American airport and was a real hotshot, a "cowboy", you said. That's what we've been calling him ever since.'

'Yes, of course, but,' Thornie paused and squinted at Flynn, then leaned towards him and said in a low, hesitant voice, 'are you telling me he can finish training and be licensed in only four more days? That would be unheard of. It would be ...' He turned his gaze to me and whispered, '*remarkable*.'

'You should have seen him this morning moving airplanes!' Flynn moved his finger around in the air.

'Really?' Thornie rubbed his chin as he looked at me approvingly.

'And he has excellent eyesight.'

'You could license him today,' Flynn assured him. 'But why put pressure on him? Give him a couple more days to settle in.'

'Yes, of course, why indeed?' Thornie smiled. 'Don't want you to work too hard, my boy. Take your time. Relax. I'll schedule a Licensing Board to convene at nine o'clock on Friday morning. My word, this is exciting!'

Flynn got up and walked out. I hesitated for a moment, alternating my gaze between Thornie, beaming in admiration, and Flynn's back. I caught up with Flynn at the base of the stairs.

'Hey.'

Flynn stopped two steps up and turned.

'You really think that? I mean, that I'm that good?'

'Based on what? That you had one airplane and couldn't even get that right?' He grinned maliciously. 'What I think, *mate*, is that you'd better get to work and pray for a miracle.'

'Then why the hell did you get me into this?' I screamed as loud as I could whisper.

'You want a job, don't you?'

'Well, yeah, but —'

'Look,' said Flynn as he took a step down and lowered his voice, 'you've got two things going for you. When things start moving here, this place is a madhouse at the best of times. You won't ever control anything here. The pilots only occasionally follow instructions. The best you can learn is to not try to make any sense of it and just keep your head down.'

'What's the other thing?'

Flynn grabbed my shoulder, squeezed hard and smiled as if he had just seen Amanda fall down three flights of stairs. 'Mate, I'm going to teach you how to do that in just four days.'

'Great,' I said, though not completely convinced. 'With all that on my side, how could I lose?'

Six

'All in all, Carlton my boy, I'd say that went pretty well,' Freddie said, sliding into his chair and savouring the smooth caress of fine leather as it gently massaged his butt.

'Are you kidding, Freddie?' He looked at his watch as he sank into the seat opposite Freddie across the wide oaken span of desk. 'It's after two o'clock. That little welcome ceremony was supposed to be a morning tea break.'

'Well, you have to take the time to get to know your staff one on one. Besides, there was plenty of food to carry us through to make it a working lunch and I think we accomplished a tremendous amount of work.'

'Your staff? Don't forget, Freddie, they hired you. They think of you as part of their staff. And that's another thing — you've got to show these guys a little respect. You slapped the Chairman of the Board on the back and called him "Archie". I doubt even his wife gets away with calling him that.'

'Which is why he probably just wants to be treated like a regular guy, I'm sure.'

'Not this guy, trust me.'

'Oh, he just wants someone to go bowling with.'

'Ten-pin? Please don't ask him to, Freddie. The guy plays polo.'

'Too late.'

'Jesus Christ!' Woodcock started rubbing at his lower abdomen and looking at the window like he was considering taking a flying leap. 'I think that ham might have been a bit off.'

'You're aggravating your ulcer is what you're doing, Carlton. You need to find yourself a relaxing hobby,' Freddie said soothingly, 'or a woman,' he added with enough emphasis to annoy Woodcock. 'Anyway, we got a lot of work done today and I learned a lot.'

'Like what?'

'Like where the money is — we control a huge chunk of the Pacific airspace with a lot of money coming in from overflights through what you call your, uh ...' Freddie snapped his fingers.

'The Oceanic Sector.'

'That's the one. And the main centres — all those big jumbos produce a lot of revenue in landing fees.'

'So?'

'But what about all these other little airports around the country. We're employing people to sit around there doing nothing.'

'Well, I wouldn't exactly say they're doing nothing. Some of them can be quite busy. Sure, they're not big revenue-earners, but they need to be there.'

'We'll see about that. Anyway, I've got our whole week's schedule planned.'

'*Our* week's schedule? Don't forget, Freddie, I don't work for you. I'm not here for you to —'

'Straight from the top, Carlton. It was Archie's idea to team us up this week.'

'I bet it was.' Woodcock stopped rubbing his abdomen and squinted at Freddie. 'So what is our schedule for the week?'

'Tomorrow we're having meetings with each of the departments and I'm going to do a bit of motivational management — get them thinking outside the box and thinking more in terms of commercial opportunities to be had.'

'Freddie, you're not their boss.'

'But this is my job as Commercial Manager.' He lifted a finger to stop whatever Carlton had planned to say next. 'On Wednesday we have the managers from the three main centres coming up here: Auckland, Wellington and, uh ...' he snapped his fingers.

'Christchurch.'

'That's the one! Anyway, we'll basically do the same tap dance for them. We'll get everyone motivated for the big changeover on Friday, and it will also give us a good chance to weed out the bad eggs.'

'Bad eggs?'

'The ones who are not a hundred and ten percent behind us.'

'And Thursday?'

'On Thursday and Friday, Carlton, you and I are going to take a road trip.'

'A road trip?' Carlton's eyes suddenly went wide.

'Yes, I understand we own a lot of provincial real estate out there.'

'You mean the domestic airports?' Carlton was shaking his head. 'No, Freddie, no road trip for me. I get carsick, and some of these places are at the far ends of long, windy roads.'

'It's got to be done, Carlton.' Freddie stood up from his desk, walked over to the window and continued to speak to the view. 'We've got to meet the small people, soothe the masses, reassure them, instil them with the corporate spirit.' He spun around. 'And then we can figure out for ourselves how many of these little money pits we really need to hang on to.'

At 4.30 on the afternoon of my first day on the job — a day I had planned to spend sleeping off jet lag, but instead found myself thrown into the thick of training with Flynn as my assigned on-the-job instructor — Flynn finally introduced me to a place I had heard referred to a dozen times that day. The Tie Down was what he explained as an aviation 'social club', but I would have called it a bar attached to a flying school. As we reached the front door, we were met by a middle-aged cop coming out, who paused and at first blocked our way. Unlike his American counterparts, he carried no gun or truncheon, nor did he have anything dangling from his belt. At first glance, I thought he was a flight instructor in his casual blue slacks and light blue shirt. He was returning his hat to his

head when he recognised Flynn and stared for a moment with that semi-pleased, semi-disgusted look of finally finding the man who owes you money.

'Well, well, Mr Flynn,' he said.

'Constable Tucker,' Flynn said cheerfully and nodded towards the club door. 'Is this a shakedown, or are you drinking on the job these days? Wouldn't blame you if you did, though, with the kind of stress you must have to endure in a job like yours.'

'Just making my rounds.' Constable Tucker did not look like he was easily amused.

'Oh yeah — we're part of the beat, are we?'

'Mr Flynn ...' said Tucker as he took one step threateningly close to Flynn and tilted his head as if in challenge, 'I've heard a rumour around this flying club that you've been aiming your signal pistol rather low again.'

'Just scaring the birds away, sir,' Flynn shrugged and smiled. 'Why, have they complained? If so, tell them I'm sorry and if they'd agree to not fly around my airplanes, I'll agree not to shoot at them.'

'This is not a joke, mate.' He poked a finger at Flynn. 'And if I ever see you aiming that in the direction of any person, structure or car, I'll have you up for it.'

'Of course you will, Eddie.' Flynn's defiant grin did not flicker. 'But if you cut me some slack this time, I'll give you a tip-off that will be sure to get you that promotion to detective.' He leaned into Tucker and whispered, 'Amanda Sheppard is operating a major international drug ring through the control tower.' He leaned back. 'Now, if you'll excuse us.'

'Flynn,' Tucker grabbed Flynn's arm and stopped him. 'I'm not kidding, mate. These antics have got to stop. You can't afford to get yourself in trouble. Not now.' He looked Flynn in the eye for a moment and they traded some unspoken knowledge before he stepped aside. Tucker eyed me suspiciously, too, as I cautiously moved past him to follow Flynn inside.

The room adjoined the Milton Gorge Flying School. It was

nothing fancy, but functional, with a bar, a pool table and a scattering of tables and chairs. The walls were adorned with various framed posters advertising long-past air shows, old but highly polished propellers and antique flying paraphernalia, and one area had a display of photos that were, presumably, lost mates and comrades. When we arrived, there were a few people sitting at the bar talking in low whispers. A group of four pilots sat a corner table, noisily trying to outdo each other's flying tales. One of them had been pointed out to me as Brandon, but it was another who turned and yelled at Flynn, 'Hey Flynn, you're looking a bit pale today — something scare you?' which brought a round of laughter from everyone else in the room except Brandon, who just stared at Flynn and smiled.

'First round on me, boys,' he said to his antagonist, and then turned to the bartender, who seemed to be just another instructor doing his turn behind the bar. 'Cutter, my shout — everyone in the place,' which brought a round of cheers, a few applauding.

By five o'clock there were four times as many people in the place and it was getting considerably noisier. I was surprised at how cheerful so many of these pilots were with Flynn, considering he had fired on this place with a signal pistol. But, as he had predicted, all was quickly forgotten once a few beers were poured and Flynn had told them a few completely fabricated stories about how I ended up being called Cowboy. He perpetuated a few more myths about what I had done to the President, and how I had personally told the President of the United States, to his face, that neither he nor his fucking airplane were welcome at my airport — a lie that even the weakest mind among them must have recognised as an impossible tale. But they seemed to be unusually quick to welcome me into the brotherhood of the reckless, the legion of liars: pilots.

An hour later, Flynn and I were still sitting at one of the tables when the old man walked in. His appearance did not create an absolute hush, but the noise level dropped noticeably as he paused in the doorway and scanned the room. He was still dressed in the olive green flying suit with several patches sewn on it that he had pulled on before dawn that morning.

I was facing the door and saw him first, and would not have paid any attention had it not been for him stopping his scan of the room on us. Seemingly satisfied that we were who he was looking for, he moved towards us in a slow but steady pace. Although he looked old with his deeply lined and weatherworn face, he did not look frail; he stood straight and tall as he approached Flynn and me. It was not until he was almost upon us that Flynn noticed my distraction and turned in his seat.

'Scuffs,' Flynn smiled at the old man, 'you're still alive.'

'Mr Flynn,' the old man nodded but did not return the smile, and then inclined his head towards me and offered another nod.

'Tom Hardy,' Flynn said, jabbing a thumb towards me. 'We call him Cowboy. He's the new guy in the tower. He's from America.'

'I was stationed with the Americans during the war for a short time,' Scuffield offered, but did not indicate whether that was a good experience or not.

Flynn then reversed his position and looked at me while he turned his thumb to indicate the old man. 'Amos Scuffield, last of the great airborne warriors and the guy who tried to kill you this morning.'

'Nice to meet you,' I said, raising my glass of beer.

Flynn turned back to Scuffield. 'A little closer than usual, eh Scuffs?'

I noticed the room was still quieter than it had been before Amos Scuffield entered and several of the people in our proximity seemed to be interested in the exchange. The old man obviously commanded reverence from these younger pilots.

Scuffield turned his attention to me and studied me with icy grey eyes. 'I sincerely hope that I did not frighten you, young man.' He barely inclined his head towards me but did not unlock his gaze. It sounded more like a challenge than an apology, like a commanding officer might issue a new recruit.

'No, sir,' I said and held his gaze. 'I have no sense of fear. I was a flight instructor.' This brought a round of laughter from those around us who were listening in, and I detected the slightest upturn to Scuffield's leathery old mouth.

'So, Scuffs,' Flynn said, 'it's not like you to be flying mid-week. You guys coming out this weekend? I only ask, of course, so I know to wear my flour-coloured shirt.'

'No, that's it for me, Mr Flynn. You were my last duel today, and I acknowledge your victory. In the end, if youth doesn't defeat age, then age will defeat itself.'

'What's up?' Flynn asked.

The old man took out his wallet, pulled out two twenties and tossed them onto the bar. 'Mr Cutter, please take care of these gentlemen for me, thank you.' He returned his attention to Flynn. 'I'm afraid it's taps for ol' Scuffs.' Then he turned and walked out.

'What did he mean by that?' I asked Flynn when Scuffield was out of earshot. '"Taps for ol' Scuffs"?'

'I'm not sure.' Flynn looked truly concerned as he watched the old man depart but said nothing more.

Seven

'Sounds like a pretty exciting first day.'

'Yeah, that would be a bit of an understatement.'

I looked around his office and the paintings on the wall: all abstract. Lines and shapes and shadows. There was more of a picture going on outside the window as the light faded and the clouds and darkness slowly crept in.

Amos Scuffield. I thought about the old man for a moment — I hadn't really thought about him much since that one and only face-to-face meeting in The Tie Down. I didn't even know if he was still alive. I sure hope he was. We needed him now. I wondered if I would hear from Flynn.

'As you can imagine, trying to get a grip on that place in four days was hard going. It was all pretty exciting.'

'How many times do I have to tell you before it sinks in?' Flynn was sitting on the counter in the rear of the cab, leaning on the window and polishing his hunting knife in what, to me, was an unreasonably threatening manner. 'They're not listening to you anyway, so you're better off saying as little as possible.'

I was finding little encouragement in his methods. It was Thursday, my fourth day on the job, and I had no more of a clue what was going on than on the first day. There were so many new reporting points to remember with difficult Maori names, the accents were hard to understand, and the pilots seemed to do as they pleased. Even some of the airplanes were new to me.

Flynn had assured me that Thursdays were always fairly quiet days, and that it didn't really get busy until the weekends when the Warbirds went out to play. While he was making vague unspoken threats with a hunting knife, I had four aircraft in the circuit doing touch and go's, three aircraft on the ground waiting for take-off, four inbound from three different directions joining to land from places I still couldn't pronounce, one non-radio Auster Aiglet circling overhead waiting for a light signal approving him to land on the grass strip, and a helicopter hovering around on the east side of the field doing God-knows-what.

'Try ignoring them,' Flynn said, holding the knife up to inspect the sheen.

'It's not what I was trained to do.'

'They'd probably be safer if you'd shut up.' He squinted at the blade of the knife. 'Why don't you have yourself a cup of tea, Cowboy?

'Why don't you have a cup of tea?' I turned to Flynn, but my attention was caught by something over his shoulder, through the window in the bright sunlight — a spot in the sky that was hard to see in the glare of the sun. It was something else I would have to deal with in the next four or five seconds. But I had a more immediate concern — the Piper Cub on short final was trying to land on top of a Cessna that was supposed to have taken off thirty seconds ago, but was still sitting on the runway. I aborted the Cub's landing and told him to re-circuit, and then turned my attention back to the Cessna to clear him for take-off again. Meanwhile, a Piper Cherokee was trying to descend into the traffic circuit on top of another Cessna, and an impatient chap in a Beechcraft was causing more radio clutter by repeatedly requesting take-off clearance, apparently oblivious to the existence of the two aircraft in front of him.

'Why, thank you, I think I will have a cuppa.' Flynn dropped off the counter and pointed the knife at me again. 'You know what your problem is — you need to learn to relax.'

I told the Cherokee to stop his descent until he could spot the Cessna, told the Beechcraft to stand by, and turned to say something nasty to Flynn about his habit of brandishing weapons.

'My problem is —' But before I could fill in the blank, a biplane went roaring past the tower not fifty feet outside the glass and scared the crap out of me. It proceeded to land on the grass directly in front of the tower.

'Oh, that's Warren,' Flynn said. 'I probably should have warned you about him — Wacko Warren in his Waco. He doesn't have a radio and he's too old and too colour-blind to understand light signals, so he just looks for a spot on the grass and lands.'

'Did you see how close he got to the Auster?' My heart was pumping at three times its normal rate.

'Don't worry about him — everyone knows that when Warren's out flying, you just got to work around him.'

'Work around him,' I grumbled to myself. 'I'm sure that's in the book somewhere.' I returned my attention to my immediate concerns, the chaos in the circuit. Somewhere out there, the Cherokee finally spotted the Cessna and slipped in behind him. There was nothing I could do to protect these aircraft from such stunts. Only sheer good fortune and a few feet had prevented the Auster from falling to the ground a crumpled, shredded and bloodied tangle of fabric and aluminium tubing. There was no air traffic control procedure to apply, no commands I could issue. But at the ensuing investigation they would grill me on what I had not done, and why I had not performed some miracle to prevent it.

Investigation? What was I talking about? There wouldn't be any investigation. This was the third insanely illegal act I'd witnessed in four days and the most serious response yet was a disgusted sigh as someone went to make the tea.

'This place is a madhouse,' I said aloud, hoping the sound of my own voice would wake me up.

'Yeah, but it's home,' Flynn said as he noisily pushed dishes around the cluttered counter top. 'Sure you don't want any tea? You really should start drinking the stuff. It'll make you feel better. Anyway, it could be worse.'

'How?' I glanced over my shoulder at Flynn, who was deeply

absorbed in something at the bottom of one of the cups, and turned my attention back to the Auster without the radio that was now trying to cut in front of the Piper Cub.

'Shit, that's gross,' Flynn said at whatever was down in the bottom of his mug.

'You could try washing it, Owen,' Amanda's voice came drifting up the stairwell. She appeared at the top of the stairs with her armful of books.

'There,' Flynn said, pointing at Amanda. 'It just got worse.'

Amanda took so little notice of Flynn's comment that I guessed she had been ignoring him for years. Following Amanda up the stairs was another person I had not seen before. He was small, probably no more than five foot four, and thin, possibly not breaking a hundred pounds. He had a dark complexion and a boyishly young face. He wore jeans and a T-shirt with a flight jacket that was too large for him and probably not necessary on such a warm day. It would have been easy to have mistaken him for a thirteen-year-old, but when I noticed the purpose with which he proceeded to look over the daily log and sign his name to it, and then take a look at the traffic moving around the circuit, I realised he knew exactly what he was doing and what he was looking at.

'Ah! The rest of the afternoon shift is here. Hey, Kenny,' Flynn said to the young man, 'how was your holiday? Islands still there? Haven't floated away or been submerged by global warming?'

The kid called Kenny nodded, but said nothing.

'And the family? Mum? Dad? The eight sisters? All okay?'

Again he nodded.

'Kenny doesn't speak a lot,' Flynn said to me. 'Kenny, this is the Cowboy. Says his real name is Tom Hardy. He's the new guy.'

Kenny turned his attention to me and offered his hand.

'You're a controller who doesn't speak?' I asked, shaking his hand.

'I said he doesn't speak a *lot*,' Flynn piped in. 'He's a hell of a controller.'

'You really have eight sisters?'

'Two,' he said in a soft voice.

'And how are you today, Thomas?' Amanda asked, dropping the books onto the back counter. She was sparkling clean and nicely dressed, with her hair tied back, and as she leaned in closer, the smell of lilac wafted in the air.

'Fine, and you?' I said automatically, but was more concerned with the chaos at the runway.

'Busy?' Amanda placed her hand on my shoulder and gently, almost imperceptibly, massaged it with her thumb.

'Not any more than Custer was at Little Bighorn,' I said, trying not to let the gentle motion of her thumb distract me from what was going on outside. The Cub positioned number two behind the Auster for landing on the grass. A warm tingle spiralled into my shoulder muscle. A vision flashed through my mind of Amanda giving me a full body massage, rubbing almond oil into my naked muscles. I felt the stirrings of an erection and leaned forward in an attempt to escape her thumb.

'Well, you look like you're not having any trouble settling in,' she said as her hand followed the forward motion of my shoulder without interrupting the rhythm of her thumb, 'despite the lack of guidance.'

'He doesn't need guidance,' Flynn barked as he made his tea, splashing more hot water over the counter top than in his cup. 'He's a natural. A regular cowboy.'

Kenny was engrossed in filling out some paperwork and not paying attention to any of us.

'Really?' Amanda's thumb increased its tempo on my shoulder and I considered the possibility that there was more passion in her thumb than my ex-wife had had in her whole body. Maybe that's unfair. Janey had passion — just not for me. Amanda, on the contrary, she was smouldering. The warm, tingling sensation was working its way into my spine. The Auster, the Cub, the tingle — I suddenly understood what drives a cat to purr.

'Well, tomorrow's the big day.' Her thumb dug deep into my shoulder muscle.

'Yeah,' I said, briefly closing my eyes and thinking about that massage with the almond oil and both of us fully nude. Then I opened my eyes. 'Big day for what?'

'Your checkout,' she said, briefly stopping the massage. 'And tomorrow night I'll fix you dinner to celebrate.'

'Oh man, is she hot on you, Cowboy.' Flynn looked up and grinned. 'You never fixed me dinner, Amanda.'

'Bring your dog food bowl in, Owen, and I'll keep it full.' She resumed her thumb massage for two more turns then abruptly pulled her hand away, sat down next to me and picked up a pen. 'What do you have?'

What do I have? I considered the many things I had at the moment: a boner in my lap and a flying circus that was positioning for one big, twelve-way, mid-air collision as its grand finale. Amanda sat down next to me and made notes as I identified each aircraft, working from the runway out. Then I slowly stood up behind her and watched, making sure I hadn't forgotten anything.

'How did you do that?' Flynn asked in feigned awe, stepping up behind me. 'You got Amanda to work. I'm impressed.'

I ignored Flynn and watched Amanda take control of the traffic. She issued instructions with the clipped efficiency of someone who does not invite doubt as to who is in charge. I looked down at her shoulder, wondering if I should return the favour.

'Must be your pheromones, Cowboy,' Flynn said, persisting for his amusement only, 'to make them come running like that. They must be screaming, "Amanda, Amanda, I'm gonna lasso your heart. Giddiup." Come on, what's your secret? Are you a natural with women, same as you are with moving airplanes and cattle around?'

'It's called a shower,' I suggested. 'You should try it.'

Flynn grinned. 'May be hope for you yet, Cowboy.'

'Well, it was nice to meet you, Kenny,' I said turning to Kenny, but was suddenly stopped by the movement under the breast of his jacket.

'That's Kenny's friend,' Flynn explained.

Kenny held his jacket open and a white rat crawled out from an inside pocket, up his shirt front, onto his shoulder and around the back of his neck to the other shoulder.

'It drives Amanda crazy,' Flynn added with a certain amount of glee. I just stood staring at the rat.

'At least it's cleaner than you, Owen,' Amanda said without turning around.

Kenny smiled. I had to admit, he did look like a happy, though very quiet, guy, but my eyes were still fixated on the rat, which was sitting up on its hind legs on Kenny's shoulder twitching his nose and looking at me with red eyes as if he were judging me — a judgement I somehow feared.

'You know, they tried to take it away from him,' Flynn said. 'Turns out, the rat is really the brains in this team. Kenny's a completely useless controller without the rat, yet brilliant with him.'

Kenny's grin widened, obviously enjoying Flynn's ragging on him.

'Just one thing,' Flynn added, 'we probably should have told you on the first day — if you see something around here that looks like a raisin, don't eat it. Come on, Cowboy,' Flynn said as he headed down the stairs. 'Your shift's over.'

'Well, it was nice to meet the two of you, Kenny,' I said as I stepped down one and stopped. 'By the way, Kenny.'

Kenny stopped and turned back to me.

'What's his name?'

Kenny grinned again and said in his soft voice, 'Garry.'

'Well, it was nice meeting you too Garry,' and I continued down the stairs for some reason hoping that I met with Garry's approval too.

'Have you ever killed anything?' Flynn asked as we walked out the tower towards our cars. I had the air traffic manual under my arm and was looking at a long night of cramming its contents into my brain.

'Not yet.'

'Well let's go over and talk about it over at The Tie Down.'

'Are you kidding?' I held the book up. 'Don't you think I should be trying to learn a bit of this stuff before tomorrow morning?'

'No, I don't. But if it makes you feel any better, bring that along, and I'll quiz you on it while we have a couple beers. After all, I know what they're going to ask you on your oral exam tomorrow.'

'You do?'

'Yes.'

'You promise?'

'Scout's honour.' He held his hand up in the Vulcan salute.

I took a step closer to him and looked him square in the eye. 'One beer, one hour — because I know you're bullshitting me. One beer, one hour, and then I'm on my way home.'

'And I will personally see to it that you get there safely.'

At The Tie Down I settled into a chair at a quiet corner table while Flynn went up to get the beers. By the time he returned, I had the manual open to Section 1: Definitions and Abbreviations.

'Now, I'm not too worried about the first part of this because it's pretty standard stuff,' I said as Flynn brought the beers back and took the seat opposite me. 'I think the biggest problem area is the section on separation because, quite frankly, I have no idea what type of separation we're using out there.'

'It's called Milton Gorge separation, and we have special dispensation to use it,' Flynn said, and then reached across the table, slammed the manual shut and tossed it onto an unused table behind him.

I closed my eyes. I knew this was a bad idea.

'Now, I repeat my question: have you ever killed anything?'

'No, for God's sake, will you leave that alone. I didn't kill the President. I never spoke with the President. All that happened was I got in an argument with his pilot and refused him landing clearance. That was the extent of it. I thought I was trying to make a political point to impress someone, and it turned into a stupid prank. I was immediately relieved from position. I lost my job, and I lost my career. Now for God's sake will you just stop trying to make a big deal out of that. It may be a game to you, but I lost a fucking lot. So if you don't mind, I'd appreciate it if you would stop making a joke out of it.'

Flynn stared at me in silence for a moment, and for the first time in the four days I had known him, I actually thought I saw something approaching sorrow. He sat quietly.

'That's not what you were talking about, was it?' I finally asked.

'No, I just meant shooting. Hunting. I thought maybe we could head up to the mountains and see if we could bag a deer this weekend.'

'I don't think so. I sort of lack the killer instinct.'

We sat in silence for a minute, both sipping our beers.

'So who were you trying to impress?' he finally asked.

'What?' I stared into my beer. 'Oh that. My wife — I mean, my ex-wife.'

'Ah, divorced.'

'Yeah, divorced.'

We each took another awkward sip of beer, and again it was Flynn who broke the silence. 'So then that's bullshit that you lack the killer instinct.'

I looked at him.

'How about fishing? Ever been fishing?'

'*Och, my wee laddie is lost*!' I heard my dad's voice inside my head. '*But he will grow to be a great protector of worms and fish and man! Please, watch over him and guide him as you have me.*' Yeah, I like fishing, I thought, but for some reason answered, 'Not particularly.'

'You like the mountains?'

'Yeah, I like the mountains.

'*You're weird, Dad*,' I had said then, but now wished I hadn't.

'I could show you some of the most scenic country in the world. We could go down to the Rangitikei and pack our stuff in.'

I stared at him for a moment, trying to dislodge a scene in the woods from my head. 'Don't you think I should concentrate on getting through this checkride tomorrow?'

'I'm talking about Saturday. That'll be over with one way or another, tomorrow morning. Either way, you're going to have the weekend off.'

'That's right. Tomorrow. I'm screwed.'

'What do you say?'

'Okay,' I said. I'll go camping this weekend. But do you think you could at least quiz me on the oral exam first?'

'I'm going to do better than that, I'm going to give you all the answers right now.'

'Right now?'

'Three minutes,' he said. 'Just remember three minutes.'

'Three minutes? What is that, some sort of wake turbulence separation? We don't have heavy aircraft flying out of Milton Gorge, so as far as I remember, the greatest wake turbulence separation we have to apply for aircraft on the same runway going in opposite directions is two minutes.'

'Just trust me. Remember three minutes.'

'That's it?' I could feel the anger rising from the pit of my stomach. This guy didn't care that I was going to make a total fool of myself in the morning when my answer to every question they asked was 'three minutes'. He didn't care — he had a job, a home.

'No,' he added. 'Heat the cups with hot water first.'

'I don't even want to know what that's supposed to be the answer to. Listen, Flynn, you've had your fun this week. Next week I'll be gone and maybe they'll give you someone else to fuck with, but —'

'Hang on to that thought,' he said as he got up. 'We need more beer.'

This was ridiculous. It was a ridiculous idea from the very beginning. Trying to run away from my life and mistakes in the US. Why did I ever think I could just go to a different country and I would somehow change in the process? I was sitting there thinking Flynn had made a fool of me, but he hadn't. I had. Exile

Tower. A guy who fires signal pistols at cars and possibly airplanes. Planes that actually attack the control tower. A guy who carries a rat around in his pocket. A boss who thinks it's still 1962. It was a lunatic asylum, but as I sat there, it dawned on me — this was it. I had proven myself a lunatic. Maybe the Americans had some deal — hell, maybe the whole world had a deal — that there would be one airport where they would send all the nutjobs.

Flynn returned to the table with two more beers and sat down.

'Okay,' he said. 'Where were we?'

'I forgot,' I said and took a long, slow drink of my beer.

Eight

'Through all the turmoil of that first week, you actually completed your training as well. Doesn't that say something positive about your own skill?'

A great protector of worms and fish and man. I remembered the woods by the Russian River, lots of trees, they were so tall, the shadows long and there were so many places he could hide. A great protector of worms and fish and man. An' let poor damned bodies be. I was looking out the window and turned back to him. 'Skill? What?'

'I said, doesn't the fact — '

'Yeah, I heard you. But this is what I'm saying. I don't think anyone cared about my skill or whether I could actually do the job or not.'

'Of course they cared. They'd have to. I mean, you did finish the training programme, didn't you?'

'That's what I'm telling you — that was pretty much the extent of it. I never got a grip on the insanity. I only got an introduction to it. You know, a taste of things to come.'

'But you still went to the Rating Board the next morning?'

'In America I went through four months of training in Oklahoma, followed by over a year of gruelling on-the-job training. I faced a frightening oral examination on the regulations, plus several days' worth of evaluation on the job to get rated. Here, I stayed up most of the night before trying to memorise that damn book. I didn't stand a chance — not in one night, not in four days. In the real world, I didn't stand a chance. But this was not the real world, this was a land where everyone was living out their own fantasy, their own private fiction, and I was just various characters in their strange worlds. No, this wasn't the real world.'

✈

It was 9.30 when I got to Thornie's office.

'Ah! Come in, Thomas. Please have a seat.' Thornie was sitting behind his desk. Seated to his right, in the leather wingback, was another man in the same age group as Thornie, whom I had not met before, though his face was vaguely familiar. 'This,' Thornie said dramatically, 'is our star pupil, a man of immense talent, a man who has turned air traffic control into an art form. May I present Mr Thomas Hardy.'

'Not *the* Thomas Hardy.' The old man laughed as he took my hand, which was good because I was hoping he was taking it all as a joke. 'I thought *the* Thomas Hardy had died a century ago.'

'Just a mere imitation at your service, sir,' I said as I shook his hand. 'I apologise for being so late. I was, ah …' I was going to tell them how I had been up all night cramming an endless assault of numbers: runway lengths, emergency phone numbers, types of airfield lighting, regulations, radio frequencies and countless other pieces of information that I would probably forget within hours, but even the excuse seemed pointless, so I left it with a shrug.

'Oh, you don't need to explain to us. After all, we were young men once too, weren't we?' Thornie looked sideways at the other gentleman and giggled.

In my state of exhaustion I could not imagine what Thornie thought I had got up to the night before and decided not to try.

'Thomas,' said Thornie as he held a hand up to the other gentleman, 'I'd like you to meet Norwynne Skidmore, from the CAA Head Office. He'll be conducting the test with myself.'

'Oh, yes, of course.' Then I remembered the face from one of Thornie's photographs and offered a hand. 'I thought you were, ah …' I didn't know how to finish and turned to Thornie for help.

'Dead?' Skidmore offered. 'Did he tell you I was dead? Damn you, Thornie. How many times do I have to tell you I'm not dead?'

'Oh, silly me,' Thornie chastised himself. 'Did I say that? I keep forgetting, you didn't die, you just went to Head Office.'

'Well, I'm glad you're alive,' I said with a smile.

'Oh, thank you. That's very kind of you to say,' Skidmore seemed genuinely touched. 'I say, Thornie, he is a good man, isn't he?'

'Quite,' Thornie said, smiling as if I were a favourite child. 'Now, shall we get this messy licensing business over with?'

I sat down in one of the wooden chairs facing the two men, suppressed another yawn and blinked several times in an effort to look more awake.

'As you know,' Thornie began, 'the licensing process is broken down into two parts: the oral exam, which is what we're going to commence now; and the practical exam, which, of course took place yesterday. Now —'

'Excuse me?'

'Yes?'

'What practical exam was that, that I took yesterday?'

'Well, of course, the on-the-job test where we observe you practising what you do so well — even, might I say, magnificently.' He held his hands out like a maestro reaching for the grand finale. 'That is, controlling airplanes.'

'I don't recall this taking place. When did you observe me?' I squeezed the bridge of my nose but it had no effect on my exhaustion or my current level of comprehension.

'Oh, I don't do that myself. I'm far too out of practice to be judging you. Besides, I wouldn't want to place any undue stress on you.' He smiled gently. 'No. I rely on your trainer for that. And, of course, Mr Flynn speaks highly of you. I'm sure if I were to ask him he would tell me how remarkable you were. But then, of course, I know how modest you are and I didn't want to embarrass you. So let's just take it as said then, shall we?'

'If you say so.'

'Now, first we need some tea. Would you like some tea, Thomas?'

'Ah, no, I ...' I hesitated, but then considered the benefits caffeine might provide. 'Well, okay.'

'Very good! That is correct.' Thornie annotated something on his notepad.

'Huh?'

'Now, do you remember how to make it?'

'Ah, yeah. Hot water, tea bag.' I shot a quick glance behind me to see if there was an audience of some sort.

'Remember, heat the pot first, a little hot water and gently swish, swish.' Thornie made a slight circular motion with his fist. 'And what do we do with the mugs as well?'

I stared at them for a long moment, my mouth hanging open. Then, despite all the information, all the numbers, and all the rules I had crammed into my head the night before, I recalled what Flynn had told me the day before. 'We,' I hesitated and they both leaned forward in anticipation, 'heat them? Swish, swish?' I copied the motion.

'Excellent! Now, Thomas,' Thornie looked at me seriously, 'how long do you let it steep?'

I smiled. 'It's nothing to do with wake turbulence.'

'Sorry?' Thornie raised his eyebrows.

'Why, three minutes, of course.'

They both stared for several seconds in silence.

'You were right, Thornie,' Skidmore finally said. 'He's a natural.'

'Well, didn't I tell you?' Thornie turned to Skidmore.

'You told me, but I didn't believe you,' Skidmore said to Thornie, then shot a quick glance at me that I can only describe as awe-filled. 'And to think, ranching, too.'

I laughed and shook my head. I was sure they were having me on. Perhaps it was a joke so elaborate that they had planned it all from the first day.

The funny thing was, I wasn't offended. This was probably all part of my punishment, which could have been much worse, all things considered. They were all nice people — perhaps all in need of some competent and intensive psychiatric care, but nice, nonetheless. They couldn't help what had happened to the organisation. Maybe, if I went along with it good-naturedly, this ControlCorp would compensate me for the week and give me a few days' holiday. I could spend another few weeks wandering around the country, then head down to the South Island. Hell, I could spend as long as I wanted — I had a three-year working visa. Admittedly, it was a good gag, and I had fallen for it.

I leaned back and decided to show I had a sense of humour too. 'Well, they say I was born into it — ordained at birth, that I was sequencing and separating the toys in my crib.'

'Really?' Skidmore leaned forward.

I laughed and looked from Skidmore to Thornie and back again, hoping they might join in. But they waited, in hushed awe.

'No, not really.'

'There's that modesty again,' Thornie piped in proudly.

'I was just kidding,' I tried to explain. 'Weren't you?'

'Your modesty is admirable,' Skidmore said in a fatherly tone, 'but you should be proud of your gift, son.'

'Yes, sir. I am. But, maybe I've given everyone the wrong idea.'

'Personally,' Thornie jumped in, 'I happen to find Thomas's modesty most appealing. Such a delightful change.'

'Well, I agree, Thornie. I'm just saying, the young man has a gift and he shouldn't be shy about it.' Skidmore was talking as if I had disappeared.

'Oh, pish-posh.' Thornie dismissed Skidmore with a wave of his hand. 'Thomas doesn't have anything to prove.'

'Yes, I do.' But I don't think either was listening by this time.

'Okay,' Skidmore rubbed his neck, 'I see what you're saying Thornie, and I'll concede that he doesn't have to prove anything to us. I guess I'd just hate to see his talent go to waste. He should be ... I mean, what's he doing out here in Milton Gorge?'

'I assure you, Wynnie, he won't be wasted. But give him time to settle in.'

'Yes I do!' I said, louder.

The two men stopped their debate and looked at me.

'You do what?' Thornie asked.

'I *do* have something to prove.' I looked from one to the other, hoping to get a chance to use some of my knowledge before it fell through the sieve that is my memory. 'The runway, for instance — ask me how long the runway is.'

'The runway?' Skidmore exchanged a perplexed look with Thornie.

'Runway three-zero/one-two is the larger of the two. Two thousand two hundred and ten metres in length. It is composed of reinforced concrete with an eight-metre reinforced bitumen edge and a three hundred and twenty metre reinforced bitumen overrun on runway three-zero. The lighting is composed of high-intensity, aviation white —'

'I should say, that sounds long enough,' Skidmore interrupted me again.

Thornie nodded agreement, then giggled and wagged his finger at Skidmore. 'Although, I do recall, Wynnie, there was at least one occasion when you found it a wee bit short. When was that? 1965?'

'Oh, bloody hell, Thornie, you know damn well it was 1966. It's the one thing you'll never forget as long as you live.' He wagged his finger right back as if he were challenging Thornie to a sword fight with fingers. 'Besides, I still blame you for that. You were in the tower, and you should have told me about the wind shift. I swear there must have been fifteen knots up my arse.'

'Oh, there was not,' Thornie snorted. 'There was no wind shift. You just can't admit you were coming in too high and fast.'

'High and fast!' Skidmore's voice jumped up a full two octaves. 'Listen, I reckon I have a few more hours logged in Tiger Moths than you, old man.'

'Well, perhaps you should consider logging a few more until you learn to fly something without flaps. I told you thirty years ago, Wynnie, that you were using flaps like a crutch and you'll forget how to fly without them. And that's exactly what happened, and you still can't admit it.'

'The only thing that I admit is that I knew the day would come when I'd regret saving your life, and, by golly, I do now.'

'Oh, saved my life, indeed.'

'Well, do you deny that it was me who brought your attention to Abercrombie trying to land his DC3 on top of you? Another second and you would have been history, and I'd be sitting here with Abercrombie today.'

'Abercrombie,' Thornie huffed. 'Now there was a man who had no business sitting in an airplane.'

'Oh, of course not,' Skidmore raised both his palms to Thornie and leaned back in his chair. 'No argument from me. Everyone knows he couldn't fly if God had given him wings and a jet engine up his arse. And what a shot!'

Both men simultaneously burst out laughing.

'Do you remember?' Thornie asked between gasps of air. 'The day he dropped a load of DDT from a hundred and fifty feet and the wind blew it over Edna Bascom's rose garden?'

'Do I *remember?*' Skidmore's eyes were glazing over as he tried to catch his breath. 'Hell, we lived six houses down from her, and he still managed to kill my wife's hydrangeas. Thought I'd never hear the end of it.'

'Oh, and what a state Edna was in. As I recall, she didn't speak another word to him for the rest of her life.' Thornie took a handkerchief from his pocket and dabbed his eyes.

'She had a few choice words to say to him the day she drove her Vauxhall through his tomatoes.' This brought another round of reminiscent laughter from the two men.

'Excuse me?' I was not sure if it was safe to interrupt the two old men, but if I had to listen to them much longer, I thought I might start crying. 'Do you want to ask me any questions?'

'Oh, no. I think that pretty much covers it.' Thornie turned to Skidmore. 'What do you say, Wynnie? About …' he shrugged, 'shall we say ninety-five percent?'

'Sounds good. After all, he did struggle there for a moment, but ninety-five sounds about right.'

'Well then,' Thornie held his hand out to me. 'Congratulations, son, welcome aboard and keep up the good work. You are a credit to your profession.'

I was acutely aware that my mouth was hanging open, but could do nothing about it. 'You're joking, right?'

'Now, now, don't be modest. You truly are a credit to your profession.' Thornie gently slapped his desktop. 'I say, I'm parched. Thomas, would you care to join Wynnie and me for a cuppa?'

'No.' I stood up. 'You know, I think I'll just go and do something.'

'Good heavens,' Skidmore said. 'He is a good keen man, isn't he?'

'Very dedicated,' Thornie agreed.

I backed out of the office, nodding and smiling and making no sudden movements until I was out in the hall. As I approached the stairs, I hesitated. I had one hand on the oak banister that would lead me up, and with the other I reached out for the wobbly old doorknob of the front door. I could take a hard right out that door, make a break from this loony bin and never look back. I could have my bags packed in ten minutes and by tomorrow morning be half way across the ocean. They'd take me back in America, right? I mean, they would have to, I think. In any case, the FAA was still short-staffed — probably desperate enough. Perhaps they could give me a job as a weather observer in the Aleutians.

I stared at the door. It would have been the original one installed when the American army built the tower sixty years earlier — now pockmarked and peeling and worn with age, but still standing strong to whatever it kept out — or, perhaps, whomever it kept in.

'Tom,' came Thornie's voice from behind as I grabbed the doorknob. 'I'm sorry, there is one thing I forgot to ask you.'

He approached me from his doorway. I could still hear Skidmore laughing at something in his office.

'What?' I dropped my head.

'I'm afraid we have a rather delicate staffing situation to deal with.'

'What?'

'Well, you see, normally we would have Amanda and Kenny working this afternoon's shift. But I was told only late yesterday that we were getting a visit from some of these new corporate headquarter types this afternoon around two o'clock. It's dreadfully short notice, I know, but it did leave me with a bit of a scheduling conflict.'

'Kenny's rat.'

'Yes — Garry. I see you're following me perfectly. I don't think they would respond well to the issue of the rodent.' He paused, then looked at me quizzically. 'Do you?'

'No, I don't think they'd appreciate having a controller who brings a rat to work with him every day.'

'Yes, so I did some late rescheduling and had Kenny do the morning shift, so he and Garry should be long gone before these chaps are due to arrive.'

'And Flynn?'

Thornie smiled. 'I see, once again, you're way ahead of me. Heavens, I should be careful, or you'll have my job before the day's out.'

'Trust me, I don't want it.'

'Yes. I had to reschedule Flynn to work this morning too, which didn't work out either because ...' he hesitated, 'well, please don't tell him I told you this, but he doesn't like Garry too much. So I let him go home early.'

'Okay, he'll face down a T6 at full throttle, but is afraid of a big mouse. So who went home early? Flynn? Kenny? Or Garry the rat?'

'If only,' he laughed. 'No, I'm afraid I had to let Flynn take the rest of the day off. I'm sure he could use a little extra break anyway.'

'That he could. So you want me to cover for Flynn for the rest of the morning shift.' I did not believe, for one minute, that I could control airplanes on my own up there without killing someone. But still I said, 'Sure,' and released the doorknob.

'In fact, would you mind terribly much staying around until these corporate types have come and gone? You know, you and Amanda, put on the best face and all. I assure you, as soon as they leave, you'll be free to take the rest of the day off. Amanda will be fine on her own. I understand you and Flynn are going fishing. That'll be grand. He really knows those mountains like he was born in them.'

I just stared at Thornie's smiling face and could think of nothing to say except, 'No problem.' It was at that moment that I realised I was now an inmate here, and there was no escape. There were no more choices to make. I started my slow ascent of the stairs to work with the silent Kenny and Garry the rat until Amanda came on duty at one, as Thornie returned to relive some memories with Skidmore.

'Oh, and Thomas …' Thornie paused at the door to his office. I stopped mid-flight and stared at him. He wagged his finger at me. 'If you see anything up there that looks like a raisin.'

'I know,' I interrupted him. 'Don't eat it.'

'Oh, I tell you Wynnie,' I heard his voice disappearing with him into his office. 'He is always one step ahead of the rest of us.'

NINE

'They gave you a BMW?' Woodcock was grumbling from the passenger seat, though Freddie paid little attention. He was too busy thinking of real estate as it flew by the window in a 120-kph blur, and trying to remember to stay on the left side of the road. 'I can't believe this. You get a BMW. They gave me a Honda.' He turned accusingly to Freddie, 'An Accord. They gave me an Accord.'

'Carlton,' Freddie said soothingly, hoping to quiet Woodcock down so that he could get back to his fantasising. 'I told you, it's just the image thing. I have to schmooze execs and dignitaries, and I've got to look good doing it. Believe me, to not have to kiss up to them, I'd sooner ride a bike to work.'

They were into the second day of their executive drive-through, stopping off at all the pissy little facilities in the provinces to reassure the peasants that they were all safe and secure and that life in the Corporation was going to be like living in the Emerald City. Freddie considered himself an infinitely patient man, but a day and a half listening to Carlton Woodcock gripe about cars was wearing him down. He could not wait to get to Auckland that evening, where he could put the little moaner back on the plane to Wellington.

In an effort to block out Carlton's whining, Freddie let his mind roam freely with the beautiful countryside they were sailing through. Real estate — so much of it, so untouched. He had not forgotten how badly he got burnt with the last real estate venture. But he had learned from his mistakes. He recognised the flaws in that plan. The important thing was always to learn from your mistakes. Don't be afraid to get right back up on that high horse or however it went. In any case, the new plan would be foolproof.

'Okay, Freddie, give me the BMW and I'll buy you a pushbike,' Carlton said.

'You want a BMW?'

'Yeah, I want a BMW.'

'Then I guarantee you'll be driving one by the end of the year. Just trust me. Now, we were supposed to be using this travel time to do some brainstorming. Have you come up with anything?'

'For what?'

'For anything. Carlton, my boy, you got to learn to think outside the box. Give me five new ways the Corporation can make money right now, without thinking about it. Go ahead — on your mark, get set, go!'

Woodcock snorted. 'Freddie, my job in Financial is to save the Corporation money. I don't have to think of ways to *make* money. That's your job.'

'It's our job. We're all part of the Commercial Group.' Freddie gripped the steering wheel tighter.

'No, I'm part of the Operations Group.'

'Carlton, you need to keep up with the memoranda.'

'What's that supposed to mean?'

'Financial falls under Commercial Group now. We've been restructured.' Freddie clenched his teeth, knowing what came next.

Carlton whipped his head around so fast he almost lost his glasses. 'What the fuck are you saying? We're not even in business yet and you're telling me they have already restructured?'

'Well, what better time to? At least we don't have to change the stationery. It's no big deal. I was just breakfasting with a few of the Board members yesterday and we all agreed it made more sense this way.'

'So I'm working for you? Is that what you're trying to tell me? You've been here five fucking days, and already I've been reduced to your employee?'

'Well, I don't look at it that way, Carlton. You're much more to me than that. You're my most trusted advisor, my right hand —'

'Oh shut the fuck up, Freddie!' Carlton turned towards the window and stared out his side at the blur of scenery.

It was like driving around with an angry fifteen-year-old. Freddie shook his head. 'You see, Carlton? That's one of those things that gets in your way — that language. For goodness sake, sometimes I cannot tell the difference between you and those controllers we had to talk to down in Palmerstonville. And you should always be able to tell the difference, even before you open your mouth. We need to work on that Carlton.'

'It was Palmerston North we visited, and the only thing we're working on is my ulcer,' Carlton snorted as he struggled with the lid on a bottle of Mylanta.

'Just relax, Carlton. Enjoy the scenery.' He looked again at all that beautiful real estate rolling by. 'Enjoy the game.' He glanced across at Woodcock and decided to change the subject quickly to divert the guy from giving him the silent treatment. 'All right, let's talk about cost-saving if you like then. Show me the expense analysis you've been working on. I know, show me the pie chart. I like pie charts; they remind me of … well, pies.'

Woodcock rolled his eyes in Freddie's direction. 'Right, Freddie, I'll show you a picture of a pie. It's right here in my briefcase.' He reached into the back seat, snapped open the briefcase and retrieved the top document.

'Hold on a second …' Carlton looked at the document carefully. 'What the hell's this?'

'Oh, that's mine. You must have been in the wrong briefcase.'

'It looks just like mine.' He twisted in his seat and inspected Freddie's briefcase. 'It's the same as mine.'

'You see, Carlton, there is equality in the world. Nice one too. Real leather.'

'What do you know about that?' Carlton offered a smug smile.

'We're all equal in ControlCorp, Carlton. It's what I've been trying to tell you. We're all on the same team. And there's no 'I' in team, unless you're a really bad speller.'

'Yeah, Freddie, I get it. I read the Corporate handbook, too. Hell, I wrote it.'

'I'm just saying cheer up and be patient. The Corporation is going to treat you right. Hell, they've already given you a nice expensive briefcase.'

'They gave you yours? They made me buy mine.'

'Yeah? But at cost, right?'

'So what is this anyway?' Woodcock held up the document he had retrieved from Freddie's briefcase and pushed his glasses up the short bridge of his little nose.

'I'm glad you asked. It's something I've been toying with. You know, just some ideas to toss around, get some feedback on ways to modernise, that sort of thing.'

'The Corporate Held Units Modernisation Plan?' Woodcock squinted at the cover, then turned to Freddie. 'CHUMP?'

'Yeah,' Freddie smiled, 'it's got a certain ring to it, don't you think? I was trying for SCHMUCKS, but that was too much of a stretch. Anyway, it's just a few ideas. It's the reason for the whole restructuring. It needs us working together as a team. So, can I count on you, Carlton? Are you a team player?'

Woodcock took another swig from his bottle of Mylanta and turned back to the window.

'You got to learn to trust me,' Freddie said.

'That'll be the day,' Woodcock said. 'I swear to fuck, Freddie, one of these days you're going to get me thrown into jail.' He continued staring at the passing scenery for a few moments of moody silence. 'First thing, we can't call it the CHUMP Project.'

Freddie smiled and shrugged. 'You have no sense of whimsy, Carlton. But, when you're right, you're right.' He reached across and tried to pat him on the shoulder, but Woodcock pulled away. 'So what's the next stop on our little tour today?'

Woodcock remained motionless for several moments, then let out a slow, resigned sigh. He bent forward and retrieved a different folder from the floor of the car. 'Milton Gorge Aerodrome. Let's see … mostly flight schools, small charter outfits, top-dressing. Typical provincial shit. The staff consists of a tower manager, one Thorndike Rumbold, who has virtually ignored every Head Office directive for the last eighteen years. And the staff are … well, the place is known as Exile Tower, for good reason. Six controllers, all of them dumped there in Rumbold's lap, for various reasons ranging from the positively whimsical …' Woodcock looked down and read from the file, 'one Kenneth Lima, who broke all previous records for the number of mid-airs he had during his simulator training and now refuses to stop bringing a pet rat with him to work. Says the animal's love and loyalty keeps him focused.'

'Yuck.' Freddie shuddered. 'Any mid-airs since?'

'No, of course not. But he was ultimately blamed for the rodent infestation of Gisborne Tower, so there has been speculation he may be breeding an army of them.' Woodcock glanced again at the file. 'There are a couple of old-timers — Quincy Weston and his life partner of over twenty years Bryan who had his name legally changed to Weston too; both are in their sixties and ready to be put out to pasture.' Woodcock flipped another page. 'Ah! Then, of course, there is our man, Owen Flynn.'

'What's with him?'

'Oh, you haven't heard? He was legendary for trying to put two Boeing 737s nose-to-nose down on the same track in Canterbury a few years back and refused to resolve the conflict until the two pilots agreed — and I now quote from the transcript of the radio frequency — "to stop acting like a couple of knob-headed fuckwits".'

'And, he kept his job?'

'Turns out they were twenty miles apart. He never told them that. Had them sweating though.'

'Anyone else of interest?'

'That Yank — the name's Tom Hardy. He's the guy who had a run-in with the President's plane. You probably didn't hear about it. It was a CAA kiss-up job. Figured they might get in well with the FAA if they offered jobs to every deadbeat loser the Americans wanted to unload.'

Freddie shrugged, 'Basically, the same philosophy behind importing toxic waste.'

'I think they figured it would ultimately get us back into ANZUS or something. Anyway, we didn't think he would ever show up. But when I talked to Rumbold this morning, apparently the guy not only showed, but he finished training just in time to be employed by the CAA. So, unfortunately, he gets in on a technicality.'

'Hmm,' Freddie nodded, 'so, what you're saying is: one useless airfield, seven useless employees. We sell the place off as a nuclear test site and we get rid of eight problems and make a bit of money.'

'Yeah, except we're supposed to be a nuclear-free zone.'

'A minor technicality, Carlton. Let me make a few calls.'

That first morning, after the checkride that confirmed me not only as a CAA-soon-to-be-ControlCorp controller but as an insane asylum inmate, was also the first morning I worked with Kenny as a controller. I had to admit he was unexpectedly pretty good at it. He spoke to the aircraft in the same soft but authoritative tones he used on the few occasions he actually spoke to me directly, which he did only when it was required for coordination purposes. He was not much of a conversationalist.

The rat, Garry, would move around the back of his neck from one shoulder to the other and nibble — or perhaps whisper in — his ear. At the time, Flynn's suggestion that Garry was the real brains behind the team seemed perfectly plausible. The rat was merely issuing instructions to Kenny, who on occasion would turn his head and speak in imperceptibly low whispers to Garry, as if they were conferring.

Still, the rat did give me the creeps. It was much less busy on ground control, so I read the ATC manual in the vain hope that I still might learn something before I killed someone. I was glad when Amanda showed up at one o'clock to let Kenny and Garry go home.

Amanda occupied the tower position, while I continued to work ground control. The mid-afternoon was mercifully quiet.

'So,' Amanda said, attempting to draw my attention from the ATC manual, 'at last, we're alone. I don't know how you're going to stand it, having to work with Owen Flynn.' She had her legs crossed, exposing just the right amount of thigh to draw attention.

'But you have to work with a rat,' I reminded her, only glancing up as far as the exposed thigh.

'Oh, Kenny is quite a sweet boy, and compared to Owen Flynn, Garry has a certain amount of charm too.' She kept her eyes out the window, always attentive to her job, ever vigilant. All was quiet over the airfield.

I glanced up from the book, this time all the way to her face. 'Why do you work here?'

'What do you mean?'

'Well, they call this place Exile Tower, right?'

'So I've heard.'

'I know why I'm here. I can see why Flynn and Kenny are here. I haven't got to know Quincy and Bryan, but I can imagine why they're here. So why are you here? You seem to be a perfectly competent controller with no visible mental malfunctions.'

She smiled and actually blushed.

'So why are you here? Why were you sent to Exile Tower?'

'Me?' She looked out the window and didn't say anything for so long I thought she was going to refuse to tell me. Then she turned to me, leaned forward and, rather unexpectedly, smiled — not a smile that radiated warmth or pleasure, or even sarcasm or wickedness. Her lips did not quiver with doubt — her mouth, her eyes, her whole face was fixed in certainty. Her expression was that of an Olympic gold medallist who has just turned in the winning performance, knows it, but now must wait those few moments for the official results. 'Why, I surely wouldn't know. Perhaps they needed one person to bring order here.'

'Oh.'

'Of course, that's all going to change very soon. I won't be here much longer, I assure you of that.'

'How's that?' I asked, though I was suddenly more interested in getting back to the ATC manual and memorising minimum weather criteria for landing and taking off at Milton Gorge. *Eight hundred feet cloud base and one mile visibility. When the weather closes in, when the blackness covers you like a shroud ...*

'When the Corporation is running this business, it will be run the way a business ought to be run — efficiently. There'll be no room in it for the likes of Owen Flynn or his primitive behaviour.'

I looked up again, but did not say anything.

'This is a once in a lifetime opportunity for me — for us.' Her eyes lit up, the blueness accentuated by the flawlessness of the white. 'The Corporation will be for us, Thomas.'

'Us?'

'For people like you and me: open-minded professionals who are ready and willing to embrace change, people who know opportunity and when to seize it.'

I half expected her to reach out and seize her imaginary opportunity, but she remained composed and ready for traffic, pen in one hand and the other poised near the radio mike.

'I just wanted to find somewhere quiet,' I said, but Amanda was not listening. She was only talking.

'You and me, Thomas — we're the people who can change things.' She turned her head slightly towards me, her eyes travelling the remaining distance until she met mine.

'Do you have an aspirin?' I asked.

'Of course.' She reached for her purse and began digging through it. 'You should probably put the book away when they get here,' Amanda suggested. 'It wouldn't look too good to be reading on position.'

'Not even the air traffic manual?' I held it up for her to see, but knew she was right and had no intention of looking like that much of a geek in front of the new bosses. I closed the book.

Amanda handed me the pills and smiled, seductively, alluringly, as if she was inviting me into a secret. 'This is the first time we've actually got to work together alone.'

'Yes,' I said, but thought to myself it could be our last. I took the pills and popped them in my mouth. The only thing within reach to wash them down with was a cold cup of tea that I had not finished.

'We could ask Thornie to make it permanent.'

'Really? Is he like the captain of the ship? Can he marry us?'

She laughed. 'He can on the schedule.'

'Well,' I hesitated. I was getting used to Flynn and drinking beer with him after work. On the other hand, I briefly imagined what kind of things Amanda and I could do after work.

She leaned back in her chair, exposing an inch more of her thigh, and directed her attention to looking for any unannounced movement on the airfield. 'So, tell me about yourself.'

'What's to say? Just a controller. Did some flight instructing for a while.'

'I know that much. What about your family?'

'Dad's been dead since I was a kid. My mom's remarried and is living in Phoenix. No brothers or sisters. It's a small family.'

'No, ah …' She gave her shoulder a little shrug as she finished her scan of the airfield for movement, then turned to face me. 'No, partner?'

'Not at the moment.'

'I see.' She turned back to the window and smiled again. 'Then I guess it's been a while since you've had a nice home-cooked meal. Why don't you come around tonight and I'll cook?'

'Absolutely.'

'7.30. Don't be late,' Amanda said decisively as she turned to face me again and was about to say something else but stopped at the sound of voices in the stairwell.

'Yes, since 1965 it's been like that.' Thornie's voice drifted up the stairs with other mumbling voices and stomping feet. 'Here we are.' Thornie appeared first, followed by a tall, portly man and a short, mousy-faced guy with glasses perched on the end of a button nose.

'And how lucky we are, indeed,' Thornie waved towards us. 'Miss Amanda Sheppard.'

'Ms,' Amanda corrected with a humourless smile. She stepped forward, ignoring the mousy-faced man, and offered her hand to the obvious highest power in the room. 'A pleasure to meet you finally. We've been looking forward to it.'

Thornie wrinkled his brow. 'This,' he said, 'is Mr Moore, manager, of, ah — well, something important.'

'Commercial Operations Group,' Moore said. 'The pleasure is mine. We're just working our way up the country, calling in at our airports and meeting the staff.'

The mousy-faced man looked around nervously.

'And this is Mr Woodstock,' Thornie said, 'manager of something equally impressive.'

'Woodcock, Carlton Woodcock,' he said with an agitated sigh and a resentful glance at Moore. 'It used to be Chief Financial Officer, but it's changing daily.'

'Oh my, it does sound a bit like royalty, though, doesn't it?' Thornie giggled. 'And this is Thomas Hardy, a countryman of yours, Mr Moore.'

'Hardy?' Moore first exchanged a glance with Woodcock, then turned his attention to me and offered his hand. 'I've heard so much about you.'

'Well, I'm not actually a Canadian, but close enough.'

'Tell me, Tom — do you mind if I call you Tom?' Moore asked but did not wait for an answer. 'What brings you here?'

'Work,' I said, deciding against any further attempts to offer any explanations on how I was run out of town on a rail. 'So what have you heard?'

'Oh, Thomas is so delightfully modest,' Thornie piped in proudly. 'He's the best in the business and has even been using his skills to teach our own controllers a few things.'

I could see Amanda stiffening up through the corner of my eye, or maybe I just felt it. There was definitely a chill in the air.

'Is that so?' Moore said, rubbing his chin and squinting at me.

'Well, now, I wouldn't say that.' I tried to offer some argument, but was saved from further conversation by an aircraft calling ground control, and so turned my attention to the radio.

Thornie, speaking quietly so as not to disturb me — the master of ground control — was pointing out various buildings on the field for Moore, who appeared to be only half-listening. Woodcock cowered under Amanda's grilling over the business plan and escaped under the pretence of having a question for Thornie. Moore then turned his attention back to me.

'It's good to see a man who knows opportunity when he sees it,' he said and slapped me on the back. 'And don't worry, Tom. We don't care so much who you were or what you did. I suspect you could be going places. The future is an equal opportunity employer.'

'Yes, sir, I sure hope so.'

'Well, Amanda,' Thornie said, turning to her. 'Mr Moore has expressed a desire to see more of the aerodrome itself. Would you mind keeping an eye on things for me for thirty minutes?'

'Of course not,' Amanda said. 'You know you can always count on me.'

'So you leave the girl in charge?' Moore piped in. 'Excellent. Good to see them having an equal go of it.'

Amanda stood rigidly still. 'Yes, sir,' she said crisply, lips slowly disappearing into a single thin line. Her eyes were locked on Moore, though he did not notice. He had turned away.

While Thornie's attention was briefly with Amanda, Moore leaned over to Woodcock and whispered something through the corner of his mouth. I could not hear what he had said, but it elicited a knowing nod from Woodcock.

Thornie led the two men out of the cab. Amanda's cold, savage glare followed them out and remained frozen on the empty space they left behind for several seconds.

'So, there's one of your new corporate bosses for you,' I said, trying to break her trance. 'Anyway, I wouldn't take him too seriously if I were you — sounds like he hasn't attended his political correctness training seminar yet.'

Amanda turned to me and smiled. As she did, the grimness once again melted away into something approaching radiance, though I thought a shadow of it remained.

When the blackness moves in, when the shadows cover you like a shroud.

She sat down. 'So, I do believe we were discussing dinner.'

Ten

I arrived at Amanda's house at 7.40. When she came to the door, the first thing that struck me was that she was even more attractive after hours than she was at work. Maybe it was the light of the setting sun, or the soft glow of the porch light that was on too early, but her blonde hair glowed with just a hint of red, and her eyes seemed a deeper shade of blue in the twilight. She wore blue jeans and a snug-fitting T-shirt that accentuated a striking and, probably, well-managed figure. Her fragrance smelled of lilac and was, perhaps, just a little too strong.

'Hello. You're late,' she said as she motioned me inside. 'You must have had trouble finding the place.'

'No, not lost, just misjudged the timing of the drive,' I said, handing her a bottle of Australian red. 'I'm a pilot. I don't get lost.'

She looked at the label on the wine and, though her smile only flickered slightly, I could see it fell short of her approval. 'Yes, you are a pilot, aren't you? Can I get you something to drink? Gin? Scotch? A glass of white?'

'Yeah. A G and T sounds good.'

'Make yourself comfortable. Put some music on,' she said as she showed me into the lounge and indicated a stereo on the bookshelf, then continued into the kitchen to get the drinks.

The lounge was tastefully decorated — a little too much so for three single people sharing a flat. There was no mismatched furniture, or stereo cabinets made of apple crates, or walls decorated with posters of James Dean, or cats poking their heads out of toilet bowls, and no rubber tree plant dying in the corner. All these plants were alive and thriving, the walls were adorned with modern art, the leather lounge suite looked too expensive to be comfortable, and the whole room was bathed in the glow of a half-dozen candles.

I selected a disc and perused the label.

'Ray Charles, okay?'

A quiet groan came from the kitchen. 'I'd prefer some classical, if you don't mind,' she said.

'Fine.' I returned Ray to his place and continued through the stack. Rossini — nothing like the Italians for romance. I fumbled with the stereo. 'So you say there are three of you here?'

'Yeah,' she called back. 'Myself, Anthony and Kelli. But flatting is only temporary for me. I've got better ideas than this for my lifestyle. Besides, I don't have much use for Kelli.' Then she added matter-of-factly. 'She's a slut.'

'Lucky Anthony,' I said to myself, but hadn't seen her re-enter the lounge.

'He's gay,' she said, standing in the doorway with a glass of wine for herself and handed me a water glass-sized gin and tonic. She held a glass out and glanced at the stereo as Rossini started playing. 'Oh, Anthony likes that Italian stuff, too.' She reached over and turned the volume down, then returned to me and held her glass aloft.

'Cheers,' I offered, tapping her glass and, raising it to my mouth, took a long thirst-quenching slug. My guess was it was at least half gin with the tonic sharing the other half with the ice cubes.

'Don't give me this "cheers" business.' She held her glass still, poised, waiting for me to return my glass back to the toast position. 'To our newest controller, congratulations,' she said, proudly.

'I'll drink to that.' I tapped her glass again and took another long drink, but still hers remained unmoved.

'To the Corporation. A new age.' She glowed as she spoke the words, as if she were proclaiming the birth of a new religion.

'Whatever you say.' I tapped her glass and took yet another drink. At this rate, it was entirely possible I was going to finish the entire drink before she got around to taking one sip.

'To us!' she proclaimed loudly.

Again, I tapped her glass, hesitantly. 'To controllers, worldwide.'

'No,' she said emphatically. 'To us. To you, me — us!' This time she tapped my glass and raised it to her lips.

'I'll drink to that,' and downed the rest of my drink, my words echoing in the glass.

'Let me make you another,' she said as she took the glass from my hand, looking mildly disapproving that it had disappeared so quickly.

'Listen, don't go through the trouble,' I said as she disappeared into the kitchen. 'I'll just have what you're having.'

She returned with the bottle of wine and handed me a filled glass.

'I must say,' she said, 'after meeting our Mr Moore today, I should say we won't be encountering much trouble moving up the ladder.' She moved to the sofa, sat down and leaned back, holding her glass delicately, seductively.

'What ladder?'

She smiled at me as if she knew I was playing stupid. 'Promotions, my dear. I mean, if that's the calibre of executive, then I'd say we both would easily meet the standard.'

'Executive?' I laughed at the thought of me as an exec and took a big gulp of wine. The transition from gin to wine made me feel a little light-headed at first, but I shook that off and moved over to the sofa. 'I don't think —'

'Just a second,' Amanda set her glass down and jumped up. 'Stir-fry's almost done. Why don't you take the bottle and have a seat at the table?'

I refilled my glass, filling it to the rim, then emptied the rest of the bottle into her glass.

A few minutes later, she re-entered and placed a ceramic dish on the table. 'I hope you don't mind, but it's nothing fancy. I'll just get the rice and we can get started.'

I leaned over and smelled the dish of chicken and stir-fried vegetables. 'Smells great.'

'Oh, it's nothing, just something easy enough for me not to ruin.' She reappeared with a bowl of rice in one hand and a large green salad in the other. 'I'm really not the kitchen type.'

'No, I'm sure you're a great cook,' I smiled and raised my glass to her, but I knew that didn't come out right even before I felt the chill.

'Being a woman doesn't mean I have any natural inclinations towards cooking.' She set the bowls down on the table with a thump and eyed me cautiously, as if it was my turn to serve the ball.

'Not at all — what I meant was it smells good and figured you must be a good, or a pretty good, cook. What do I know? I'm hardly a connoisseur of fine dining. It might be crap for all I know. No, that doesn't sound right either. Well … maybe we should open that other bottle of wine. I believe Australian red goes well with food. Anyway, you know what I mean.'

'Yes I do.' She offered a slight smile, not so much out of kindness as victory, and went to the sideboard, returning with the bottle of red. 'I'd suggest giving it plenty of time to breathe.'

While I wrestled with uncorking the wine, she served up the dinner and looked to be relaxing again as she motioned me to take a seat — not across from her, but at an intimate right angle. Having decided against saying any more than was necessary, I asked about the classes she was taking, a subject that warmed her up considerably. She told me about how hard she had been working to complete her course of study in business, how she had had the foresight to see the changes in the wind, and that she believed she would have her masters in less than a year. She had little intention of remaining a controller any longer than was necessary and knew I could understand that. She talked for ten or fifteen minutes on the fascinating things she's been learning without pause enough to take a bite of food. I listened politely, smelling the stir-fry as it cooled off, and, when she sounded like she was winding down on the subject, picked up my fork, hoping she might follow my lead.

'It looks, ah …' but I saved myself the hazard of finishing a sentence by sticking a forkful of food in my mouth. And it was good, certainly better than any of the fast-food meals I had had since my arrival. 'Mmmm, very ...' I hesitated, nodding my approval. 'Sufficient. Adequate. Completely functional.'

She laughed, which I took as a minor victory for me: fifteen all. At my best, I'm sure I could have made Stalin laugh.

'Thomas.' She raised her glass of white, still not half way through her first. Once again, her eyes were bright, her smile easy. She looked safe.

'Yes?'

I finished off the last of my white and eyed the bottle of red, wondering how much breathing would be enough.

'Thomas,' she said again. 'You and I.'

Enough breathing — I poured a glass of red.

'Do you see the potential for people like us?'

'Oh, yeah.'

'I knew you would. That's why you came here, for the opportunity.'

'I say, "Never pass one up." Ask anyone. That's what I say.' My head was already starting to feel the buzz that I knew would turn into a roar.

'Exactly. With new economic policies constantly being introduced in New Zealand, we are quickly becoming the land of opportunity.'

'And opportunists.' I held my glass up in toast.

'A man like you is attracted by that.'

'Absolutely, I like someone who knows what they want.'

'Yes!' She leaned back and smiled. 'You know, I never believed that ridiculous story about you refusing the President's plane landing clearance from the start and arguing with the pilot over the air. I was sure it was a complete fabrication.'

'It was blown out of proportion by those who enjoy a good story. One hundred percent bullshit — for the most part. Not more than forty percent truth. Maybe fifty, sixty max. In any case, the man's still alive, isn't he? So what does he have to complain about?' I had another bite of chicken stir-fry, but was more interested in the wine at that stage.

'I can't tell you how good it is to have a like-minded person finally show up at that God-forsaken airfield. Thanks to Mr Rumbold, that place has been permanently stuck in 1963. Do you know, he's the reason we've become known as Exile Tower?'

'Is that right?'

'Yes. Because Thornie created his own little kingdom where nothing ever goes wrong and there is no such thing as problems, the ministry took advantage of that and began using the place as a dumping ground for every controller they never wanted to deal with. Really, can you picture Owen Flynn being employed anywhere else? He's completely uncivilised.'

'Oh, I don't know. For all his faults, Flynn isn't too bad.'

'Oh, please. He's a Neanderthal.'

'Possibly.'

'Even if he has managed not to kill anybody yet — and it's only a matter of time before he does — he's so out-dated. There's no place in the new system for a man as unprofessional and uncivilised as him.'

'He's a little rough around the edges.' I really did not want to talk about Flynn with Amanda. There were so many other things we could be talking about — or doing. Nor did I want to have to defend him. He was the only person in the country that I, sort of, considered a friend. I'm not exactly sure why. Maybe it was because out of all the lunatics, Flynn was the only one who knew he was a lunatic.

'You need to be careful that you're not identified too closely with him.' She gently waved a finger at me that suggested I was on my way to detention. 'You and I are the only two people at that airport who are really suitable to carry on this business into the future. And they'll see it.'

For the first time since I had known her — and drunk as I was — I felt something radiating from Amanda Sheppard. Something else. It was not just passion or ambition as I had thought earlier.

This was power. This was real power. She thought she wanted it, but she already had it. What she wanted — needed — was to make it tangible. She wanted to feel it in her hands. At that moment, to me, she was frightening. And so damned hot.

'Now, Thomas,' she leaned further forward and lowered her voice to a seductive whisper, 'we were discussing us, and our future.'

'Oh yeah.' I took another long drink of the red wine, then set my glass down and reached over to place my hand on hers.

'Networking, alliances are extremely important, and it's never too early to start. We each have the potential for rewards here, individually, but the two of us ...' she reached her other arm across the table and placed it on mine, 'as a team, we could be ...' she squeezed my arm, 'synergistic!'

'Oh, yeah,' I whispered. 'Sounds fantastic! Count me in.'

'We could join forces.'

I leaned forward until my face was only inches from hers. 'Let's.'

'Yes, an alliance.' She smiled mischievously. 'We could be going places.'

'But let's stay in tonight.'

'Oh, we're so much alike.' She pulled her hand out from under mine and placed it on top. 'We both know just what we want. There's no competition between us because we can both have it, and we're both willing to do what we have to do to get it.' Her hand squeezed my arm harder. 'There's nothing wrong with that. The meek may, possibly, inherit the earth in the end. But it's us, the ambitious, the ones willing to work for it, who will earn it!' She was raising her voice and increasing the pressure on my arm. 'We're the ones who cause progress. We shape the future with our own hands. You, me, we have the chance to make a change, a change for the better. The power to right the wrongs of the past.'

'Let tomorrow deal with regrets. That's what I say.' That was supposed to sound poetic, but I was drunk and horny, and it was the best I could do as I went forward and met her lips over the table. I knew, from that moment, I would be regretting it long before tomorrow though. I was already scared of her. I knew I was walking right into her web. I could feel the silk threads encircling me and tightening around my throat as vividly as I felt her grip cutting off the circulation to my arm. I grabbed her by the shoulder, knocking over my glass while she came forward and snaked her arm around to the small of my back as the red wine blossomed into the white linen tablecloth.

'Thomas, Thomas, Thomas,' she breathed heavily into my ear.

'That would be pretty much all of us.' I tried to roll her over into the stir-fry, but she had better leverage and somehow reversed the tactic.

'I want to be a major player in the Corporation.' She didn't seem to mind that she had an elbow in her own plate of stir-fry. 'I want you to be a major player, Thomas. I can make you one. Right by my side. Together we'll be magnificent.' She rolled me over through the salad, knocking her own wine over so that her white mixed with my red. 'I want it all, Thomas! I want us to have it all. Thomas! I want you!' She planted her lips firmly on mine, the force of which brought us both to the floor and the whole of our dinner following closely behind. 'I want you to be my ally.'

I groped at her tight fitting T-shirt; she pulled at the buttons of my shirt even as she was pushing me away.

'But not this, Thomas.'

'Yes! This here, now. I've never done it on rice before.'

'No, we can't.' She pushed me away as she sat up. 'Don't you see? Our potential goes way beyond sex. We have the chance to form a business merger.'

'So let's merge,' I said as I was unbuttoning her jeans.

'But we don't want to spoil it with a physical relationship.'

'Yes. Yes, we do.'

'No, Thomas.'

'I'm pretty sure I want this very much right now.'

'What you want is what we want. We have a chance to change the world. What we want is power.'

'No, it's just the sex I want for now.' It was amazing, I hadn't even had sex with her yet and I was already regretting it — regretting it and begging for it all at once. I could see the fangs coming down and all I wanted was what was due me before death. Does the spider do the same thing? Is the male black widow spider aware that he's going to die shortly after sex saying to himself, 'Well, this better be good'? Is that human nature too? Or just spider nature?

She leaned away. 'Thomas, try to think clearly here. Try for one moment to consider the future.' She began re-buttoning her jeans.

'What?'

'The future.'

'How am I supposed to think of the future? I'm lying under your dining table in chicken stir-fry and rice with something dripping on my head.'

'I think you're getting carried away.'

'I'm getting carried away? You were breathing pretty heavy, too, you know.'

'Your advances were uncalled for, a typically male response. You misunderstand your own animal instincts for actual intellectual discourse.'

'What? You're insane.' In retrospect, that was a really bad thing to say. Her head snapped around, her eyes filled with the fires of hatred. At that moment I was sure she could have killed me with her bare hands.

'Don't you ever call me insane.'

'I'm sorry, I didn't mean it. But listen, Amanda.' I was still catching my breath. 'You got the wrong idea. All I want is to be a controller. That's all I am; that's all I want to be. I'm not executive material, not a manager, not an aspiring mover and/or shaker, not a rancher and I've never even been on a horse. All I want is to live quietly somewhere that I can talk to airplanes and not worry about one minor infraction being turned into an international incident.'

I slowly got up, letting chunks of sticky rice fall to the floor. She remained sitting on the floor, back against the sideboard. A devilish smile was tugging at the corners of her mouth.

'Thomas?'

'Yes?'

'If you're not with me, you're against me.'

'No, no, no.' I said shaking my head. 'Don't even try using that one on me, or it will be Air Force One all over again.'

'Being a male gives you the competitive edge only for now. That won't be the case forever, or even for long. Despite having allies like Mr Moore.'

'Allies? What are you talking about?'

She smiled again. 'Oh don't deny it. You don't need to be ashamed of it. You know as well as I do that Mr Moore was at Milton Gorge this week just to scout for talent. The way he was looking at you, the way he was looking at me. He knows where we're headed.'

'For now, I'm headed home.' I picked another clump of rice out of my hair and looked around for my car keys.

'I don't blame you for trying to impress him. And I'm not afraid of a little competition myself. We could go so much further if we were to stick together, but just don't think you could ever betray me and not pay for it.'

'Okay, got it.' I headed for the door. 'Thanks for dinner, Amanda, it was, interesting if nothing else.'

'Thomas?' She had stood up, but kept her distance.

I paused at the front door.

'Don't leave,' she whispered. 'Stay.'

'I've got an early day tomorrow. Listen —' It was at this point that I would normally want to apologise for being me, but I didn't, which I consider a moment of personal growth. Instead, I just stared at her for several seconds in silence. She reminded me, in several ways, of my ex-wife, Janey. It was hard to put my finger on just what they had in common. Perhaps it was because they both wanted me as a foot soldier in their crusades.

'We'll be okay. Okay?' I said and offered a gentle smile. 'I'll see you at work next week.'

It's happening all over again, I thought as I fumbled with my keys. I drove three blocks away from Amanda's and pulled to the side of the road.

Too god damn drunk. I was feeling more sober than I was, but I was sober enough to know I wasn't. I groped around the back seat for my jacket, got out of the car, put it on. I looked around the ever-increasing darkness on an unlit street.

I have been guilty of calling my ex-wife a bitch on occasion, and I had reason enough to support the claim. She dumped me after three years of spending all my money; she left me for a pilot and, worse yet, a guy I knew and didn't like. At the time of her departure, my career was down the shitter and she was not entirely without blame there. In fairness to Janey, however, I should say she was not really a bitch.

She was a passionate person. She was a strong and intense person. But passion can be a dangerous chemical when it meets the wrong catalyst. And maybe that's what I was. After all, when I met her, she seemed pretty nice. She was caring to animals and the elderly. She took in strays — I think that's the qualification I got in on — and she joined every liberal activist group within a fifty-mile radius. In Northern California, that's a lot of joining.

We had a lot in common. I just cannot remember exactly what that was now. I thought I was a liberal, but she made me feel like a right-wing extremist just because I worked for the federal government. The guy she referred to as 'my boss', that is, the President, was a Republican. Hell, I didn't vote for him. I didn't vote for anybody.

The dirty money these Republicans paid me every other week, however, was not so tainted that she did not funnel a considerable amount of it towards her causes. I always thought I deserved at least some credit for pretty much funding that entire demonstration down at the stand of redwoods that they opened up for logging, even though I couldn't be there myself to get thrown in jail with my wife and the rest of the local heroes because I was on morning shifts all that week.

When I suggested to her that social injustice was too big and widespread for one person to take on single-handedly without being driven completely off their rocker, she did not take it well. Apparently, it all became clear to her that I was just another closet Republican who was probably actively working against activism. And like an idiot, I responded by attempting to prove her wrong. Like a bloody idiot.

Too god damn drunk.

I zipped the jacket up to my neck against the encroaching chill and walked off into the blackness in a direction I wasn't sure about, but thought there might be a McDonald's.

Eleven

I was in the middle of this dream. I was in the woods down by the Russian River outside Santa Rosa in Northern California. I was the age I am now, but I was with my dog, Wiley, that I got when I was a kid and is now long dead. We used to go there a lot when I was a teenager, so Wiley knew the place as well as I did. The trees were tall and the shadows long — there were many places he could hide if he wanted to. But I knew where he was headed — to the big green meadow that lay beyond the trees — and he dashed ahead in anticipation of what he was going to find to chase.

'Come back here, Wiley,' I yelled after him in vain. If the park ranger caught me letting my dog run free, I'd be in trouble again. I thought it was a stupid rule, and one that needed to be broken every now and again. There was seldom anyone else around here during the week, and a dog needed to be unleashed from time to time. Everyone did.

'He never listens to me. You'd think he was a pilot,' I said to Janey, who in my dream was walking at my side, although it made no sense, since I did not meet her until long after I left Santa Rosa. But, it was not Janey's voice that replied. 'Och! My wee laddie is lost!' my dad said in his pretend Scottish accent, and then laughed loudly, 'Then you, ye auld, snick-drawing dog!'

'What are you talking about?' I demanded.

He stopped laughing. His expression was as grey and lifeless as it was in the casket, as he leaned his ashen face to within inches of mine and, in a low, slow rumble, growled, 'Remember, Cowboy. Or others will die.'

'Remember what?' I asked.

'Remember me,' he said.

'What? But I haven't forgotten you. How could I?'

Then I was jolted awake.

'Hey, Cowboy!' Flynn kicked the bed frame. 'Wake up.'

The room was the dark grey glow of pre-dawn. I recognised the voice of the shadowy figure standing over my bed, but too late to prevent my body from twitching in momentary fright.

'I didn't scare you, did I?' Flynn said, grinning.

'You're a God-awful thing to wake up to. What the hell are you doing here and how did you get in?'

'We're going camping today, remember? And I let myself in.'

'Let yourself out and lock the door on your way. I don't want to go. I changed my mind.' I pulled the blankets up to my chin and rolled over, hoping against hope that this, too, was just an extension of a bad dream.

'I don't think the lock works any more. Besides, you'll change your mind once we get there. Now come on, we're late.' Flynn grabbed the blankets, and in one swift motion left them in a pile at the foot of the bed.

The sharp coldness of the morning air hit me like the snap of a wet towel and all I could do was moan in agony, curl up, shivering in my underwear, and bury my face in my pillow.

'Come on, Cowboy. We're wasting daylight. We've got distance to cover,' Flynn said. 'I'll go and fix you a cup of coffee.'

'Daylight?' I clutched the pillow for warmth.

'It'll be light soon enough,' Flynn said from the kitchen as he made an unnecessarily loud show of preparing a cup of instant coffee, banging cupboard doors, rattling dishes and kicking chairs around the kitchen.

I rolled out of bed and struggled into my clothes. The wine from the night before had worked its way into my cranium and set my brain afloat, banging against its moorings and making sloshing noises inside my head.

'You're not a morning person, are you?' Flynn handed me a cup of instant coffee as I stumbled into the kitchen, wrestling my way into a sweatshirt.

'I had a late night.' I took a sip of the strong, hot coffee and closed my eyes in pain. 'Jesus, this coffee is terrible.'

'It'll do the trick,' Flynn said, looking mildly hurt. He took a seat at the table. 'So — did you pork her?'

'Pork who?' My hand trembled as I searched through the assortment of junk collecting on top of the refrigerator until I found the container of aspirin. I sat down opposite Flynn and fumbled with the inebriate-proof cap.

'You know who,' Flynn said, snatching the aspirin and ripping the top off without regard as to whether the little arrows were lined up or not. Nothing could keep Flynn out if he wanted inside, be it an aspirin bottle or my house. He set the open bottle in front of me. 'Her Royal Harness. Weren't you going to her place last night for a little pork?'

'I think we had chicken. And, no, I didn't. I'm pretty sure she hates me. Unless, of course, I misunderstood her threat to ruin me.' I struggled to wash a couple aspirin down with the hot coffee.

'Thank God, you're saved.' He got up from the table and looked around. 'So, I don't suppose you're ready?'

'Not quite. Look, have you checked the weather? Maybe this isn't the best —'

'The weather's fine. Trust me, everything's going to be perfect. Now, you go get your gear together and I'll fry us up a couple egg sandwiches for the road.'

I suspected Flynn would not hesitate to use force, club me over the head, or perhaps hold me at gunpoint, and then lock me in the trunk of the car. So I decided to go quietly.

'You never congratulated me on passing the test yesterday,' I said once we hit the highway.

Flynn looked at me and rolled his eyes back. 'You still haven't figured it out yet then?'

'I haven't figured anything out yet, Flynn. When I was in school,

I got stuck on Reaganomics and haven't been able to tackle another riddle since. And yesterday was one heck of a riddle. They didn't ask me a single question that had anything to do with anything. I'm not even sure if they knew I was there.'

'They knew. You're just a controller who probably knows more about it than they do, so how are they supposed to test you?'

'What about the questions though? All that stuff I've been trying to cram into my brain over the last few days. I thought he might be interested to know if I knew any of it.'

'Thornie's a practical guy. He knows there's not a lot of the rulebook that applies to Milton Gorge. He also knows you're going to learn what you need to survive.'

'Yeah, well, you could have saved me a lot of hassle.'

'And spoil the fun?' Flynn laughed. 'We ask for so little.'

I forced a laugh to prove to the son of a bitch I was a good sport.

'I'm sure he would have liked to have given you a month or so to get comfortable,' Flynn continued, 'but he didn't have the time. Besides, he likes you, and if he likes you, he'll bend over backwards to help you out.'

'He doesn't even know me. He still thinks I herd cattle in my spare time.'

Flynn laughed again. 'He knows he likes you. You're lucky that way. I'm lucky because he likes me. That's something Amanda hasn't figured out. She can bad-mouth me all she wants, but when it comes down to it, he likes me and he doesn't like her.'

'Really? He seems to be pretty nice to her.'

'He's afraid of her.'

'Afraid of her?'

'You have to remember that in Thornie's prime it was a boys-only club. He's not intentionally sexist. He's just old-fashioned.'

'I see.' I turned to watch the scenery in the early morning light. The rolling green hills reminded me of Ireland. When I was a kid, my dad took us there on a holiday one summer. I was too young to remember much of that trip, except that I saw very little of my dad. He was giving lectures at the university most of the time.

I had never thought to ask Flynn where this river he wanted to go to was. I just assumed we would drive for an hour, back the car into an open space next to the gently tumbling mountain stream, pitch the tent and start pumping the Coleman stove. My assumptions were incorrect. In the first three hours we covered the distance a law-abiding driver might have done in five. I alternated my time during the drive by trying to doze off and clenching the armrest hard enough to inhibit the blood flow in my arm — much like a soldier in the trenches tries to catch a few minutes of shut-eye while knowing death is imminent. Flynn attacked the road as if he had a personal vendetta against the benignly winding ribbon of asphalt, snapping the car around bends, rocketing past the other cars in his way without pause or hesitation and, I was certain, on two or three occasions, went airborne over bumps.

It was somewhat ironic, I thought as I watched the gentle, placid farmlands pass by my window in a serene blur, that I could die in absolute horror like this here. The landscape at dawn was a tranquil blend of greens and golds, the sky a smooth, polished granite. The low mountains appeared on the horizon, the land rose and the hills became steeper. The agriculture industry gave way to timberlands, which in turn gave way to native bush.

We headed south, west of Lake Taupo, hit the Desert Road — the tops of the volcanic peaks to our right were all hidden in cloud — and at some point I barely noticed, turned east and headed into the bush. Flynn slowed down only marginally when the sealed road gave way to unsealed gravel, and, again, when the gravel gave way to dirt. The dirt road deteriorated into ruts and potholes. Possibly not a road at all, I considered, but a riverbed, or a washout, or some other naturally caused phenomenon serving as a reminder that we would probably never be found again should we suffer a mechanical — or nervous — breakdown.

The noonday sun was just burning off the overcast when Flynn announced our arrival. I stumbled from the car, stretched my back, massaged my sore arm in an effort to restore circulation and took a look around at the surrounding forest.

'Not bad, eh?' Flynn said as he unloaded the car, tossing the packs onto the ground.

'Nice, ' I murmured, although the fragment of serenity I felt was not so much from the surrounding native bush, but more out of the gratitude to whatever luck or God had kept me alive over the last several hours. 'Is there a campsite around here?'

'Nope. We need to walk a bit to get to it.' Flynn had both packs open on the ground and was transferring some of the food from his to mine.

I slapped an insect that was biting into my arm. 'There are mosquitoes here,' I announced as I wiped away the spot of blood and the little diner's crushed body. Another chomped into my neck and met a similar fate. 'Shit, they're all over the place.'

'They're sandflies. The mozzies won't be out till dusk. I'd recommend you get your gear together before they devour you. They won't bother you once you start moving.'

Flynn slung his pack on, walked up to me and slapped me in the face, then examined his palm and grinned as he showed me the squashed sandfly. I rubbed my cheek as I watched Flynn walk away and pondered the intelligence of me disappearing into the forest with this guy. I should have left word with somebody. Maybe they could have warned me that Flynn has been a suspect in several cases of disappearing foreigners. But it was a bit late now, and, against the certainty of death by sandfly, I might be better to take my chances with him. I picked another sandfly off my arm, rolled it between my fingertips and inspected it. At least death might be quicker with Flynn.

The bush was dense, the track overgrown. I stepped carefully through the thick, twisted roots that laced the path. Flynn was waiting for me on the other side of a muddy patch, which I attempted to step gingerly around.

'You think you're going to keep those boots dry?' Flynn laughed, shook his head and continued ahead.

When I was a kid, in California, I had done one or two backpacking trips in my brief and inglorious career with the Scouts, but it did not prepare me for this. Those trails were well graded and dry; this was more like the Amazon. The foliage was lush and often obscured the track, which itself was mostly muddy bogs or masses of twisted roots. My dream of dry feet lasted nearly ten minutes. There was no way to avoid the ankle-deep mud, and occasionally a harmless looking damp patch turned out to be knee-deep. By the time we reached the first stream to ford, I was grateful enough to wade through, if for no other reason than to wash some of the thick, sticky mud from my boots and lighten the load.

Flynn was several strides ahead, and the hard, steady pace he maintained was not conducive to carrying on idle conversation, so I was content to occupy my ears with the songs and the screeches of the forest birds and the *squish-suck-squish-suck* sound made by my boots with every step I took through the mud. As my foot hit the ground, the mud and water that was saturating my socks would ooze out between the laces in sync with the squish-suck-squish-suck. At first, it made me giggle. Then it started to lose its entertainment value, became merely monotonous, then hypnotic — *squish-suck-squish-suck-squish-suck*. Occasionally the screech of a forest bird would jump in on cue as if it had all been orchestrated as part of a forest symphony: *squish-suck-squish-suck-screech-squawk-squish-suck-ooze*.

This was enough, I thought, to drive a perfectly sane man crazy. Certainly it would be a problem for a perfectly sane man. Here I was, alone in a jungle, up to my knees in mud, with a man known to be, at the very least, borderline insane, if not a full blown psychopath. I reached for a moss-covered log that crumbled in my grip and left me with a handful of green, squooshy fluff. I grabbed at another branch that offered slightly more support in my tug of war with Mother Earth.

After the first hour, I was beginning to doubt Flynn's concept of time.

'Where the hell is this campsite?'

'Just up ahead a bit.'

'That's what you said when we started out.'

'Yeah, well, it's still ahead of us.'

Flynn showed no signs of slowing down or even being out of breath. The track rose sharply and he went up the steep zigzag climb like a mountain goat. As the track continued to get steeper, there was a slight change in the vegetation, from the thick rainforest to what Flynn explained was mostly beech, though I wouldn't know. To me, if it's green, it's poison oak.

By late afternoon, we had worked our way around to the south-eastern side of the mountain and were making our way down towards the river again. The cloud cover had burnt off and the sun was high in the sky.

'There it is,' Flynn said, pointing ahead.

'There what is?' It took me a minute to make out the small green shack that blended in well with the background. 'Who would build a house up here?'

'It's not a house, it's a hut. It's not the flashiest of huts in the backcountry, but as far as I'm concerned, it's the best. And I'll show you why.'

The inside of the hut smelled of dampness and age, but was, all things considered, in good shape. It was small. Each wall was no more than eight feet long. There were four solidly built bunks, two on each side, with a potbelly stove in the centre, and a heavy, scarred wooden table. The bunks looked like they had seen a lot of use, but were holding up and comfortable enough.

I eased the pack off, letting the weight slide from my aching muscles and feeling like Atlas taking a smoko. I sank onto a lower bunk and would have gladly surrendered to it, but Flynn wasn't about to let me.

'Come on. We won't eat dinner if we don't catch it.' He pulled some gear from his pack and began assembling a fishing rod and reel.

I paused as I watched him.

'I know. You don't like fishing, either,' he said, rolling his eyes. 'Give it a try. You might learn to like it.'

'I have given it a try,' I said, but was thinking that maybe I should try it again.

Flynn shrugged. 'Suit yourself.'

Maybe that's what I needed — a hobby. Go fishing, just like in the good ol' days. I rolled the idea around for a few minutes. *'Och! A wee laddie he is, but he will grow to be a great protector of worms and fish and man.'*

'Okay,' I said jumping from the bunk. 'But you might have to remind me how it works.' I followed Flynn down to the river and perched myself on a nearby rock to watch him fish. I have never been clear on fishing. It is not so much that I enjoy the act as I enjoy the idea. My dad took me fishing once when I was a kid — 'a wee laddie' — I went because I wanted to do something with my dad, not because of the fish. In fact, I was really quite concerned that I might actually catch something. My lack of killer instinct extends that far.

'But you're not averse to eating them?' Flynn asked.

'No, I'm not,' I said, knowing very well what his point was and how easy it was for him to make it, but I still didn't buy it. There is a big difference between seeing something on the plate and being the one to squeeze the life from it.

'The problem is, you think of it as a friend. If you think of it as an arch foe, I bet you wouldn't have too much trouble killing and devouring it. You've had enemies before, haven't you?' He turned towards me and grinned. 'I mean, besides heads of state.'

'So who's the fish to you? Amanda?'

'Not at all. She's not my enemy.'

'You're kidding, right? You hate her.'

'No, not at all.' He turned back to me and was dead serious. 'We don't hate each other.'

'Could have fooled me.'

'She's just got a lot to live up to.'

'How's that?'

'Sir Richard Sheppard, that's how.'

'Sir who?'

'He's huge in the corporate world, a textbook bastard by all accounts. He was married to the woman who put him through school and struggled with him through the early years. But she only produced two daughters, so he divorced her in favour of a younger woman who would provide him with male heirs — a real Henry the Eighth type. So, you get one guess who daughter number two is.'

'You're kidding — Amanda?'

Flynn nodded. 'The little girl who broke up mommy and daddy's marriage because she wasn't good enough, or the right sex, from the very beginning.'

'Ouch.' I considered the impact such an idea might have on a little girl, but was at a loss. 'But certainly, this Sir Richard guy must have to offer some support.'

'I don't know. I doubt very much she would take anything from him. No, she's very much into proving she can do it all without assistance. Put herself through school, honours, all that. It's a pity she has to be motivated by vengeance. That's what clouds her thinking. Anyway, she graduated top of her class at the Aviation College.'

'Top? Really?'

'Yeah, she's a good controller — a bit too by-the-book for me, but efficient and professional.' He turned and glared menacingly. 'Don't you ever repeat that.'

I nodded. 'So how'd she end up in Milton Gorge?'

'In Exile Tower?' Flynn smiled. 'She scared the bosses down in Wellington. She was already better educated than anybody in management when she started in air traffic. When she finished her course at the College, they sent her right to Wellington. But she was too ambitious and it was too obvious, and it scared the shit out of them. It was made even worse because she was a woman, and young.'

'And attractive.'

'Yup. So they made up an excuse that she needed more experience in a domestic centre and packed her off.'

'So her paranoia is actually justifiable?'

'Yup.'

'Unlike mine.'

'Oh no, trust me, yours is justified too. Anyway, when she first arrived at Milton Gorge, all perky and pleasant, hell, I actually felt sorry for her. First thing she tried to do, though, was to organise the place.'

'Organise?'

'Yeah, tried to get the pilots to comply with regulations and standard operating procedures. Tried to get the controllers to use only approved phraseology and radio techniques, and to file incident reports for every minor infraction, which in itself would have been a full-time job at that place. Hell, she even tried to organise a social club — I mean a regular one, not the one at The Tie Down. It's the most sociable airfield in the country, and she wanted to introduce a social club.' Flynn laughed at the thought. 'What a trooper. It was enough to keep Thornie locked in his office for a week.'

'So, if you felt so sorry for her, how come you guys are always going at each other?'

'She can detect pity and she won't have any of it. She'll go for your jugular if you try pity. Besides, it's about life in the balance, you know? We're just playing out our roles. She's an extreme person. So, to keep things balanced out there, I got to be extremely opposite. Yin and yang and all that shit. She knows it as well as I do. In the end, we're all in this together. We the unloved, the unwashed, the unwanted, the orphans of air traffic control.' He stared into the water for a moment in silence and then started reeling his line in. 'Come on, they're not biting. Time for a drink. I think the pub's almost open.'

'There's a pub here?'

'Just follow me.'

'To the end of the earth, Flynn. Or are we there yet?'

Flynn disappeared into the hut and returned a minute later, held up a canteen in one hand and a hip flask in the other, giving both a little shake. They sounded temptingly full.

'Grab your mug and follow me,' he said as he took to the path that rose behind the hut. A moment of panic seized me as I rushed into the hut and dug through my pack for the mug, as if I let this pie-eyed piper get too far ahead I'd be lost.

Flynn must have jogged the rocky hill behind the hut because I did not catch up with him until the top, despite feeling a hundred pounds lighter without the pack.

'More climbing,' I said, trying to catch my breath. 'Jesus, what a great view.'

'It's more than a view, mate,' Flynn shouted, his arms were spread wide as if he were awaiting crucifixion. 'It's the whole universe.'

It did not seem like such an overstatement. We were perched on top of a rocky hill with a nearly 360-degree view of mountain scenery, the river twisting and tumbling a couple hundred feet below, the jagged peaks clawing the sky above, deep green canyons and dense forest below. Twilight had touched the deepening blue of the sky, and one of the planets was already glowing brightly.

'Venus,' Flynn pointed out. 'We'll be able to see Jupiter tonight, too.'

Flynn set the mugs up and poured out equal portions of what he called 'mountain screwdrivers' — powdered orange drink and vodka. 'Raro and vodka — best drink in the world. Drink up.'

We toasted the mountains and sculled the first mug. Flynn set up a second round as I stood and took in the view.

'It's really beautiful. A pity it's so difficult to get to.' The vodka was making itself known, my brain unwinding, but not yet spinning.

'It's the journey that makes it worthwhile,' Flynn laughed. 'I'll tell you what, mate — living a dull, easy life is easy. And dull. It takes effort, imagination and lots of hard work to have some fun while you're here.'

It seemed to me that something was happening to Flynn up there on that hilltop. He was not merely enjoying the view — he was breathing it in, reviving something, feeding something. The cloud of intensity that usually swirled around him was dissipating, burning off like the morning overcast so that he, too, was becoming a flawless, blue sky.

'Have you seen your place in the corporate structure?' he asked, still gazing out across the river valley. 'It was in the briefing file yesterday.'

'The corporate tree? I glanced at it. Didn't know I was actually on it.'

'You're not — not as an individual, or even a human being. You're down at the bottom. The very bottom. Barely on the page. Bottom of the food chain — bacteria. You're one of the six hundred people they lumped together in that last little box: "ATC staff." We comprise eighty percent of the employees and we barely get a mention.'

'Oh well, try not to take it personally.'

'I don't.' He turned to me. 'You want to know why?'

'Why?'

'Because only I understand the real corporate structure, the natural and unchangeable corporate structure.'

'How's that?'

Flynn pulled a small maglite torch from his pocket and tossed it to me.

'Take a look at your feet.'

I looked down at the moss-covered rocks on the ground.

'Not moss. Lichen,' Flynn pointed out. 'It's the oldest living thing on earth.' He knelt down by the rock. 'Now look closely and tell me what you see there.'

I turned the light on and illuminated the lichen.

'Lichen,' I said, shrugging my shoulders.

'What else?'

I leaned closer. 'Just lichen and,' I squinted, 'oh, some tiny little bugs. Jeez, you can hardly see them.'

'That's right — it's a whole different world in there. Almost microscopic to us, but in their world, shit, we'd be God-size.'

I leaned back in and returned to sitting on my rock, checking first to make sure I wasn't sitting on any lichen worlds.

'Okay,' I conjectured, 'so up here, you're the CEO?'

'Not quite.' Flynn nodded towards the sky. 'How could I be?'

The sky had taken on a deep twilight hue, Venus blazing brightly near a crescent moon and another planet faintly visible. I stood up to get a closer look.

'And that,' he continued, 'is just our own patch of lichen out there. Wait until the stars come and you'll see what makes our own solar system look like a speck of dust.'

I nodded. 'So I'm back to dust, bacteria, ATC staff.'

'Take a deep breath, take in that view.' Flynn stepped behind and out of my field of vision. 'Right now you can see farther than you can walk in two days. Look at the size of the sky, those mountains, the depths of those valleys.' He paused. 'Close your eyes, pull it into your lungs.'

I closed my eyes and swayed from the vodka, but followed his instructions.

'Draw it in slowly,' Flynn continued, 'the stars, the planets, the moon, the mountains, the river — pull it in as deep as you can, and then ...' he paused again, leaned closer to my ear and whispered, 'exhale it through your feet.'

I confess, I was not sure how one exhaled through one's feet, but instead of questioning his instructions, I did my damnedest to follow them and, I swear, without trying, I almost felt it was happening.

'Let your breath flow through you, into the ground, into the rocks, into the lichen, into the vastness that's too small for you to see. Just let it flow like a conduit. A flow of energy that moves smoothly, naturally, back and forth through a continuum.'

I kept my eyes closed, but could hear him moving around to the front again.

'Tell me now, Tom,' he said quietly, using my name for the first time I could remember. 'What do you feel like? A speck of dust or a god?'

'Neither. Or maybe both. I feel ...' I opened my eyes to find him staring intently at me, 'a part of it. I can't really explain it.'

'Don't try to explain it. Just feel it. Know it.' He smiled. 'That's the real corporate structure, mate. We're all part of an infinite chain and every link is as important as the next, whether it's the size of dust or the size of God. And the more you try to fuck with that natural structure, the more the natural structure will reject you, spit you out.'

'Very philosophical,' I said, out of nervousness, but I wished I hadn't. I got the feeling Flynn didn't share this with many.

'Just the truth,' he said, 'which is not hard to see when you open your eyes.' He turned his face to the sky again. 'You know, Cowboy, they're going to give you a higher branch on that corporate tree one of these days.'

'I doubt that very much.'

'Oh, they will. I promise you that.' He turned back to me again. 'All I'm saying is, don't look to someone else's diagrams to tell you where your place is. If you lose it, you won't find it in the briefing file. You'll need to come back here, and stand right here, on this very spot.'

I nodded. I didn't know what to say to him. Over the preceding week I thought I was getting to know this guy — the wild man of air traffic control, the borderline psychopath, the bolshie, brash, uncivilised farm boy from Southland who could fix anything with a piece of number 8 wire and a staple gun. And though he scared the crap out of me at times, the way he lived his life at full tilt as if he was on one long, high-speed chase, at least I was getting used to it. I thought I was beginning to know what to expect. But, suddenly, in the encroaching darkness I was facing a different man, a universe-pondering Buddhist, a monk in gumboots. And in a way, it was even more frightening. In any case, I realised, I was never going to know this guy.

'Man, I'm starving,' Flynn said. 'Let's eat.'

'We didn't catch any fish.'

'To hell with the fish. Next time. Besides, we don't need fish.' He grinned. 'If I recall correctly, I might have slipped a couple of kilos of beef in your pack along with the potatoes, onions, carrots and another bottle of vodka. Shit, we have a feast waiting to happen.' He slapped me on the shoulder as he passed. 'Come on, Cowboy. Don't forget my torch. You'll need it to light your way.'

TWELVE

'Enjoy the sunshine, Carlton, my boy,' Freddie said, leaning back in the wrought iron chair. 'You'd never get weather this beautiful so late in autumn back where I come from.'

They were sitting at an undersized table on the terrace of one of Wellington's many cafés, conveniently located only a half block from ControlCorp Head Office.

'It's still too chilly to be sitting outside,' Carlton grumbled into his mug of heated milk. 'Can't we find a seat inside?'

'Not chilly at all, Carlton,' Freddie smiled. 'It's brisk! You always need to look on the positive side, and always put a positive spin on things.' Freddie gave his wrist a twist as if he were launching a child's toy top. Then he reached for his latte and took a gentle sip. 'Besides, it's good for the circulation.'

'Circulation? My feet are fucking numb, Freddie. I can't feel my feet.'

Freddie took another sip of his latte and tried to ignore Carlton Woodcock. Sometimes he could only take so much of his attitude. Even Freddie had his limits.

'So tell me again why we can't just fire this Rumbold fellow up in Milton Gorge? He must be past retirement age by now.'

'Not as a manager,' Carlton huddled around his mug and shivered. 'And he's too entrenched. There's no dirt to find on the guy. Everyone likes him. There's not a single complaint, and not a single operational error has ever been filed, because he's never filed one in his life.' Carlton looked up with a flash of anger in his eyes. 'And he's very old chums, old flying buddies apparently, with our own Chairman of the Board, Archibald Hampton, who promised him, get this: "a lifetime job".' Carlton stuck his face down into his mug. 'They might as well call him Sir Thorndike. As if anyone would ever promise me a lifetime job.'

'Well, not with that attitude.'

'And I'm sick to fucking death of you telling me about my attitude. I've got an education, you know, a real one, and I would like to put it to use. I don't just waltz into places and sweet-talk my way into taking over like you. I work for what I get and I can rise to the top through hard work and recognition, not some hocus-pocus card trick. I've got an education, you know.' He leaned forward again to warm his face on his steaming mug.

Freddie stared at him for a second and said, 'Then, god damn it, use it.'

'What?' Carlton looked up, surprised at the sudden change in Freddie's tone.

'I said, god damn it, use it!' Freddie leaned forward menacingly across the table. 'You know, sometimes it's hard even for me to stay positive around you. But if you're so smart, why don't you start solving some of your problems yourself instead of running into my office snivelling and whining all the time. Come up with your own solutions and act on them.'

Carlton's tiny nostrils flared to almost a normal size.

'Have you got a brain in that giant forehead of yours, Carlton?' He made the short reach across the table and knocked on Carlton's forehead as if it were a door. 'Then use it!'

This did not produce the reaction Freddie had expected.

Carlton leapt to his feet, knocking over his mug of steaming milk as he jumped back three feet and took on the look and stance of a tomcat ready to fight. He was panting and snorting so hard, spittle was coming from his mouth. 'You don't ever do that again!' He yelled at Freddie. 'You don't ever touch me again, you understand?'

Freddie was profoundly surprised by Carlton's vicious, animalistic reaction. He stood up and held his hands out calmly as if he had just found himself in a cage with a wild tiger. 'It's okay, Carlton, it's okay,' he said soothingly. 'I'm sorry, I was just fooling around.'

Carlton Woodcock continued to eye Freddie and breathe heavily through his mouth. His face was beetroot red.

'Honestly, Carlton,' Freddie said quietly. 'I swear I would never intentionally hurt you. You're my friend and trusted ally. I never knew you were sensitive about people touching you. I was just horsing around, just like friends do sometimes.'

'Friends!' Carlton snorted.

'Yes, friends. Carlton, you're my best friend. I'm not ever going to hurt you. I just didn't know you were so sensitive about some things. And for that, I am truly sorry.' Freddie glanced around. 'Now let's not make a scene on the street.' He smiled. 'Let's go find a table, inside, where it's warmer. I'll buy you another mug of hot milk and will talk about how you can put that education to work. You know, Carlton, in a couple years, you could be CEO of this Corporation.'

This idea seemed visibly to relax Carlton Woodcock and he eased his tense stance. 'CEO? Really, or are you just bullshitting me?'

'Really. I swear to God.'

'What about you?'

Freddie laughed. 'Not for me. You can do the political side of it. I'll stick with commercial opportunities all the way.' He held an arm out to lead Woodcock into the café and went to pat him on the shoulder as they walked in, but then thought better of it. 'And the odd card trick.' Freddie added with a chuckle.

Woodcock was still pondering the idea of himself as CEO as they went inside. 'You'd take orders from me?'

'Of course I would! Whatever you say, because we're partners and I trust you completely. In fact, any good idea you come up with in the meantime that you want to project manage, I'm your loyal servant.'

'There are a lot of efficiencies we need to make in the system,'

Woodcock said, as if his mind was getting back on track and his momentary insanity was already fading into a dim memory. 'Particularly around some of the domestic aerodromes.'

'Of course. Let's make this a working lunch, which is on me, and we'll discuss what needs to be done to tighten the ship, so to speak.'

They took a seat at a table inside and Freddie made a mental note to himself never, ever to touch Woodcock's enormous forehead again. And above all else, never to trust him either.

Thirteen

'That was our little social structure. I had Flynn on one side, Amanda on the other. Between the two of them it felt like they cut me right down the middle. Flynn hated everything about the Corporation and everything it stood for. He repeatedly said, "They need to be taken down."'

'Really? You think he was serious?'

'Of course he was. This is the guy who taught me to dig a hangi pit with gelignite.'

'Gelignite? How would he know how to handle dynamite?'

'Oh, he knew how to handle it all right. He lived in this caretaker's shed on a local farm and paid his way by helping out a lot around the place. I guess some of the farmers use it to clear fields or whatever.'

'Interesting, I didn't know that.'

'And talk about a small world — the farmer was Amos Scuffield's son, Garrett, a grumpy bastard, but I guess he was less inclined to kill Flynn than his old man. I guess you get a lot of that in a small community.'

'Yes.'

'On the other hand, there was Amanda, who wanted nothing more than to be a part of the Corporation, to rise to her glory. And the funny thing was, they both thought I wholly agreed with them. Flynn knew I would be a starter for any commando operation he had planned, and Amanda, despite her threats, figured I was going to be racing her up the corporate ladder. Thornie loved me because he was convinced I was an exceptional controller and — this is the most bizarre one — that guy Freddie Moore, the Canadian from Head Office, liked me too.'

'Well, you're a likeable guy. There's nothing wrong with that.'

'No. I decided it was because I was malleable — like a lump of clay.

They all saw me as someone who could be shaped into someone else, an ally, someone to flesh out a role in their play. And there is something wrong with that.'

'Okay,' he said slowly, as if he had to choose his words carefully. 'I still don't understand what that has to do with the current incident we're investigating. You understand, of course, that this evaluation of you —'

'This psychiatric evaluation,' I corrected him.

'Yes, of course. Be that as it may. It's only to determine if there were personal factors that contributed to the incident, and to determine your fitness for a return to duty, which I'm more than happy to sign off on right now.'

'And that is what I'm saying — there were personal factors, and I don't know if I am fit to return to duty. So how can you just sign me off like that?'

'Well, it's not that. I'm happy to hear you out, and help if I can. Or perhaps I can refer you to someone who can help you with your more… long-term issues. For the moment, however, we really are only concerned with those matters that were a contributory cause of the events of last week.'

'And this is what I'm telling you — it all matters. It's important to what happened. I mean, Flynn, Amanda, Thornie, they all had something to do with what happened last week. All roads lead to here. None of this would have happened if we hadn't all been the way we were. We were all contributing factors. I'm telling you, just as sure as the Corporation killed Thornie, the Corporation made Amanda a fascist, Flynn a terrorist, and me —'

'And you, what?' he raised his eyebrows. 'What did the Corporation make you? A rebel without a cause?'

'No.' I looked at him and wasn't sure if I appreciated the insinuation, but it was the only chance I could see to get through this, so I pushed on. 'They made me one of them. At first I rebelled, but I was losing my malleability. The clay was drying and I wasn't sure I liked the shape.'

'Interesting.' He leaned back in his chair and put his pen to his mouth.

✈

The first thing the Corporation did, once they were installed, was to begin to clean the house. Some of the quieter, more distant facilities were simply shut down as uneconomical. Towers were closed and the airfields left as 'uncontrolled' fields for the pilots to fend for themselves. The staffs of these towers were mostly made redundant and turned out into the cold.

Milton Gorge presented a special problem, however. It was far too busy to shut down and just walk away from. Its centrality and proximity to the biggest population centres of the country would make such a move politically unfeasible. And, besides, the manager there just refused to acknowledge that the Corporation even existed, and Head Office was finding that increasingly frustrating to deal with. It took them three months to come up with a solution.

The coroner decided that Thornie had died of a heart attack while sitting at his desk, drinking a cup of tea. I found him face down on the desk, still clutching his cup.

Flynn and I were on duty in the cab that morning. Woodchuck arrived at 8.30 to nose around the books and made only one brief appearance in the cab when he first arrived, in which he asked if there was any milk available for his tea and we directed him to the downstairs fridge as none of us up in the cab used it — which was a lie, but we didn't want to give him any of our milk. We did offer him a bowl of raisins which he wisely declined.

When Thornie had arrived that morning, shortly after nine o'clock, he was a little flustered to have found Woodchuck nosing his way through the tower budget records — not that Thornie had anything to hide, but he thought the man was terribly impolite for not warning him he would be there. So Thornie retreated to the cab for a yarn with the troops until Woodchuck left.

Aside from Woodcock, Thornie said he had a meeting later with that chap Mr Moore. Obviously having to see both of them on the same day had him agitated, perhaps more stressed than he was ever used to. I suspect Thornie was driving the guys in Head Office nuts. Milton Gorge was his airport and he refused to make changes. When the Corporation started dictating changes to him, he'd simply say, 'Oh, absolutely. I'll get right on with that,' and then would turn around and completely ignore, or forget, the directive. When the Head Office boys started coming by more often and suggesting to Thornie that maybe it was time for him to consider retirement, he'd giggle and say, 'Oh, don't be silly. What would I do with myself?' And then offer them a cup of tea. They even tried promoting him to Head Office once. He said, 'Oh, good heavens, I'd be sure to cause a nationwide disaster. No, I think I'll just stay put. But thank you very much.'

Moore telephoned the tower cab from his car at 11.15 that day and said he was not getting any answer on the office line, and would someone please go and find Mr Rumbold, and advise him that Mr Moore was going to be arriving at 11.30, not eleven o'clock. That alone was enough to start me wondering. Why would this high-flying corporate exec bother to call just to say he was going to be there in fifteen minutes? And the fact that Thornie did not answer the office phone was not, in any way, unusual. Since the Corporation took over, it was quite common for Thornie to ignore the office phone completely — as he put it: 'Nobody nice ever rings on that phone any more.'

I went downstairs and found Thornie at his desk, slumped forward, clutching a cup of tea and stone dead.

'No!' I yelled. 'God damn it! No.' I took a step back, and then forward again to touch Thornie as if I could wake him up. But he was not asleep. He was dead and I backed up against the wall and stared at the whole scene — Thornie, face down, at his desk, and a puddle of tea on the blotter.

This is not happening. Not again. I approached him slowly and reached out to the puddle of tea. It felt warm. I tried to breathe, but couldn't. This is not happening.

Then I thought of Flynn. He was home. He could help. I mean, he was here with me in the tower. I pushed the intercom to the tower and told Flynn to get the rescue fire service over right away.

Then I felt for a pulse, but there was none. Not knowing what else to do, I sat down in the chair opposite and stared at him. There was coldness in the air and a stale, dusty smell that stung my nostrils. I heard the creak of floorboards and turned my head, but realised it was just the natural groan of an old building and not the ghost I expected to see. I turned back to Thornie and saw him there, still clutching his tea. Dead. It was the first time I had ever seen a dead body.

'*But fare-you-weel, Auld Nickie-ben*!' I whispered.

'What?'

'Nothing.'

'No, what was it you said?'

'It was Robert Burns' "Address to the Devil", I think — I don't know, it just came to mind at the time. It's the only poem I ever learned. My dad made me learn it. Now it's just become a bit of a nervous chatter I think.'

'But why whisper it then?'

'I'm not sure. It just came out. Like I said, a nervous twitch, if you will.'

'But where did it come from?'

'Scotland. I think around 1780-something.'

'I mean —'

'My father was an English professor. He was an authority on Burns, among other things, and that was the one he had me memorise. Another trauma of my childhood you might say. Why else do you think I ended up with the name I did?'

'Tom Hardy, what's wrong with that?'

'Think about it over a drink tonight.'

'You said he's dead, right?'

'Thomas Hardy? Of course.'

'I mean your father.'

'Yeah, he's still dead too.' I turned my attention towards the window

and watched as the first droplets of rain began winding their way down the pane, connecting with other droplets, forming little rivers of rainwater on the glass.

Okay, it was the second time I had seen a dead body.

Be prepared. That was the only thing I learned in my brief association with the Scouts. My mother had thought it was just what a fatherless boy needed. She was wrong, though. What a fatherless boy needs is a father. I was not prepared.

Sitting there, staring at Thornie, may not have been the first time I'd seen a dead body. I saw one once before.

Flynn came down the stairs like a commando team.

'Oh, Jesus Christ,' Flynn said when he came into the office. He pressed two fingers to Thornie's jugular, then leaned him back in his chair and gently began CPR. But it still did no good and did not bring Thornie back to life. Flynn finally stopped, leaned over and pressed an ear to the chest. 'Oh Christ, oh Christ, old man,' Flynn's voice was shaking. 'What has happened to you?' He stood up and stared at him.

The puddle. I leaned forward and squinted at the tea.

'Tea's still warm,' I said. I put my finger in the small puddle of tea soaking into the blotter again.

'What?' Flynn said in a choking whisper.

'The tea.' I could not take my eyes from the puddle on Thornie's blotter. 'Thornie's tea is still warm.'

'It's stone cold, Tom.' Flynn stood there in silence. 'Fire rescue should be here in a minute,' he finally said. He was choking back tears. The sirens could already be heard. 'You stay here with him, I'll go talk to the airplanes.' He departed and left me alone with the other recently departed.

'*Great is thy pow'r an' great thy fame*,' I whispered. My eyes didn't move from the tea-stained blotter. I could smell a faint odour of smoke. Or maybe it was just the dust of an old building; a building, like a man, whose time has passed.

The fire rescue crew were the first to arrive. They checked for a pulse, and one guy took the cup from Thornie's grasp and moved it to the bookcase behind the desk. Constable Tucker was the next to arrive. He paused and looked at me as if I had done it, then went to join in hushed conference with the rescue fire boys. Within fifteen minutes, the ambulance, more police and Freddie Moore were there as well.

I watched them remove Thornie from his desk. It was not until he was gone, and Tucker was asking me a couple questions, that I noticed the change in the scene.

'Where's the tea?' I asked.

'What? You want a cup of tea now?' Tucker asked. Then put his hand on my shoulder with an awkward and by-the-book sincerity and added, 'Of course, we'll see what we can do.'

'No, I just want to know.' I looked around the desk, on the bookcase behind the desk. 'Where'd it go?'

I walked out of Thornie's office into the hall and stood in the hall for a minute, pondering my surroundings. For a moment I forgot where I was, and it seemed weird that the staircase was on the left when it seemed like it was supposed to be on the right. I reached out, first with my left hand, and then accepted the change and used my right to grab the polished oak banister and slowly ascend the stairs to the second floor. That's where I found him, Freddie Moore, in the kitchen. He had the tap running in the sink and was dumping the carton of milk down the drain.

'What are you doing?' I asked.

Moore turned around a fraction too quickly at the sound of my voice.

'Tidying up,' he said and returned to his task. 'Just tidying up a little. Making myself useful.'

'But why are you dumping the milk?'

'It had gone off,' Moore said without hesitation. 'Past its use-by date.'

Like Thornie? I wondered.

Thornie's recently washed cup was drying on the dish rack next to the sink. I picked it up and looked at it.

'You washed his cup.' It was an old RNZAF squadron mug that, despite its age, was always kept clean — completely free of tea stains.

'Yeah, just tidying up a little,' Moore shook the excess water from the milk carton and crushed it, neatly folding it into a square. Then he put his arm on my shoulder and led me from the kitchen and back down the stairs. 'It's Hardy, right? Tom?'

'Yeah.'

'You're the American.'

'Yeah.'

'We were just talking about you down in Wellington the other day. We think you could have quite a good future with ControlCorp. I'm glad to have met you finally — just sorry it's under such sad circumstances.'

'We've met several times.'

'Right, of course. Anyway, you're under a lot of stress today. It must have been traumatic for you.' He led me to the hall, to the front door. 'You need to take the rest of the day off. I know Mr Rumbold meant a lot to you.' He opened the door. 'I've already called in those two queer controllers to take over for you and Mr Flynn upstairs. They should be here in a few minutes. Why don't you go home now? Or find a pub that's open and have a drink for your friend. Now, if you'll excuse me.' He gently pushed me out the front door. 'Oh, and Tom?'

I turned back to face Moore in the doorway.

'Grieve for him today, but don't dwell in the past. The future holds much more promise.' He nodded as if he was satisfied with that as a pearl of wisdom. 'And just remember, Tom — my door's always open.' Then he closed the door in my face.

By late that afternoon, Flynn and I were sitting across from each other at his kitchen table with a nearly empty bottle of Johnny Walker Red Label between us. The sun was low and leaving an orange glow on the towering cumuli that were collecting on the horizon, over the airport. Thunderstorms. Didn't seem right for the time of year, this late in autumn.

There must be an explanation, I thought. This can't happen.

'*An' let poor damned bodies be*!' I whispered.

Flynn looked at me for several moments before he said anything. 'What?'

'He was murdered,' I said. It had taken me that long and that much drink to find the courage to say it aloud. It was the only explanation.

'What?' Flynn repeated.

'I've been thinking. All the evidence points to murder.'

'You mean a heart attack,' Flynn said, looking at me as if he was wondering if I was going to need some medication — some *more* medication.

'He did it: Freddie Moore did it.'

'Jeez, Cowboy, come on,' Flynn shook his head. 'I don't have much use for the guy, either, but even I'm not that paranoid.'

'How do you explain a man that fit and unstressed having a heart attack, while sitting down, relaxing?'

'How the hell should I know? I'm not a doctor. These things happen to the healthiest of people all the time. Maybe he just had a bum heart. He was, by the way, getting on in years.'

'That's not the only thing, though.' I poured another shot of Red Label and refilled Flynn's glass. 'I've been thinking, and something's bugging me. First, it's Moore and him cleaning up before anybody had a chance to look around. He washed Thornie's mug, he dumped out the milk, said it was "past its use-by date". Woodchuck had said it was "nearing its use-by date." Bullshit. As if Thornie would ever let the milk go off. Not just that, though, Moore rinsed out the milk carton and I don't think he threw it away.'

'You're losing me. What's his tidying up got to do with —?'

'Exactly! Tidying up. In times of stress, what do we do? We rely on something that comforts us. Have you ever noticed how Amanda, when she gets busy, keeps fussing with her hair, tucking it behind her ear, stroking it, knotting it up. Or how much more Kenny whispers to his rat. I knew a controller who used to start humming show tunes whenever he got busy.'

'And you start babbling lines from long dead poets,' Flynn added.

'And you shoot at the airplanes with the signal pistol.'

Flynn shrugged. 'I find it relaxing. What's the point?'

'The point is, all those things come naturally to us. We just intensify our habits when we're under stress. But Moore, he was tidying up, and said he was trying to stay out of the way — two things that I doubt very much come naturally to him at all.'

'I'm not following you.' He leaned back and studied me suspiciously.

'I remember seeing him in Thornie's office earlier. He was moving around, but not really talking to anybody. I bet that's when he got the cup of tea out.'

'No, still not following you.'

'Remember a couple months back when Moore gave me a lift into town after he had made one of his surprise visits to tell Thornie they'd give him a bonus if he'd retire early? My car was in the shop that day and when he was stomping out of there in frustration, I asked him if he could give me a lift into town. It was right on his way. He didn't like the idea of me sitting in his BMW, but then warmed to the idea because he spent the entire trip talking about what a promising future with ControlCorp I could have. If it weren't for Thornie standing in my way, he said, I could be manager of Milton Gorge. I didn't listen too much to his bullshit because I thought he was crazy, but I remember one thing about that trip into town.'

'And what was that?'

'He had this beautiful, brand new BMW, but the backseat was like a pigsty. The floor was covered in junk food wrappings and debris. It looked like the contents of the trash bin at the back of McDonald's.'

'Okay, so the guy's a pig.'

'Yeah, he's a slob! It's not natural for him to be tidy. He only looks tidy on the outside because he has to.'

'You're stressed, Cowboy,' Flynn said. 'I don't think you should go around reasoning that Freddie Moore washing dishes proves he's guilty of murder.'

'He was getting rid of the evidence.' I got up, paced to the sink and returned. 'He must have put something in the milk. That's the only thing Thornie ever put in his tea. Everybody who knew Thornie knew that.'

'Something that causes heart attacks?'

'Yes! Certain poisons do. I saw it in a movie once. Like arsenic or something.'

'Yeah?'

'Flynn,' I said as I sat down again, 'what was the most important thing in Thornie's life?'

'Well, at his eulogy I hope they say his family and his work, but, okay, I'll play along — you're right, it was tea. So that has some connection here?'

'He had just made himself a cup of tea and had taken only a sip or two before he died.'

'And?' Flynn said hesitantly, but I could see he knew what I was getting at.

'Thornie would never leave a good cup of tea unfinished. He would not have died, he would not have let his life finish, if he hadn't finished his tea.'

'So you think they murdered him? Based on that evidence, you have concluded that Freddie Moore murdered him?'

'They couldn't get rid of him. They'd been trying to retire him ever since they took over, but how could they fight him when he just ignored them?' I stood up and walked over to the phone. 'We've got to call the police.'

'And just how are you going to explain your theory to the police?'

'Just how I did right now. It makes perfect sense.'

'Cowboy ...' Flynn picked up the bottle of Johnny Walker and topped up my glass to the brim. 'Let's talk this through a little first.'

'So you think Moore had something to do with Mr Rumbold's death?' he asked. His eyes narrowed and he looked like he was seriously reconsidering that quick sign off of my sanity.

'I did.'

'And do you still?'

'Flynn talked me out of pursuing it at the time. There was just no evidence.'

'That's not what I asked.'

I turned towards the windy, black rain hitting the window and thought for a moment. 'Can I tell you a story?'

'Isn't that what you've been doing?'

'That's just the opening act. I wanted you to know about the good old days, so you would understand them. But they lasted for exactly three months after I was checked out at Milton Gorge, and then they came to an end.'

'Well, we all miss our own version of "the good old days", don't we?'

'No. These came to a conclusive end on a specific day. These good old days ended with murder, scandal, corruption.' I hesitated as I turned back to face him and our eyes were locked on each other. 'And a tremendous explosion.'

Part Two: The New World Order

FOURTEEN

'Are you sure you want to do that?' Simon asked from his seat on ground control. For a minute I thought he had been dozing off. So he was awake after all.

'Never let 'em see you sweat, kid,' I said.

An Air New Zealand 747 had just touched down on the runway. A United Airlines 747 appeared to be on a seven-mile final. That was what it looked like on the tower radar display, which was built into the desk between the tower controller's position and ground control. In reality, the plane was now on about a four-mile final because the radar picture froze a couple of minutes ago. It was a particularly annoying bug in the new radar equipment that every once in a while the picture just stopped, the planes held fast, unmoving in space and time.

If only we could really do that, I thought. Old Thornie came the closest to pulling it off, but even he succumbed to the juggernaut of progress. That was over a year and a half ago already, and in that time it was as if progress was making up for lost time.

It was easy to not notice a frozen radar screen because, as tower controllers who were generally looking out the window most of the time, we only glanced at the radar display to help us determine spacing. The technicians, we were told, were working on the problem, but in the meantime we had to live with it and try not to kill with it.

I confess that when I told the Inland Airways Banderainte to taxi on to the runway and to be ready for an immediate take-off, I really did think United was on a seven-mile final, which would have been plenty of room. But when I realised that the radar had gone belly-up again, and the 747 was much closer than I first thought, instead of stopping the Bandit, I decided to work with it, and, above all, to act as if it was what I had planned all along.

'It's not going to work,' Simon said. 'There's not enough room to get him out.'

'It'll work,' I said, turning to him and seeing the deepening panic in this kid's face. He had been corporate trained and that's one thing they didn't teach down in their new school in Christchurch — how to stay cool. 'What did I tell ya? What's Rule Number1?'

'Ah,' he shot a glance that suggested I was insane.

'Don't choke on me,' I said calmly. We had several seconds to spare here, and there was no need to get worked up into a lather. 'What's Rule Number 1?'

Simon struggled to find some words. 'The safe, orderly, expeditious flow of traffic.'

'No, that's your purpose in life. What's Rule No 1?' I glanced at the runway. Air New Zealand had thrown in his reverse thrusters and was standing on the brakes. He was going to make the second high-speed taxiway as instructed. Good boy.

I keyed the mike, directing my voice to the pilot of the Bandit, but keeping my eyes on Simon. 'Inland four-one-one-two, be ready immediate.'

'We're ready,' the pilot said drolly, his voice nearly drowned out by the sound of his engines roaring up to full power. He, too, was standing on his brakes, waiting for the word 'go.' Good boy.

'You sure this is going to work?' Simon asked and, as if on cue, the pilot of the United 747 piped in too.

'Tower, is this going to work?'

I answered them both as one: 'It'll work.' Then I took another slow sip of coffee for a little dramatic effect. As Air New Zealand nosed onto the high-speed, I keyed the mike again. 'Inland four-one-one-two cleared immediate take-off,' putting just the right amount of stress on the word 'immediate' to let the Bandit know, if he didn't get that thing off the ground real soon, we're all screwed.

'Rolling.' The Bandit had already started its take-off roll.

'So, how many times I got to tell you?' I said back to Simon. 'Rule Number 1: never let 'em see you sweat.'

'What kind of separation are you applying?' His face betrayed a flash of anger that quickly settled into confusion.

'Milton Gorge separation?' I shrugged.

'Which didn't exist when Milton Gorge existed.'

'Oh, you've still so much to learn.' I turned my attention back to the runway. The Bandit rotated, pulling his nose up, and a moment later his wheels left the ground. At the threshold end United's main gear was moments away from touching down. 'Wheels up. How about runway separation then? What do you know, it's even legal.' I turned my attention back to Simon. 'They can hear you sweat. Don't let them, or they'll walk all over you and you'll never control shit.'

'But why give yourself an ulcer if you don't have to?'

'Give myself an ulcer? What are you talking about? I live for this. The closer, the better.' I was kidding him, of course, but with an absolutely straight face. 'Besides, you have to look ahead a little at what's coming up. Approach is backed up, which means that Bandit's going to fly slow as shit straight out for ten miles. After United clears, we have another 747, followed by two 73s, and an Airbus is pushing back at the international terminal. And see that VFR target at fifteen hundred feet over the city?' I pointed towards the frozen radar screen in the desk between our two positions. 'I bet he calls us up any second to transition southbound. He just has that look about him. You're supposed to keep things moving, aren't you? So fill up the holes when you got them.'

'I wouldn't have considered that a hole. What if —'

'What if? That's your job, to know how the "what if" plays out. If it doesn't work, then you do something else. That's what you're paid all this money for, that and looking at the big picture, which requires taking in all available information — like knowing who you're dealing with. Look.' I pointed at the Air New Zealand jumbo lumbering towards the international terminal. 'You know that guy. You should recognise his four-pounds-of-gravel voice by now. And you know, if he says he's going to make the second high-speed, then he will. And United — hell, he's just coming in from LAX where he's used to tight squeezes. Ask him to fly his airplane ten knots slower than his handbook says is possible and he'll make it happen, especially with fifteen knots of wind on his nose. And the Bandit,' I pointed into the morning haze in the direction of the departed aircraft, 'that's Ian Powell flying. I ran into him at the pub last night and I said, "So, Ian, if I give you an immediate take-off tomorrow morning, will you promise not to piss around on the runway so I don't have to kill you the next time you come in?" And he promised he wouldn't piss around.'

Simon laughed. I think the last bit was pushing it and I don't think he believed me any more. 'I still think one of these days you won't get away with it. This isn't Milton Gorge.'

'And it's a pity we don't have the place to send you to for training — maybe it would turn you into a good controller. Because, one of these days, you might learn how to do it and then they could put you in charge of the training department.' I reached over and tapped the radar screen 'Now, if you've got a moment, call the techs and tell them this piece of shit froze up again.'

Simon Henare was, in fact, already a good controller — certainly the best of the new lot that arrived from the air traffic control school in Christchurch last August. They were the first fully corporate-trained group of newcomers. There was nothing necessarily wrong with any of them — they just had a few holes in their training. The first thing they used to teach new controllers was their purpose, the reason for their very existence: the safe, orderly, expeditious flow of traffic. In that order: safe, orderly, expeditious. The second thing they used to teach them was that the first thing came before all else — that was unchanging. Whatever regulations come into it, whatever procedures are used, whatever directive distracted, whatever whatever — never forget what your purpose is, and you'll be okay.

The Corporation cut this out of the curriculum. I guess it fostered disobedience and independent thought. They replaced it with their mission statement — something Freddie Moore had unveiled at a management meeting a few months ago.

'Ladies and gentlemen,' Freddie announced as he turned the first large piece of cardboard on the easel over, 'our mission statement. Now, you won't need to commit this to memory, I've had it printed on convenient wallet-sized cards for everybody.' Freddie looked at the cardboard with a gleam of pride and began to read: 'ControlCorp will be a world leader in the aviation business community, servicing the needs of its customers on a sound commercial basis. We will respond cost effectively to our customers' legitimate business requirements as best we can, while maintaining an adequate rate of return. We will develop a qualified, motivated and committed management team and treat them with respect in a climate of trust, growth and reward. We will continue to seek and develop business opportunities nationwide and worldwide.' Freddie's eyes were moist when he finished reading. 'Isn't that a work of art?' he asked the group.

'But,' I said hesitantly, 'it doesn't say anything about "safe, orderly, expeditious".' I was hesitant to criticise something that the man obviously held dear — in those days I still had one or two ideals that had not been completed defeated. It was when I was still malleable enough to have a little of Flynn's rebel attitude, before the clay had completely dried hard.

'Huh?' Freddie looked at me.

'Well, you know. Airplanes, safety, stuff like that.'

Freddie returned his admiration to the cardboard. 'Yeah, well, we didn't want to make it too wordy.'

Too wordy? They turned three words into about a hundred and they thought my three words were going to make it too wordy? I might have pursued the argument, but I was getting 'the look' from Amanda, who at the time had been facility manager for only a few months. Even when we were both senior controllers, I quickly learned when Amanda gave me 'the look' it acted as a pretty good barometer that I was approaching thin ice and my New Year's resolution about not stirring the pot, which was in turn supposed to make my life quieter and hassle-free. It was a theory.

So I dropped it. After all, I was still the senior controller in charge of all the training in the tower and not without influence over the new arrivals. The Corporation could have their mission statement, and I could have mine.

The first group of corporate-selected and corporate-trained controllers they sent us arrived in late October. Simon was the best. He had a natural talent for the job. He was just a little inflexible, a little too stuck in the book. He needed to develop his instinct a bit more. In any case, I had to be careful not to be overly praiseworthy of him. The last thing young Simon needed was an ego that grew faster than his skill.

'It's about time,' I said to Ryan as he climbed the stairs. 'I sent you on a break an hour ago.'

'But there was cricket on the telly,' he said. Ryan was also a new controller who arrived in the same group of four as Simon. He was safe and competent, but not great.

'Then I'm glad it wasn't a five-day match.'

Ryan took over at the tower position from me, and I stepped back to watch them for a few minutes until there was a lull in the traffic. The Airbus had started its nearly two-mile taxi to the runway, the incoming rush of traffic was tapering off. It was the kind of airport most young controllers were just itching to get to — big, international, lots of fancy equipment. The runway here was five times as long, the tower three times as high, the airplanes twenty or thirty times as big, and it was all possibly less than half the fun. Here the action was all on the outside, far away. Milton Gorge was an insane place, no doubt about it, but at least it was all a human-based insanity. After a while, you got used to it, began to understand it, even started to enjoy it, and then one day you woke up and realised you were every bit a part of it — an inmate, integral to the ongoing operation of the asylum.

Then, suddenly, it was gone. They took care of the Milton Gorge problem for us, got rid of that insanity and in its place installed a new kind of corporate-consulted-designed-and-developed type of insanity — which was much more complicated and harder to understand than anything Flynn or Thornie could dish up.

'Don't forget to sign on,' I reminded Ryan.

'Yes, sir,' he said with a touch of sarcasm as he reached across the communications panel to the small pad, held in place with a magnetic clip, and printed his name and the date and time he took over on the position.

'Where's our flight data person?' I asked, indicating the one unoccupied position in the tower. The flight data position was an administrative role and not usually filled by air traffic controllers, but a person who was specifically hired for the job.

'Sarah's on her way up,' Ryan said.

'Good. I have to go down and see the boss.'

'Which of your bosses is that?' Simon said, exchanging a grin with Ryan. 'Sarah or Amanda?'

'You guys just pay attention to your traffic,' I said.

'What?' Ryan glanced back at me. 'No stories? You know, Cowboy, we so look forward to your stories of the good old days — back in the pioneer days of Milton Gorge. What was it like before they invented electricity?' He let out a quiet chuckle.

'In the old days,' I said, jabbing a finger at him, 'we were allowed to shoot you for being a smart-ass.' Then I moved into my best pseudo-John Wayne voice, 'Young whipper-snappers like you would have run crying at the mere sight of an airplane. And we didn't have luxuries like radios. No, sirree. We used lights and flares, flags and raw courage. Why, I remember a time I had seventeen in the circuit at once. Hell, did I say seventeen? I meant to say a hundred and seventeen. Yes, sir, winds were all over the place. Twenty knots of tailwind on both ends of the runway, six emergencies all going on at once, my underpants were on fire and it was time for my tea break.' This elicited a round of laughter, but I was losing my enthusiasm for the joke myself. 'Yes, Sir, that's the way it was back in ol' Exile Tower. I remember I had to take a tennis racquet, climb onto the roof and start swatting them like flies. You girls would've gone a-cryin' to your mamas and it would've been the wall, a blindfold and a last cigarette for you.'

'Just as long as it wasn't a smoke-free firing squad, eh?' Simon piped in.

I let them enjoy a moment of levity, then pointed in the direction of the runway. 'Okay, men, the airplanes are out there. I'll be in Amanda's office if you need me.'

They both turned their attention to the outside and scanned for something they might have missed, something they might get in trouble for, something that might bring their careers to a premature end. They had the same fear all young male controllers had — that it would all come to an end before they were finished using their profession as a means to meet impressionable young women who were awed by their cool.

I hurried down the stairs to wait at the lift on the floor below for Sarah to arrive. I could already hear the hum of the lift as it rose to the tower sub-floor and the kerplunk sound it made as it reached its destination and pressed my body against the wall so as to be unseen the moment before the door opened.

She stepped out of the lift and I sprung my attack. 'Ha!' I said and she jumped at the surprise. I pressed my body close to hers and led her backwards into the equipment room.

'Tom, no,' she protested weakly with her voice, but her mouth was more than willing to accept mine. I nuzzled her neck as I fumbled my hands under her blouse.

'No, Tom,' she said, more emphatically, 'not here, not now.'

'Why not? I'm in the mood, you're in the mood, and we're both in the equipment room. And I don't think we've ever done it in the equipment room before.'

'You know as well as I do we've done it at least twenty times in the equipment room.' She pushed me back. 'Lying back on the air conditioner is not the most comfortable of positions.'

'How about standing up then?' I slowly lowered myself to get better leverage, but she grabbed my shoulder and stopped me.

'And I'm not in the mood.' She pushed me away to arm's length.

'What's wrong?'

'Not now,' she said, tucking her blouse back in and smoothing down her hair. 'We can talk tonight.'

'It's not talking I want to do tonight.'

'Well, I've got a lot on my mind right now, and this isn't helping.'

'Oh, sorry. How's your mum doing?' I asked. Sarah's lovely mother had had a minor heart attack a couple weeks ago and although she seemed to be recovering nicely, it still seemed to weigh heavily on Sarah.

'She's fine, but it's something else. Look, if you don't mind, I'm already late for work.'

I stepped to the side to let her pass and followed her out of the equipment room.

'Tonight, then?' I pleaded.

'We'll talk tonight,' she said, and disappeared through the door and up the stairs towards the cab without saying another word.

I had fallen in love with Sarah Gregory the moment I laid eyes on her. The day she arrived at Auckland Tower almost a year earlier I knew there was something different about her. She had applied for a job as a tower assistant and when she walked through those doors, she had the job immediately. There was a quality about her that was hard to define. She had been a pre-med student and said she was taking a break from that to clear her mind, so she wasn't, technically, qualified for the position. But she had an interest in aviation, and her dad was a pilot, so that was good enough for me. I gave her a job and she was a great addition to the tower. A person could talk to her about subjects other than airplanes and drinking. She was educated, well read and could talk intelligently on many issues. I came in to work on one particularly quiet day to find the three of them all reading at their respective positions. Simon had his nose stuck in the sports section of the newspaper, Ryan was numbly thumbing through a *Woman's Day* in his pathetic search for an underwear advert, and Sarah — for God's sake — she was reading Dostoyevsky. *Dostoyevsky*!

But it wasn't just the fact that she was smart — there was something else I could not put my finger on. Perhaps I stared too much trying to figure it out, but Simon accused me of being smitten with her and encouraged me to ask her out.

Maybe I was smitten with her. I couldn't ask her out though — supervisors dating subordinates was one rule the newly appointed unit manager Amanda was sure to enforce, particularly when it came to me. But in the beginning she was just intriguing to me because she was not like most women I'm drawn to. Janey wanted to save the world, and Amanda wanted to conquer the world. That may not sound like a similarity, but it is because they both had big plans that included them and the world, and both had determination and focus on how to achieve their goals. And in both cases, I would only play a supporting role. Sarah didn't appear to have plans that involved the whole world — maybe that's what intrigued me.

I don't know if anyone else noticed it, but there was something about her that radiated from within, behind those deep brown eyes and the smooth, even glow of the South Pacific complexion she inherited from her Fijian Indian mother, and those straight white teeth. Something in the way her shiny brown hair bounced cheerfully in a pony-tail one day, or cascaded alluringly down her shoulders another, highlighting the graceful, sensual curve of her collarbone.

It took me almost six months of watching her, of thinking about her, until I finally worked up the courage to break Rule Number 1 in the Amanda Book of Conduct.

Fifteen

From his corner office, Freddie looked down on the flow of summertime foot traffic on the streets eight floors below. He smiled. Tourism was a good sign — good for the country, good for the airlines, good for the 'made in Korea' ControlCorp souvenirs and, thus, good for Freddie. The souvenir trade, of course, was never supposed to be more than just beer money, but even that might have been setting the bar too high — they weren't selling all that well.

Rule Number 1 in Freddie's book was to never pass up an opportunity, no matter how small. Or maybe that was Rule Number 2 — he could never remember. He met his souvenir supplier in the sauna at the Seoul Hilton, while he was unwinding from a day of coercing the Koreans into signing a contract for ControlCorp to assist them on a major upgrade of their air traffic facilities, an upgrade that included off-loading a bit of old equipment mixed in with the new. As long as it was polished to a high shine, it was new to them.

These little Asian contracts served two very important purposes. First, they kept the money coming and going in so many different directions it was hard to keep up with what exactly was financing what — a little corporate card trick. Second, they also helped with the unexpected cash flow problems attached with all the new equipment they bought from the French — also a bunch of cheap crap, but it had a nice shiny new polish to it. He was not expecting to have to employ a full-time team of French technicians to keep it up and running. Of course, that was only meant to be until they could work all the bugs out, or until they could phase out this whole messy service business entirely and make a decent living out of being consultants.

Evolution, Freddie pondered, indulging himself in an extravagant moment of fantasy as he closed his eyes and felt the warmth of tinted sunlight flowing into his office. It was the obvious evolution of business. First you needed raw material and a labour force to produce the goods. Then you get rid of the raw materials and just have the labour force to provide the goods and, *voilà*, the service industry is born. Then you develop a halfway decent management team, get rid of the labour force and, *abracadabra*, the consultancy is born. Hell, all you need now is to get half a dozen Third World countries to skip the bullshit and send him money straight to a Swiss bank account and you would be set.

Freddie opened his eyes, looked at the tiny specks on the streets below and smiled. Stupid assholes with your real MBAs. You wasted your time. No university in the world teaches you what you really need to know, like how to strike up a casual conversation with a guy in a sauna and end it twenty minutes later with a handshake deal and another few grand to be made — all the while dressed in nothing but a towel.

Buy cheap, sell high — that was Rule Number 1. Freddie enjoyed philosophising about business. The main thing about business was that it was about people, and Rule Number 3 was knowing people one person at a time. It was about human nature, and how to sense the weaknesses, fears, likes and dislikes in your opponent. It was a talent, a skill, a gift. Hell, he could teach a class in this shit. Or was that Rule Number 4? Must remember to write these things down.

Carlton Woodcock entered the office carrying a manila folder and let out a little snort as he dropped into the leather chair.

'Carlton, my boy,' Freddie said as if he had been expecting him, 'just the man I wanted to see.' He sat down behind his desk, leaned back and tucked his hands behind his head. 'Everything taken care of for Fiji next week?'

'Yes, Freddie,' Carlton reported unenthusiastically. 'Reception should have the tickets by Friday afternoon.'

'Good.' Freddie eyed Carlton carefully. 'Everything okay? You look a little blue around the edges.'

'I got my new car today.'

'Great! How is it?'

'It's a Hyundai, Freddie,' Carlton said.

'Great car — reliable, economical —'

'It's seven years old! And I don't want economy. I want a BMW. You've been promising me a BMW for a year.'

'And you'll have it. But we have to play the cards right. We're not that far behind schedule.'

'The point is, it's a *Hyundai*! And it's used!'

'I know you're a little disappointed, Carlton, but it wasn't my decision. It came down from above,' Freddie said, pointing at the ceiling.

'We're on the top floor.'

'You know what I mean. The Board doesn't think it would look too good for us to go around buying a BMW for every executive in the building. People might start asking questions in these sensitive economic times.'

'Yet, you're on your second.'

'Yes, but that's different, isn't it? I have to maintain an image. I'm the one facing the public. When people look at me we want them to say "Success!" But if everybody in the building drives around in a company-paid-for BMW, people will say "Waste!" It's a fine line, Carlton. Besides, if you recall, mine was lost rather tragically.'

'Yeah, I remember.' Carlton grinned. 'Tragic.'

'Look, you're making a good salary, why don't you go down to the BMW dealership this afternoon and buy yourself one?'

'It's not the same. I'm supposed to get a company car.'

'So you shall. But for us to present the right image — it's economy, for now.' He leaned back again and laughed. 'Shit, Carlton, when we see the cash from the M & G deal, you'll have enough money to buy the BMW dealership. How about a different BMW for every day of the week?'

'M & G,' Woodcock shook his head. 'What does the M and the G stand for, anyway?'

'Milton and Gorge,' Freddie said. 'Money and Growth; Monkeys and Gorillas — what does it matter? The point is to have a nice innocuous name, that doesn't call attention to itself. Anyway, don't worry about what our little side business is called, it's going to make you enough money to buy a fleet of BMWs. In the meantime, I'll let you drive mine this afternoon when we hit the road.'

'Hit the road?' Woodcock stared at Freddie for a moment, then shook his head when it sunk in. 'No way, Freddie, I'm not doing another road trip with you. We're due in Auckland tomorrow, and I'm flying this time. I already have us booked.'

'Sorry, Carlton, we've got business to take care of on the way in Palmie this afternoon.'

'What business do we have in Palmerston North?'

'Chief controller has reached retirement age.'

'What are you talking about? He can't be more than fifty.'

'All I know is that he's thinking in the wrong century. His mind has been rather closed to many of our suggested new policies up there, especially concerning foreign students training up there, and the price structure we've incorporated.'

'Why is this sounding new to me?'

'Because you probably haven't read my memo on it yet, or maybe Tania was slow in getting it out. In any case, I'll fill you in on the drive up. By this afternoon he will come to the reasonable conclusion that it's time to retire. He doesn't know that yet. That's why I need you to cook me up a pot full of numbers to make his transition easier on all of us. We get that little business out of the way, then take the Beamer out to stretch its legs on the Desert Road, have dinner in Taupo with Sir Dickhead to sell him on this deal, and tomorrow morning we'll make a quick stop on our way into Auckland to see how our little investment is transforming Purgatory into Eden.'

'We're stretching our necks out on that, Freddie.' Woodcock grimaced. 'You said there'd be more funding by now. I can't keep juggling —'

'Don't worry. The funding is as good as there. The risk is minimal.' Freddie offered a reassuring smile. 'Now, back to the Fiji travel plans. Were you able to blow Amanda off?'

'No, of course not. You know she would never miss a chance to mix with upper management.'

'Dammit! I was hoping we'd be able to lose her. She always puts such a damper on the fun. Ah well, it was worth a try. Guess we'll have to make time to do a little team-building during our team-building weekend. Maybe we could play some beach volleyball or something.'

Freddie Moore could not figure out Amanda Sheppard. She seemed to be immune to his charm, which annoyed him, but didn't deter him. Just switch tactics. Always have a Plan B ready. She said her ambition was to get more women in the business, and what the hell did he care? If it made her happy, she could hire trained chimpanzees. But it didn't make her happy — nothing did. The more free rein he gave her, the more she wanted. And she never showed any gratitude. Every time he tried to compliment her on something, she would take it as an insult. What he would like most of all was to see the end of Amanda Sheppard. Unfortunately, she seemed intent on staying around and, as long as she did, he needed her support. Otherwise, she could cause a lot of trouble for him at this delicate time.

What she needed, Freddie rubbed his chin as another brilliant idea surfaced, was more of a personal life. What she needed was a damn good screw. He would not want to do the dirty work himself. Maybe that hard case Hardy should be doing it, he figured. He thought he picked up on some sparks there before. But that boy had a lot to learn about schmoozing and seemed to be resistant to success. And, besides, she would probably never go for a subordinate. For her to be interested she would have to see some potential for influence, someone from Head Office at the very least, someone ...

Freddie grinned.

'What?' Woodcock shifted in his chair. 'What's with the grin, Freddie?'

'Oh, nothing. Just in a good mood, I guess.'

'Why does that make me nervous?'

'So Amanda's coming to Fiji with us, then?' Freddie leaned back and pondered the ceiling.

'Yes, I think that's what we've decided.'

'Good. I may have a special project for you.'

Woodcock squinted. 'Like what?'

'I'll let you know. It'll be fun.' He looked back to Woodcock and smiled.

Woodcock leaned forward and stared at Freddie suspiciously. 'When am I getting my BMW?'

'When we get our money from the man.' Freddie held up his right hand in a Boy Scout salute. He had never been a Scout himself, but learned a lot about Scout life twenty-five years earlier when he was running a shell game at a jamboree in Calgary. 'Which reminds me,' he glanced at his watch. 'Did you meet with his point men yet?'

'No, not yet. And I still don't think it's a good idea.'

'We need his support. Besides, don't worry about what anyone else may think. It's a legitimate investment opportunity for him.'

'I know, but he's pretty savvy — and powerful. I don't like messing with him. He might not approve of some of M & G's tactics.'

'Standard operating procedures in business. He'll understand.'

'Maybe so, but you don't think he would be pretty suspicious if he knew we were working both sides of the ControlCorp–M & G fence? I don't think he would be too happy to discover we own two sides of this triangle. And, you know, it wouldn't be that hard for him to make a connection if he talks to his children at all.'

'Which he doesn't. Rest assured, they are very much estranged. Give me some credit for prior planning,' Freddie leaned forward and lowered his voice. 'Don't get wussy on me, Carlton. This is business in the real world, my boy, not that textbook stuff you wasted your time on. You know you want to play with the big boys, and this is how you do it. Besides,' he leaned back again and grinned, 'don't play it so innocent — after all, we both know you have a healthy little mean streak yourself. You just need to channel that energy in the right direction.'

Woodcock glared at Freddie and worked his mouth as if trying to dislodge a stubborn morsel of food.

'Anyway, remember your ulcer,' Freddie continued. 'Everything we're doing is perfectly legal, nothing more than normal practices for legitimate investment interests.'

'Perfectly legal? Jesus Christ, Freddie.' He put his face in his hands and started rubbing his forehead. 'If anyone discovers our connection to M & G Properties, I'm going to jail.'

'Oh, don't be so melodramatic. Name me one thing we're doing that isn't entirely legal.'

'What? Are we talking about the same thing?' Woodcock wrinkled his forehead and lowered his voice. 'Was that one of the days you cut class in law school? The day they talked about the difference between the legal way and the illegal way to acquire property? Did you miss the day on falsification of legal documents, too? How about insider trading? Misappropriation of corporate funds? Bribing public officials?' He lowered his voice until he was only mouthing the words, 'Collusion?' Then raised his voice again. 'Exactly what part of what we're doing is not wrong?'

'Oh, Carlton, you worry too much,' Freddie waved off his concerns. 'It may not be exactly letter-perfect legal, right now, but it's not wrong. Do you know it was once "illegal" for women to go out in public; for them even to be seen in public was punishable by death. But all it took was a few brave souls to disobey. And now we can acknowledge the important contribution they make —'

'Where was it ever illegal for women to go out in public?'

'Oh, some place … how the hell should I know? Afghanistan I think. My point is, times change and progress is only possible if someone of vision is willing to take an occasional risk. I guarantee you, when all is said and done, you'll be remembered as a visionary and for your great contribution to your country, its economy and its people. The pursuit of wealth is what progress is made of. Sure we may make a little money out of the deal, but look at what we're creating — we're creating homes for people and what is more noble than that? We're a regular Habitat for Humanity.'

'Habitat for ... these are half-million dollar homes!'

'Well, the middle class are part of humanity, aren't they? We're not going to make any money on poor people, for God's sake. Where's your business sense?' He shrugged. It was obvious enough even for a moron to see. 'Carlton, close your mouth. You look silly. Look, it's a short-term thing. As soon as all the sections are all sold, we sell our shares to someone else and we're out of M & G without a trace. Now,' he pointed at the manila folder in Woodcock's lap, 'is that something for me?'

Woodcock shook his head slowly and let out a mournful sigh as he looked down at the folder in his hand. 'A little problem with Douglas Malahide.'

Freddie looked soberly at Woodcock. 'The Inland Airways CEO?'

Woodcock nodded.

'What's wrong?'

'Well, it seems your ever-efficient staff at Auckland Tower have a problem with the way his Learjet was being flown last week and have filed a safety incident report. Malahide is very unhappy.'

'Damn that Amanda.' Freddie shook his head. 'She just loves causing trouble.'

'Actually ...' Woodcock looked at the paper, 'it's Hardy's name on the bottom.'

Freddie relaxed. 'That's not so bad then. Hardy won't take it so seriously.'

'Don't be too sure. It says here, "The pilot's failure to comply with clear and specific ATC instructions resulted in a hazardous situation and threatened the safety of a Boeing 737." The guy may not be much for rules, but he has this thing about air safety.'

'So what happens to those things?' Freddie said pointing to the paper.

'The usual chain is the supervisor submits it to his manager and he, or she, sends it to us. We're required to submit it to Civil Aviation. They'll investigate. Then, depending on the seriousness of the matter, either issue a reprimand, a fine or, in rare cases, suspension of the pilot's licence.' Woodcock looked again at the paper. 'This sort of case would probably just be a reprimand if it were a private pilot. But since it's a Lear getting in the way of a 737, there'd be a fine too. But there's also another complication.'

'Which is?'

'Well, it seems Malahide enjoys getting behind the controls from time to time. That's what he was doing here.' Woodcock waved the paper. 'So, not only is he the one who has to take the blame, but he never bothered to get a rating to fly that particular type of aircraft. It would put him in a lot of trouble. He could lose his licence, and I don't think it would look too good for the CEO of Inland Airways to be considered a hazard to air safety.'

'Damn,' Freddie whispered.

'And,' Woodcock continued, 'he says, if you can't fix it he's seriously going to reconsider his relationship with us — and I'm not talking about ControlCorp.'

'We need his participation.' Freddie scratched his neck. 'So what's the problem? Why don't you just throw the report away?'

'Because, one thing I can't do from my office is fix parking tickets.' He dropped the paper on Freddie's desk. 'Hardy's responsible for filing it and he has. Now the only one between him and the CAA who can stop it is the unit manager, Amanda. Or you can get Hardy to rescind it and rewrite is as a minor pilot deviation.'

'Great,' Freddie said with a sigh. 'I wonder what that's going to cost me? Okay, leave it with me. Tell Malahide it's been taken care of and I'll think of something. What time are we due in Auckland tomorrow?'

'Eleven. It's a strategic management seminar. I told Amanda you would meet with her senior controllers and pretend to be interested for an hour.'

'Fine. Find out what Hardy drinks and throw a couple of bottles in my briefcase. I'll see if we can nip this little Malahide misunderstanding in the bud. Now,' he stood up and readjusted his belt, 'let's go grab a burger. I'm starving.'

Sixteen

The senior controller's office was the first along a pastel-hued corridor, the far end of which was capped by the heavy wooden doors of the executive boardroom.

Leanne was in there typing away on the computer. She was the newest of the tower supervisors. She was a short but athletic and strongly built woman with closely cropped hair and a face that glowed of fitness and a recent trip to the gym.

'Good morning,' I said as I went to my desk and immediately began moving things around to create the illusion of purpose.

'Morning,' she said engrossed in her typing. 'Oh, Tom, I've added a few notes to your training plan.'

'What?' A sudden wave of guilt punched me in the gut. 'How did you get into my training plan?'

'I didn't. It was password protected.' She glanced over and rolled her eyes. 'I swear I don't know why you're so paranoid about people reading it.'

I looked around my desk for something else to move from one basket to another. 'Security, that's all. Remember what they told us about guarding the Corporation's intellectual property — all that stuff.'

'Oh, you turn me on when you talk dirty like that.' Leanne smiled in disbelief and turned her attention back to her project. 'Anyway, don't worry. I put it in a separate file. It was just some stuff I got out of an ICAO document on developing training plans that I thought you would be interested in.'

'ICAO, of course.' Why didn't I think to check with ICAO? They regulate aviation worldwide. Of course they would have notes on developing training plans.

'Just a few suggestions,' she said diplomatically. 'I thought it might help us all to review each other's work. But you seem to be somewhat sensitive about people looking at yours.'

'No, it's not that. I don't mind. It's just that I never claimed to be a writer or anything.'

'Touchy, touchy.'

'So have you already finished your standards plan?'

Each senior controller was responsible for a different area of the operation. Mine was training, Leanne's was standards, and Denise, the third senior controller, was in charge of document control. As part of the modernisation plan, we were each obliged to write a manual on our area of expertise. This, the Corporation said, was to enable a consistent nationwide standard, though I suspected it was so they could get rid of me and replace me with a book.

'I thought I had, until my meeting with Amanda today.' She looked up and lowered her voice. 'She reminded me that I had more to prove than you, and that I ought to prove it.' She turned back to the computer, shaking her head.

'Well, you understand, she's doing it for you. For the Cause.'

Leanne rolled her eyes back again.

I liked Leanne. She was a bit of a cynic. Denise, on the other hand, was a little hard on the nerves — not because she was unpleasant, quite the opposite. She was bubbly and energetic, and took to corporate jargon with the same enthusiasm as a Kiwi climber tackles Everest. Her career goal was to get into the office of Corporate Communications. That would be the fulfilment of her dream of 'Show Business!' It was a small consolation to me that, being on the opposite side of the roster, I seldom saw Denise, except at our regular management meetings.

'Right — well,' I grabbed a few pieces of paper out of my in-basket that had no relevance to anything we were going to talk about. 'Wish me luck.'

'Good luck,' Leanne said as I left the office.

I went back around the corner to the executive wing where the pastels took on a slightly deeper hue and paused briefly at Amanda's office. The door was closed, as it often was, and I had never completely resolved the issue of whether I should just enter; or knock and wait to be invited in; or tap lightly and open the door carefully. I opted for the third option. I think I always opted for the third.

'Good morning, boss.'

Amanda was seated behind her desk, making notes on a notepad. She was dressed in conservative grey business attire, stiffly buttoned up to the neck and down to the wrists. Her hair was pulled back tightly — a serious-looking style she took to wearing when she was appointed unit manager. Personally, I thought she would accomplish much more in the still mostly male-dominated industry if she had stuck with the well-maintained and sexually alluring look of our days at Milton Gorge. But there was no way I was going to be the one to suggest it.

'Good morning, Thomas,' she said. 'I thought you promised me you were going to try to wear a tie more often.'

'I am,' I nodded. 'Trying, I mean. But it's casual Wednesday.'

'There's no such thing as casual Wednesday.' She glanced down at a pad of paper in front of her — her ever-present, ever-ready agenda. 'Anything I should know about this morning?'

The agenda must have been a good one for her to not pursue the tie issue. Neckties were not something I was being defiant about. I had one in the top drawer of my desk in case I needed to meet with someone from the airport company, or give a tour to a bunch of school kids or something. But they made my neck stiff and itchy and I don't think there was anything in the air traffic manual about wearing one. In fact, I'm pretty sure Amanda only wanted me in one to remind me which end of the leash I was on.

'All ops normal.' I took a seat opposite her and glanced around her office, wondering where the listening devices were hidden. I had this flashback to Thornie Rumbold's old office, with its 1940s solid wood furniture, the shelves crammed with books and manuals, and the smell of age and dust permanently in the air — all of it gone now, all of it a memory gathering dust in storage or in ruin.

Flynn and I were the only two to pack up Thornie's office; we thought it better for us to do it with a certain amount of love and reverence than to have the Corporation hire a cleaning crew to come in with a bunch of rubbish sacks. Some of the stuff had to have significant historical value, so we volunteered for the job of packing up the carefully preserved photo albums, volumes and mementos — some valuable, some worthless. Even his leather-bound blotter — when I picked it up and saw the stain left by his last cup of tea, I could smell the dust and the smoke again. The calendar page was current and, other than the tea stain, was utterly spotless; not a phone number, not a note, not a scratch to get the ink in his pen working. He hadn't picked at the edges and, even as he tore off the pages of each month, left no 'hanging chads'. He was a meticulous man.I tucked it into one of the boxes along with some photo albums and we moved it all over to the storage room in the Warbirds hangar until a permanent home could be found for the collection.

'Your interpretation of "ops normal" is what worries me,' Amanda said. 'The centre supervisor complained that you've been doing your squeeze plays again.'

'They wouldn't be squeeze plays if they would give me more than four miles between arrivals.' I could have told her about the radar freezing up again, but she knew about the problem and if I used the term "piece of shit", it would only be interpreted as a poor corporate attitude.

'Did you ask them for five miles in-trail?'

'Don't worry about it, boss.' I waved it away and remembered how Thornie used to wave his troubles away. *An' let poor damned bodies be.* 'The approach controller's not complaining. It's just the centre supervisor trying to get even with me for being witness to his contribution to Ryan's deal last week.'

Amanda nodded, as if she was weighing this information carefully, but I knew she knew I was right and was not concerned about the petty squabbles the controllers had between themselves. She was just fulfilling her duty to pass on the complaint.

Despite our aborted roll in the rice, I still wanted to be friends with Amanda and, on occasion, still felt a strong urge to be more than just friends. I was her moth, she my flame — and I always got burnt. That's why I worked almost exclusively with Flynn for those last three months at Milton Gorge. Flynn may have been a wild man, but I learned a lot from him. When we worked together, there were no other two controllers who could turn chaos into an aerial ballet and have as much fun as we did. We never saw Amos Scuffield again, but there were plenty of old farts like those in the Wild Blue Squadron who thought they could scare us with the odd buzz-and-break over the tower. They couldn't. And I even got used to working around old Whacko Warren in his Waco.

It's one thing to watch things fade away and get used to the idea of their ultimate disappearance. But the day Thornie died was the end. It came so abruptly, and I knew it then. It was the end of me and Flynn kicking butt around the circuit. It was the end of me and Amanda and unfulfilled sexual desire. It was the end of Kenny and Garry's efficient working relationship. Even Quincy and Bryan Weston were 'disestablished' with a small redundancy payment and they ran off to Hawaii to be properly married. Last I heard they had opened a health food café in Wanaka — with a Warbirds theme no less.

I looked around at these current surroundings. Amanda's office, compared to Thornie's, was positively spartan. The polished wood of the furniture didn't have one scratch, dent or coffee stain. The coloured spines of the few books she had on one shelf behind her desk looked like they were chosen for their tie-in to the décor more than their content. The plants were real and very much alive — they were tended to by a company that did nothing but tend to office plants. In one corner, she had a sofa and a couple overstuffed chairs arranged around a coffee table, with a liquor cabinet to the side.

'How's the first week of the new roster working out?'

'A bit of grumbling, but they'll settle into it.'

'And the new noise abatement policy?'

'That might need a bit of tweaking. Maybe we should use it only after 11 p.m. There's still too much traffic at nine to try departing aircraft off in the opposite direction to the landings just to please a group of citizens who should have had more sense than to buy houses next to an airport if they were sensitive to noise.'

'Well, they are an organised group of citizens, and we have to show we're making some sort of effort. See how it works for another week at nine and report back to me on it. Of course, don't compromise safety.'

'No more so than I do daily.'

She ignored my quip and looked down at her list. I wished she would lighten up sometimes. It wouldn't kill her to just relax the jaw muscles a little, undo her bun and let that beautiful hair tumble playfully down her shoulders.

We could still be friends, I thought, Amanda and I. But she never really forgave me for once trying to be more than friends. What was it she wanted, then? Synergism?

'That incident you filed last week regarding the Learjet, let's see ...' She looked up from the notepad. 'That was Ryan on duty.'

'Yes.'

'And you've listened to the tape? Are you sure he didn't make a mistake himself?'

'He said everything he was supposed to say — he did his job.'

'And his tone to the Learjet?'

'His tone? Rather angry, I would say, but the guy deserved it.'

'The guy,' Amanda said looking down at the report, 'was Douglas Malahide, CEO of Inland Airways.'

'All the more reason for him to know better than to be out in a Learjet for a joy ride, not talking to radar, and cutting in front of 737s.'

When he called the tower, Ryan had sequenced him to follow the B737, making a visual approach. Then he briefly turned his attention to other traffic and when he looked up again, the Learjet was cutting right in front of the B737, probably with less than 200 feet separation. Immersed in my own administrative duties over the daily log, all I heard was Ryan yell 'Shit!' and looked up. 'Send the 737 around,' I yelled at Ryan. He had frozen, but he did what I told him to and let the Learjet land first. Always work around the dickheads. I had told him so many times always to rely on the more trusted component in a situation like that. No, Ryan could have done better, but he was young and stupid and he had learned his lesson — at least, he would know what to do if that one ever happened again.

'Yes, well,' Amanda said, 'Mr Moore called from Wellington a little while ago and said there may be some problems with that one and that your report was incomplete. You'll need to redo it before it can go on to CAA.'

'Of course.' They were going to sweep this one under the carpet. I could already see it coming. The Learjet pilot had political sway and ControlCorp was going to buckle. They would call it diplomacy. Never mind the issue of air safety, never mind the fact that the Learjet's little stunt almost took out a B737 with 120 people on board. Because he had money, he had far more influence than me in the court of corporate law. The ruler of the land.

'Make sure it's letter-perfect,' she said, but meant to leave enough doubt in Ryan's performance so that they could dismiss it. 'Mr Moore and Mr Woodcock will be up from Wellington tomorrow morning and I'll take it up with them then. Now, next item ...' She looked at the agenda again. This was a trick of Amanda's — I think she got it out of one of her textbooks. She discouraged any debate on the subject by running it right into the next item on her list. What she didn't understand was, I wasn't arguing as much as I used to. There was no point.

'The billing system.' She pushed her notepad a few inches away as she leaned back and crossed her arms, looking at me as if I had been caught red-handed drawing pictures on the walls with my crayons. 'This isn't going to be a rebellion, is it?'

'What do you mean? Who's rebelling? I told you guys what

I thought a month ago. There was no secret. Freddie Moore and Woodchuck were there. I just think it's wrong to introduce an accounting department task into the tower cab. It's supposed to be a focused environment — eyes out the window, stuff like that. By requiring the controller to turn his attention away from the planes to enter billing information into the computer is, I believe, asking for trouble because it breaks his focus.'

'Or hers. And please try to refrain from calling Mr Woodcock "Woodchuck" — it's all right for the controllers to have nicknames among themselves, but I don't think Mr Woodcock would appreciate it if got back to him.'

'Sorry. It's just too easy.'

'Now, back to the billing system. Your argument was all very convincing.'

'But not convincing enough.'

'I wasn't enthusiastic about the idea when they first suggested it to me either, but it does make sense, and it does streamline the operation to have the task done at the source.'

'You mean it allowed the Corporation to eliminate a few more jobs down in accounting.'

I could see the muscle in her jaw twitch and knew she was getting bored with this exercise. She did not like debating because it implied a challenge to her rule, which is why I had largely given up trying — but there were still a few of my buttons left she knew she could push.

I was sure she considered herself quite a good manager and in some ways she was; she certainly gave it her best shot. The problem was one of respect. She didn't get enough of it from the controllers because she didn't offer them the same. To the workforce, she embraced everything that came out of Head Office with passion and was quick to censure those who did not share her enthusiasm. When the Corporation announced that ATC salaries were the bulk of the Corporation's costs and thus the number one target area for cutbacks, Amanda readily volunteered that she could run her facility with three fewer staff. Then she was surprised when the staff baulked. 'They lack the proper corporate spirit,' she said of the entire controller staff. But to them, she was the Corporation. I personally did not feel as strongly about her as some of the others. Once you've rolled around the stir-fry with someone, it's just hard to forget the good times. I really did want to like her. Or maybe it was because she was really my last link to Milton Gorge.

Well, not quite my last link. But the other was doomed. Kenny Lima was sent downstairs to the Oceanic Sector. He and I were not close at Milton Gorge. He was pretty shy and, I admit, there may have been a certain reluctance on my part to reach out to him — after all, I didn't think his pet rat Garry approved of me, and I wasn't sure he if he had an army of friends to do the whole *Willard* thing on me. There was no evidence to support the theory that Kenny was training an army of rats. But even so, Garry had to go and the Corporation ultimately forced the break-up of that partnership. They wouldn't let him bring the rodent to work with him in Auckland. And, minus the rat, Kenny had a problem with focusing on his job. He was becoming legendary for the number of incidents he's had. The poor guy's career was now on shaky ground, all because they wouldn't let him bring his furry little friend to work. I just felt sorry for him because he was going to have one too many incidents, and then he'd be out. Besides, the Corporation was being unreasonable — Garry wouldn't have been the only rat in the building. Some were making six-figure salaries.

So Amanda was, in a way, my last remaining link to Exile Tower. And I still had hope that she could one day pull her head out of her arse and start leading her troops instead of trying to face them down. After all, she was a good controller. She was intelligent, and she was not afraid to stand up for herself — if she could just learn to stand up for others.

'In any case,' Amanda reminded me, 'your views were listened to. The decision to introduce the billing system into the tower as proposed was made, and it is now your job to support it wholeheartedly.'

'I accepted that and we've been doing it.'

'Your crew has been leaving some undone on the evening shift for the morning crew to finish.'

'That's because flight data goes home and there's no one to do it.'

'The controllers.'

'No.'

'And so we get to the heart of the matter.' She leaned back slowly, getting maximum protest from the leather chair, the corners of her mouth turning slightly upwards, not so much as a smile as a lack of a poker face. She was manoeuvring me back into place.

'It's not a rebellion. I just don't want the controllers turning their attention away from the airplanes.'

'Come now, they're not that busy all the time. The reason we even send flight data home at 8.00 is because it slows down.'

'The point is —'

'The point is, the decision has been made. It's not open for any more discussion, and I expect you to comply.'

Yes, of course. That was the point. Indeed. The decision was already made. By the time the decision reached us, they were not interested in discussion, only the appearance of having a discussion.

'Yes, ma'am,' I said, trying to stop the sarcastic downbeat.

'Thomas ...' she began, but then paused and looked like she was reconsidering her direction. She picked up a pencil and quietly tapped the tip on her pad, her agenda. I wondered what was next. 'You realise some of these new members of your team look up to you — Simon and Ryan for instance. You need to be very conscious of that fact, of the effect you have on them.'

'What effect would that be?'

'Well, your manner can be rather ... flippant, at times. It's not professional.'

'You think I'm unprofessional? That's pretty harsh, don't you think? I mean it doesn't seem that long ago when you were boasting what a good controller I am ... or was.'

'Your technical skill is not in question, but it's only a very small part of being a good corporate citizen. You're not doing anyone any favours by being militant towards the Corporation.'

'I'm not being militant! If you haven't noticed, I've been the picture of compliance.' I took a deep breath to bring myself down a notch. 'It's not as much fun, I admit, but I have been toeing the line. And I think it should be noted.'

'Maybe,' she said. 'But you only embarrass yourself with your sarcasm and lead the more impressionable down the wrong path. Promise me you'll make an effort to present a better corporate spirit. I would hate to have to turn this minor issue into a disciplinary action.'

Or else. You will become good corporate citizens or else there will be — a disciplinary action. It sounds much more civilised than a firing squad. I wonder if there is a ControlCorp equivalent to the Lubyanka? I mean, now that Exile Tower had been reduced to rubble and a suburb, where will they send the misfits? The rebels? The unbelievers?

And I wonder how this New World Order is working out for them and how long before they will plan the new New World Order. One of the most basic, primal qualities of the nature of man — no, it is basic animal behaviour — is to be driven by instinct to repeat the same activities over and over again. We wake, we kill, we eat, we shit, we sleep, we wake again. All evolution does, every one hundred or one thousand years, is to put a new spin on the same cycle and to give us more tools with which to conduct our affairs more efficiently and to kill on grander scales. We rise up, we revolt, we enjoy the spoils of war, we shit, we sleep, we rise up again. Round and round we go without really going anywhere. We become enlightened, we incorporate, we globalise, we shit, we sleep, we become enlightened again. The New World Order is really just variations on the theme of musical chairs, except that in this game, those that are left standing when the music stops are not merely out of the game ...

They're out of the game.

SEVENTEEN

I poured myself another cup of coffee from the executive brew in reception before heading back to my office. One improvement I had no complaint about was the coffee-maker — no more instant. I do not remember exactly when the Corporation moved from providing tea to providing coffee for the office staff to drink. Coffee, apparently, was the corporate drink. They brought in a team of research consultants to determine what was the appropriate drink, the drink that made the right statement, the drink of success, the new power drink. In any case, I suspected the cup I was holding was the most expensive cup of coffee this side of the space station.

'Good afternoon, Mr Hardy.'

I turned my attention from the coffee-maker to the voice. 'Why hello, Eddie. Shouldn't you be out looking for hijackers. I hear there may be some about.'

'It's Captain Tucker. And I'm more interested in bombers.'

'Well, I'll let you know if I see any today.' I carried my coffee towards my office, hoping he would not tag along, but he did.

Captain Edwin Tucker was now the head of aviation security and loved to hassle me. He had been just a local constable out in Milton Gorge, but by signing on with the newly formed Airport Company as their head of security, here he was: The Man. And the airport was his beat. Ever since our first meeting outside The Tie Down out at Milton Gorge, he permanently associated me with Flynn and his signal pistol antics. To Captain Tucker I was synonymous with trouble. Now, if I forgot to display my identification badge, if I put my car in the wrong place, or broke the pedestrian speed limit through the terminal,

Captain Edwin Tucker was there, lying in wait. I suspected he was having a bit of fun with me, just as I did with him back then. I also suspected he thought that if he kept after me, sooner or later I'd lead him to his Public Enemy Number 1: Owen Flynn.

'Would you?' he asked as he walked alongside me. 'Would you tell me if you heard from any bombers?'

'Of course I would, Eddie.' I turned and smiled. 'I mean, Captain Tucker. You know I have your number on my speed dial, right between pizza delivery and the fire department.' We approached the door to my office.

'You know, Tom, I know you like to make jokes.' Tucker stepped in front of me at the door. 'But all I'm after is the truth. It doesn't seem like much to ask for. With truth we can have justice. You can understand that can't you?'

'Except that I don't believe Owen Flynn is guilty of anything.'

'Then why did he run? Why did he not just stay and tell the truth?'

'I don't know.' I shrugged to make it look more convincing. 'Maybe because some of us believe truth doesn't always lead to justice — not when you're being framed. The truth is, sometimes there is no justice. And you can't fight big money.'

'Yeah.' Tucker smiled, then took a step closer and turned, vaguely menacing with his conspiratorial whisper. 'Sometimes you and I think alike.'

'How frightening.'

'Which is why I may be your only friend,' he said with a smirk, his eyes locked on mine.

'Great. Do you golf? I'm not very good at it myself, but want to get more into the game. Maybe we could do that. Now, if you'll excuse me, I have a very important meeting to attend in my office here.'

Tucker moved to the side. 'You were his best friend.'

'He had other friends.'

'Not many. I checked.'

'I'm sure you did.' I pushed the door open and was sorry to

see that Leanne had left, thus blowing my story about having an important meeting waiting for me.

'It's hard to believe you don't have any idea where he is. And if you do, that's complicity, which wouldn't be so funny. I'm just trying to help keep you out of trouble. And you know something else?'

'What?

'Just maybe I could help him, too — I mean, if it's true what you say about his innocence.'

Much like my feeling towards Amanda, I actually liked Tucker, if for no other reason than the entertainment value. He and I could banter endlessly as if it were scripted by overly tired TV writers. When I was a kid, all I ever wanted was to live on a TV show, and this was as close as I ever got. Tucker made me feel like I was living my life out on the set of *Dragnet*, which was better than some TV shows I could have been trapped in — at least it didn't have a laugh track. I think having a laugh track in my life might push me over the edge.

I sat behind my desk and took a sip of coffee. It tasted particularly bitter today and I set it down, unsure whether or not I really wanted it any more. I linked my hands behind my head, leaned back and stared at the tower through the office window. What I appreciated about Tucker was that he was relentlessly dedicated to his job and his melodramatic search for truth, justice and the Kiwi way. He figured I could lead him to the would-be terrorist Owen Flynn. Even though it was not within his jurisdiction any more, he was determined to track the guy down. It was something he would do because he felt it was the right thing. Tucker was okay. But as long as he continued to try and ambush me on the whereabouts of Flynn, it was my duty to continue to play dumb — or smart. We both had our parts to play, and mine was that of the wrongly accused. It was like a game. It was like a TV show.

Los Angeles, California. City of Angels and fallen teen idols. Five million people with five million stories to tell. This is just one of them. It was a balmy summer evening. We were pulling a late shift. My partner is

Bill Gannon. My name is Friday. It was Tuesday.

I smiled and silently laughed at myself. Sergeant Joe Friday never harassed the innocent. I don't think he ever once turned on his own. '*Hey Bill, I know what you're up to: marijuana. That's right: pot, weed, grass, dope, reefer. Call it what you will, it's all a ticket on the express train to LSD, angel dust, blow, and the big H.' I knew he was guilty, I could see it in his guilty blue eyes. That's right, baby blues, ol' blue eyes, jeepers creepers where'd ya get those peepers? Call them what you will, they were eyes and they were blue.*

At least, I don't remember seeing that episode during any of my TV binges.

'*Thomas, turn that thing off*,' my dad commanded as he walked in the front door, down the hall and into his office without ever pausing. His sudden appearance in my fantasy startled me as much as my dad bursting through the door unexpectedly had back then. I followed him with my eyes, and when the door to his office closed with a solid *thump* behind him, I turned back to the TV. It was another one of those oddities about my dad I was learning to ignore at an early age: an order without power, without follow-up. He was not a disciplinarian; he was an excessively rational man who tried to reason his way through every situation — even with a little kid. I knew, even back then, after that one little burst from him, if and when he re-emerged from his office in ten minutes, he would not say anything more about turning the TV off.

Why that particular memory came back, I don't know. Maybe it was the similarity between Tucker's search for truth and justice and my dad's hopeless crusading for the same. I stood up and walked towards the window. Part of the domestic terminal, ramp-side, and the control tower occupied most of the scene outside my window — it seemed oddly appropriate that the corporate structure had turned me inside out. They used to pay me to sit in the tower and look out, now I am here, outside, watching the tower. Leadership by remote viewing — that's when wars became most lethal, when the leaders disappear from the front line and start watching from their offices while holding a cup of freshly brewed coffee. I reached for my cup of stale black coffee and continued to stare at the tower.

I should be up there — something's going wrong.

'*Your place.*' That's what my dad used to say. '*You must always know where you belong — it's your place. Defend it.*'

My dad had his place and he defended it with his life to the very end. He was a professor of English literature. He loved literature passionately and teaching it was everything to him. He loved teaching it; he loved finding that one kid out of twenty or thirty or fifty whose world would be opened up by it, whose life would be changed and who would end up understanding what my dad understood. Maybe he liked teaching too much.

He had his own brand of privatisation to deal with — the university didn't exactly go corporate, but the politics and the selling out of ideals was pretty much the same. And, in the end, it's what killed him. Ambitious new deans who were eager to make the English department more cost-effective by cutting courses and driving dusty old professors like my dad into early retirement so they could have the budget to fund a new course on the interpretation of 1960s television shows. Sure, I would take a class like that, but … well, my dad, for God's sake, had met T.S. Eliot, Robert Frost and exchanged letters with Ezra Pound when the poet was locked up in an insane asylum.

You would think that being subjected to his obsessive love for books would damage a kid — drive him away — after all, he made me read a hell of a lot, and then he would quiz me on what I had read. Difficult stuff too — it was kind of daunting for a little kid. But he did it gently, and I think it was just his way of counteracting my obsession with television. He had his obsession and I had mine. Although we never exactly shared the same obsession, I didn't mind partaking a little in his. It was something. He could be cold and withdrawn much of the time. He never knew how to be a family man — he had married late in life to a woman fifteen years younger and was already forty-nine when I was born. We were never very close, but I wanted something, some part of him. So there were two things I pretended to like as a child so that I could try to own part of him: books and fishing.

I thought of the woods — down by the Russian River where I used to take my dog Wiley in my teenage years after my dad had died. My dad only took me on one fishing trip down there. I was eleven at the time. It was just me and my dad. He was carrying the fishing tackle and one rod. I was struggling with, and trying not to keep tripping over, the other rod.

'My secret spot,' he called it. 'Only men allowed. Just you and me, Thomas, and Mr Burns.'

'Where is Mr Burns?' I asked him over and over again because there was no one else with us. I never knew my dad to have friends, so I was anxious to meet this guy he spoke so highly of. I assumed he was going to meet us at the river. The more evasive Mr Burns appeared to be, however, the more frightening he became to me. I half expected a crazy old man with no teeth, one eye and a hunched back to jump out from behind a tree laughing like a madman, at which point my dad would introduce Mr Burns. But my dad just kept saying, 'Patience my dear boy. You will meet Mr Burns all in good time.'

It had taken months of begging finally to wear my old man down enough to allow me to come along on this fishing trip. Those few times a year he took a break from his work to go fishing were something important to him — times he wanted, or needed, to be alone — and I wanted a part of that. I wanted to share a part of him. So when I was old enough to figure out my dad could be reasoned with, I begged and begged until he relented and said I could come.

'I guess Mr Burns won't mind the company of *me fair wee laddie*,' he had said in the funny Scottish accent he loved to use when he was in one of his good moods.

When we arrived at his 'secret spot', no one else was there. I cautiously eyed the trees, but didn't see any signs of crazy old men. I watched in quiet awe as my dad showed me how to bait the hook and adamantly refused to do my own.

'A man needs to learn to bait his own hook,' my dad said. 'Look, son, they're just worms. They can't hurt you.'

But it wasn't myself I was afraid of hurting.

'They're just worms,' he said. 'They don't feel anything — it doesn't hurt them.'

My dad had acquiesced on the worms and, instead, put a small piece of cheese on the end of my hook. But the problem was not the slimy, wriggling worms either. It was the fish. I had wanted to go fishing with my dad for a long time, but had never really thought about what fishing involved. I sat quietly praying that no fish would bite the cheese on my hook.

My dad found that extraordinarily funny. 'Oh, Thomas, my boy, men have been fishing for many thousands of years — but leave it to my son to find the cruelty in it.'

I suggested that he wouldn't much care for it himself if he had, say, been walking past the kitchen table and found Mom had made him a nice grilled cheese sandwich for lunch, and so he takes a bite and bam! — suddenly he finds himself in the tug of war for his life with a hook firmly embedded in the roof of his mouth. My father had laughed long and hard over that. 'Bravo, son. The argument is logical and carries a certain weight of compassion.'

We laughed together that day. His laughter still echoed in my ears. He didn't laugh often. He was more often an angry man, angry at the world, at the university, at people. Angry about things I did not understand. We were sitting there, both laughing, holding our fishing rods with the lines dangling in the water. When he had regained his composure, he announced that Mr Burns had finally arrived. I stopped laughing and turned my head in trepidation, which brought another round of laughter from my dad. Then he reached into his rucksack and removed a small, leather-bound volume.

'Thomas,' he said. 'May I introduce Mr Robert Burns of Ayrshire, Scotland.' He then turned to the book and said, 'Mr Burns, I'd like to introduce my only son, and indirect descendant of one of your fellow pantheon members, Thomas, of Sonoma-shire in the Land of Moral Void.'

That was when I realised my dad, talking to a book, was more than just a little odd.

'Och! A wee laddie he is,' my dad said in his funny voice again. *'But he will grow to be a great protector of worms and fish and man. Please, watch over him and guide him as you have me.'*

'You're weird, Dad,' I said, but wished I hadn't.

My dad looked at me in mock dismay. *'Ay, that I may be, laddie.'* Then he laughed again.

I remained silent.

'A man needs guidance in his life,' he said seriously, 'and inspiration. There are not many sources of true inspiration.'

I stared, but continued to say nothing.

'Read all that you lay your hands on, son. Be inspired by it. Give something of yourself to the words and they will repay you tenfold. Allow yourself that at the very least.' He held the book up. 'Just be careful of that Bible. I can't save you from it, just be careful with it and with those who will beat you to death with it. Some find a lifetime of inspiration and guidance in its pages, whereas I find its words too often twisted and used to bestow grief on others. No, it's not for me, I'm an atheist.' He leaned closer and added with a whisper, 'But please don't tell God.'

He laughed at his own joke and then fell silent, looking thoughtfully, lovingly, at the book in his hands. He gently stroked the well-worn cover. 'No, I thought Mr Burns might be more up your alley. He faced great adversity, yet he knew how to be happy and to rejoice in life. If you know how to be happy in the face of the blackness, then you have risen above mere mortals.'

My dad sometimes referred to 'the blackness' when he spoke, but it scared me too much to ask him what he meant. I could only piece it together over those few short years: what it meant to him and what it meant to me. I did not understand completely until the end. Then he opened the book, there on the banks of the Russian River that day, and read in a loud clear voice as if he was on stage.

'O Thou! whatever title suit thee —' he recited in an overly dramatic voice, *'Auld Hornie, Satan, Nick, or Clootie, Wha in yon cavern grim*

an' sootie, Clos'd under the hatches, Spairges about the brunstane cootie, To scaud poor wretches!'

To me, it sounded like Dr Seuss.

'Hear me, auld Hangie, for a wee, An' let poor damned bodies be; I'm sure sma' pleasure it can gie, Ev'n to a deil, To skelp an' scaud poor dogs like me, An' hear us squeel!'

He read on for a long time, savouring the words as if they were chocolate-coated. When he finished, he closed the book and smiled as he gazed upon it.

'You'll understand someday,' he said quietly. Then, as was typical of my dad, he gave me homework. I was to memorise just one verse from that poem, which I would have to recite the next time we went fishing. And then he presented me with the book as a gift. I learned two verses, though I could no longer recall the title. But we never went fishing again, so I never got to recite them to my dad. At least, not when he was alive.

I looked around my office. There was something I was supposed to do, paperwork of some sort. The incident — Ryan's incident, I had to re-file that.

Bullshit.

'*An' let poor damned bodies be.*' I remembered that much.

For a moment I thought I could smell the stale mustiness of my dad's office and the blackness creeping in.

EIGHTEEN

'The incident? That was the one between Pacific West and Tasman Airways?'

'No, of course not. That was the following day. Am I boring you so much that you can't follow?'

'Not at all.' He shook his head. 'I find it all very interesting.'

'I think you were dozing off.' I smiled at him. 'Am I taking up too much of your time?'

'No. I have all the time in the world. Besides, I'm billing the Corporation $250 an hour.' He smiled back at me. 'Talk as long as you want. And I promise I'll stay awake. But I never heard of this related incident you spoke of, the one with the Learjet.'

'That's because they're sweeping it under the carpet.'

'So what has it got to do with the current investigation?'

'Maybe something, maybe nothing.' I turned and watched the rain on the window for a moment and wondered why I had thought this was a good idea.

Because, it had to be said. This was the second step of my purging. Flynn's orders.

'It's just to give you an idea of who gets to investigate whom. I mean, exactly why are we not investigating that incident? Why do they want it dismissed? I'll tell you why,' I turned back to him, 'because the rules don't apply to those who can buy "justice" — and believe me, it's for sale, like every other public service in this world. Ryan's incident was every bit as dangerous as Simon's, two jets getting within two hundred feet of each other as opposed to two jets having to take evasive action to miss each other. One was clearly the pilot's fault, but he happens to be a guy who can buy his way

out. And so he would. I knew it then, even before I had to file a second set of paperwork.'

He narrowed his eyes and stared at me for several moments. 'Simon's incident?'

'What?'

'You said "Simon's incident".'

'No I didn't. What are you talking about?'

'You said "Simon's incident".'

'Well, I meant this incident I was involved with, the one I am currently being psychiatrically assessed for.'

'It was Simon's, wasn't it? And you're taking the blame to protect him.'

'I'm taking the blame for the Corporation. Simon was downstairs taking a break.'

'Why are you protecting him? Is he a fish, a worm, or a man?'

'Simon's a tomcat. You want to play word association?'

'Do you feel a need to protect others?'

'I guess that would be as good as anything to stand up for, but no.'

'What are you protecting Flynn from?'

'I'm not protecting Flynn.'

'Yes you are. You're protecting him from Tucker. After all, you know where Flynn is, don't you?'

I thought long and hard before I said anything. It was a confidence I had not want to betray — not yet. But, damn it, I had chosen this road to go down and could see no way out but through to the other side now. 'Of course I do.'

'So, I ask again, why are you protecting him?'

'I'm not. I'm just keeping his secret. He's my friend.'

'But he's a wanted man.'

'Only as a scapegoat.'

'The police say he's dangerous.'

'They don't know the truth.'

'Why don't you tell them?'

'Because I don't know the truth either — not yet at least.'

✈

Closing down the tower at Milton Gorge did not go down well with a lot of people. The Corporation referred the complainants to their bottom line. There was just no way to make a profit at an airfield that could only charge the users $6 per landing. To support the infrastructure fully they would need to charge five times that much. And no pilot would go for that. 'Sure we understand your feelings,' the Corporation would say. Then they'd sniff and shrug and say, 'Okay, if you don't want us here, we'll go.' And they were gone. The controllers were gone and the pilots were left to figure it out for themselves.

Y'all be careful now.

Mr and Mr Weston were disestablished, which was the Corporation's nice way of saying they were sacked. I bet my dad the English professor would say — if he were still around to voice his opinion — that Thornie was the only one who could be correctly described as being 'disestablished'; that is, made to no longer exist.

They offered Flynn a position as a weather observer at Scott Base. Kenny, sans rat, was sent to the Oceanic Sector. Amanda and I were the up-and-comers — we were sent to Auckland. Freddie Moore himself pulled me to the side and told me I should apply for the newly advertised tower supervisor position there, said that forward thinking people like me were just what the Corporation was looking for, and he had it on good authority that I would be a shoo-in for the job. Then he winked and squeezed my elbow. I had no idea what he meant.

Amanda also applied for the job. If I had been doing the hiring I would have hired her. She was far more qualified, far more ambitious. Even without her implied threats of sexual discrimination, I still would have hired her. Instead, the Corporation chose another route. They decided they needed two supervisors and hired both of us — which worked out so well they decided to call us senior controllers instead of supervisors and hired a third. They've recently hired a fourth, although he has not shown up in Auckland yet and, if I'm not mistaken, I believe they are now looking for a fifth. Or maybe I'm wrong on that, maybe they're just planning ahead and looking for my replacement.

As for Amanda, it was just the first rung on the ladder that would, in less than a year, allow her to climb to manager of the facility. She knew how to play the corporate game, and I had to respect that. Every time the music stopped, she always had a better chair.

But I had no complaints going to Auckland — the place suited me fine. It gave me a chance live in the big city and to continue my search for a halfway decent Mexican restaurant. That search continues, but the city had a few more benefits. There was enough variety of pubs to allow me to develop my drinking skills further without gaining a reputation in any one particular establishment. It was also sufficiently cosmopolitan — in its own quaint, provincial way — to enable me to go for whole days without having to answer for my American accent, explain I didn't know anyone famous, be blamed for the President of the United States, or try to explain American foreign policy. I always found that amusing, not only because I did not vote for the man — that is, had I voted, I would have voted for someone else — but also because I was probably the only person in this country who had come close to having a real run-in with the guy. Of course, I'm talking about ordinary people. Some heads of state might argue that they had a relationship with the President. After all, it was the Prime Minister of New Zealand who pointed out to the President of the United States at last year's APEC conference that he had some salmon pâté on his tie. Who could forget? It was in the news here for three days.

By the time I had finished my training at Auckland and settled into my new role as senior controller, I think it was safe to say that my career had reached the highest point in its trajectory — something that usually took a retrospective perspective to determine. But I knew it then. It was all going to be downhill from there.

Trajectories were a problem for Flynn, too — not career trajectories, but, specifically, the difference between the trajectory of a bird-scaring cartridge and a flare. I was only kidding about his position as a weather observer at Scott Base. He didn't stand a chance of being offered a position anywhere. All they needed was an excuse. And who better to find some dirt on Flynn than Freddie Moore, who was up from Wellington with his lapdog, Woodchuck, on one of their housecleaning tours. It only took Freddie Moore one round of drinks at The Tie Down to dig up a good enough reason to get rid of Owen Flynn forever.

'What?' Flynn was genuinely dismayed at their reasoning for dismissing him. 'It was only a pea-green Corolla.'

'Nevertheless, destroying a flight instructor's car with a signal pistol shows a dangerous level of negligence.'

'Even if it was an accident?'

'And was it? I wonder, Mr Flynn,' Woodcock piped in, 'if you do not use the term "accident" a little too loosely to explain your own unprofessional conduct and simple negligence.'

'Well,' Flynn shrugged, 'I know the difference between an accident and on purpose.'

'Nevertheless,' Freddie said, 'you're fired. Now go away.'

Early the next morning, Freddie Moore emerged from his motel room to find a piece of notepaper under a brick in the place where Freddie had previously parked his BMW. The neatly printed block-lettered words on the paper offered very little clues as to the whereabouts of his car — all the note said was: 'For instance — this is on purpose.'

All was explained in less than hour when Constable Tucker found the smouldering ruins of Freddie's BMW in the middle of the runway at Milton Gorge.

That only ensured Flynn's dismissal. It didn't turn him into a fugitive. To his credit, he denied having stolen and set fire to Freddie's car. I respected his adamant proclamation of his own innocence, although I didn't believe him. He was my friend and I know I was supposed to believe him, but I mean it was so like him. Looking back, though, I wish I had believed him because I think I had something to do with turning him into a fugitive.

At Milton Gorge he rented a foreman's shack on a local farm and, besides job at the tower, put in a lot of hard work tending to Garrett Scuffield's farm. That job gave him access to gelignite, a piece of circumstantial evidence that would not work in his favour. The locals all seemed to know him and like him, but he still kept to himself and had few people that could honestly be classified as a friend.

Yet he was my friend. And I think he considered me the same because, like him, I had trouble fitting into the system — although, as I often argued with him, I did try to fit into the system. I wanted to fit, whereas he seemed to go out of his way to disrupt the system and certainly took a good deal of pleasure in his disruptions.

'You only think you want to fit,' he said as he flicked his fishing line across the water during what was becoming one of our regular trips out to the river. He was trying to teach me to fly-fish. My attitude to the act of fishing, the hooking and killing bit, had not changed from the time I was a boy, but I still liked the idea of the fishing trip. Or maybe it was the 'ideal' of the fishing trip. I'm not sure. What I do know is that Flynn just smiled and said, 'Sure,' without asking a single question when I told him I would let him teach me how to fish if he would listen to some Robert Burns while we were fishing. That was a joke. I would never have put him through that. Some stuff is just private.

And now, once again, I wish I had the chance to go back and do something differently. You just don't know when you're never going to have the chance again. All I needed to say was, 'Of course I believe you, Flynn. If you say you didn't steal Freddie's car, then I believe you.'

But I didn't say that and Flynn, without friends, disappeared so completely, one could easily start to wonder if he ever existed. Garrett Scuffield said he went looking for him to load hay bales one day and Flynn was gone. He had packed what few things belonged to him, left everything else, and was gone, feeling somewhat betrayed, if my guess is right.

One thing he did not take with him was something he left on my doorstep the day he disappeared. Although it was gift-wrapped, it was pretty obvious what it was — a brand new fly-fishing rod. The attached note said 'Happy Birthday', though my birthday was many months away. Maybe it was meant to be a gift. I only thought of it as a reminder of my betrayal.

Freddie never pressed charges on the car. He got the two things he wanted most: to be rid of Flynn and a new BMW. So, at that point, Flynn was still not a wanted man. He didn't reach that status until a few weeks after his disappearance. And this time, a lot of people wanted him.

Had there been any actual witnesses, my God, it probably would have been a spectacular sight. One moment, Milton Gorge Tower was standing there as it had done for nearly sixty years, and the next moment, just as the morning sun was casting its first few rays on the sky, there was a thundering boom of an explosion that shook the walls and rattled the windows of every building on the field and every farmhouse within a two-mile radius. It must have been spectacular. It was not just big, it was precise — it was absolutely professional. Other than the tower being completely demolished, the only damage recorded on the airfield was twenty-three broken windows and some superficial damage to three aircraft from flying debris.

The preliminary police investigation decided that the tower had been demolished by someone who had a reasonable knowledge of what he — or she — had been doing; that the explosion — or perhaps more precisely, implosion — had blown the base of the tower and probably sent the tower cab straight up before it fell back and was, itself, smashed to bits leaving little more than a pile of splinters for them to sift through.

As soon as I heard about it, I drove down to Milton Gorge to see for myself. It was stunning to see something that had become such a part of the landscape so completely gone. I stood by myself at the far end of the runway staring at the emptiness, in utter shock, the acrid aroma of destruction stinging my nostrils and flooding my brain with a jumble of confused and blackened memories. I just stood there and wished I could cry — for the tower, for Flynn, for Thornie, for me, for my dad, for everything — but couldn't. I just stood in stunned silence.

After a quick consultation with ControlCorp executives, Flynn was chosen, as the number one suspect. As the Corporation pointed out, he had the motive and access to the materials. The police agreed to commence a dragnet for him, but did not rule out other possible suspects or the possibility it was the work of a terrorist group, a hostile foreign power or, possibly, France. However, they were unable to locate Flynn or anyone else that looked like they might be out to blow up an airport.

The day Milton Gorge Tower was blown to bits and all evidence suggested Owen Flynn had become a dangerous, vengeful man on the warpath — a domestic terrorist — that was the day I realised the depth of my betrayal. That was the day I realised he was, and always had been, an innocent man.

How could I have been so stupid?

I also knew then what the fishing rod meant. And so I waited.

Nineteen

'How much do you drink?'

'Ha!' I looked at my watch. 'It took a long time to get to that question. I thought that would be one of the first.'

He shrugged.

'The usual, I guess.'

'And how much is the "usual"?'

'Well, do you mean how much do I drink at work? Is that what you want to know? Or how pissed do I get before I go to work?'

'Do you?'

'Of course not. I do take my job pretty seriously, you know. Why would anyone suspect me of breaking a basic rule of the job?'

'I didn't say anyone did,' he said without offering even a polite grin.

I stared at him. What the hell was he getting at? Suddenly, the trust I had in him was dissipating rapidly. Something told me he knew a bit more than he had let on about Ryan's run-in with the Learjet.

After all, this was a corporate selected shrink I was talking to, to whom I was required to explain my actions of the previous Thursday evening, a night in which the air traffic system failed. I was tired then. But did he actually think I had been drinking that day? As he leaned back and studied me like I was a lab rat with a new twitch, was he thinking I had been drunk at the time? I had been at work for more than ten hours when the incident occurred. So what did he think — that I had a bottle stashed in the back of my bottom drawer? Or was spiking my coffee with booze? How do you explain to a guy like this? You'd have to be an idiot to be dipping in while on the job. It would be fatal. Maybe that's why some pilots and controllers did drink to excess when they partied, because they were stymied so much of the time.

Yeah, I drank sometimes. Had a few beers with the boys down at the pub occasionally, or a glass of wine or two when I went out to dinner. And spirits? Yeah — only one though — I liked the odd nip of Scotch. That, I started at an early age. In fact, I believe I was savouring the occasional wee dram before I had my first beer. But it was not because I was a teenage alcoholic — hell, it usually was just a little sniffing and rolling a bit across my tongue and could hardly be considered drinking. No, it was because I wanted to know something and for some reason, the way Scotch tickled my senses and numbed my tongue seemed to help me know it.

And yes, I had a bottle stashed in the bottom drawer of my desk.

The blackness, I thought, that's what nothingness was — creeping in along with the night. It would envelop my dad and drive him deep within himself. It would start with the silence. My mom could notice it and she knew I could. We would exchange a nervous glance as we passed the mashed potatoes around the dinner table and she would struggle to find a conversation in quiet small talk to cover up the shatteringly quiet clink of cutlery on dishes.

'Thomas got an A on his math exam today, didn't you dear?'

'Yes, Mom.'

'That's very good — was it a difficult exam?'

'No, not really.'

'Well, I'm glad you don't have too much trouble with math. I never was very good at math myself.' And with the exhaustion of that subject, she would fall silent again for a few minutes until she could see the tension rise in Dad's chewing, and then she would find another innocuous topic to cover. She always steered clear of asking me about my English exam.

Silence was the beginning for him. First his words and thoughts receded from us, and eventually he would disappear himself. Either he left the house without a word or went into his study. My mom, always apologetic, would explain it to me as 'one of his states', that he wasn't himself and usually sent me to bed early.

But silence was sometimes only the beginning of 'his state'. Sometimes in the morning he would be back to normal and talking as usual, and other times it would get worse and turn violent — never towards me, and never towards my mom, but on more than one occasion I would be awakened late in the night by a sudden crash of something in his office as his anger turned outwards. That's when it was worst. That was when he acted as if no one else in the world existed.

Once, when I was eleven or twelve, I ventured down the darkened stairs after hearing one such outburst. Perhaps as I approached adolescence I was just getting braver, perhaps not, but I was torn between fear and courage. I listened at his study door for a long time, without making a sound, my ear pressed to the door. All had seemed quiet inside. I cautiously turned the knob and eased the door open. In the dim glow of the lamp, in the dusty smell of old books, I could see my dad slumped down in his sofa clutching a nearly empty bottle. I watched him without moving from my position at the half-opened door. His eyes were open, glazed and staring at nothing. After what seemed like a long time, he slowly turned and squinted at me as if he did not know who I was. My hand clenched the doorknob.

'Come here, Thomas,' he finally said in a low, hoarse voice.

I inched forward slowly. I could see his cheeks were wet.

'Are you sick, Dad?' I asked, barely above a whisper. 'Do you want me to get Mom?'

He shook his head, 'Come here,' he repeated and held his hand out to me.

As I approached him, I could smell the alcohol on his breath.

'I'll be okay,' he said. 'I just had a bad day at work. Some people who don't know how to do my job want to tell me how I should do it. Isn't that crazy?'

I nodded.

'What do you want to be when you grow up?' he asked.

'I want to fly airplanes,' I told him without hesitation.

'Oh my, a pilot,' he smiled, but his eyes were full of tears. 'That is good news for your mother and me. You'll be able to fly us all over and you probably won't even charge us for the tickets.'

'I'll give you free tickets.'

'Thomas.' He pulled me into him and hugged me. He hugged me so tight it frightened me — not because I thought he would strangle me, but because he seemed so afraid to let go. The foul smell of alcohol was strong. Mostly I think it came from him, but when he had let go of his bottle to hug me, the contents started to drain onto his leather sofa. It was the smoky, musty peat smell of Scotch whisky that reminded me of my dad in this mood, the smell of his darkened room, his kind of night. Still hugging me, he said, 'Whatever you want to be when you grow up is okay with me, but promise me whatever you do, you'll be very good at it. No matter what other people say.' Then he released me and held me at arm's length. 'Promise me that, Thomas.'

'I'll try,' I said, my voice cracking.

He stared at me in silence, then began to nod slowly.

'Well,' he said as he tousled my hair, 'that's all I'll ask then. Now go to bed.'

That is what the blackness was for my dad. I did not understand it then, but I began to on that endlessly dark night. A long time after he had died, maybe a full year, I went into that study which had remained unchanged and unused from when he was alive. In his lower left-hand desk drawer there was another bottle, about one-third full. It was Glenfiddich, I remember that. I sat behind his desk and opened the bottle, putting my nose to the neck and slowly pulling in that aroma. If I closed my eyes, it became easier to see my dad, but with that vision of him also came hints of that blackness. Sitting alone in the musty, smoky smell of that old study, the room was cloaked in shadows. The first time was frightening, but I went back and did it, again and again.

'I tried,' I whispered to myself. I had been a pilot, but never went beyond flight instructor — never went on to the airlines, or crop-dusting, or bush flying or anything else that might have made him proud. Never got my mom free tickets. Never did anything.

Coincidentally, in my office at the airport, in my desk, in the lower left-hand drawer is another bottle of Glenfiddich. It is there simply because a pilot friend picked it up in duty-free on his way through one day and gave it to me. It's only a pint bottle; the seal is unbroken. I never drank at work and I was not about to start now. I should take it home and drink it, but instead I leave it there. Someday, after a long, hard shift, when the work is done, while Amanda is entertaining a few execs in her office with a drink, I could pull it out and offer a drink to Simon or Ryan or Sarah or anyone else who had also put in a good hard day's work. I fully intended to do that some day. But somehow, for now, the bottle in my desk drawer still seemed a little illicit.

It was not the bottle of Glenfiddich, however, that I was reaching for in my bottom drawer. It was my mail. On my desk I had an in-basket and an out-basket along with a few other baskets, but this was mail I had pulled out of my letterbox as I left home that morning. The personal mail I usually put away in the bottom desk drawer until I had a chance to get to it for the simple reason that I was paranoid and afraid that, left in the open, Amanda might tuck her corporate letter opener in her belt, slip in here while I'm up in the tower and read what my mom has to say about Uncle Frank's impending hip-replacement surgery.

Today's was an especially good haul: some junk mail, a real estate brochure, another phone bill, the latest copy of *ComTalk* — the ControlCorp staff magazine — and two of particular interest, a padded envelope with no return address which I didn't need to open to see what it contained, and this letter, which I had been waiting for for so long I had almost forgotten. I turned it over in my hand and inspected the return address again: Federal Aviation Administration, Regional Office, Los Angeles, California.

USA.

My fingers trembled as I began to tear it open. I did not know what the answer would be. I was stopped abruptly with a gentle tap on the open door.

'Sarah,' I said, catching my breath just short of a gasp. Guilt washed over me as if she had just caught me jerking off. All I was doing was opening my mail — it wasn't even porn.

'Busy?'

'No,' I looked down at the letter in my hand. 'Just sorting through the junk mail.'

She glanced at the mail scattered across the desk. 'Oh, I see you got *ComTalk*.' An almost imperceptible smile tugged at the corners of her mouth. 'Anything interesting? I haven't seen my copy yet.'

'Oh yeah, Freddie Moore has just won Azerbaijan in a card game and ControlCorp has contracted to supply one controller named 'Tom' to Rangoon — I'm thinking about applying.' I dropped the letter on top of the junk mail, then scooped it back into the drawer. 'Just junk actually.'

She smiled, but had not moved from the door.

'Come on in. Close the door.' I got up and walked over to her. She closed the door behind her and leaned back against it gently as I leaned in closer.

'Tom,' she whispered. I was close enough to feel her breath on mine.

'Yes, Sarah?' I whispered back, then leaned into her and gently touched her lips to mine before she could speak another word. Her hands came up to my chest as if to push me away, but did not.

'We can't,' she said as I briefly released her lips. 'Not here, not at work.'

'I'm on a break and you're finished for the day.'

'We need to talk.'

'We need to act.' I pressed my mouth against hers again and my hand was running up her thigh on its long wonderful journey to her breast when we were both jolted by the muffled sound of someone about to come through the door. I jumped back and turned towards the window. As the door opened I pretended to be in the middle of a sentence. 'And from now on the billing system will take highest priority and we will no longer … Oh, Amanda,' I said as I turned back and did my Oscar-winning best to look surprised to see her standing in the door, shifting her gaze from me to Sarah and back again.

She was not an idiot. She had bumped the door into Sarah's back when she walked in. Sarah's hand was instinctively smoothing out her hair. I paused in my speech and became suddenly, overwhelmingly, self-conscious of my mouth, rubbing my lips on each as if I was trying to even out my Chapstick. Sarah did not wear layers of thick red lipstick so there was probably not a trace, and I would have been a lot cooler to stand there and stare back at her, but instead, my own hand reached instinctively across my mouth.

'Oh, Thomas ... ' Amanda was saying, but paused and shifted her look between the two of us suspiciously. Her eyes moved from Sarah and returned to me as if in her quick assessment she decided she had just walked in on a plot to assassinate her and I was the obvious ringleader. 'Thomas,' she finally said, 'stop in and see me before you leave today. We need to go over next week's schedule.'

'Yes, of course, I'll do that,' I stumbled to fill a verbal void. 'I'll be finished at about four and then —'

'Yes, Tom,' she cut my babbling off with a wave of her hand, 'just before you leave.' She turned and headed back down the corridor.

'Shit.'

When Amanda left I pushed the door shut, locked it and took a step toward Sarah, but she raised her hand and stopped me.

'We need to talk.'

'Right.' The phrase 'we need to talk' has never preceded good news. Besides, talking is overrated, and I would know. I've been in a few talk-heavy relationships. Talking is like a drug. At first they find a good conversationalist is stimulating, even fun. Then they want it in heavier doses and it gets to be dangerous fun. By the time we get to 'we need to talk', what they're really saying is 'I *need* to talk — and you, my supplier, have dried up, so you're out and some guy named Ramón is in. Ramón, I tell you, is such a good listener. What a sensitive guy and he knows shiatsu.' I walked back to the chair behind my desk, dropped into it and quietly waited for her to begin talking. 'I thought we were going to talk at home tonight, you know,' I raised my eyebrows and waggled my head. 'Between fooling around? We can talk about anything you like, I promise, even redoing the kitchen if you like.'

'Tom,' she said as she sat down across from me and leaned forward. 'I'm resigning.'

'You're quitting? Why?'

She shook her head. 'I just think I've been here long enough. I want to get back to my studies and finish my degree.'

I shrugged. 'We can work your schedule around your classes. I mean, if that's all it is, it shouldn't be a —'

'That's not all it is.'

I stopped and stared at her.

'I'm not going to be there when you get home tonight. My mother needs me and I'm going to stay with my parents for a while.'

'So you're not quitting your job, you're quitting me?'

'I'm sorry to have to say it so bluntly and here at work. I wanted to wait until I could break it to you gently, but ...' she was starting to tear up. 'I just can't put it off any longer. I'm just going to stay with my parents until I can figure this out.'

'This is crazy.' I turned towards the window and stared up at the tower. 'For starters, it's your apartment. Don't you remember, I moved in with you?' We had a lovely little two-bedroom flat in St Mary's Bay with a deck and a view of the marina. 'What's to figure out? We have fun together, we have great sex, we have so many things in common.'

I turned back to her.

'Do you love me?' she asked. 'I mean, beyond the sex and the fun things we do together? Do you love me beyond that?'

'Do I ...? What do you mean? Aren't my feelings to you obvious enough to you?'

'I want to hear them, Tom. Do you love me? Or are you just in lust?'

'Oh don't be ridiculous! For Christ's sake, we've been living together for four months, haven't we? Of course I feel that way about you. You're everything I've ever needed or wanted.'

'Yet I need something more.' She stood up. 'I'll give you four weeks' notice for the job. As for the apartment — don't worry. I need to stay with my parents for a while anyway. Just take as much time as you need.' Then she turned and left.

'Sarah!' But she was gone.

From the first day I saw her, I felt that pull towards her, like a magnet. I just couldn't help myself. I tried to keep my distance, for professional reasons, for my own safety or hers, but I couldn't help but feel that intrigue. It wasn't until Simon Henare showed up in Auckland Tower for his training, cocky young smart-arse cad as he was. He noticed my attention towards her and wasn't afraid to rib me about it from the very start when most trainees would have shown a certain amount of respect towards their supervisors.

So I made a move before he could. I asked her if she wanted to meet a couple of us for a drink after work one day and she said, 'Sure' and then I failed to mention the invite to anyone else. It even seemed devious to me, but I pretended to wonder where the others were. She wasn't much of a drinker — an occasional glass of wine and, if I recall correctly, that day she only had a Diet Coke.

She was laughing at something I had said and I was mesmerised by the curve of her collarbone. For some reason I was thinking of a luge track, a smooth, graceful arc, so delicate yet so strong, so flawless. At the time, I was not consciously thinking of having sex with her. I was just thinking she had a quality I had not seen before. It was not anything I had interpreted as perfection; it was more like completeness. She was just different. It was her lack of cynicism that made her seem out of place.

What I did not know that first time we went out socially was that, as I followed that collarbone along the curve of her neck, I had already launched myself down that track.

She liked literature and music — so we could talk about something other than airplanes. She just seemed to be interested in everything, from my dad the literature professor to the many social causes I was pulled into by my ex-wife, though I may have given her the impression I was slightly more of a leader in that area than I really was. I'm not sure what she found interesting in me and was content not to ask, or maybe I was afraid to ask. Even then, I was not thinking of sex — or did not think I was thinking of sex. I didn't even realise at the time how fast my toboggan was moving.

At Simon's birthday party a few weeks later, I was pretty loose after a few drinks and we were in a quiet corner having an intense discussion — she loved to prod me on American literature, and she was proposing the argument that *Huckleberry Finn* was a homoerotic fantasy.

'Feminist claptrap,' I protested, knowing a little something myself about what buttons I could push with her too. 'Can't it be simpler than that? Maybe it just harks back to the simplest time in a person's life: that moment before puberty when the kid has the maximum freedom without being terrorised by hormones, that moment before sex and relationships screw us up. Can't it be a simple juxtaposition of the brutal realities of slave life as seen through the perspective of youthful ignorance?'

I'm not sure why I felt such a strong urge to sound like I had any idea of what I was talking about, or even to debate an issue she possibly knew more about than me. All I know was that the passion I felt was invigorating, and no matter how hard I tried to keep my mind on her argument, I kept being pulled back to the collarbone and the smooth skin of her neck.

'But don't you agree that the relationship between Huck and Jim is covertly homosexual?' she countered. She let out a quiet, kind of sultry laugh and moved closer to be heard over the loud music filtering in from the lounge.

'Ridiculous. Can it be that the orphan just longs for a father figure before society forces him prematurely into the role of man himself? Maybe he just wants someone to go fishing with one more time before the world changes forever. Maybe ...' I paused, or maybe I kept talking and my words just faded away to my ears. At that moment, without any conscious plan, I reached up and stroked her collarbone, caressed her neck. At that moment, I started thinking of Sarah and sex in the same frame.

Instead of pulling away, she leaned forward to meet my lips. Her hand reached around and gently touched the small of my back. It was the beginning of a long passionate night that never once considered the consequences. She cared about me and that's all I cared about, and the more she cared, the more I would come to her needing her as if this time she was the drug and me the addict.

After that night we spent so much time together, it seemed to be the natural step for me to abandon my shabby little flat in Panmure and move in with her, where, until a moment before, I had thought we had a pretty good life together, enjoying the simple things — movies, dinners, concerts, mountain biking. Our tastes in videos differed widely, but that just made it more fun. It gave us something safe to debate. Her parents lived in Howick, and they seemed to like me because I could make them laugh. It all seemed so right, so complete then.

As for work, by the time we took up residence together, our relationship was well known around the facility. Even Amanda with her imaginary Book of Conduct would have known about it. Regardless of whether she approved or not, there was nothing she could do and, to her credit, she never tried.

Did I love her? Yes, I loved her. It was just something I found hard to say out loud. I had been in love before, and I was wrong. I didn't want to be wrong again.

'I'm sorry, Sarah,' I said, though she had long gone. I felt like a guy opening the divorce papers for the first time — irreconcilable controller, you're out, the pilot's in because he's focused, he knows what he wants, he's mature and he knows shiatsu.

'Shit,' I said and looked around my office, wishing momentarily for something to break. But even if everything in this fucking office hadn't been made of unbreakable plastic or oak-veneered particle board, a smash attack would call more attention to myself than I needed right now. So I just sat in my chair, glancing around at the mounds of bullshit paperwork and documents that were supposedly making life so much more efficient, prosperous and successful than before. My eyes stopped on the opened bottom drawer, the bottle of whisky and the stack of mail.

I took the bottle of whisky out and set it in front of me. Then I pulled out the half-opened letter and set it down in front of me too. Was it what I thought it was? What I had been waiting for? Forgiveness for a past betrayal?

Then I took the padded envelope out — a past betrayal already forgiven. I ripped it open and took out Flynn's torch.

TWENTY

Freddie Moore's jet black BMW was doing almost 150 kph down the Desert Road. Woodcock gripped his armrest tightly and had both feet pushed as hard as he could against the floor mat.

'Slow the fuck down, Freddie,' he pleaded.

'Not a chance. We have a lot of ground to cover. Sir Dick doesn't like to be waiting and we have to be in Taupo in …' He glanced at his watch. 'Shit. Why did that guy in Palmerstonburg put up such a fight?'

'Watch the fucking road!' Carlton shrieked. 'If you want to know what time it is, just ask me. And it took so long because I wasn't expecting him to have been so meticulous with his own set of books, that's why. It was a hard argument to make. And it's Palmerston North! Now slow down.'

'So what is south of Palmerston North?'

'What?' Carlton turned to Freddie and kept his glance shifting between him and the winding road ahead. 'We just drove up from Wellington today. That's the only city of any note south of Palmerston North. There are some other smaller towns — Levin, Otaki. What's your point?'

'My point is: where is Palmerston South? You're always telling me about this Palmerston North place, but I've yet to drive through Palmerston South before I get to the north part of town.'

'What the fuck are you going on about, Freddie? There is no north part of town, and there is no Palmerston South. And what does this have anything to do with anything at the moment? We finally managed to get the chief in Palmie to agree to go without a fight. We only have 140 km to go before Taupo — we'll be there in plenty of time if you just slow down. They do have plenty of cops on these roads, you know, and 50 kph over the speed limit would be a fairly pricey fine.'

'A business expense.' Freddie waved casually.

'Like offering the chief of Palmie a $30,000 bonus on top of his redundancy if he'd go quietly? What was all that all about?'

'Just thinking ahead, Carlton. Always think several projects in advance. Haven't I always told you that? It's the number one rule in The Book of Business. St Miltonville Estates is soon to be a done deal. And a done deal is a no-fun deal. Got to keep thinking ahead.'

'I thought rule Number One was —'

'Rule Number One is not to be overly concerned with the rules, Carlton. Rules are made for those that need to be ruled.' Freddie thought about that one for a moment. 'I like that one, I think I'll write that one down.'

'You can't possibly be thinking of carving up Palmerston North.'

'Of course not; it's an important airport. A lot of training goes on down there — lots and lots of training.'

'Freddie,' Carlton was starting to pout. It was not a good look on him — what with the mousy nose and big glasses and big square forehead.

The poor kid must have hit a rock when he dived into the gene pool, Freddie thought.

'Tell me what you're planning, Freddie,' Carlton said in the most threatening tone Freddie had ever heard come out of his mouth. 'You tell me right now or I swear to fuck, you find yourself another accomplice. I am, after all, supposed to be kept informed on all your upcoming commercial projects, so I can do a financial risk and viability assessment.'

Freddie considered the threat for a moment. He didn't like the idea of Carlton growing some balls and starting to stand his ground, but he also learned to be a little afraid of him when he got that look he seemed to be getting now. He really was one of the best book-cookers in the business, and he would hate to have to break someone new in at this late stage in the game. Still, after the St Miltonville deal went through, it might pay to keep his eye open for a new right-hand man. That chap Hardy might be worth checking for potential. From what he's heard from Amanda, his balls were shrinking daily. He was also smart, if not a bit too much of a smart-arse, but he seemed to remember the guy had a bit of a record or something. And he liked the way he could get Amanda riled up.

Mental note to self — do a thorough background check on Hardy. Find his weakness, find his record.

Freddie looked over at Carlton and smiled. 'I'll tell you my idea if you tell me where Palmerston South is.'

'I'll tell you where Palmerston South is,' Carlton said, his eyes glued on Freddie, 'if you slow the fuck down!'

Damn. He was growing balls. This was not good. Not good at all.

Freddie eased up on the accelerator and let the speed drop to 110.

'Are you happy, Carlton? We'll just take a nice slow, meandering drive up to Taupo tonight and enjoy the sunset drenched scenery of this barren land. Is that Mt Fujiyama over there?'

'It's called Ruapehu.'

'It's pretty. It looks Japanesey. I like Japanese food, except it's not really very filling.'

'It's an active volcano.' Carlton said, returning his eyes to the road ahead. 'So what is this next scheme of yours?'

'Where's Palmerston South?'

Carlton let out a long, disgusted sigh and stared out the window. 'In the South Island, just north of Dunedin, there's a town called Palmerston. That's where Palmerston is. The town we left an hour ago with one more unemployed person is in the North Island and is called Palmerston North.' He turned to Freddie. 'Got it?'

'So why don't they call the one in the South Island —'

'Freddie!' Carlton almost shouted in exasperation. 'What is the Palmie plan?'

Freddie looked across and stared at Carlton for a good long moment.

No, not good at all.

'Well,' Freddie started slowly. 'I'm just thinking out loud here — just throwing some ideas out for new business opportunities and such, you understand?'

'Of course, nothing on the record.'

'Well, I met the most delightful chap the other day at the club, and we started talking over a drink. He really was a most interesting fellow. An academic, I believe.'

'You belong to a club?'

'Yeah, the Mustang Club.'

'The Mustang Club is a whorehouse, Freddie.'

'Such a vulgar term, Carlton. Really, you should join and they'll show you how to relax. They're very good. You might meet a nice girl down there, too.'

But we don't want it to happen before we can hook you up with Amanda, Freddie thought. A chill ran down Freddie's spine at the very thought of those two assuming the position.

'The plan? The one that just cost us thirty grand?'

'Oh, I wouldn't call it a plan — just tossing some ideas around under the influence of fine wine and beautiful women. But this chap has a flying school down there, and he had me convinced the next big market for flying training is China.'

'So you want to have him train Chinese pilots down here?'

'Oh no, they can train themselves. What I'm thinking here — just a little thinking outside the box — why not sell the whole place, lock, stock and tower, to the Chinese?'

'Jesus fucking Christ, Freddie,' Carlton squeezed his eyes shut like he was trying unsuccessfully to have a bowel movement. 'You can't sell off all our domestic aerodromes.'

'Like I said, just thinking outside the box, Carlton. Anyway, this chap was much more open to the plan, so I thought, for the time being, he could be the interim manager down there.'

'I can think of no way you'd get away with that one,' he gulped hard and looked like he might throw up. He reached for the glove box. 'No one on earth could, Freddie. Now where is my Mylanta.'

'Oh look, Carlton, here comes the windy bit. I love this stretch of road.' He punched the accelerator.

Twenty-one

'So, Sarah dumped you the day before the incident. That had to be hard. And a big meeting coming up the next day. I can see you were under a lot of stress. But what were you doing with Flynn's torch?'

I stared at him and didn't know what to say. I had to think about this for a moment. Was I going to betray Flynn now? But they had already known, at least Tucker knew, which probably meant Freddie and Woodcock knew, too. I had meant to talk about the bottle of whisky and my dad, or the half-opened letter and Janey, but I told him about the torch. I stood up and walked over to the window. It was pitch black outside and raining. All I could see was the reflection of the room and him looking at me.

'It was sent to light my way.'

I had driven out to Howick, completely sober, and went to her parents' home.

'Please, Mr Gregory,' I had pleaded with her father to let me in to talk to her, but he was obviously under strict instructions to keep me out. He liked me, he was a kind man, but he was trying to protect his daughter too.

'Give her time, son,' he said. 'Just go home and get some sleep. She just needs time. Her mother and I have been through hard times before too and, trust me, sometimes you just got to give them some time —'

'Mr Gregory, please don't take this to mean any disrespect, but I'm not in the mood for any relationship lectures, I just want to talk to Sarah for five minutes.'

'Well, mate, I can't help you then. I'm under strict orders to not let you in and I'm the one who has to live here. So just —'

'It's okay, Dad.' I heard Sarah's voice from the dark of the hall behind him.

'You want me to let him in now?' Her dad turned to her, sounding more than a little perturbed. 'Because I wish you'd make up your mind. For this I'm missing the footie.'

'I'll come out. Mum's asleep.'

'I thought you might need a friend,' my dad had said when he gave me the puppy for my twelfth birthday, then he switched to his funny voice and added, '*Your wily snares an' fechtin fierce.*'

I lifted the puppy from the box up to my face. 'Wiley,' I said and the puppy approved by slurping his smelly little tongue across my nose.

'Wiley?' My dad asked in mock dismay. 'Well, I was hoping for something a bit more classical like Wordsworth for instance. Or perhaps abstract whimsy like Phaedo, but if you must take it on down to the working class, then I should say, "Mr Hardy meet your Mr Laurel."'

'Can we take him fishing with us, Dad?' I asked. I had been trying to convince my dad to take me fishing again and now summer was over, school had started, and the weather was showing the blustery signs of autumn. But there was still the weekend.

'Of course, son.'

'When?' I knew if I didn't pin the old man down on these promises, they would soon be forgotten.

'Oh, you're a cunning negotiator, my boy. Let me see,' he rubbed his chin in serious thought. 'Can't do it this weekend, but how about next weekend? On Sunday?'

'Yeah!'

'Now, Edward,' my mother interrupted, 'I don't want the boy missing church.'

'Well, I can't do it Saturday, I'm meeting with the dean that morning for breakfast.' He looked like he was about to brush it off for another week or two, but then turned back to my mom. 'Now, Marion, I'm sure the Lord won't mind if we spend one day worshipping Him in his greatest temple — nature.'

Mom thought about this carefully.

'Please, Mom,' I pleaded. 'I want to take Wiley fishing.'

'Well, okay,' she said reluctantly. 'Just this once, and we don't want you making a habit out of this.' She walked back into the kitchen shaking her head as if she was worried about my soul.

My dad winked. 'Small victories will win the war, son,' he whispered. I smiled. I had no idea what he meant, but was smiling because it made me happy to see him in high spirits and joking. It had been a good birthday. Wiley was the only gift I remembered. My mom made my favourite dinner — hamburgers — and a chocolate birthday cake. My dad had even put a tiny piece of birthday cake on a plate for Wiley. Before I went to bed that night, I studied a bit of the Robert Burns poem that I was going to recite for my dad when we went fishing. It was not easy to learn because the words all sounded made up, but I decided if I could learn just one line a day, by the time we went fishing, I would know a whole verse, maybe even two, which would please my dad.

As the week progressed, the days got cloudier and my dad got quieter. I was reprimanded more than once that week by my teacher for letting my mind wander, but I was unrepentant; I had a dog to get home to and a fishing trip to think about. And this time, I would use real worms on the hooks.

But we never went fishing again. On Saturday morning it had rained. My dad had been most of the morning with the dean and, when he returned, he went straight to his den and shut the door without saying anything. He was not feeling well.

Later in the afternoon, my mother called me into the house. She was going out to the store to pick up a few groceries and wanted me to play in the house until she got back because it looked like it might start raining again. She reminded me not to bother my father until he came out of his den.

'He's not feeling well,' she said. Her face was pale.

So I went to my room and worked on the Robert Burns poem, while my mother went to the supermarket. After a little while, Mr Burns' funny language was making me dizzy so I took a break and tried teaching Wiley again how to fetch a ball. The tennis ball had been too big for the puppy to get his mouth around, so we switched to the smaller red rubber ball Mom had brought back from the store a few days earlier. But every time I tossed it across the room, Wiley would go grab it and then didn't want to give it back. We'd end up playing tug of war with it until I would finally get it back and was able to toss it again. I was starting to think it would be impossible to teach this dog to fetch a ball and drop it at my feet.

I heard a thud downstairs — as if someone had bumped their head. I figured my dad had dropped a book on the floor or something. Wiley pricked up his ears, dropped the ball from his mouth and let out a short whimper.

I don't know why I cared if my dad had dropped a book, but something didn't feel right. So I thought I would go to investigate.

'Dad?' I called quietly at the door to his office.

There was no response, no sound, no movement. It was, by nature, a quiet house — but this was different. This was being alone. I could feel the aloneness.

'Dad!' I called again, but still no response.

I pushed the door to the study open just a couple inches. 'Can I come in, Dad?' I whispered through the opening. I peeked around the door. It was dark in my dad's study, the light was off and only a dim grey glow seeped in through the shades. The room had a bitter, musty smell.

'Dad, I'm learning some Mr Burns for you. Do you want to hear it?'

At the desk, I could see the dark figure of my dad with his head down on his blotter.

'Dad? Do you want to hear it?' I stepped inside and walked towards my dad. I thought maybe he was having a nap. I reached up to nudge him awake and put my hand in a puddle of tea that had spilled on the blotter. It was warm. It was still warm.

My dad had died at his desk. A heart attack. I knew it then, I guess, when I touched him and he wouldn't move. Maybe he was just napping, but I think I must've known he was dead then because all I could think of to do at the time was recite him some poetry. As if that was going to wake him.

'*Great is thy pow'r and great thy fame*,' my voice trembled as I whispered the words slowly, *'Far ken'd an' noted is thy name; An' tho' yon lowin' heuch's thy hame, Thou travels far; An' faith! thou's neither lag nor lame, Nor blate, nor scaur*. Dad?'

'That,' I said to Sarah. 'Is something I've never told anyone. It was a secret that I wanted you to know. I don't know why I felt anyone else needed to know that. But I want you to know. I can't exactly explain. It's just hard for me sometimes to express certain things. I grew up in a lonely, empty house.'

'You found your dad dead?'

'Yeah, just like I found Thornie.'

'I'm sorry. That must've been really hard for a kid.'

'Yeah, it was.'

She reached for me and pulled me close.

'I'm sorry,' she whispered, her face was buried in my shoulder. 'But, Tom.'

'I know,' I said as I pulled away from her. 'It may not be enough, but I just wanted to tell you anyway, because you were right about me.' Then I turned and walked back to my car. I knew I had a long day the next day, but I was going to find a liquor store on my way home.

'So your dad and Thornie Rumbold died in very similar ways?'

'Yeah, I guess so.'

'And you found them both?'

'Yeah, I guess so.'

'I don't understand the tea though? How could it still have been warm? I mean, tea would cool within minutes, even seconds if it had puddled.'

'Maybe it just felt that way to me.'

'Of course, that must be it. But it's funny though.'

'I'm glad you're amused.'

'No, I don't mean it that way. I just think it was odd that your dad was drinking tea in his office. Didn't you say he was, like you, a confirmed coffee drinker? And he liked his Scotch.'

'Yeah, I guess I might've said that. So what? Maybe he was trying something new.'

'Or maybe it wasn't tea you remember — maybe it was coffee. Trauma can play tricks on your mind.'

'Yes, of course. It probably was in fact.' I turned back to him and looked at my watch. 'It's getting late. You must have enough for your assessment by now.'

'Why don't you stay just a bit longer?' He shrugged. 'After all, I have an expensive ex-wife to pay for, too.'

Twenty-two

I was reconsidering my position on the backward shift rotation the next morning, lying in bed, staring at the ceiling and careful not to move too suddenly lest I upset my delicate condition. We were all generally opposed to the idea of starting our work cycle on an early shift and ending on the late. Traditionally, it was the other way round, which offered a longer break between cycles. At the moment, however, I was thanking the god of all things corporate for not having to drag my damaged body out of bed at 5.30 in the morning to get to the early morning shift. Perhaps the Corporation was onto something after all when they hired a whole team of consultants to decide they could save the cost of seven-tenths of one controller by switching the rotation of shifts around. This new set-up allowed me to drink more during my shift cycle instead of waiting for the end of it.

Allowed? No, that doesn't sound right — that sounds dependent or too master–slavish. I had promised someone, I believe it was the facilitator at our Team Building for Team Players seminar, that I would choose my words carefully to focus on positive attributes. The new roster 'enabled' me to drink more. It 'proactively empowered' me to explore new directions in my body chemistry.

Shit. I could do this; I could be a corporate guy. Just give me one more chance. I promise I'll make good this time.

As I lay on my back I noticed my bedroom had a slow turn to it. That was never a good sign. I carefully tilted my head just enough to see the large green numerals of my clock radio: 8.47. That was late for me, but had we been on the old roster rotation, I would have been two and a half hours late already. Bless those corporate boys. Maybe they were right about all these cost-cutting measures. Maybe this is a better world. I'll have to ask someone to send me a postcard someday and let me know how their New World Order worked out in the end. Was it better, worse, or just different?

The fact that I had slept through from whatever time I had decided to stop drinking last night to the relatively late hour of 8.47 in the morning without waking up was not entirely by chance. I used the last swig of Scotch to wash down a couple of sleeping pills, knowing how shitty this alcohol stupor would make me feel compounded with the lack of sleep that too much alcohol usually caused.

Today was going to be a hell of a long day. My shift normally started at 2.00 p.m., but there was that damn management meeting I had to attend today at eleven o'clock. Two hours of that bullshit, then a full shift. And I would have to talk with Sarah again tonight. Had I stayed in her arms and squeezed her just a little bit harder last night, I know exactly what she would have done. She would have forgiven me, because she was a kind and forgiving person, and things would go on for a while longer. Instead, I left. Not because I wanted to, but because she had been right. I needed her because I had an emptiness that needed filling. She didn't need me. It was the hardest thing I ever had to do in my life, but I turned and walked away.

At the end of our marriage, Janey had complained about the same thing. Here I thought I was proving to be supportive of her, trying to be something she wanted me to be. But in the end, all she wanted me to be was to be a whole person on my own without needing anyone else to tell me what to do, what to believe, what is right.

Synergistic. That's what Amanda thought we could be, but she was wrong. For synergism, as far as I knew from being a mere Liberal Arts major, it took two wholes that would make the union stronger. Didn't work with only one and a half wholes.

I thought Sarah made me feel whole because she was whole, and by association, I felt whole. But she was right, there were pieces of me I had lost and wouldn't have a clue where to look for them.

Did it feel this bad when I left Janey? Or did she leave me? I think we both just started walking in opposite directions. There were good times with her, too, in the beginning. Ol' Janey and I hit it off from the very beginning. I met her at a party.

'Oooh, a G-man,' she said when I told her what I did for a living.

I had only been a controller for six months. I was still in training, but I was getting a lot of mileage out of the job title.

'And you can still sleep at night?' she asked.

'No, not really. I'm an insomniac.'

'Maybe it's your conscience keeping you awake. After all, your boss is an environmental rapist.'

'Who? Big Ted — he seems all right — but I don't think he's much of an outdoorsman. I mean, the guy must weigh 300 pounds.' I was serious. I honestly and quite stupidly thought she had something against Ted Kazniak, the tower manager.

'I'm talking about the President,' she corrected me. 'You work for the government — he's your boss.'

'Oh, yeah, him — right. Yeah, he's a real prick. Won't even say "Hi" to me when I see him at the water cooler.' That made her laugh, which was a great relief to me.

'Well, next time you talk to him, why don't you ask him what he's done to the EPA?'

I had no idea what she was talking about, but was quite turned on by her militant spirit. Our first date was to a Greenpeace protest of a nuclear power plant. We ended up in jail. How many people can say that about their first date?

I gently rolled my eyes over to the clock: 8.54. Shit, I wish I had taken a couple of ibuprofens with those sleeping pills last night.

It wasn't really jail. The police came around and herded us into a van, emptied us into a high school gymnasium, where they separated the boys from the girls and let us cool our heels for a few hours. When they 'processed' us, they were really only looking for the hardcore troublemakers. Guys like me they just threatened with the prospect of having a criminal record, then turned us loose again. Actually, with me they didn't even do that. When I told them I was an air traffic controller — a fellow G-man — and that I got roped into this whole event by my infatuation with a radical, we all had a good laugh and they looked her name up and told me that she was spending the night. They told me to come get her in the morning.

'And, hey buddy, good luck.' Laugh. Wink.

I was there in body only because I wanted into her body. I knew I should have cared more, but I never even opened my mouth to join in the chant. When the police came and started pushing and shoving, Janey said, 'Go limp!' and I just quipped, 'I bet you tell all the guys that.'

Ha ha. I didn't go limp. The cop said, 'This way,' and I said, 'Thank you, officer.'

When they let me out, I figured it was too far away to drive home and come back the next day for her, so I checked into a motel, ate dinner at McDonald's and went to a movie, by myself. It was an Arnold Schwarzenegger film. I don't remember which one, but he saved the world.

The next morning, I collected Janey from the gymnasium-jail.

'I just got out myself,' I lied. 'But it wasn't so bad, Jackson Browne sang us a couple songs and I actually had a pretty good night's sleep.'

Janey laughed, but said nothing. I must have scored some points, however, because we started seeing a lot of each other. It was exciting — always having that threat of a criminal record hanging over my head. At the time, I also felt like, for once in my life, I was making a stand — doing something to make a difference. Of course, I wasn't doing anything. I was just standing close to someone making a stand.

As I rolled over slowly and focused on the clock: 9.02, and very slowly eased myself into a sitting position, I realised now there was a difference. I was just getting a thrill sharing part of someone else's spirit.

I proposed to Janey at a rally for the National Organization for Women. In retrospect, it seems quite ironic and in fact uncharacteristically brave on my part, judging from the scowls I got from a lesbian couple who overheard my proposal and promptly urged Janey to reject my offer to enslave her.

Some wannabe politico was waffling on about something or other on stage. I was bored out of my skull and, without even thinking about it, turned to her and said, 'Hey, why don't we get married?'

Janey was momentarily at a loss for words, which gave the lesbians a chance to put their suggestion forward about having me castrated. Janey smiled at them, which turned into a smirk as she looked back to me and said, I think for their benefit, 'No, I won't marry you. But how about if you marry me?'

'I don't know.' I shrugged. 'Let me think about it. Do you make much money?'

Anyway, we got married a couple of months later, and I never told her that I never did any jail time — that, instead, I did time in a reasonably priced, clean and comfortable motel, and paid my dues by having to sit through a hundred bad quips from Arnold Schwarzenegger. That was just the first of many lies I lived with Janey.

Shit. 9.08, and I finally made it to the bathroom and stood under a hot shower. It offered only minor relief from the pain.

So why do I miss Janey so much? She was a good person. Militant, yes — but it was because she believed so strongly in acting against social injustice and not being one of these pretentious, BMW-driving yuppie twats who sit around and talk, talk, talk, but do nothing until tax time, when they send a $50 cheque to World Vision. No, Janey wasn't like that. She was all heart and soul, and she lived truthfully to both. And she followed through with action. She gave something more valuable than money — she gave her time. Hell, she gave something even more valuable than her time — she gave my time. But I let her. I let her spend my money, too. I let her tell me what to believe and how to show it, so I could feel like I was living truthfully.

For the nearly four years that we were married, I grew more and more jealous of her causes. They got her attention, they were important, and I was jealous. I was angry, and it got in the way. Our marriage was running its course in record time. Suddenly we were 'over' but not before I did something really stupid in an ill-thought attempt to impress her.

We had a fight that lasted well into the night. She had finally decided that my support of her causes was disingenuous and I admitted it was — but not because I did not believe the causes were for the good. Hell, I was all for protecting the environment and civil rights and putting more into the education system and righting social wrongs. After all, I was a liberal. However, I just could not handle the guilt associated with that any more.

What I truly loved, in my heart — I mean, besides my wife of course — what I loved most was airplanes. I loved flying them and I loved my job controlling them.

The fact was, I didn't want to spend all my weekends chained to trees. I wanted to buy an old Citabria and fix it up and fly it. And I was sorry if the CEO of Domino's Pizza publicly supported the pro-life campaign. I didn't give him money for his political beliefs. I just wanted a pizza. And I liked war movies. I've probably seen hundreds of movies with men killing men in them, and they never made me feel like it was okay to kill other people. Except for the occasional porn, movies never made me feel as guilty as my wife did, going on about catering to the Hollywood machine that was corrupting our minds. One can only take so many three-hour Czech films about a woman's internal struggle for freedom, told in silent, poetic, black and white imagery and almost always ending up in suicide — either the main character's or mine.

Then there was the Air Force One incident. I was an air traffic controller, and it was a pretty big deal for me to be chosen by my boss to be the one to handle that aircraft when it was due to land at our airport the next day.

I didn't care about the dumbfuck passenger on the plane —

this was just about an airplane and my career. There was nothing I could do to change the political climate at the time. It was just the *plane*.

But, boy, did it get her started.

The President was apparently coming out to speak to some audience about opening up more national park lands for logging and oil exploration. We were in total agreement on the issue politically, but we were in a screaming fight over the matter. It was insane. If the neighbours were listening in that night, they probably thought I had just confessed to owning a sweatshop in Indonesia or being a Republican.

I slept on the sofa that night. No, I take that back. She slept on the sofa that night — we were a totally liberated household.

'It's your total lack of commitment,' she accused.

'I'm committed to the safe, orderly, expeditious flow of traffic,' I said.

'And how often do you stick your neck out for it?' She took her pillow and a blanket and headed towards the sofa.

Janey was right in a way. I was controlled by a certain amount of fear. I did not know if I really wanted to stay married to her, but I was more afraid of being divorced. So on my drive to work early the next morning, I hatched the plan that I thought would impress her. I would put something on the line. I would stick my neck out.

There was a procedure we follow strictly whenever Air Force One was scheduled to arrive. All traffic at the airport stopped fifteen minutes before and fifteen minutes after the President's plane. That was a lot of empty space surrounding that airplane. Before arrival and again before departure the runway and taxiways were 'swept' by an army of security personnel and then kept sterile — that is, no one uses it until the President has finished using it.

Security was tight, with secret service and CIA swarming the airport, including inside the tower. Facility management is expected to put reliable, seasoned professionals on the control positions. When Ted Kazniak told me I was going to be on the tower position, talking to Air Force One after it was established on final approach, I should have taken it as a compliment — that he trusted me enough to not embarrass him, the facility or the profession.

When Air Force One checked in just inside the ten-mile final, and since there was not another aircraft in the sky, the correct procedure was to issue a landing clearance. The book said something like: 'A controller shall not unduly withhold a clearance.'

Not me, though. Instead, I said: 'Air Force One, unable to issue landing clearance at this time.'

There was a flurry of confused movement around me. At first, it was probably assumed I did not know the correct procedure.

'Just give him the wind and altimeter and clear him to land,' Ted said, as if I was just forgetting that part. He was listening in from the coordinator's position.

There was a short pause from the pilot. Obviously he had to consider something he had never heard before. 'Tower?' the pilot said, 'are we cleared to land?'

'No, sir,' I said in as commanding a voice as I could come up with. 'You are not cleared to land at this airport. You can overfly the airport and just keep on going because that warmongering environmental rapist is not welcome in our city.'

That little flurry of activity instantly turned into a whirlwind of which I was the centre. A secret service agent made his move at me from my left, but it was the one on my right that caught me by surprise. And I was surprised by the speed at which Ted could move, given he was such a big guy and on the verge of a heart attack. In one fluid motion, he yanked my headset plug out and plugged in an external microphone, leaned forward towards the mike; his face had gone a deep red and he looked like he was in the middle of aforementioned coronary. Yet, as soon as he keyed the mike his voice was utterly calm. It was magical how soothing his voice sounded in contradiction to his current emotional state. It was Zen.

'Air Force One,' he said in his gentle, dulcet tone. 'Disregard the previous transmission. You are cleared to land runway three-zero left, surface wind now two-seven-zero at one-two knots, altimeter two-niner-eight-seven.'

But Air Force One was already on the go, making a steep climbing turn away from the airport until the terrorist controller could be neutralised. It looked like I might get that criminal record after all.

It was at that moment, while two secret service agents pushed me to the floor and tied my hands behind me with a plastic band, and I was watching Ted do his job despite everything else, that I understood what professionalism was. I instantly respected him and instantly became aware of how I had just betrayed this man who should be idolised, not mocked.

A secret service agent escorted me down to Ted's office first, where some conferring was done out of my earshot. Then I was taken on to airport security the back way.

Somehow it reminded me of my first date with Janey — I don't know why, but it was like coming full circle. They put me in a room with a mirror on one side — presumably someone was on the other side of it observing me — and a table and some chairs. After almost an hour, someone came in and cut the plastic bands from my wrists, which was a huge relief as I tried to rub the circulation back into my hands.

I continued to sit there in silence for another half hour or so before a man in a suit and tie came in and asked me lots of questions: name, date of birth, address, simple stuff like that. After he left another man in a suit and tie came in and questioned me on my terrorist associations. I said I was a member of the Sierra Club, but that was only a birthday gift from my wife — I never went to any meetings or anything and was not much of a joiner myself. But if they wanted, they could talk to my wife and see what other organisations we belonged to. Lots of tree hugging, but not much more than that.

Jesus, my wrists hurt.

It was a full three hours — technically my shift had ended a half hour earlier — before I heard more men conferring outside the door and, at last, the door opened and Ted Kazniak walked in. Despite how embarrassed I felt at how I betrayed him, I was sure glad to see him. And I fully expected now that all the questions were over, they were giving him a half hour to beat the living shit out of me. I had already decided that I would not fight back, that, finally, I would just go limp and accept it. When he came in, he took a seat opposite me and remained silent for what seemed like an eternity.

'Why?' he finally asked, barely above a whisper. 'Why did you do that, Tom?'

My plan was simple enough. Knowing that the newspaper would be listening in as well, I figured they would report it that some brave controller tried to refuse the President's plane landing clearance. I figured there would be some confusion and some dismay, but ultimately — say when Air Force One was on about a three-mile final — he would get his landing clearance and that would draw attention to the President's poor record on his environmental policies when he addressed his audience that night. I knew I would get in trouble, but frankly, I sorely underestimated this overreaction on everyone's part.

I didn't realise they were going to have to revector Air Force One around until the 'terror threat' had been secured on the ground. Nor did I expect them to keep me locked up until the President had safely landed and was quickly hustled off the airport.

I knew I'd get in trouble, but figured it would blow over. Janey would be impressed that I was willing to stick my neck out and look at me with the same adulation she did on our first date when I was, supposedly, willing to go to jail to make a statement. That was the plan at least.

I grossly miscalculated the outcome.

'I'm sorry, Ted,' I said quietly. I wanted to explain it all to him, but I couldn't. I just stared at the table and waited for him to take a swing at me.

To his credit — and considering what I had just done to him, his integrity, and probably his career — Ted did not hit me once. In fact, he was very gentle and kind, which made me hate myself all the more for doing it.

'I've talked to Janey,' he said. 'I know things are not good between you two. You should have told me how much stress you were under.'

'I didn't know.'

He glanced back at the door, then looked me in the face and continued staring until I was forced to look up and look back. Then I understood we were under very close surveillance — the mirrored wall behind him, probably microphones. I understood then that he wanted to save my life.

'I guess I got you in a lot of trouble,' I said.

He shrugged. 'I'll get chewed out, but I've been chewed out before. I'll survive. I'm just sorry I was so busy not to notice the obvious signs of stress in you.' He stared at me unblinking.

'Yes, I guess I should have told you I was under a lot of stress. I fell in love with a militant Democrat and now our marriage has fallen apart. I was too embarrassed to tell anyone at work about the stress. But you know, Ted, you understand, I love my job and would never do anything to harm anyone.'

'I know.'

'What's going to happen to me now?'

'Well, from what I understand, they want to keep this as small a news story as possible, so they'll have some shrink come and talk to you and confirm you've been under a lot of stress due to your impending divorce, and when the President is safely out of town, they'll probably let you go.'

'Can I come back to work tomorrow?'

'I'm sorry, Tom,' he looked down at the table and folded his hands in front of him. 'Part of this deal is that we're going to have to let you go. But if you quit in lieu of dismissal ...' he shrugged.

I nodded. 'I understand.'

By that weekend I was sitting in a folding chair in a T-shirt and boxer shorts in my now empty apartment, staring at the wall. Janey had taken pretty much everything, leaving me only the overdue rent. She moved in with her friend Natalie who would eventually introduce her to Ray the pilot — who by coincidence I knew from our flight instructing days.

There was a tap on the door.

'It's open!' I yelled.

Ted Kazniak came in. He had a six pack of beer with him. 'Just thought I'd see how you were.' He took a look around. 'Jeez, she really cleaned you out. You have another chair?'

I nodded to the one leaning up against the wall.

He unfolded it and I was surprised it supported his weight as he lowered himself into it. 'Did she leave you some trousers?'

I nodded.

'Good.' He handed me a beer. 'If you can find them, you can come stay with me and Carla until you get set up somewhere. We finally got the kid to go back to school, so you can have his room.'

We drank in silence for several minutes.

'Somewhere, where?' I finally asked.

He skulled the last of his beer, then opened two more, though mine was hardly half gone.

'Listen, Tom,' he said. 'Don't lose your confidence. You're still a good controller — you just did something really stupid. But it's not the end of the world. Controllers are in short supply all over the world. You still have your licence, the shrink pencil-whipped your records as completely sane, just a momentary lack of judgment due to stress and lack of sleep. You may have been in love with your wife, but take a look around you.' He spread his arms. 'She cleaned you out. So what the fuck, man, you're free. Go anywhere you want, the Middle East, Canada, Australia, wherever.'

'The end of the world?'

'Sure, if they need controllers.' He leaned forward and the chair strained under his weight. 'Find yourself a nice, quiet, sane little airport to work at for a year or so. Most of this has blown over already, but will be long forgotten in a few months. Give it a year. I'll work on it — I'll get you your job back. Just give me a year or so for it to go away completely.'

'You'd do that for me? After what I did to you?'

'Sure,' he said waving his hand like I had done nothing more than make a fat joke.

'Why?' I asked.

He leaned forward and said in a low, conspiratorial whisper, 'Because I hate that motherfucker, too.' And we both burst out laughing.

A week later I was sitting in the now spare bedroom at Ted and Carla's reading an advert in *Flight International* — air traffic controllers were wanted in New Zealand. That sounded far enough away. By sheer coincidence, it was also the day the Sierra Club voted me Man of the Year. I declined the honour.

Then a resurrection and a career was reborn, and I became a corporate citizen. Did I ask for this? No. But I accepted it as I have always done when choices were presented and I chose not to choose but let the impatience of time choose for me. Now there was another choice and a chance for me to put things straight. To go back to where I made a wrong turn and take the right one. There was a way out for me — the way back. I had to take it. That's why I had to let Sarah go without a fight. I had to go back home.

TWENTY-THREE

'It's the land of opportunity,' Freddie said as he gazed across the empty, grassy field that would be his shopping mall. 'That's what this place is. No, even more than that. It's the Promised Land.' He turned to Woodcock, seated next to him in the BMW. 'Don't you see it, Carlton? Can't you smell it?'

'I can smell something, Freddie,' Carlton said distractedly, as he looked over the documents in his lap. 'You know, if they were to do an audit on ControlCorp right now, somebody might get curious as to why the Corporation has invested so much money in M & G Properties.'

'Because it's a good investment — and it's part of my job to make sure we make good investments.' He turned his attention back to the subdivision rising from the ashes of Milton Gorge Aerodrome. 'And look what we're creating. It's beautiful. Look how they can just cut the top of that hill off; isn't modern technology amazing?'

Carlton looked up at the once rolling green hills that now looked like an open wound and the block of houses with terracotta-coloured roofs. 'There's a group of lefty environmentalists that don't share your sense of wonderment with the place.'

'Screw them. They don't have vision.'

'What I had in mind was something a little more conclusive.' Carlton smirked as if he just remembered the punch line to a fond old joke.

'Yes, well,' Freddie glanced over his shoulder. A chill ran down his spine at the thought of what was running through his creepy little friend's mind. 'You might want to keep that plan to yourself.'

He turned his attention back to the view of his new development. 'Before you know it, there'll be waves of terracotta lapping at the horizon, as far as the eye can see.' Freddie sighed and tried not to get misty-eyed. 'I see they finally got rid of that Aeroworks eyesore, and not an airplane in sight. It's so …' he paused.

Carlton looked at Freddie.

'So peaceful,' Freddie whispered. 'Peace on Earth — that's what our sign should say. Don't you think? 'St Miltonville — Peace on Earth.' What do you think, Carlton?'

'Catchy,' Carlton mumbled, then returned to his documents.

'You need to work on that sense of vision, my boy,' Freddie said. 'Or maybe not — that's what you have me for.'

'Yeah, and I'm the guy going to jail.' Carlton shook his head.

'Never. Just stick close to me, and you'll be okay.' Freddie turned the key and the engine purred to life.

'We need to stop by the M & G office, to pick up the papers for our meeting with our man Dick.'

'Of course. On our way.' Freddie pulled back onto the highway and punched the accelerator.

Another long car ride with this sour puss. Freddie did not know why he bothered.

He could have flown to Auckland, but he was having too much fun in his new car. Besides, this gave him a chance to stop in and see how his idea had become reality. He had this vision the first day he saw Milton Gorge. It was prime real estate cluttered by hangars and machines and noise. Through that, however, he had seen this — and this was beautiful. He got burnt on real estate once, so it was fitting that it would be real estate where he would redeem himself.

Fate must have been on his side, even if it did need a little nudging here and there. First Rumbold dies, then the tower is reduced to rubble. Hell, no wonder the operators were so nervous. Leak a little document suggesting the CAA was going to decommission the aerodrome entirely and open it up for developers and watch how they crumble. They were like rats off a sinking ship. Chumps. When Aeroworks finally bailed, that was the end. Milton Gorge was gone forever.

And from those ashes rises a whole new community. Affordably priced housing for all who could afford it. St Miltonville Estates.

'Milton Gorge Estates?' Freddie had scoffed at the suggestion, 'Sounds like it belongs in the Bayou.' He thought his original suggestion of 'Miltonborough' had the classiest sound to it, but that was thrown out by the other partners when Carlton Woodcock came up with those bullshit numbers to his bullshit survey in which eighty-seven percent of the respondents thought the place was to be called 'Milton Berle' and of those, sixty-four percent approved.

Smart-arse.

The partners decided on 'St Miltonville Estates' — which only brought a small protest from the religious community who claimed to have never heard of any 'St Milton'. Then it was Freddie's turn to come to the rescue and reassure them that they had done extensive and expensive research and discovered the existence of St Milton — who lived in Scotland a thousand years ago and is now the patron saint of corporate attitudes and stray cats. That was enough to quiet the church groups who were quite fond of both Scottish saints and stray cats. They also appreciated the large donation Freddie was willing to make to help spread the word.

'You're looking terribly stressed out,' Freddie said. 'Remember your ulcer, Carlton. We don't want you getting sick in the car again.'

'Believe me, I haven't forgotten my ulcer, Freddie.'

'I just do not understand why you are so worried about this. We, as private citizens, saw an opportunity and seized it. We invested in real estate. We found a few investors, we formed a real estate development consortium and we invested in your country.'

'What if we get audited? What if the ControlCorp Board wakes up from its naptime? What if — '

'And what if the sun explodes tomorrow? Screw it. Live for the day, Carlton. Besides, none of that is going to happen, I promise you. You take care of your end, and I'll take care of mine. Trust me, the Board has far more important issues to focus on, and the IRD — well, just never mind, I got that covered.'

'Where's my Mylanta?'

'I think you left a couple of bottles in the glove box. Look, Carlton, you're a good man, and you're doing a good job. You've just got to learn to be more trusting here. The day will come when you can write your own ticket. Hell, if you want to spend all your time thinking about airplanes, no problem — you'll be CEO by this time next year.'

'You think so? That soon?' Woodcock perked up, he paused the bottle halfway to his mouth.

'Sure — why not? You're the perfect man for the job. I'll personally put your name forward to the Board.'

Carlton narrowed his eyes. 'Would you really take orders from me?'

'I have already, haven't I?' He looked across at Carlton. 'I swear I don't want the job. Too much work. I'm perfectly happy being the ideas man and all. That's more my style. After all, diversification is the name of the game, and that's what I'm good at. Diversification.' Freddie smiled, then quietly sighed as he turned his attention toward the scenery rolling past his window.

Boredom — that was the real reason he could never be bothered taking on a job like CEO. It would be just too bloody boring. He needed more variety in his life. Leave the actual management tasks to the hopelessly boring, unimaginative chumps like Carlton Woodcock.

Freddie glanced across at Woodcock who was suckling from his bottle like an addict. He would probably make a bloody good CEO, come to think of it. He was a first-rate number cruncher. Twist them this way to make it look like a profit when a profit was needed, or that way to make a loss when a loss was needed, or just so when it was needed as evidence. It took a certain talent to do that. Freddie could not be bothered, but Carlton was a regular whiz-banger. Manipulating numbers was Carlton Woodcock's talent, and recognising other people's talent was Freddie Moore's.

'But you'd be willing to work for me?' Carlton said, his lips ringed with Mylanta.

Freddie shrugged. 'Gee, Carlton, I think of us as more of a team, but if you want to put it that way, sure, why not? I'd be honoured to be your humble servant.'

'You're so full of shit, Freddie.' Carlton's hands shook as he fumbled the bottle top back on.

Freddie miled. 'I'm just getting warmed up, Carlton — after all, we've got a strategic management meeting to get to in Auckland.'

TWENTY-FOUR

The ControlCorp boardroom at Auckland airport was on the mezzanine level of the admin section, at the far end of the corridor from my office. The room, with the tables removed, was large enough to accommodate an audience of sixty or more comfortably — which they did from time to time whenever the management wanted to sell the general staff their latest and greatest new idea or to explain the latest restructuring.

I sat quietly, looking up at the ceiling. Denise was chatting away with the woman across the table from her, but the rest of us remained subdued. I wondered if any of them felt as hung over as I did.

Oh, the pain. I closed my eyes and tried to block out Denise's perky voice and senseless chatter. Play some music. Ah, that's better, the Restructuring Waltz. When the music stops, if you're not sitting down, you're out.

They hold a gun to your head while you write a memo to the staff explaining how you've voluntarily decided to leave ControlCorp to pursue other career opportunities, get some business cards made up calling yourself a consultant and go on the dole.

Oh, to be that important.

They sometimes went to great lengths and expense to restructure, depending on how high up the person who was being restructured out of existence rested on the corporate food chain.

Me, they would probably just fire. Or murder.

I pondered the possibility as I sat at my position at the table. For a smaller meeting, like today's, the tables were arranged in a long rectangle. One end was reserved for Freddie Moore and Carlton

Woodcock, who had yet to show up. Then, along the left side would be Amanda, who would probably show up when Freddie and Woodcock did, and Leanne and Denise, who sat to my left. I was on the end opposite the head — that is, the foot of the table. On the other side of the table was a skinny guy with a large nose, bad skin and an overly prominent Adam's apple that someone had introduced as Linus Boswell from accounting. He had come up from head office for this meeting and none of us had any idea why he was there. He was very nervous looking and was pretending to be deeply engrossed in his own paperwork so as not to converse with any of us.

To my right was another Head Office person, an attractive woman in her early thirties with a friendly smile. Her name was Tania, and she was apparently an administrative aide to Freddie Moore. Why Freddie needed to fly his own secretary up for our meeting escaped me, especially since, according to Tania, Freddie had not flown up himself, but was driving up with Woodcock.

Between Tania and Linus was possibly my least favourite person in the entire Corporation, and the one whom Denise was at present busily kissing up to — a severe-looking woman with a sharp, angular jaw, and closely cropped, coppery red hair. Her name was Gloria LaCoste, and as a rule she hated all pilots, and all controllers and TV news people, who were all overpaid prima donnas as far as she was concerned, as were politicians, all other people who worked in TV, and, oddly enough, stevedores.

I had met Gloria on several occasions — each time as unpleasant as the previous one. Any time there was something newsworthy going on, she and her long pointy nose would be there, digging around like a kiwi looking for grubs. More than once I would turn around and find myself face to face with her and her notepad. She talked a lot, asked a lot of dumb questions, listened very little, and scribbled vigorously on her notepad. She was the corporate communications manager. 'Corporate communications manager' was a modern term, but Joseph Goebbels had exactly the same job description in Hitler's administration as this woman. Her job was to add the saccharine to bullshit, and she considered herself very good at it. Whenever there was an article in the newspaper about ControlCorp, it was Gloria who was quoted, offering the slogan of the month. Whenever there was an air traffic news story on the TV, it was Gloria fronting up to provide a face to the industry and offering the subtlest of implications that it was someone else's — usually the controller's — fault. Personally, I found her horrifying, I'm not sure why, but she reminded me of a character out of a B slasher film. I suspect she hated me too. Not only was I a controller, but I was American as well, a people she had a basic contempt for. I had the feeling she was just waiting for the opportunity to work me into a story.

At the moment, Denise was rabbiting on about something to Gloria, who was nodding at her, but eyeing me suspiciously.

'So by giving them a schematic on the organisational fit,' Denise said, 'we can then determine who is, and who is not, working within the matrix.'

If Denise had been speaking Urdu, I would have had a better chance of understanding her. Gloria was nodding her agreement, but did not take her eyes off me as if she expected trouble from me or my kind. I wasn't planning any. I was just wondering why any of these Head Office people were here. Originally, this was supposed to be a senior controller meeting with Amanda — something that happened once a month, during which she would spend an hour grilling us on what we'd done for the Corporation lately, and end with a hearty 'keep up the good work, team', and a friendly reminder of how tenuous our careers could be. As of last Monday, however, 'meetings' were out and 'strategic management seminars' were in.

When she told us there would be Head Office people there to address us, I figured they were going to unveil another restructuring — or something they thought equally impressive. I was kind of hoping for a restructuring. Sometimes there was a lot of money to be made. It could be the best of all possible worlds: 'senior controllers' were being disestablished and we would all be paid off two years' salary, as per our union agreement. Not likely, though — I'm not usually that lucky. Perhaps they were going to get rid of us more cost-effectively. I looked up at the sprinkler system.

Gas. That would be it. Quick, clean and probably cheap.

My theory on our dispatch was immediately shot down when Freddie Moore bowled in through the doors, closely flanked by Amanda and Woodchuck.

'Thank you for coming, everyone,' he said, as if any of us had a choice. 'It's good to see you all again. Hey there, Leanne,' Freddie waved, then nodded at Denise with the familiar kind of grin people offer when they don't have a clue what your name is. 'Tom,' he snapped his fingers as he pointed at me, then flipped his wrist in a drinking motion, 'you and I have to do some serious catching up.'

'Sure thing, boss,' I nodded back, but dropped my smile when I caught the glare from Amanda. She did not like too much of the boys-will-be-boys stuff.

'Okay, exciting times on the ControlCorp horizon,' Freddie launched into his speech without hesitation as Woodchuck and Amanda took their seats. 'And you're all going to be a part of it.'

Dammit. No restructuring.

And if it wasn't restructuring, it could be only one other thing. Reimaging.

'But as we rapidly expand on all fronts, we cannot forget how utterly important it is to maintain the right corporate image.'

I wasn't sure about the 'utterly important' — it seemed like an odd choice of adverb.

Freddie's pep talk went on for longer than it needed to be. At first I tried to follow what he was saying about the new ControlCorp Culture and the values it espoused.

'We've created a new culture?' I asked but my question was ignored or unheard through Freddie's apparent enthusiasm for it and I was not interested in a reply enough to care to press it. I was having a hard time keeping my eyes open. I hadn't had enough sleep, and I was still hung over — not to mention a few issues I had on my mind that I considered somewhat more important than the new society Freddie was trying to create out of the ashes of what had been, I thought, a perfectly good society and had missed the point in which it had ceased to exist.

I turned toward Tania, who turned her head toward me and offered a warm smile. She must be a very nice person, I thought. She was wholesome looking. But she was not Sarah, and it was Sarah I was thinking of when I was exchanging smiles with Tania. Maybe I was making a mistake.

I don't think I would necessarily have described Sarah as wholesome — not that she wasn't — but she had a kind of sophistication about her that belied wholesomeness. Or maybe it's just that once you've had passionate sex, the idea of 'wholesomeness' is tainted in my mind. Maybe that was my problem — I mean, it's not like we did anything kinky. It was good. Healthy. Wholesome.

I realised I was probably holding my attention on Tania just a little too long, so I turned back to Freddie and nodded as if I agreed with whatever he was saying, although by now I had pretty much lost the thread. He was still waffling on about the ControlCorp values and the need for a consistent corporate image, two things that seemed to be incongruous, but apparently the crux was that ControlCorp needed to be represented as a modern, efficient and progressive organisation and this was the ultimate solution.

Safe, orderly, expeditious. Why did we have to keep changing it? Keep them apart and keep them moving. My hand trembled as I tried to take a sip of coffee.

Maybe it was just caffeine and lack of sleep that made my hands tremble. I had to talk to Sarah today — she had to understand why I had to do what I was going to do.

Maybe she would come with me.

I had to talk to her, and I was a little nervous about it. I was not planning on talking during this meeting — this strategic management seminar — beyond the occasional 'here, here' or some other show of support for the New World Order. I really had every intention of being supportive — it was going to be my gift to Amanda. My parting gift.

I was just not expecting to be called upon by Freddie Moore.

'Huh?' I said when I heard my name.

'Don't be shy, Tom,' Freddie said. 'We're all looking forward to your training plan. Did I tell you we're going to use it as the model for the National Training Plan?'

'The national ...' I opened my mouth but nothing more came out.

'The National Training Plan — the NTP — it's a vital part of everything we've been talking about today — that is, standardisation. Every unit in the country will follow the same standardised procedures, whether it is in training, standards, document control, et cetera, et cetera.'

'I thought we already did — I mean follow the same procedures.' I looked around the table. All eyes were on me, and suddenly I knew what it must be like to stand before a firing squad.

'Tom, my man, you are going to set the standard.'

'Oh.'

'Yes. Amanda has been telling me your training plan is brilliant — a regular work of art.'

'She has?' I looked at Amanda and she smiled back. I'm not sure what she was up to. Her mischievous smile was getting harder to distinguish from the compassionate one. Either she was trying to build me up so she could look good as my boss, or she was just screwing with me. Or maybe she was just being nice. At the moment, I wished I had taken the time to know just a little more about Amanda Sheppard. What was it like to be success-oriented, to set your goals higher than others? What was it like to have a rich and powerful dad whom you didn't get along with? What was it like to have a dad?

'We are all eager to hear about it, Tom,' Freddie said as he lowered himself into his chair, 'so please share it with us. The floor is yours.'

'Well — it's not actually done. It could still use a bit of tweaking.'

'That's okay — a rough draft is fine with us.'

The truth is it needed more than just a little tweaking. It needed to be written. We had been told to get started on our prospective plans two months ago, but I figured it was just another one of those empty, time-consuming projects to keep us busy as worker bees. At the time, things were going great with me and Sarah, and it was hard for me to stay interested in a pointless assignment. I didn't understand it. I even went back to Amanda and asked her, 'What did you want me to say about training? They send us a trainee from the aviation college, we give him or her a headset, plug him or her in with an instructor, who then teaches him or her how to keep them apart and keep them moving.' Seemed simple enough.

Amanda said that was the old way and what they now wanted was, 'The corporate way. Get with the programme, Thomas.' So I sat down at the computer and I started writing my corporate training plan, which was probably overly simple:

Stage One: Throw trainee into shark-infested waters. If trainee:

a. Survives
    i. continue to Stage Two and
    ii. bill trainee for swimming lesson
b. Does not survive
    i. find new trainee and
    ii. bill sharks for lunch.

It took me exactly eight minutes to write it — and that was including the formatting. Since then, I've been having fun with Sarah and not thinking about writing an NTP. The password-protected file on the computer that was marked 'Hardy-TrngPln. ver.3' was really something I found on the internet about fly-fishing and how to tie your own flies. Nobody told me we were going to be asked to present these things to Head Office personnel and now, sitting there, scanning the eager and expectant faces, I wished I had at least come up with a Stage Two.

'Well …'

'Tom, please stand up,' Freddie said.

I got to my feet slowly, my head still swimming. 'What I was going to say was, well, that the National Training Plan — or rather the NTP — ' I looked around the table. They were all looking at me — even Linus Boswell from accounts seemed interested. It didn't seem fair. After all, I wasn't interested in anything they had had to say. I took a deep breath, picked up a couple of pieces of paper and looked at them closely — the top one was a memo I had collected from my in-box, reminding everyone to please leave the coffee-making facilities clean and not to leave dirty cups on the countertop.

'Well, basically, it is a three-stage modular training programme that takes a proactive discourse in addressing the training needs of the …' I spoke slowly enough for my brain to stay one or two words ahead of my mouth, 'Training Development Unit and to ensure the training programme is at all times aligned with corporate values and objectives and meets the organisational fit for the development of and exploration of various commercial opportunities and market potential in the global marketplace.' I couldn't think of any place to fit the word 'matrix', but otherwise thought I was doing okay.

'Wow!' Freddie was looking overly excited. 'This sounds fantastic. "Training Development Unit" — I love that name — that's what we're going to call the aviation college from now on.'

'So, Mr Hardy, what exactly is Stage One?' Gloria LaCoste asked as if she was in the pressroom at the White House trying to nail the President down on a lie.

'Yes, of course, Stage One.' I glanced around the table — at least Boswell was looking down at his documents again — that was good. One down, six to go. Woodchuck looked like he could drift away at any time. 'Well, Ms LaCoste, that's a good question. Stage One is simply the pre-programmed computer-assisted theory-based procedural learning, uh, matrix. That is, the classroom training, Ms LaCoste.' I offered a smile, but she still looked hungry.

'So what would Stage Two be then?' Her smile was nothing

more than a stretched out smirk. She turned towards Freddie, to remind them to keep watching this space for how she was about to skin my Yankee arse.

'That would be the modular on-the-job training stage, Ms LaCoste.' Again I offered a smile.

'So then, could you explain to us Stage Three?' Her smirk widened further into something approaching a genuine smile as she stuck her chin out and shifted her eyes again towards Freddie and Woodcock.

'Stage Three?'

'Yes,' she said, turning her attention back to me, 'you said it was a three-stage plan.'

'Of course it is.' Shit. I could have as easily said two stages. 'But, Stage Three, obviously, is our overseas market enhancement programme that is designed to attract our foreign clients, and to establish us as a leading supplier of air traffic training in the global marketplace.'

'Excellent!' Freddie Moore jumped to his feet. 'That's exactly the kind of thing I'm talking about, people. Tom is thinking outside the box — he's not limiting his ideas to the domestic market. And the only three words I have for you, Tom, are *brilliant, brilliant, brilliant*!'

'Thank you, Mr Moore,' I said as I eased myself into my chair. With just a cursory scan of the faces around the table, I learned at least two things: Gloria LaCoste and Amanda Sheppard both wanted me quite dead, and Freddie Moore — dazzled by gibberish — was at least as much a phoney as I was.

'I am looking forward to seeing this thing, Tom. When will it be finished?'

Finished? Probably not until long after I'm finished.

'Give me a couple of weeks,' I shrugged. What did I have to lose? I would be long gone.

The meeting was not over, not by a long shot. It went on for another hour and a half, and we all had our turn. Leanne was next up with her Standards Plan, something she put a considerable amount of work into, and her idea of setting up a quality assurance programme that would ensure a high standard of service nationwide.

'Very good, Leanne,' Freddie said when she had finished. 'Remember, though, if you set the standard too high, you'll be excluding people. ControlCorp is an inclusive organisation. Remember always to think positive.' He then quickly moved on to Denise, who was bouncing in her seat in anticipation of sharing her schematic for the organisational matrix with the group. Freddie gave her less than two minutes to explain what the hell that meant before he dismissed document control with a quip about 'the drudge of paperwork', a chuckle and a wave of his hand. She looked like she was about to cry when he told her to sit down. He must have noticed, so added, 'But I would like you to provide a full, in-depth briefing to Mr Woodcock on this one.' And then Woodchuck looked like he was about to cry.

Even Linus Boswell had a chance. Turns out, he was the guy who came up with the idea of the billing system, and now he wanted to explain his new system of charging that would substantially increase revenue. What it meant was, they were raising the rates — but he was able to make it sound better than that.

After we had been there for almost two hours, it was time to hear from Gloria LaCoste about the spit and polish they were adding to the corporate image. A new logo — which meant all new stationery. We were no longer supervisors, or senior controllers, but were now to be 'team leaders' — which meant new business cards. So far I had used only one of the 500 business cards I had been given, and that was to scrape an especially stubborn bird turd off my windscreen.

'So, what about everyone else?' I asked. 'I mean, the people on my crew — are they still air traffic controllers, or do they get a new name, too?'

'As a matter of fact,' Freddie piped in, 'they're "air traffic specialists", and it's no longer your "crew", it's your "team".'

'Are they still people?'

'Nope,' Freddie said. 'They're "human resources".'

'Okay,' I nodded my approval. 'I'll be sure to pass that on to my resources this afternoon.' I looked across at Tania, who was smiling at me again.

'We'll also be doing a little remodelling around here,' Freddie added.

Amanda fidgeted in her seat. 'Mr Moore, we have only recently completed a refurbishment of this facility. We just finished repainting six weeks ago. There's yet to be a single coffee stain on the new carpet.'

'There's one, Amanda,' I said, though she ignored me. 'I was going to tell you ...'

'We're redoing it,' Freddie said.

Amanda stiffened, her lips slowly disappeared, her fingers started drumming the blue diary that sat on the table to her left. 'You realise, I chose the colour scheme myself,' she said, her voice had the slightest tremble to it. She took great pride in her tastefully subdued pastels, neutral tones and easy-on-the-eye watercolours. She had done a pretty good job of it and, at the moment, I was feeling a bit sorry for her.

'You did fine. Enjoy it until next week. We're talking a consistent corporate image, dear.'

Amanda's nostrils flared, her fingers increased the tempo of their drumming. 'Then why,' she said coolly, regaining control over her tremble, 'did you not tell me this a few months ago before we went over budget refurbishing this place?'

'Because the consultant team hadn't finished doing their study on the optimum colour scheme.'

'And *what* is the optimum colour scheme?'

'Well, for the carpet we have a lovely shade of navy,' Gloria LaCoste interjected, trying to regain control of her presentation.

'Not "navy",' Freddie interrupted. 'I think they called that one "James Brown-on-a-Bad-Day-Blue",' he laughed at his own joke and held his hand up. 'But now, it's "Corporate Blue".'

'Corporate Blue?' Amanda looked to be dying a slow and painful death by bad taste.

'Yes, we'll also use that colour for all our drop files for consistency in our look,' Freddie said. There was a tense edge to his voice I had not heard before. 'It's one of our team colours. Every team, in every corner of the world, has team colours and the ControlCorp team colours are Corporate Blue and Successful Silver. Blue for the sky we rule.'

'And silver for the loose change we get to keep,' I offered, unable to let the moment go by.

'Thank you, Tom,' Freddie said sincerely. 'I'm glad someone can get into the spirit of things.'

While Freddie and Amanda entered into a brief and diplomatic debate on the subject, I leaned towards Tania again who was not bothering to record the tense exchange between the two. 'I had them one time,' I whispered so only she could hear.

She looked at me with raised eyebrows.

'The corporate blues — doctor said I had 'em bad.'

She laughed silently.

'That's why I started drinking. You want to go drinking with me?'

She smiled and mouthed, 'I don't think so.'

'Tom,' Freddie said loudly, 'if you're done hitting on my secretary, we can finish up.'

There was a relieved round of polite laughter from the others except for Amanda, who was giving me a laser-beam look. I could feel the colour rising in my face — red, I assume, and probably not the approved blue. 'Of course,' I said, looking down at my stack of meaningless memos in front of me, and for no reason jotted down 'blue.'

I wasn't hitting on her. I glanced up at Tania, but she was no longer returning my glances. Just having a little fun, I thought. What's wrong with that? It's not like I was really asking her out for drinks. I'm out of here. History. If I was going to stick around, then I would not be looking for a date with Tania. If I was going to stick around, I would do everything in my power to show Sarah I can be a whole person, to say the things she wants me to say to her.

'Very, very productive,' Freddie was summing up the meeting.

Yes, it has been, hasn't it? We decided on new colours and new job titles and the new summer collection of bullshit and, in over two hours, I don't think the word 'airplane' was actually mentioned once.

At the end of the meeting, I left the boardroom and headed straight for the men's room. I was standing in front of the urinal when Carlton Woodcock came in and stepped up to the urinal next to me.

'That was pretty funny, Hardy,' he said, letting out a little snort. 'Ha! The small change we get to keep. Went right over Freddie's head, too.'

I tried to ignore Woodchuck. I don't think I've ever exchanged more than a few words with the guy — we've never actually had a conversation — and at that particular moment, I didn't really want to start having conversations with him. Some guys were urinal-talkers; some of us prefer to keep the moment somewhat more private and don't consider it the best time for making new friends.

'Yeah, that was pretty funny all right.' Woodchuck was worse than a urinal-talker; he talked without encouragement. 'Freddie thinks he's so smart, but he misses stuff like that because he's too busy listening to himself blow. You're lucky, you can get away with saying stuff like that.'

'Yeah, I'm lucky no one listens to me,' I said as I finished up. It felt safer to say something. I turned towards the basin.

'But I'm like you. I've had about all I can take.'

Like me?

I turned the tap on and put my hands under the warm water.

I wonder what he means by that. How would he know? I dismissed the thought.

'Is that right?' I asked, though I really did not want to encourage him to talk any more. I concentrated on lathering up the soap and rubbed it slowly across my hands.

'Yeah. A guy can only take so much of the bullshit. Am I right?'

'You're right.'

'Yeah, well at least you don't have to work for Freddie — "Carlton do this, do that, buy this, shred that, burn this, go fetch" — like I'm his own personal gofer boy or cook or something. But I tell you, I've had as much as I can take.'

'What?' I briefly glanced at Woodchuck. 'You cook for him?'

'He likes some things cooked,' Woodcock mumbled almost inaudibly, then looked around and let out a nervous laugh. 'I said I wasn't hired to be Freddie Moore's personal assistant. I got a fucking MBA. Did you know that?'

I shrugged, though he probably didn't notice.

'I mean a real MBA. I could be running this damn business. And I'm in it for the long term too.' He lowered his voice as he looked down at himself and fumbled to get himself put away. 'Anyway, I can wait him out. One of these days … one of these days it'll be taps for ol' Freddie Moore.'

I looked at Woodchuck's back in the mirror. 'It will be what?'

He was shaking his head as he turned around and stepped up to me — too close. 'You ever come down to Wellington, Hardy? We should go drinking.'

'Sure,' I said, drying my hands with a paper towel. 'Sure thing,' I said again as I turned to face him, but I would rather dig my eyes out with a spoon than to go drinking with Woodchuck.

'Think about staying, Hardy.' Woodcock rubbed his hands on his trousers. 'Stick it out here for a while — put up with Amanda's bullshit while I put up with Freddie's bullshit — before you know it, there'll be a New World Order.'

'Another one?'

'A better one. For guys like us.'

Guys like us? Like what?

'I'm serious,' he said, leaning even closer. I leaned back. 'I could use your help — a guy with your knowledge of the coal face.'

'I don't know anything about coal,' I said, but he had already turned to leave. Except that we were both males of the human species, I could not think of one thing that Woodchuck and I had in common. Guys like us? 'Hey, Woodcock.'

'Yeah?'

'What do you mean "it'll be taps for ol' Freddie"?'

He shrugged. 'Just an expression, Hardy. Haven't you ever heard it before?'

'Yeah,' I said, though he was already gone. 'Once before. A long time ago.'

TWENTY-FIVE

'Long day after a hard night. First the meeting, and then you went on shift?'

'Yeah.' As I glanced around this guy's office, it had just dawned on me that he didn't have a single book on display. No bookshelves full of three-inch thick psychology textbooks, no colourfully covered, easy-to-read self-helpers, no novels, no books with his name on the spine. I wondered if he was just not a reader, or if he thought books wouldn't fit in with his minimalist approach — the leather and chrome chairs and glass-topped table, the vaguely erotic abstract wood sculptures or the paintings on the wall. Lines and shapes and shadows. Or the blackness creeping in.

'Synergism.'

'What?' he asked.

'Synergism requires two complete and separate wholes joining together.'

'Still not following you.'

I wonder if she would come back with me now that she really knows the rest of the whole of me? Does she like the rest of me? The lines and shapes and shadows and blackness creeping in from the borderlands?

'Yeah,' I said again. 'It was a long day before a hard night. Along with everything else, I was faced with the new and most disturbing idea that Woodchuck was trying to be my friend now too by giving me disturbing little clues. But it was nothing compared to the private little meeting with Freddie immediately after that.'

'Oh? What did he want to meet with you about?'

'Blackmail. What else?'

'Tom, walk with me.' Freddie Moore caught up with me as I walked down the hall to my office. It sounded more like he wanted to walk with me, but I wasn't going to split hairs. 'You were dynamic in there.'

I looked up at him, but said nothing. He was a good four or five inches taller than me, and sometimes he could step just a bit too close so as to make you to look up at him.

'The whole training thing, I mean,' he said, leaning into and over me.

'It was nothing,' I said, and really meant it.

'You have so much potential. Have you ever thought about applying for a Head Office job?'

'No, not really.'

'You really ought to — I mean, how does something like national training manager sound?'

'It sounds impressive.' I stopped at the door to my office. 'But, you know, I'm not really …' I shrugged, not knowing how to complete the sentence.

I'm not really what you're looking for? Not really interested in being another Woodcock? Not really qualified? Not really going to be here more than another week? Not really much of a coffee drinker any more now that I'd decided to switch back to tea?

'Don't dismiss the idea until you've had a chance to think about it. You've got plenty of time — hell, the job doesn't even exist yet — but say the word and it could. Just think of the influence you could have. Something like that would be a great opportunity for you to get away from controlling.'

'But I like controlling.' And I did. That was the whole point of my existence. I did like controlling and I was good at it. Once. My dad would have been proud of me. How did they drag me into this New World Order?

'Of course you do. Let's talk in here.' Then he pushed me into my office and closed the door behind him. Besides the height, he had forty pounds on me and the way he shoved me was just like a bully had done to me in the schoolyard when I was about ten. I briefly thought I was in for another thrashing.

'You see, thing is, Tom — I got a problem.' Freddie started a slow pace around my office. 'Well, I guess we all have our problems — I got a problem, you got a problem. But that's all the more reason why we need to help each other out — you know, teamwork, networking and all that jazz.'

'I got a problem?'

'My problems — you don't even want to get me started on my problems.'

'No, I don't.'

'Politics. That's what my problem is. Bullshit politics. Don't you hate politics?'

'Yes, I do.'

'Of course you do — but then you don't have to deal with it on the level I have to deal with it.'

'Just the Presidential level for me.'

'Believe me, you wouldn't want to have to put up with the crap I have to put up with. It's enough to drive you to drink. Which reminds me, come on down to Wellington some time and we'll go out and tip a few back. I understand you're a man not averse to a wee drop now and again.'

'So I keep being told.'

'Just not during work hours.'

'Of course not.'

'Yeah.' Freddie suddenly stopped and got a pained look on his face. 'Yeah,' he said again slowly, looked away from me and shook his head, 'that's where we get into this messy political bullshit. Such a nasty business really.'

'Could you please just get to your point?' I had no idea what Freddie was leading up to, but I was wishing he would just get to it without this constant prattle of bullshit. I was not in the mood for pretending any more. My head felt like it was trying to hatch a komodo dragon. I needed to talk to Amanda about my change in career plans, and find Sarah to see if I could get her to change her mind. I was facing the usually busy Thursday afternoon shift, and I was still feeling a bit queasy from Woodchuck's attempt at friendship in the toilet. Now Freddie was trying to soften me up for something by implying I had a future down the hall from him at head office, plotting the economic overthrow of the Third World. It was all too much.

'Tom,' Freddie said, shaking his head as if in disgust, 'let me be honest with you. I think it's all bullshit. I think Amanda's out to get you.'

'You think so? I don't think it's that bad?'

'Apparently she's got friends, too.'

'I should hope so.'

'Friends in high places.'

'And who would that be?'

Freddie walked around my desk, tapping his fingers along the oak-veneered edge near the spot that was already starting to peel. He continued around until he was on the far side from me, then looked down at the desk and, with his foot, gently nudged the bottom left drawer open. 'A Mr Malahide, it seems.'

'The Learjet pilot?'

'Yeah. He says the supervisor he talked to on the phone about his alleged incident last week sounded a little ...' Freddie looked down at the drawer, then leaned forward and extracted the bottle of Glenfiddich. 'He said the supervisor sounded a little intoxicated and he wanted us to conduct a full investigation.'

'Hmm,' I said, nodding. 'That sounds unlikely, since the supervisor he spoke with that night was the centre supervisor, Craig — and, if I'm not mistaken, the guy's a Mormon and doesn't touch the stuff.' But it was too late. I could already see the set up. The bottle of Glenfiddich was half empty — or half full, depending on your perspective. To me, it was half empty.

'I believe you, Tom.' Freddie set the bottle on the desk and walked over to me, standing too close. 'I think this is some kind of political manoeuvring going on here. I mean, I wouldn't let this guy push you around. I would still throw the book at him. But, dammit,' Freddie shook his head in disgust again. 'He must've got to Amanda, because now she's hot on your trail. She found this and wants me to give you the sack for it. Damn her. This is going too far. I tell you what ... ' he put a hand on my shoulder, 'I'm going to stick by you on this. There's no evidence whatsoever that you were drinking on duty. This,' he waved towards the bottle, 'doesn't mean anything. Nothing says you can't have a nip or two after work, right? What I'm saying is, I'm going to stick by you on this one. No matter what.'

'In exchange for?'

'I'm talking about the big stink Malahide and all his solicitors and Amanda are going to make just because a man enjoys the odd drink. They're probably going to get the incident thrown out anyway but I'll make sure Amanda doesn't get this drinking on duty business to stick. I'm behind you, Tom.'

'You want me to drop the incident?'

'Well,' Freddie shrugged and pretended to think it over, 'I can see your point of view on that, the big picture so to speak. Dropping it would be the quickest way for it to go away, which would save us wasting our time and resources. And sometimes it's better to just bite the bullet, make it go away and get back to the more important business. Yes, I see what you're saying, but, you know if you want to fight it, I'm on your side.'

'Good. Then we'll fight it.'

And that was it — that was the first and to date only time in my life I've been properly blackmailed. It was easy; it was simple. Freddie sends Woodcock into my office while I'm out under the pretence of making a few phone calls or something, then he closes the door and rifles through my desk looking for anything that might be frowned upon by Amanda. There are many things she frowns upon, so they figured the odds were good there would be something they could use. And they hit the jackpot. Woodcock finds the bottle of Glenfiddich and drains half of it — God knows where, but if my rubber plant dies, I'll know who to blame. The fact that I would insist the seal was unbroken and the contents undisturbed would work even better because nobody would believe I had no intention of opening it and it would look like I was deep in an alcoholic's denial. That gave Freddie more ammo than he could have dreamed of for getting Malahide's incident swept away forever.

Woodcock, however, found something else — a letter from the FAA — and being the nosy bastard he is, he would have read it and learned they were offering my job back in California and requested I start back as soon as possible because of staff shortage. Big Ted Kazniak really pulled through for me. My guess is Woodcock did not share that much with Freddie because he thought he, in turn, might use it to his own advantage. So he tries to make friends with me while we're peeing.

The bottle would be too circumstantial to actually get me booted out, but it would be enough to cause more trouble than Freddie Moore figured I wanted.

Toe the line. You have a future; don't blow it. Learn how to play the game. Do that and become one of us.

I wonder if this is how they got my dad in the end? I never knew who his enemies were — if they were real or imagined — but something drove him deep into his blackness, from where he never returned. I wondered if that was where I was headed. So the choice was to sell my soul now, to give in and be assured of an immediate survival and a little high-flying success — but to pay the eventual price by a corporate-sponsored heart attack at my desk, face down in my puddling tea when I was no longer useful. Or I could stand up, tell Freddie Moore to go fuck himself, and accept the cost to my career. That's when I understood a fight was only worth fighting when you had something to lose.

'What did you tell Moore?'

I stared out the window and pondered it. 'Well, I was leaving. I had nothing to lose. So I would like to say I rose up on the balls of my feet and got right in Freddie Moore's face, within an inch of his nose and told him I had had enough of his New World Order, had had enough of him and mission statements, and Gloria LaCoste and her new, more positive corporate image, and the corporate vision that was blind to the one thing they should never lose sight of. I would like to say that I was no longer going to sit around and watch him rape and pillage an industry that I had once thought of as a pretty important public service. But I didn't. I was tired. I was thinking of what I had to get through in the afternoon before me and, besides, I had a better idea. So I stepped back to a respectful distance and told him I had to go to work. And then I left my office and went on shift. It was a busy afternoon. Sarah was there and we kept avoiding each other's glances until it was time for her to go home. Ryan had gone home by then and it was just me, her and Simon. She went downstairs at about a quarter past eight. But Simon could tell what was going on between us. We weren't fooling anyone. The traffic had quieted down and he told me he would cover upstairs, but that I shouldn't let her leave without sorting something out. So I caught up with her in the parking lot.

'She was not interested in hearing me plead, and we argued. I asked her to come back to the States with me, and we argued. Then I asked her to marry me, and she said no.'

'I'm sorry.'

'Then I asked her to go fishing with me. And she said yes.'

'Fishing?'

'Yes. Then she went home to her parents' house, and I went upstairs to give Simon a break. The rest, you know.'

Twenty-six

'Did you ask for the early turn?' the captain asked as he slipped into the left seat of the 737.

'Affirm,' the first officer said without looking up from his technical log. 'Said they'll advise on take-off.'

'Good. Let's try to make this as short a flight as possible. Been a long day and I've got a firm-breasted redhead with some almond oil and a bottle of champagne waiting to give me a full body massage in Wellington in about an hour.' He grinned. Captain Dave Nelson loved being one of the youngest captains on the 73s. He loved his four stripes and being single and good-looking, and he loved being able to talk like this to the older, married and more staid first officers. And he loved that they had to listen because he was the captain.

'Well, let's get there first,' the first officer said. Wayne Perry was typical of the sort of first officer that Dave liked to rib. He was a good, reliable and professional pilot. While Dave was busting his nuts flying the regionals for eleven years, waiting out the comings and goings of Tasman Airways hiring phases, sweating out the years as each one made him older and less desirable, this young hotshot went straight from his stint as a flight instructor into Tasman and has been on a fast track to 747 captain ever since. While Wayne spent another three years flying Metroliners, Dave started as a first officer in a 737 right from the start.

Wayne was not angry. He had long ago resigned himself to the fickleness of the airline industry. He knew it was not skill or experience that decided their seats. It was timing. And through a fluke of timing, Wayne Perry sat in the right seat and answered to

Dave Nelson instead of the other way around. No, he was not angry. However, he disliked these rosters that put him in the seat next to this cocky little prick, because Dave had no idea that it was luck and timing that got him the job. He was certain he was the best damn pilot in the air and that was a dangerous position to take. If Dave was smart, he would be more respectful towards the older first officers — he might even learn something from them — and less arrogant towards the younger ones.

Company procedures called for both pilots to be in their seats while they did their pre-flight checks and received their ATC clearance. But Dave liked showing off the four stripes on his epaulets to the passengers and the flight attendants, which cut into his pre-flight time, and it was left to the first officer to pick up the slack. As soon as Dave dropped into his seat, he did a quick run-through of his pre-start checklist, tapped the flight plan details into the onboard computer and was ready to crank her up and get going. He did not like waiting around, especially when he had a firm-breasted redhead waiting for him in Wellington.

'So what's the hold-up?' Dave asked Wayne as he impatiently drummed his fingers on the control column. 'We have any ramp rats down there to push us back, or are they taking another coffee break?'

'They're just throwing on a few more bags. Should be just about done.' Wayne glanced down at his route clearance and the note he scrawled on the side. 'We need to be airborne in nine minutes, though — they're positioning a 747 sixty miles out for runway zero-five, and we have to be in our turn southbound before he hits the outer marker.'

'Why? Since when does he get priority over us? Isn't two-three the runway in use?'

'They just switched to their noise abatement configuration — calm wind, no traffic after 9.00 p.m. means in over the water and out over the water. And I believe they consider the landing traffic having priority.'

'I know that. Fuck 'em.' Dave drummed his fingers for a few seconds in silence. 'Who's on up there tonight?' he asked, nodding in the direction of the tower.

'One of the new guys.'

'Shit. All right, then let's get moving. We'll take an intersection departure. Give me the Before Start Checklist down to the line.'

Several more minutes had passed by the time the ground crew had finished loading the bags, securing the cargo doors and pushing the aircraft back into position for taxiing. Another minute lost on unhitching a stubborn tow bar. They were crucial minutes.

As soon as the start sequence had been completed, Dave pushed the button on his steering column that keyed his mike as he fast-taxied off the tarmac. 'Tower, Tasman four-two-two, request taxi. We'll be ready at the intersection.'

Several moments passed without a response from the tower. Wayne was still doing his pre-take-off checks, trying to keep up with Dave.

'He's probably asleep up there,' Dave mumbled. He was about to push the mike button again to repeat his request before he had to slow the plane down when the tower responded.

'Tasman four-two-two, taxi runway two-three, speedway three, be ready immediate.'

'Roger.'

'We don't have cabin clearance yet,' Wayne said, indicating the flight attendants were not done securing the cabin.

'Shit!' Dave shook his head.

'Tasman four-two-two you're cleared for take-off,' the tower said.

'Tower,' he keyed the mike, 'we're going full length.' He unkeyed the mike and glanced at his co-pilot. 'That should give them one more minute to get them all strapped down.'

Wayne nodded.

Again the tower was slow in responding, and when he did, he sounded unsure.

'Ah, Tasman four-two-two, yeah, roger, full length — no delay though, traffic being positioned for zero-five seven miles outside the marker. You're cleared for immediate take-off.'

'Roger, cleared for take-off,' Mike repeated, then unkeyed his mike. 'Seven miles outside the marker — you'd think with seventeen miles between us, the guy could relax a little.'

'I think he's more concerned about us being clear of the localiser signal before the seven-four reaches the outer marker,' Wayne suggested.

Dave shot a quick glance at Wayne. He would rather this guy keep his lessons in air traffic management to himself at this hour of the night.

By the time they reached the end of the runway, the flight attendant had called in the cabin clearance and they were ready to go. Dave lined the plane up on the runway, set the break and pushed the throttle up to forty percent as Wayne ran through his last checklist items.

'All checks complete,' Wayne announced.

'Let's roll,' Dave said as he released the brakes and throttled up to max. The aircraft started its slow roll bumping along the runway, picking up speed.

'Pacific West five-two on final,' they heard over the radio, and, again, the tower seemed to take an inordinately long time to respond, before the same hesitant sounding voice came back and uttered, 'Pacific West five-two, number one.'

'V-one,' Wayne called off as the airspeed indicator climbed past 136 knots. 'One thirty nine, rotate.'

Dave eased the nose up to fifteen degrees and the aircraft bumped a few more times before it broke free of the runway. 'Gear up,' he instructed his co-pilot.

They climbed through one hundred feet.

'Right, let's call radar and see if he'll turn us out of a thousand direct on track so I can get to that redhead.' He grinned and glanced across at Wayne who was keeping an eye on the speed indicator waiting until it passed 190 knots to start retracting the flaps.

Then another voice came on the radio — a different controller — his voice calm, but the very weight of it commanded attention. 'Tasman four-two-two make an *immediate* left turn southbound — 747 traffic opposite direction.'

Dave exchanged another quick glance with Wayne, and keyed the mike to confirm they wanted him to turn the aircraft at their present altitude, passing 300 feet or at the usual one thousand feet. After all they knew the 747 was approaching the outer marker, but that was ten miles still. He keyed the mike just as he saw it. 'Confirm Tasman four — shit!'

They had both seen it at the same time, the landing lights of a 747 bearing down on them — through the blinding glare it was impossible to say how close it was. For a moment, frozen in time, Dave Nelson knew he was going to die. The normally darkened cockpit was flooded in bright white light. The moment could have been a half a second or it could have been half his life — but in that single moment he both resigned himself to his fate and fully gave in to his survival instinct. It was pure reflex — rules, procedures, even thought had nothing to do with it — he just responded instantaneously. He put the weight of his body behind a hard bank to the left and in a split second the light went out and a thundering roar filled his ears momentarily and then subsided. When they were still airborne, climbing through 400 feet a second later, it began to sink in that he was still alive.

'Fuck!' Dave shouted as his faculties returned. 'Son-of — ' he positioned his thumb to key the mike, but the controller was already talking, apparently to the 747: 'Affirm. Climb straight ahead to two thousand feet contact approach now for vectors back to final. Break, break — Tasman four-two-two stop your climb initially at one thousand, maintain your present heading for vectors on track and contact radar now.'

Dave looked across at Wayne — even in the dim glow of the cockpit, he could tell the guy was white as a sheet. He keyed the mike, 'Roger, heading two-seven-zero, stop at one, going to control.' He unkeyed the mike and paused for a moment before switching frequencies, then went back to the tower controller. 'Tower, someone's going to pay for that one.'

The tower controller responded almost immediately. 'Roger that, Tasman four-two-two. Please contact the centre supervisor on the telephone when you get to Wellington.'

'You bet.' Dave unkeyed his mike. Shit — this was going to be a long night of paper work. So much for the redhead.

Part Three: Taps

Twenty-seven

I sat in my chair opposite him, but my head was turned to the window. I could make out nothing out there in the night. No lines or shapes, just blackness and a cold southerly tapping at the window. I was staring out the window, with the little rivers of rainwater forming on the glass, and was reminded of something Flynn said: 'A whole different world — almost microscopic to us, but to their world we'd be God-size.'

God-size.

He glanced at his watch, despite there being a clock mounted on the wall directly above my head, ticking away, too loudly — tick, tick, tick. It was especially designed, no doubt, for a psychiatrist's office. Tick, tick, tick. The mind games they play on the mentally tired people sitting here wondering where their lives have gone.

'So,' he said, 'the facts are: one, that a controller was responsible for the traffic at the time; two, that the controller was remiss in not paying attention to his primary duty at the time of the incident.'

'Yes, those are the facts.'

Tick, tick, tick.

'They are the facts — disputed by no one. The only question that remains is: was that controller you? Or Simon?'

'I guess that is, indeed, the only question for you to answer. And here I've put you through hours of torture to get you to boil it down to just that one question. You could have asked me that in an email.'

'No, on both counts. I've enjoyed this session and, shit,' he laughed, 'with what I'll be able to charge the Corporation, I could buy a new car.'

'Get a Beamer. Freddie Moore might be ready to sell you his cheap.'

He laughed. 'But there's still the simple question, which is not for me to answer — it's for you to answer. Was it you or Simon on duty at the time?' He stopped smiling. 'Look, Tom, in either case, the other fact is, you stepped in and prevented a catastrophe. No matter how guilty you are of being a contributing factor, you still stopped it in the end.'

'Luck saved us in the end. Luck and the Big Sky Theory — which is, if all else fails, it's a big sky, and the chances are they'll miss each other.'

'No — it never went that far. It was stopped before that. The system didn't fail because you did your job.'

'You sound like you're trying to get me off the hook, doc.'

'I am. Tell me the truth. Tell me it was Simon's incident.'

'No.'

He shook his head. 'Don't you understand? Simon has already confessed. I can help this go away. It will be easier if you work with me here. Tell the truth and you can come out of it as a hero.'

'A hero?' I turned and faced him, truly surprised at the suggestion.

'That's right — the way Simon tells his story. If we can just get the two stories to gel, we won't even have to have the hearing on Wednesday.'

'But now it's you who does not understand.'

'All I need,' he said, his hand nervously tapping his desk top as if he was sorely missing Happy Hour down at the shrink's lounge, 'is for you to tell me, in your own words, what happened when you went back upstairs that night. If it fits in with Simon's story, this is over — it'll just be paperwork.'

'What you don't understand, doctor,' I said, 'what you have failed to understand is that I'm perfectly aware of the easy way out. However, it's not going to happen. Not this time. You have my statement — I stand by it as given.'

'You want to force a hearing?' He narrowed his eyes. 'Why?'

'Because it's time. It's my turn. It's their turn. It's what my dad would have done; it's what Janey would do; and because I finally understand why they would have felt they had to do it.' I lifted my jacket from the chair and walked towards the door. 'Thank you for hearing me out, doctor. But now,' I turned and smiled, '"There will be time, there will be time ..."'

'For what?'

'"To prepare a face to meet the faces that you meet; There will be time to murder and create."'

'T. S. Eliot?'

'Got it in one, doc. Robert Burns was not my dad's only area of expertise. I learned a lot from him, even after his death. Sometimes I'd sit in his study teasing my tongue with a drop of Glenfiddich and reading through some of his other volumes and that's just one that stuck. "I know the voices dying with a dying fall."'

I was almost at the door before he said anything else.

'Tom?'

'Yeah?'

'Did you have fun on your fishing trip?' He smiled.

'I did, I finally caught the big one.'

'How big?'

'Now, doctor, that would just be a fish story, wouldn't it? He was pretty big all right, but now I need to go catch myself an even bigger one. See you on Wednesday.'

Hero? What is a hero? I thought heroes ran into burning buildings to save babies or stormed up hills into enemy gunfire. In any case, I thought, at the very minimum, a hero had to put his or her own life at risk to save others, doing the job they were trained to do and to do it right. How does that make you a hero?

They didn't want a hero so much as a scapegoat. And if I got to be the hero, then that would make Simon the scapegoat, because faulty equipment and bad procedures can only be contributing factors. They needed a human scapegoat. They could fire Simon because he was still within his two-year probationary period. But they probably wouldn't because they would have to admit contributing factors. He had a long, promising career ahead of him and this would set that back by ten years in a provincial tower somewhere while he paid his price.

The muted amber glow of the street lamps reflected on the rain-soaked streets and cloaked the night in a feeble copper light. It had been raining again, the night turned cool — a mid-summer rainstorm? Or were we in for an early autumn? I did not notice what time it was when I wandered out onto the deck. I had fixed myself a Scotch. At a guess, it was two or three in the morning. The nightmare had driven me outside to sit out in the cool night air. To think? To ponder? Hardly. My brain was fogged in — indefinite ceiling zero, visibility zero.

So Simon had confessed to save me, and I had refused to corroborate to save his career.

It was too bad for them that they were forced to go through the process of investigation. They knew it was Simon's incident — he had already admitted it was his fault. But, I contradicted that, and so they were left with no other choice than to take it to the next step: the hearing. But it was nothing so noble as sticking up for my mates that made me do what I was going to do. The fact that I was negligent by leaving my station to chase after Sarah that night remained true, leaving an inexperienced controller alone to cover for me.

I had caught up with Sarah in the parking lot and stumbled over 'I love you', but it came out all wrong and sounded like a dirty secret. I almost choked when I asked her to marry me and come back to the States with me, even though I knew she wouldn't leave her mum at this time. I offered her a poor explanation of why I still had to go back — trying to make her believe that by going back, by getting my job back and by acting like a professional in it and doing what I was good at, it would be the right thing to do, even if it was only to redo a small piece of my life.

I tried to explain that I had given up a chunk of my life when I became a company man, doing something I didn't believe in. My dad had had something to believe in. He believed in education and putting his students ahead of university politics. He believed in opening young minds to the beauty, to the truth of literature, and he believed in fighting the encroaching commercialism that produced mass consumption art and short, shallow attention spans. Janey had the environment and social justice to believe in. And they were both willing to put their ideals ahead of their own comfort and security and put themselves on the line.

Of course, it killed my dad and it killed my marriage. What was I willing to put on the line? It was time to find out.

Sarah was climbing into her car when I thought of the one thing that came so easily.

'Do you want to go fishing?' I asked.

She paused. 'What?'

It had been a small point of contention that I never invited her along on my weekends away. They were what we decided to call my 'alone' time, and she inferred they had something to do with my dad. But I know it still bothered her that I was unable or unwilling to share a part of me she would have liked to have shared.

She accepted the invitation, gave me a warm embrace and I watched her drive away, to her parents home. Then I went back upstairs.

My own words?

I closed my eyes and could still see my nightmare and probably would again if and when I ever fell asleep again. In my nightmare the 737 did not turn in time. It tried to — God dammit, it tried to — but in its steep turn it clipped a wing on the lowered nose gear of the 747. The wing sheared outside the number two engine, and maybe in level flight the pilot could have controlled it still, but in my dream and in the steep bank turn, the sudden loss of lift caused the wing to stall and, already in the turn, the 737 continued to roll over. But before it finished its roll the fuel ignited and the plane was engulfed in a ball of flame. It was the technical detail I knew in my dream that made it all so plausible to my waking mind. Meanwhile, the 747 nosed over and plummeted towards the harbour. Maybe the sudden loss of lift at such a slow airspeed caused it to dive, or maybe the shock the nose section sustained after being struck by the 737 knocked the crew unconscious or killed them. But as one fireball blossomed in the sky and the 747 was a microsecond away from impact, I would wake up screaming, bathed in sweat, with my heart pounding at my rib cage.

Jesus!

So I poured myself a Scotch and came out here to the deck to search the empty streets below. I wondered if Simon was pacing his room — or does the cockiness of youth allow him to escape such nightmares? Was reality and fantasy still safely separated in his world? Did truth and fiction keep their respectful distance from each other? Or did truth and fiction blur in his mind too? And does he have delusions of Godness?

The shrink wanted it in my own words, but what were my own words? Truth? Or fiction? I didn't need words at all. I had the full-length feature film playing in my head. Why did it haunt me? It was not fair. It was not my incident; they had the facts and could read through them to the truth.

I was not lying about everything. The fact was I was responsible because I had a responsibility to be there. I had a responsibility, not to the airplanes involved, but to the controller who was responsible. I failed in that responsibility. That was a fact. The truth was, it was Simon's incident.

I went back to the tower, and walked up the stairs alone. As I hit the top step, I did a quick scan of the work area — Simon was hunched over the computer inputting the billing data and cursing his inability to type — and then the operational area. And there it was, that movie played out instantly in my mind. I froze perhaps only for the split second it took me to comprehend what I was seeing.

A Boeing 737 had just rotated, maybe 100 feet off the ground at most — too late to abort the take-off. At that moment of my glance, I also saw the landing lights of a 747 emerging from the low scud on final approach — they were on a collision course. They had four seconds to live.

'Who's that rotating?' I asked Simon calmly as I went straight for the tower controller's position. If I startled him and pointed out the situation, he could freeze in panic or take a second or two to comprehend. We didn't have a second or two.

'Tasman four-two-two. Why?' the dumb fuck said without even looking up from his task.

I keyed the mike and thought of Ted Kazniak and his serenely calm voice. 'Tasman four-two-two make an *immediate* left turn southbound — 747 traffic opposite direction, break, break, Pacific five-two go around, go around.' It was the longest split-second ever. I stood there, frozen, cold as a corpse, watching.

'Confirm Tasman four — shit!' the aircraft made a hard bank to the left as the pilot looked up and caught site of the landing gear filling his windscreen.

Simon looked up from the computer and yelled his own expletive — then went absolutely silent as the shock of what had almost happened sunk in.

'Pacific five-two is going around,' the 747 pilot said. He, too, saw what was happening and started a steep climb.

'Affirm,' I said. 'Climb straight ahead to two thousand feet contact approach now for vectors back to final.' Instead of unkeying the mike and giving him a chance to complain about the service, I held the button down and turned my attention back to the 737 without pause, 'Break, break — Tasman four-two-two, stop your climb initially at one thousand, maintain your present heading for vectors on track and contact radar now.' Again without pause I hit the comm-button to the radar controller, 'Pacific five-two is overhead climbing to two on the missed approach, Tasman four-two-two is stopping at one mid-harbour for vectors on track. It's a mess, sorry. You better get a centre sup on the phone.'

'Roger that,' the radar controller said in an unflappable voice — again, I was reminded of Ted Kazniak and why we had to keep in control of ourselves if we were ever to sort out the sticky stuff.

'Fuck! Piece of shit!' Simon was getting wound up and started kicking the radar display. It did not take me long to see why that had suddenly become the target of his wrath. The picture was frozen again and, in that still photograph, in that frozen alternate reality, Pacific West five-two was safely well outside the outer marker being vectored for his approach.

Simon was just looking for something to kick instead of himself, though. It was his fault for letting his attention get diverted — the system played him up like a chump, but, in the end, it comes down to one person who is the last line of defence. We all helped him to fail. At the end of the day, though, he was the man who should not have let his attention get diverted. This was going to cost him big. Young guy, newly rated, still on probation — this could very well cost him his career. If he was lucky enough to keep his job, he would be sent so far away he would never be heard from again. They would probably just fire him. No one was going to sweep this one under the rug.

'Simon, stop it,' I commanded. 'Get a hold of yourself.'

'You saw this piece of shit. It's frozen up!'

'I see it. Now listen to me carefully. Take a couple of deep breaths and calm down for a second.' I paused long enough to let him know I really expected him to do it.

'This fucking radar!'

'Stop going on about the radar.' I reached over and pushed his shoulder enough to turn him towards me. 'Look at me. Now do it — take a couple of deep breaths.'

He glared at me with deep resentment, but did as he was told. He was not just angry at the equipment, he was not just angry with himself, he was angry at me for interceding — for taking over his position. It was the worst thing for his mortally wounded ego. But I had no other choice — one ego up against a couple of hundred lives?

'This is what you're going to do,' I explained to him slowly. 'You're going downstairs to the ready room —'

'I can stay up here.'

'No you can't. Now I'm not giving you a choice. I'm the damn supervisor here and arguing with me is only going to make this bad situation worse. Now, I'm telling you what you will do. You will go downstairs to the ready room, you're going to have a glass of water or something, you're going to sit down at the table, and you're going to write your statement — short and to the point, one paragraph only. Just the facts, no expletives. Then you're going to sit there and wait for me to come down. But most importantly, you are not to speak to anyone about this. Do you understand?'

He looked at me, his eyes ablaze with resentment, but said nothing.

'Do you understand, Simon?' I repeated.

'Yes.'

'Good. Now repeat those instructions to me.'

He shook his head in defiance. 'I heard the instructions.'

'Repeat them.'

He turned his eyes away and remained in rebellious silence for several moments, then reluctantly gave me an abbreviated version of my instructions.

'Good. Now go.' I turned my attention back to the situation outside. 'And Simon ...'

He paused at the top of stairs.

I looked back at him. 'I'm on your side.'

He offered no response, but continued down the stairs.

I sat down in the chair at the controller's position and looked around. Simon was a good guy — he was a good controller with a future. He made a stupid mistake. At least his was not a demented lapse in judgment as mine had been. Given the chance, it might permanently clarify to him what his priorities are — what his purpose is. Unfortunately, he probably would not get another chance. This was going to cost him big.

Downstairs I could hear the lift door sliding open, then a pause and a muffled exchange of voices as Simon passed whoever was on their way up to the cab to start asking some difficult questions. I had about ten seconds to think of my next move before someone would want to know exactly what happened — what happened to whom and who made it happen.

It was not Simon's career I was thinking about when I picked up a pen and reached across the comms panel.

It's just time for a showdown, I thought. According to the digital clock, it was 2117. It had been a very long day. I scrawled my name on the position log, wrote a 2 and a 1 and paused.

It's just time. I could hear the footsteps hit the stairs.

Well, anyway — let's go out in a blaze of glory, eh? I completed my entry: 2104.

Twenty-eight

Two days later, I was standing up to my calves in the Rangitikei River, flicking my fishing line across the water, then slowly reeling it in just to flick it again. Sarah sat quietly near the river reading a novel. She was tired from the long hard tramp out here and just wanted to rest.

Everything I knew about fly-fishing I learned from Flynn. But I was still not very good at it, so a few weeks back I went down to Whitcoulls and bought the best book I could find on the subject. I would master it one way or another.

My dad did not teach me how to fish. He had only taken me to the river that once, and we sat on the bank with our lines dangling in the water, mine with cheese as bait. And, despite my best efforts not to, I caught a fish. It was probably no more than five or six inches long. My dad made a bit of a show of it as he grabbed my line and held it up to inspect the fish.

'A struggle of Melvillean proportions,' he said with a smile, 'and this time it is man who conquers nature. Look …' he turned to me and pointed to the hook that had caught just on the fish's lip, 'barely scratched him. Even as the hunter, you are a kind man.' Then he gently removed the hook, bent over and released the fish back into the river. 'Just as long as he remembers — we won this time.' He watched the fish disappear from sight. 'We won this time, old boy.'

I did not learn to fish from my dad, and I wasn't making much progress with Flynn. Sometimes we didn't even come here to fish. Once we even rafted the river in an inflatable. This peaceful, meandering river at my feet was deceptive, for there were fierce rapids around every bend. Whatever our intention was when we came out here, we usually ended up spending more time drinking mountain screwdrivers than fishing. As for Flynn giving me any lessons — sometimes I think his knowledge was more limited than he let on. Either that, or he was not very good at passing it on. His preference was for fly-fishing, which fit my image of fishing more than just sitting on the bank and dangling a line in the water. Maybe he was not the best fishing instructor, or maybe I was not the best student, but after a short time, my mind would drift away like the current and I would wander off to climb a mountain while Flynn stayed at the river's edge. Sometimes he even managed to catch us some dinner. For me, though, I think it was just the idea of fishing I liked.

Still, I was going to become at least as good as Flynn at it. So I bought the book on the subject, and another just on tying my own flies, and decided that I could, in fact, become a fisherman. The only hard part would be killing the thing — doing the dirty work would still be hard. As a fisherman, I was much like I was as a liberal — that is, willing to say I believed in the cause and willing to throw money at it, just as long as I did not have to get the blood on my hands. Maybe today would be different. Maybe today I would know the process from the ideal to the dirty end, and tonight be eating brown trout for dinner

'Watch your grip. Remember you want your thumb on top of the rod.'

I turned my head to the voice. It had always amazed me that a man who charged headfirst through life with his size eleven boots barely keeping up could move as silently as a shadow. He was standing on a rock at the river's edge.

'Gidday, Flynn.'

There was a slight gasp from Sarah on the bank behind me when she heard his voice, and I was somehow pleased with myself that her gasp had also caught Flynn by surprise.

'Cowboy,' he said slowly, 'I thought we had a rule.'

'We did,' I said as I flicked the line out again, 'but the universe is constantly expanding, so how can we expect things like rules to remain rigid?' I glanced up at him. 'I think you told me that. Anyway, Flynn meet Sarah. Sarah meet Flynn.'

'So,' Flynn stood up and smiled, 'you are Sarah. The very love of his life. It's nice to meet you.'

'So.' She stood up on the bank opposite him and smiled back. 'You are Flynn. Domestic terrorist. I thought you were just an urban legend.'

'I'm innocent.'

'I believe you,' she said as she stepped closer to the bank, into the sunshine.

'Well, that makes me feel more comfortable then.' He savoured her radiance for a moment. I think he approved of her. 'Do you know much about fly-fishing? Have you been able to get through to him where I have failed?'

''Fraid not,' she said. 'Mostly just a keen tramper.'

'Never mind all that,' I piped in. 'I bought a book.'

'Very good,' Flynn said. 'Did you bring it?'

'Sure did.'

'Good thinking. We'll need it to start a fire.'

Owen Flynn had disappeared without a trace just before Milton Gorge Tower had been reduced to kindling, and after I did not believe him when he told me he did not torch Freddie Moore's BMW. As the weeks went by, however, with me wallowing in self-pity and feeling that I had betrayed Flynn, and the fishing rod he had bought me for a birthday I didn't have sitting on my coffee table, it eventually dawned on me that Flynn would not be thinking that I didn't believe him. He was not that petty. He knew the BMW looked like his work and even if he was disappointed in me that I was sceptical of his claims of innocence, he would not hold that against me. The fishing rod that he left at my doorstep was a real gift from a friend who didn't know when my birthday really was. And as I sat in my lounge staring at it, night after night, the message changed. What I had read at first as an accusation was nothing of the sort when I started looking at it from the simple, straightforward perspective of Flynn. It was simply an invitation — one that did not need to be written down for the police to use as a lead, one that did not need to be emailed, or checked in the compendium with the corporate logo on it for availability. It was as simple as an invitation from one friend to another that is offered in a raised eyebrow and accepted in a nod. It was an invitation to go fishing.

When I understood that, I knew what I was invited to and I knew where. I just didn't know when. And that came soon enough when I received the padded envelope in the packet. What dropped out after I tore it open was Flynn's small maglite torch.

Another gift? I wondered as I turned the top end, but the light did not come on.

At least he could have put fresh batteries in it, I thought. Then I twisted it open and let the batteries spill out. A tiny piece of paper had been lodged between the batteries. I unfolded it.

'It will light your way. The seventh,' the note said.

I did not look for my compendium with the corporate logo on it. Instead, I consulted the calendar of Arizona landscapes on my kitchen wall. My mother had sent the calendar to me at Christmas with a note that reminded me never to forget where my home was — which had never been in Arizona. All it ever reminded me of was where my mom's home has been for the last eight years and how arbitrary these things can be.

The seventh was the upcoming Friday. I was supposed to work that day, but decided to call in sick and left before dawn that day. I was at the river's edge in ankle-deep, bone-shatteringly cold water by late afternoon. It was early September, and it was still winter out here. I was glad there was only a light dusting of snow and none at river level. But the days were nonetheless short and cold, and the water frigid.

There was no trace of Flynn. I climbed to the top of his hill where he might be pondering the corporate-structure of the universe. I hiked up the river and down again. I sat on a log in front of the hut drinking mountain screwdrivers until I began to sway. Not a trace, nor any sign that he had been and gone.

I built a fire in the wood-burner, boiled up my billy and cooked some macaroni and cheese for dinner. Then, despite the cold, sat outside to eat it, watching the night creep in and marvelling at how truly alone a man can make himself if he tries hard enough, and how tangible aloneness can become if one takes the time to notice. The visual manifestation of the darkness that engulfs a soul moves in around these mountains on a moonless night without a manmade light within a fifty-mile radius. Without the help of a torch, I wouldn't see five foot in front of me. That kind of blackness is blinding. And the sound was not the lack of sound, but the deafening noise of the river and the wind — a world of sounds seldom heard and usually ignored, the sounds of the universe that are tuned out of our daily existence. If I had been less drunk, I would have climbed Flynn's hill to be reminded again of my important place in the corporate structure. I should have. I needed to. At the moment, though, being alone out there, in the mountains, in the dark, at the mercy of nature with a cold, hollow breeze blowing right through me, I was afraid. And somehow it seemed appropriate.

A person can get used to being alone. I grew up alone, for the most part. It was not because of a quiet house and quiet parents. My parents had their lives, generally independent of each other's, and I suspect they had their friends — I know my mom had her circle. My dad had his, I suppose, though I can't recall. His life was elsewhere and he never really let me in to share it. Occasionally, we had our moments, but most times the door was shut and I did not exist.

Nor was it a lack of friends in my life. I had a few, though they all started drifting away after my dad died. I don't know why. It was not a lack of human contact that made someone alone — it was a lack of belonging. One must have community. My dad had belonged to a community that was dismantled. And it killed him. Maybe that was what was happening to my community. Maybe that is what will happen to me.

By lunchtime on Saturday, I figured I would head back out and make the long trip back to Auckland. But then I thought, what the hell. I had the weekend off, there was more macaroni and cheese, and maybe I'd stay another night up here by myself. It might help build fortitude to face the aloneness a second night in a row.

I sat on a flat-topped rock in the sun outside the hut, pondering what encoded message I could leave for Flynn if he showed up here after I left. A note I would stick to a nail on the wall of the hut with a cryptic message, not so much to foil any police detectives who were unlikely ever to be snooping around out here, but just to keep in the spirit of secret messages.

'Cowboy rides through when day and night are in balance.' The vernal equinox was in two weeks, and I assumed Flynn, being a man who was in tune with nature and the universe, would get the hint — assuming, of course, that he would be out here himself before then or ever again. Maybe two weeks would be too soon, but I could hardly say 'two weeks after day and night are in balance' — it just didn't have the same ring to it.

I had decided on that one, and was hunched over just putting the finishing touches on it.

'When day and night are in balance?'

His voice leaning right over my shoulder made me visibly jump enough to bump into him. He still had his pack on.

'Why don't you just say, "Flynn, had to go. We'll try again next month on the twenty-first. Cheers, Tom." What is this "Cowboy rides through again" business? You don't ride horses.'

'It's encoded,' I said. 'And how the hell do you walk around with twenty kilos on your back without making any noise.'

'How is it you can't hear me?' he countered. 'Because you're too engrossed in your own mind instead of listening to the world around you, that's why.'

'And where were you yesterday? You said the seventh.'

'Yeah, isn't today the seventh?'

'No, yesterday was the seventh.'

'Hm,' he said, shaking his head, then shrugged. 'I thought today was the seventh, but what do I know? I don't even own a watch.'

'Today is the eighth.'

'Well, thank God they haven't messed with that logical progression yet. Then it could get really confusing.' He laughed. 'Look, Cowboy, I know you're a Monday through Friday man. Just give me my torch back and the next time I mail it to you and get the date wrong, just make it the nearest Saturday, okay?'

I shrugged and dug his torch out of my pocket, only mildly disappointed he hadn't really given it to me. It was just to be used as a courier.

'And if I can't make it on the Saturday you suggest?'

'Then make it the next. Shit, I don't care, I'd walk out here every week if I could.'

Too simple, I thought. But that was pretty much our network of communication and except for the occasional hiccup, it worked well enough, and we met out here on a regular basis.

All in all, I thought Flynn had done pretty well in evading capture in a small country — although, except for Edwin Tucker, I doubt the police were putting much effort into finding him. Tucker did not have the resources of the police department behind him any more, so after Flynn had been on the run for six months, I came to the conclusion that he could quite easily remain a free man for as long as it took for his alleged crime to be forgotten. Even I did not know where exactly Flynn was living. I gathered that he was living and working on a sheep or cattle station somewhere in this region, somewhere with a 'don't ask, don't tell' policy.

'So how's life in your fascist New World Order?' he asked as he stood on the rock on that much warmer February day and watched my new, book-learned fishing technique, then added without hesitation, 'Don't pull it in so fast. Let it drift a bit and bring it in slowly.'

I relaxed my grip on the rod. 'Pretty good,' I said in response to his question. 'Slavery's been reinstated and we got approval for our corporate work camps. How's life in the terrorist industry?'

He shrugged. 'No dental plan, but otherwise okay.'

I reeled my line in and brought the rod slowly back over my shoulder to the twelve-thirty position, paused, then brought it forward in as graceful a motion as I could muster. The line was launched with a whirring across the slow moving water of the deep pool and landed with a plop.

'Getting better.' Flynn nodded.

'There's been some trouble,' I said, keeping my eye on the line as I tried to get into the rhythm of the gentle current. This was to be my final rendezvous with Flynn. I was hesitant to tell him that I had decided to go back to the States, but instead of waiting until we were drunk, I thought it best to tell him up front.

'For me or for you?' he asked, but before I could answer there was a tug on the line and our attention was immediately drawn to that.

'Let it out a little,' he said.

'I know!'

Sarah jumped on a rock. 'Oh, my gosh, I see it. He's huge.'

I started reeling him in a little and there was a thrashing in the water.

'Now let it out again!' Flynn said, stepping knee deep into the pool.

'I know! I know!' I yelled as I played tug of war with the monster trout, wearing him down, just as the Corporation has worn me down. Reel him in, give him some slack, then pull him back in. Back and forth the struggle went on. 'Jesus, this things got some strength.'

'He's a beaut, Cowboy, and he's getting tired.' Flynn was wading deeper into the pool and every time I reeled in, I stepped in deeper. Even Sarah was knee-deep by now, just getting closer to the action. We had him surrounded.

My arms were getting tired. I didn't know who would give in first, me or the fish, until Flynn reached in and pulled him out of the water, thrashing and struggling. He carried the thing, still struggling, all the way until he could lay it on a rock and hold it down with his knee. He reached into a pocket and pulled out his all-purpose pliers and started slowly, even gently, working the hook out of the fish's mouth.

'Just through his cheek, I'm surprised you didn't lose him.' He held the dislodged hook up and smiled. 'But I can tell you, we're going to feast tonight. Well done, Cowboy! You've finally caught the big one.' Then he pulled a knife from his belt and was about to jam it straight into the fish's brain to put it out of its continuing misery.

'Flynn,' I said.

He turned to me, still smiling, still panting.

I waded over to the rock. And put my hand on the fish.

Flynn raised his knee and stood.

The fish was still full of life and struggle as I lifted it and held it tight in my arms, embracing it lest I lose it.

I looked at Flynn, who just smiled as he slipped his knife back into its belt sheath. He shook his head. 'You're hopeless, Cowboy. I just hope you brought plenty of vodka.'

I lowered my whole body into the cold water, embracing the struggling fish.

'An' let poor damned bodies be,' I said as I released my embrace and watched the thing swim as far and as fast away from me as it could. 'Just remember we won this time.'

TWENTY-NINE

'So,' Flynn said as he took another long drink of his mountain screwdriver, the three of us sitting atop the hill, enjoying the sunset and a pre-dinner drink. 'There's trouble a-brewing down in the valley. For me or for you?'

'For me,' I said, then filled him in on the details of the incident, the investigation — how Simon had lost track of what he was doing and how I came back to the tower only seconds before disaster, and why I was forcing the matter before an investigation board. And then the offer from the FAA.

'Making a last stand, Cowboy? Going down with a six-shooter in each hand, eh?' He grinned, but it faded.

'Well, not quite that dramatic. At least I have a place to go to.'

'Go back to,' he muttered into his mug.

I looked at him. 'Whatever. It's just something I need to do.'

'At least you'll have a beautiful woman by your side.'

I exchanged a glance with Sarah. 'Well, we're not, exactly ...'

Flynn paused, lowered his mug and shifted his gaze between the two of us. 'Oh, don't tell me, Cowboy, you fucked this one up too? You guys are so...' He waved his mug in the air searching for a word. 'I mean, it's like you finally find someone who's not crazy, who's obviously good for you — isn't that what you've been telling me about for the last God knows how many months? You feel like you belong, like you're ...' and he waved his mug around before giving up and raising it back to his mouth.

'Synergistic?' I offered.

Flynn paused, lowered his mug and stared at me. 'What the fuck does that mean? I just mean you look good together. God, no wonder she's dumped your arse.' He took another drink. 'Synergistic! What an arsehole,' echoed in his mug.

'Well,' Sarah said hesitantly, 'I guess that is not quite the case. I mean, it's me —'

'Oh, no,' Flynn interrupted her. 'I guarantee it's him. Now,' he stood up and took a step closer to Sarah, 'you don't ever tell him I told you this,' he said, me sitting on a world of lichen just two feet away, 'but he's a pretty good guy, over there. Not a bad fisherman, lacks the killer instinct, has some dirty little secrets, I'm sure. But all in all, he's a good man — sometimes gets a bit confused what kind of man he wants to be but, what the hell, don't we all? I mean, you wouldn't, of course, 'cos you're a woman. The thing is, he's a good man, and he's a good loyal friend.'

'You're drunk, Flynn,' I said and exchanged a look with Sarah that said something more than that she was being amused by him. She was looking at me as if she saw something no one else wanted to point out — 'Excuse me, Mr President, but you have salmon pâté on your tie.'

'No, I'm not,' Flynn turned to me defiantly, almost angrily. 'But we have to go fix our non-fish dinner and get some food in our stomachs, because I have something important to talk to you about. And it's only because you're my loyal and trusted friend that I am willing for the beautiful Sarah to join us, because if you trust her, then I absolutely trust her too. Then,' he bowed to Sarah, 'and only then do I plan to get absolutely, stinking, shit-faced drunk. Now let's go eat.'

An hour later we were finishing up the feast that Flynn had packed in, and with Sarah's and my meagre, freeze-dried meals added to the pot, I would say we even overate that night. I didn't push Flynn to tell me what it was he wanted to talk about, but by now he seemed completely sober as he drank his tea from the same tin mug that would be used for mountain screwdrivers later on.

'Anyway,' Flynn finally broke the long silence as he swirled his strong, black tea around in his mug. Sarah and I were seated next to each other at the table opposite him. 'I don't think you should do it.'

'You mean take them on during the hearing? You're not one to back down from a fight, Flynn.'

'No, it's not that. It's just that you're a good controller. At the end of the day, the world needs good controllers. If you quit, then what? Maybe you've made your point, maybe not. But there's still going to be one less good controller to keep things moving. Just imagine if you hadn't been there on Thursday night?'

'What about you? You didn't put up much of a fight.'

'Yeah, well, that was different. I wasn't a good controller.'

'That's ridiculous, you — '

'No,' he stopped me, 'listen.' He took another drink and stared into his mug for a long time in silence. 'It was mostly bluff. I was the way I was because I didn't know how to do it properly. I didn't know the rules, so I made up my own. But to be honest ...' he paused again to take another drink. 'I gave them enough excuses over the years to sack me. It would have made it easier for me if they had — but with Thornie,' he looked up and rolled his eyes, 'I mean, how can you compete with a guy who puts the same single word on everyone's yearly performance appraisal: "outstanding"? He wasn't doing anyone any favours in the end.'

'Why didn't you just quit if you felt that way?'

'Scared, I guess.' He shrugged. 'I didn't know what else I could do. That's why I was so envious of Amanda.'

'Envious? Of Amanda?'

'Yeah — and you. You guys were both competent controllers. Safe. You were focused on what you were supposed to be doing, especially Amanda. She had other things going on. She was so dedicated to her studies. She could map out her whole career and where she wanted it to go. All I could do was get up in the morning and hope that I could get through the day without hurting anyone.'

'You were better than you give yourself credit for. We all occasionally struggle with our self-confidence.'

'Maybe so, but I know I was relieved when they gave me the boot. It gave me a reason to be angry with them. It gave me someone to blame. It gave me a reason to feel hard done by.'

I nodded, but said nothing.

'It worked out for the better, you see? But you — you can't bail out like I did. Like I said, they need good controllers.'

'They need them in the States, too.'

There was the tiniest flicker of anger that crossed Flynn's face. He stared into his mug again, then lifted it to his mouth and downed the remainder of his tea. 'I need you.'

'How's that?'

'I need your help. There have been some changes in my life and I can't go on being a fugitive.'

I shook my head. 'Changes?'

'I'm, ah …' he shook his head slowly, then started laughing. 'I've been a cowboy — working on a station in the Waikato.' He looked up and smiled. 'Kind of ironic, isn't it? But you know something, I think you might have been bullshitting us all this time about being a cowboy. You don't know the first thing about cowboying, do you?'

I shrugged. 'Just a single strand in the web of deceit that is my life.'

He laughed again, shaking his head. 'Anyway, I'm going to be a family man.'

'What?'

'I met this girl, Carrie — Caroline. She's a good, hard-working woman, who can toss hay bales with the best of them and drop a rabbit on the run with a single shot at seventy-five paces. And, you know the best part?' He leaned forward as if he was going to divulge a secret I didn't want to know. 'She's the boss's daughter.'

I nodded.

'Anyway — one day we were shagging like rabbits in the middle of the back paddock, and she picks me up and drops me into a fresh cowpat.'

I grimaced.

'It wasn't that bad, though. I thought, hey this isn't such a bad life. I don't know what came over me. I guess deep down, I'm an old romantic like you. So when Carrie proposed to me in that steaming cowpat, I said, "Yeah, what the hell, let's give it a try. Why not?" Anyway ...' he shrugged again, 'maybe we'll want to have some sprogs and I figured it wouldn't be any good for a kid if his old man was always on the run, so I thought I'd better pay that debt off early. You know, clear my good name. That's what I need you for. I figure if I went in and confessed to the crime, they would go easy on me. Maybe I could just get away with doing a few months in jail or something. I could do that.'

'But you're innocent.'

'Yeah, I know, but if I fight and lose, then they probably would come down harder.'

'I'm told a fight isn't worth fighting unless you have something to lose.' I swirled the last gulp of my tea around in my mug. 'Besides, maybe I have something that will help us. It might be nothing, but ...' I drained the last of the tea and stood up. 'Have you ever heard the expression "it's taps"?' I turned to him, 'You know, like "It's taps for Flynn, it's taps for Cowboy." I mean, is that a common expression here? I thought "taps" was more an American military thing.'

Flynn shook his head. 'Never heard it.'

'Actually you have — at least once. I've heard it twice here. It's just something that's been nagging me for a couple days and it got me thinking. I have a theory — at least I'm working on it. I think Woodchuck is trying to get rid of Freddie Moore. He's too smart a guy to give me that many clues over one conversation at a urinal.'

'I'm not sure I want to know any more.'

'Well, for one thing, he torched Freddie's BMW.'

'He'd never admit to that. There'd be no proof.'

'I know, he was just trying to point me in the right direction. So I took a drive down to visit our old alma mater — Milton Gorge Aerodrome. Except it doesn't exist any more. Instead they're building a flash new suburb called St Miltonville Estates.'

'So I heard. Carving the place up like a fresh kill. It's tragic.'

'Yeah. Anyway, I did some snooping around. They have an office there. I pretended I was a buyer, asking a few questions. The girl who worked there was new and didn't know anything about the place when it was an airport. But she did give me a few threads to tug on.'

'Like what?'

'Just something she said about her bosses. Anyway, I'll explain later. Let me just ask you this — are you willing to risk your freedom for this? You would have to come forward, now, this week. Not to confess, but as an innocent man. If my theory proves wrong, of course, you're screwed.'

Flynn shrugged. 'I've already decided to give myself up.'

'Right. Here's the plan. You fix the mountain screwdrivers, while I come up with a plan.'

'What do I do?' Sarah asked.

I looked at her. I loved her so much. Really, I just didn't know how to say so. 'You could do the dishes.'

She smiled. 'I will, but if you ever tell Amanda, I'll kill you.'

I got up and went out to sit by the river's edge and think. As darkness settled in over the river, I stood on the bank scanning the water for movement beneath the surface. I hope that fish was still alive and just nursing a sore cheek. I sat down on a rock and stared into the deepening shadows across the river. I wished my dad or Janey was around to give me some advice on how to take on the Man.

It was a full thirty minutes before Flynn joined me — I suspected he helped Sarah clean up and they probably did some talking of their own.

'Just one thing, Cowboy. You should be careful what you're planning. It may not be worth it. Maybe these guys are more dangerous than you think. You don't know what they're capable of. Remember what you told me about Thornie? Remember your first reaction the day he died? All I'm saying is, you never know, there could be some truth in it. Sarah and I have been talking, and she doesn't seem to think you're as crazy as I think you are. And you never told me she was a doctor.'

'Just pre-med,' Sarah interjected.

'As good as,' Flynn shrugged.

'Well, it's a bit late to be proven now,' I said. 'Thornie's been buried for a year and a half. It was already too late when Freddie Moore washed the evidence. Forget it, let's just try to support the accusations we can make.' I stood up and paced the river's edge. 'We don't have much time — only Monday and Tuesday to dig up something, and on Monday I have to go in for my psych assessment.'

He handed me my mug, filled nearly to the brim with one of his stronger mixes. Sarah was a few steps behind him. But it was what was hanging from his shoulder that caught my attention.

'What were you planning on doing with that?'

He took the hunting rifle off his shoulder and held it up. 'Oh, I brought it in case I felt like doing a little shooting this weekend.' Then he held it out to me. 'Why don't you give it a try? I bet you never even fired a rifle in your life. And you call yourself a Cowboy.'

I stared at the gun.

'Go ahead, take it. Give it a try, Cowboy. Pretend there are some Indians across the river. Or maybe a demon or two.'

I did not reach for the gun. 'No thanks, I'll pass.'

'Come on. You don't really have to kill anything. You don't even have to shoot at anything. Just shoot at a log that looks like Freddie Moore or a shadow or something. Shoot at a memory if you have to.'

I looked up at him, then the rifle, then turned my attention toward the shadows on the far side of the river.

'Come on,' Flynn urged, 'just one shot.'

Just one shot.

I set my mug down and faced him. Then slowly reached a trembling hand out to the polished wood of the gunstock.

Flynn handed me the rifle.

'Look, hold it up like this.' He stood behind me and showed me how to hold the weapon. I lined up the sight with a shadow on the far side of the river. The evening was settling in, the shadows longer and blacker. I lowered the rifle and tried to hand it back to Flynn. 'Another time,' I said.

'Come on, don't be afraid of it.'

'Tom?' Sarah sounded concerned. 'If you don't want to ...'

I raised it again and tucked the butt into my shoulder. I aimed at the same black shadow. I did not hear the wind in the trees, but could feel the cool breeze. On Flynn's instruction, I slowly squeezed the trigger. The gun jumped with a pop that shattered my silence and left my ears ringing. I do not know where the bullet went — into the shadows, into a blackness that cannot be killed, but can only be stirred into wakefulness. The bitter, burning smell of smoke stung my nostrils. It crept along my skin and seeped into my sinuses. It drifted into my brain and permeated the bone and tissue. I heard something coming out of the darkness of long ago, and then I opened a closet that held nothing but nothingness. I turned in slow motion to Flynn.

'Watch that thing,' he said catching the rifle as I let it slide from my hands. 'What is it, Cowboy?' Flynn asked, though his voice sounded muffled to me, the ringing growing louder in my ears.

'Tom!' I heard the muffled sound of Sarah's voice.

'I — ' My throat was tight and would not let the words escape. My breath was short, as if my lungs were shrinking.

'What's wrong?' He asked again.

'Tom!' Sarah ran to my side and held me.

'I — ' but still my voice was silenced. Still the ringing in my head. I stumbled a few steps and reached out to a tree for support, then slowly sank to my knees on the muddy bank. Darkness pulled in around me and wrapped me like a shroud. Tears blurred my vision. The smell of the gunpowder cut through my brain, it cut through my life.

Flynn was holding onto my shoulders, saying something that I did not hear, or could not hear. I looked up at him. *'An' let poor damned bodies be,*' I whispered.

'I don't understand, Cowboy. What's wrong?'

'I — '

'What's wrong? Are you sick?'

'I did it,' I said. I tried to breathe but my chest was so tight. I fell to my knees and threw up my dinner.

'Tom!' Sarah held me as I heaved. She was crying.

'I did it,' I said in a gagging whisper.

'What did you do?' Flynn knelt down on the other side of me and had his hand firmly gripped on my shoulder. My hearing was fading in and out.

'I did it,' I said again. The shadows of the night were gripping me, suffocating me, crushing me like an insect. I tried to breathe, but could not. I hung my head.

'What, Cowboy, what did you do?'

I looked at Sarah, then turned my head and looked at Flynn.

'I killed him.' I looked over my shoulder at Flynn. 'It was me, all because of me. I killed Thornie.'

THIRTY

At 8.30 on Wednesday morning I was at my desk, in my office. At that time of day, it was normally advisable to draw the blinds to keep the morning sun from heating the room up too much, but I was enjoying the flood of sunlight and the warmth, and focusing on the illuminated dust particles hanging in the air. What law of aerodynamics kept them floating? I wondered.

I felt purged of everything. The last few days since the river were spent house cleaning. So much house cleaning to do.

The long walk out from the river was quiet, in thought and speech. Flynn had walked out in a different direction. I had been tired, emotionally drained, and Sarah did not try to make me talk any more than I wanted to. She drove back to Auckland and we spoke little — only occasionally reaching a hand out, which I would take and enjoy her warmth, her life, her wholeness. Flynn had departed in his direction with his instructions and I hoped I would be seeing him again.

When I had described the scene in Thornie's office on the day he died in greater detail, it was Sarah who came up with an idea. We made a stop at the old Warbirds hangar, now more of a warehouse doomed for demolition in St Miltonville Estates, and dug around some old boxes until we found what we were looking for before I dropped her off at her parents' house. My instructions from her were explicit: 'Go straight home, no drinking, and go right to bed.' I had no choice but to obey her.

She hugged me tightly. 'Are you going to be okay? I could come stay with you tonight.'

'I wish you would,' I said, hugging her tightly back. 'But for my reasons and not yours.' Then I released her and smiled. 'I'll be okay.'

And every day, since then, the house cleaning had continued. I made some calls on Monday morning and did house cleaning, went to my shrink appointment and did some more house cleaning, which went on well into the evening, then went home and started packing my belongings into boxes and, finally, literally cleaned the house.

Tuesday I went into work and took care of business.

And by Wednesday, I was purged of everything and all I was left to do was ponder what law of aerodynamics kept dust particles afloat — anything to keep me from the last few tasks at hand. It was a good feeling and a bad feeling in one.

I reached for the phone again, and again replaced the receiver.

Silly me — not everything is governed by the law of aerodynamics. Some things answer only to the law of gravity — the dust particles are simply lighter than the air surrounding them. And then some things answer to no law at all.

I had picked up the phone receiver three times and replaced it three times without dialling. I wondered if my bottle of Glenfiddich was still in my bottom desk drawer or if it was in the boardroom marked 'Exhibit A'. I dared not look.

At 8.49, I finally picked up the receiver, dialled the number and held it to my ear. It rang three times on the other end before she picked up.

'Hello?' she said. Her voice was so familiar — confident, but friendly and inviting response. 'Hello?' she said again as she waited for me to say something. I was not sure if I was going to say anything, I had just wanted to hear her voice.

'Hey ...' I finally said, my voice cracked. 'It's me.'

'Tom?' She asked with some hesitation.

'Yeah.'

'Tom, what a surprise to hear from you. How are you?'

'Good.'

'Where are you calling from?'

'I'm at work — in New Zealand.'

'Still? I thought you said you'd only be there for a year. It must be two years by now.'

'Nearly two.'

'So are you staying there?'

'How are you doing, Janey?'

Amanda probably would have frowned on my using a company phone line to call my ex-wife in America, but I had already handed in my resignation the day before, and figured even if they did check their phone bill, nobody would complain. I justified it as being part of my severance package.

'I'm fine,' Janey said. 'How are you? You sound funny.'

'I'm, ah — I'm all right, I guess. I just wanted to call and say hi. See how you were doing and all.' That was not completely true. I think I had another reason for calling, but I was still undecided what that was. Ever since the idea of going back first came up, and as it came closer to reality, I had been wondering: just how far back does one go? I was picturing it as going back completely — forcing back the hands of time and being in my old life again, but doing it right this time. So it seemed natural to call Janey, not that I was even interested in getting back with her — I just wanted to know she was still there, fighting the good fight, standing up for the same things, and make sure in my absence she hadn't run off and married a Republican lobbyist or something.

'Well, things are good,' she said. 'I got a job working for the Hope Foundation.'

'Great. Must feel pretty satisfying.' I did not have a clue what the Hope Foundation was, but would not have been surprised if Janey told me we had contributed regularly and been to numerous rallies on their behalf. I smiled at the thought.

'Yeah, I enjoy the work for the most part, and the people are great, but the place has its own problems with company politics.'

'You're going to get that anywhere.'

'Yeah, I guess so.'

'Anyway, I'm happy for you.'

There was an awkward pause as she waited for me to get to the point of my call, but I had had no point.

'Tom,' she said, 'there's something else I should probably tell you.'

'What's that?'

'Ray and I are getting married.'

'Oh, really? Then I guess I should congratulate you. That's great, Janey.'

'Are you going to be okay with that?'

Okay? Why does she care if I'm okay with that? I'm her ex-husband. I'm the last guy on earth she needs to seek approval from now. It's been decreed by the courts of the state of California that I am the Other. So why does she ask if I'm okay with that?

Because she still cares. Because it is in her nature to care.

'Yeah. I am happy for you, Janey,' I said and meant it. I guess I still cared, too. At that moment, I realised I was not calling to have my old life back. I was calling to let it go.

'Thanks, Tom.' There was a momentary pause. 'How about you Tom? How are you? Have you met anybody?'

'Yeah, I think so. Listen, Janey, there's something I wanted to tell you.'

'What's that?'

'You know when we went out that first time. I mean, when we went out to the nuclear power station and got arrested?'

She laughed. 'A girl doesn't remember a first date like that.'

'Yeah, well, I've been lying to you. I was never arrested that day. They let me go after a couple of hours. I had dinner at McDonald's, went to an Arnold Schwarzenegger movie and stayed in a motel that night.'

She laughed again. 'I know that, Tom. I mean I didn't know about the Schwarzenegger film, which may not be forgivable, but I knew they released you.'

'Really? How did you know?'

'Because I asked them to take it easy on you. I was worried about you. It was your first time out. I told the police you were not actively engaging in the protest and that you only went along to get into my pants. They thought that was pretty funny and a little pathetic and then told me not to worry.'

I laughed. Ol' Janey. What a hard case that woman was. 'So why didn't you ever call me on my lie?'

'Because I liked you, and I didn't want to lose you.'

'Thanks, Janey.'

'It was a small lie, Tom. It's the big ones you have to worry about.'

'I know.' I glanced at the clock on my wall. 'I have to go now. Take care of yourself. Ray's a good guy, I hope he makes you happy. You deserve it.'

It was two minutes before nine when I hung up. I was due in the boardroom for my inquisition at nine, but they would have to wait a few minutes. There was another phone call I needed to make first. Something at that very moment I decided I had to let go of. This time I needed to work without a safety net. By my calculation it was mid-afternoon in California and I might not have another chance to call before the close of business there. I dialled the number at the bottom of the letterhead, then turned my attention to the dust particles suspended in the sunlight as I listened to the phone ringing in a distant land under the far side of the sky.

Falling, flying, tumbling, turning. Defying gravity, defying one law and living by their own.

Freddie really felt some things were just beneath him. He was upper management, for God's sake, and here they had him sitting on an Investigation Panel, questioning controllers on some petty little screw-up. But this was the Hardy deal, and he needed to be there — not only because Woodcock was getting to be a bit unstable again, but because he wanted to get a real close measure of this Hardy fellow and see what potential there might be.

He was standing on the patio outside the staff lunch room, enjoying the quiet and the warmth of the morning sun and watching the planes come and go, wondering how he got stuck with this duty that was far more suited to Woodcock or Gloria LaCoste. He took a sip of his coffee and lifted his face to the sun. It was going to be a fine summer day. Oh yeah, it was the Hardy thing, he reminded himself.

His only real concern was that it might eat into the Fiji trip. His plane to Nadi was not until later in the evening, but if for some reason this thing went into a second day, it would mess up his beach time — and, God knew, he was due for this vacation. No, not a vacation — a management team-building seminar, he reminded himself, and smiled as he took another sip of his coffee.

Still, it suited his plan to get involved in the investigation for a couple reasons. For one thing, it was Hardy they were grilling today — which might be used as leverage to speed up his rather sluggish response time in resolving the Malahide matter. Why that boy was so resistant to joining the team, Freddie couldn't figure out. Lazy, confused, drinks too much. Freddie considered the possibilities. Or just plain nuts — that was the most likely scenario.

Another reason Freddie could see for his participation in this thing was Amanda. She decided this incident was more important than her attending the Fiji function, which suited Freddie down to the ground. Amanda always put such a damper on the fun. The way these things were supposed to go was that they'd sit around for a couple of hours drinking coffee and eating pastries and talking about what to do for the next year:

'What's the plan for the coming year, people?'

'Make more money!'

'Excellent! Now, as a team-building exercise, we're all going to play beach volleyball and then see if we can get Gloria LaCoste drunk enough to do that striptease act again this year.' For a nasty looking bat, she had surprisingly nice tits.

Amanda, on the other hand, would come armed with all sorts of plans and proposals and budgets and projections and PowerPoint presentations and keep them locked up in the conference room for two days discussing an endless array of variations on her theme for making everything more efficient. So it was perfect that she found it necessary to bow out. Now, all Freddie had to do today was make sure this hearing was kept short enough so as not to encroach on his departure to Fiji, yet leave sufficient paperwork behind that would ensure Amanda was busy enough to not change her mind again.

Balance — it's all about striking the perfect balance in life. Freddie swirled the milky coffee around in his mug and turned when he heard the door to the patio open.

'There you are,' Woodcock said with the same worried expression that was becoming a permanent part of his face.

'Carlton, my boy. Good morning.' Freddie smiled. 'I didn't see you at breakfast this morning.'

'That's because you were staying at the Regal Ambassador and I was at the Mangere Motor Lodge. I had an Egg McMuffin at McDonald's for breakfast and burnt my lip on the coffee.' He set his briefcase down on the picnic bench and rubbed his sore lip.

'Oh well, don't let the small things get you down.'

'Yeah, right. Speaking of the small things, Freddie, do you know what kind of car your secretary booked me?'

'Remember what I said about economy, Carlton.'

'A Diahatsu! A fucking pinky-red Diahatsu, Freddie.' Carlton shook his head and snorted. 'It smells like urine. Do you know how embarrassing that is?'

'Surely, you can't be worried about what people think of your rental car?'

'I'm just saying, Freddie, with all the running around I've been doing since 6.30 this morning while you slept in late, you should've let me use the BMW.'

'*The* BMW — you mean, *my* BMW, don't you?'

Carlton looked at Freddie and pushed his glasses up the small bridge of his nose. 'Yeah, how could I forget? Anyway, how do you think it looks when I roll up to my meeting with Sir Dickhead in something that looks like an infected appendix? I'm just trying to remember what you had to say about presenting the right image.'

'How did the meeting go?'

Carlton glared at Freddie for a moment longer, then let out a snort and opened his briefcase. 'Signed and sealed,' he said as he extracted the documents.

'Hang on, Carlton,' Freddie held his hand up and glanced to either side. 'You probably don't want to pull those out around here — too many prying eyes, if you know what I mean. Keep them safely tucked away in your briefcase for now, and we'll go over them later back at my hotel room.'

'I've got to tell you, Freddie,' Carlton shook his head as he returned the documents to his briefcase and closed the lid. 'This is cutting things way too close. How you managed to get this far without their signatures — we could've gone to jail for —'

'Yet it's all working out just as I said it would, isn't it?'

Carlton glanced up at Freddie, 'We still need Malahide.'

'How did that go?'

'He's ready to sign, just as soon as you take care of that other little matter.'

'Yeah.' Freddie rubbed his chin. 'We'll take care of Hardy this morning. Get a hold of Malahide, and tell him his little misunderstanding with our overzealous Auckland staff will be history by lunchtime. We'll meet at my hotel room at 3.00 this afternoon for him to sign. Then we'll be on our way.' He reached across and almost patted Woodcock on the shoulder, but thought better of it. 'This is going to work out fine for everyone — truly a win–win situation. And if we can get you laid in Fiji, it will be a win–win–win situation.'

'Very funny,' Woodcock said unconvincingly. 'Either that, or we'll all be sharing a cell.'

'Never.' Freddie glanced at his watch.

'Of course not. I'll be somebody's bitch in cell block D, while you learn to play golf in minimum security.'

'That's the spirit, Carlton,' Freddie laughed. 'Now, on to other business. We've got a lynching to go to.'

'Remind me again why I have to be a part of this. I mean, they only require one participant from Head Office, which is you and — '

'I need you there, Carlton. You understand the mechanics of such things better than me. Besides, what else were you going to do?'

Woodcock shook his head. 'Nothing but hang out in the Motor Lodge and figure out a way the Chinese can buy a rather significant part of this country.'

I had not expected there would be such a crowd — five of them behind the table facing down the accused. They could have given me a table, but this was part of their carefully orchestrated mind game to make me feel as exposed as possible. A single chair, facing the panel of inquisition — alone and exposed as if I was a raft floating aimlessly adrift on the open ocean. I made a conscious effort to sit erect. I wore a clean white shirt and tie, was clean-shaven, and I even had my hair cut yesterday. I left nothing in my appearance to be interpreted as anything but the finest of corporate citizens, a loyal foot soldier in the war to advance the profit margin.

'Thomas, as you know this is just an informal hearing,' Amanda was seated in the middle. She spoke in the careful, measured style she used during formal meetings — even though, as she said, this was supposed to be informal, which everyone knew it was not. Whether she had dressed especially for the occasion or not, I couldn't tell. She had her usual well-scrubbed look, with her hair pulled back and knotted up, and was wearing a tasteful yet conservative beige suit. She was looking a little bit stiffer than usual, but that could have been the presence of her superiors from Head Office or her watchdogs from the CAA making her nervous. To her left was Freddie Moore and Carlton Woodcock; to her right were two CAA guys: one was a crisply dressed guy I had never seen before, the other was Norwynne Skidmore — someone I had not seen since Thornie's funeral more than a year and a half ago, but had spoken to recently on the phone. He looked tired and old.

'As per the civil aviation rules, Part 12,' Amanda began reading from her notes, 'we are required to conduct an investigation into any serious incident involving a loss of separation. The purpose of said investigation is to identify the facts relating to ControlCorp's involvement in the incident, and to establish, so far as those facts will allow, the cause or causes of the incident.' She looked up from her notes and addressed me directly. 'The composition of the Investigation Panel is determined by corporate policy. That is, to ensure unbiased examination of the facts, we always have at least one representative from Head Office and we invite the CAA to send at least one representative. Of course, you know Mr Moore and Mr Woodcock. They kindly agreed to act as Head Office representatives since they were in Auckland anyway.'

'Of course,' I nodded.

'Only passing through,' Freddie corrected. 'We have important business to attend to overseas and we have a plane to catch tonight.' Freddie winked at me. 'So let's make this quick, eh?'

'The importance of this matter takes precedence over the management seminar,' Amanda said, addressing me but obviously answering Freddie. Our eyes met, briefly but long enough to communicate something to me — something that told me she had resolved not to let Freddie Moore steamroll her. It was just a reflex that caused me to offer her a brief smile of support.

'Yeah, sorry you can't make it, Amanda,' Freddie said, 'but I fully understand your withdrawal from the seminar. I, however, have to be there.'

Amanda ignored him and returned to her introductions. 'We also have two gentlemen from the CAA. Mr Clive Colson, who is the CAA legal advisor.' She indicated the carefully coiffed young man sitting to her right. He was in his late twenties and dressed in an expensive looking tailored suit; he had a sun-bed tan and a small diamond stud in his left ear.

Must be on the take, I thought. No civil servant makes enough to dress like that.

'How do you do, Mr Hardy?' Colson said, when most people would have just acknowledged their introduction with a silent nod.

'I'm well, thank you.'

'And also joining us from the CAA — ' Amanda continued, but I cut her off.

'Mr Skidmore, very good to see you again, sir.'

'Delighted to see you again, young man.' Skidmore smiled. 'And how are you finding life in New Zealand?'

'A little confusing at times, but otherwise delightful. I've taken up fishing.'

'Oh wonderful!' His face briefly lit up. 'Flies, I hope.'

'Of course, what else?'

'What else, indeed! You know, it reminds me of a time Thornie and I were flying in formation over the Kaimanawas — '

'Back on this planet, pops,' Colson piped in, sounding somewhat impatient. He reached over and thumped the table with his index finger a couple of times in front of Skidmore. 'We're not here to chit-chat,' he commanded.

I was smiling at Mr Skidmore and, for some reason, perhaps just for old times' sake, was looking forward to the story. I would have liked to hear of one of Thornie's old antics again. Colson, though, put an abrupt end to that. My dislike for him was instantaneous. What would have been so bad about letting Mr Skidmore tell one little story? What right does this guy have to tell the old man to shut up so rudely and publicly? What corporate structure gave him authority over a man forty years his senior?

'Mr Hardy,' Skidmore said to Colson, apparently unruffled by Colson's admonishment, 'was the best we have ever rated.'

'Yeah?' Colson turned his smirk towards me. 'We'll see about that.'

I understood then why Mr Skidmore was looking so tired — he was subordinated to this posing prick. He was a dinosaur caged up by an ungrateful New World Order and a bunch of guys in blue suits who, combined, did not possess the wealth of life and experience this old guy probably had in his pinky. Skidmore was doomed, waiting to be culled from the system — and he looked like he knew it. All this time I was assuming that life in the CAA had remained the same from Thornie's day — but at that moment I realised the changes were across the board. The CAA had its Woodcocks and Fast Freddies too.

And the good ol' days were forever gone.

In the brief exchange between Skidmore and Colson, I was able to make a quick assessment of those who would judge me. Skidmore would never condemn me. Colson would never acquit me — he was out to make a name for himself and somehow I got the feeling, hanging controllers out to dry was the way he wanted to do it. Woodcock was probably on my side, maybe figuring I could be his sidekick in the new New World Order. Freddie's vote would be determined by which way I went on the Malahide affair, and he would hold off until I gave him an answer. Of course, he was also eager to get out of there and might acquit just to expedite things.

Oddly enough, though, it was Amanda I thought of as being my truest advocate on that panel. A week ago I would have thought she would be happy for this opportunity to demonstrate the full extent of the powers she had over me. Since my return from the river, however, there had been a subtle change in our relationship. Not on her part — on mine. On Monday she had tried to convince me not to go through with this investigation — almost begging me just to tell the truth that it was Simon's fault, and not force the issue. By Tuesday she was giving me fashion advice on how to present the most sober image at the hearing.

I was nervous, even fearful, giving her my resignation. I thought she might see it as my last act of rebellion, but I explained to her about the offer from the FAA of getting my old job back, and that it had nothing to do with the incident. In the end she looked mildly annoyed — and rightfully so, since I was not giving her any notice, just leaving — but mostly she looked disappointed and sad and nodded quietly as she dropped my letter in her in-box. At the moment, I was thinking of the first time I saw her in Milton Gorge, how we were thrown into each other's arms, and how she glowed with optimism. She wore her hair down back then — it was nicer, freer. I remembered the night when she briefly gave in to passion and we ended up wrestling around in the stir-fry under her dining room table — and how we have managed never to mention a word about that night since. Sitting there in that boardroom, watching Amanda trying to find a fair, intelligent and rational solution to a problem that had one camp wanting to hang me and the other wanting to decorate me, I was reminded of Janey. She was willing to put herself on the line for what she believed, willing to stick her neck out.

Amanda was, in a way, doing the same thing. She had cancelled her participation in the management seminar in Fiji — and the chance to mingle with upper management — because she saw this as more important. She was not going to let Freddie Moore turn the hearing into a farce so he could be on his way. Lined up as they were, I started to appreciate the difficult position Amanda was in. She was actually standing up for something here. Ultimately, she was responsible for whatever went on in this facility and, unlike Freddie and Carlton, she knew what that responsibility was. She was accountable to both sets of suits on each side of her and she was not bending to either. She was working without a net and, for some reason, I was sorry to have put her in that position.

'In accordance with Civil Aviation Rule 12.59, we are voluntarily conducting this investigation of the incident which occurred last Thursday, 17 February ,' Amanda was reciting from her notes, 'classified as a serious airspace incident, in which a loss of separation occurred between Tasman Airways four-two-two, a Boeing 737, and Pacific West five-two, a Boeing 747, during which the controller issued non-standard instructions for the pilot to take evasive action, and the pilot subsequently took that evasive action, in order to avoid a possible collision. Do you agree with that classification, Thomas?'

'Yes.'

'We have statements from the two tower controllers involved — that's you and Simon — the radar controller, and both pilots. We have transcribed the tapes for both the tower and approach frequency leading up to the incident, and have analysed all supporting documents.'

I was glad we were using the transcribed scripts instead of listening to the tapes. I had heard a snippet of the tower frequency, and listening to the hesitation in Simon's responses to Tasman four-two-two painted a vivid picture for me of him hunched over the billing system computer, grumbling and swearing and forgetting about what was going on outside the window. It broke my heart to hear that pause, that uncertainty in his voice.

'The facts of the incident are these,' Amanda continued, 'At twenty fifty one,' she glanced at Freddie, 'that is fifty-one minutes past 8.00 p.m., the approach radar controller issued advice to Pacific West five-two that they would be radar vectored for an approach to runway zero-five and then, over the landline, coordinated this approach with the tower controller, during which time he advised the tower controller that Tasman four-two-two must be airborne before Pacific West reached the outer marker and the tower controller concurred.' She turned a page and glanced around at the audience to make sure they were all still following. 'Then, at fifty-nine minutes past the hour, Tasman Airways four-two-two was told to expect departure off runway two-three and advised of the inbound traffic for runway zero-five; at eight minutes past the next hour, approach radar cleared Pacific West five-two for the approach; at nine minutes, tower an immediate take-off clearance to Tasman four-two-two; at ten past, Pacific West five-two reported on the tower frequency as being established on final and that the runway was not in sight; at twelve past, Tasman four-two-two was observed by the tower as passing through approximately 300 feet off the departure end of the runway — that's from your statement, Thomas, and is corroborated by the pilot's statement — and that Pacific five-two was observed to be passing through approximately 500 feet on three-mile final for runway zero-five — again, the numbers are corroborated by the pilot's statement — at which time Tasman four-two-two was issued instructions to make an immediate left turn to heading two-seven-zero, to stop climb at one thousand feet, and instructions were given to Pacific West to execute a missed approach and to climb on runway heading to two thousand feet. Coordination with the approach controller was then completed.' She looked up from her notes. 'Do you agree with those facts, Thomas?'

'Yes I do.'

'Well that pretty much sums it up nicely,' Freddie piped in, glancing at his watch.

Amanda glanced briefly towards Freddie then continued. 'There were a number of contributing factors: the captain of the 747 admitted that they did not turn their landing lights on until they emerged from the low cloud at about four-mile final, and the technician's log supports your contention that the tower radar display had malfunctioned.'

'I don't get it,' Colson, the CAA guy, said and looked at me accusingly. 'Why is there a radar up in the tower? I thought you were supposed to look out the windows.'

'The tower radar display,' I explained to Colson to save Amanda the trouble, 'is used as an aid to the tower controller so that he or she can better sequence departures with arrivals and to identify airborne aircraft. Since the installation of the new equipment, we have been experiencing numerous occurrences when the image on the display has frozen and thus providing us with inaccurate information.'

'Yeah, but you're still supposed to be looking out the window, right?'

'Yes, that's correct. The radar display is only an aid, but we are required to make positive visual contact with the aircraft.'

'Just so we're clear on that.' Colson was looking as if he was just wishing for three minutes alone with a piece of rubber hose and me tied to a chair.

'That the incident occurred,' Amanda continued, ignoring Colson, 'is not disputed. What we are attempting to discern today is who was ultimately responsible for its occurrence and what, if any, contributing factors were involved. Now, Thomas, we have listened to the tapes and the tower controller who issued the route clearance, pushback and taxi instructions, and take-off clearance was clearly Simon Henare ...' she paused for a moment to look down at her notes. 'The voice that issued the evasive action instructions was clearly yours — those two sound bites are corroborated by the position log. Do you agree with that?'

'Yes.'

'However, it is your contention that a changeover took place between the time in which the Tasman Airways aircraft was issued a take-off clearance and the time of the incident and that you then assumed responsibility for the position. Is that correct?'

'That is correct. I took responsibility.'

'So you're saying you assumed the responsibility for the position?'

'I'm saying I took responsibility.'

'*Assumed* responsibility?'

'*Took* responsibility.'

'For the position?'

'For the operation.'

'Hang on a second,' Freddie raised his hands in exasperation. 'You guys are losing me — what the hell are you arguing about? She says "assumed" he says "took" — banana – banahna — what's the difference?'

'I believe our debate,' Amanda said, reluctantly turning her gaze from me to Freddie, 'is one of semantics, Mr Moore. What I'm asking Thomas to clarify is whether he had signed on the position log as being solely responsible for the tower controller's position, not — ' she returned her attention to me, 'what he feels responsible for towards the operation in general as a senior controller.'

'So, Tommy my boy,' Freddie said, 'were you the controller or not?'

'What does the position log indicate?'

'Christ,' Freddie said, again tossing his hands up. 'Okay — let's just say Tom was it. We'll tell him never to do it again, wag our fingers for a few seconds, then get on to morning tea.'

'It's not that simple, Mr Moore,' Amanda said. 'The position log is not corroborated by the other evidence. For one thing, the transmission at ten past — after you claim to have taken over the position — was clearly Simon's voice. You sometimes forget, Thomas, your American accent is quite different from the other voices up there. Secondly, Simon's statement confirms that he was the duty controller at the time of the incident and did not relinquish the position until you stepped in and took it from him and then sent him downstairs at fourteen past.'

'Great,' Freddie said, 'so even better — Tom's the hero and we fire the other guy.'

'Again, not that simple,' Amanda said. 'If that was the case, Thomas would be guilty of intentionally making a false statement, falsifying documents and providing false information to an investigation.' She turned to me. 'Unless Thomas is willing to change his testimony that he had misread the clock and made a mistake about what time he signed on position.'

She's giving me a way out.

'I'm sorry,' I said to Amanda only, 'I can't do that.'

'You realise, of course, that even if it were true, Simon would still share the culpability? As part of the changeover procedure, he is supposed to remain for five minutes after the next controller takes over the position to ensure all relevant information has been passed.'

'I realise that. I'm not trying to protect him.'

'I wonder.' Amanda closed her notebook. 'Since our next participant is not due for another half hour, we will take our break for morning tea now and resume with the statements.'

'What?' Freddie turned to Carlton. 'Is it over? Why don't we just decide who's to blame and finish up? What does she mean we'll resume with the statements?'

'What it means, Freddie,' Carlton said, 'is that you should start deciding what you want to have delivered for lunch.'

THIRTY-ONE

This was going to be one of the easier moves in my life. When I arrived in New Zealand almost two years earlier, I had two suitcases with me. Going back to America, I had barely more than that — a couple of boxes of the few possessions I had accumulated were shipped off the day before. I sold my car to one of the airport security officers and left the stuff Sarah and I bought together when I vacated her apartment that morning, so she could have her own place back. As much as she loved her dear, ill mother, I think she really wanted to be back in her own place.

I leaned back in my chair, feet propped on the desk, and stared out the window at the tower. Yes, the car had been delivered to its new owner; the bank account closed; the mail redirected; my bags packed. Just one last thing on my 'to do' list for today: Bring down ControlCorp. Shouldn't take too long. Might even have time for a beer later.

Of course, it all depended on Flynn playing his part, Tucker playing his, and Sarah seeing what her friends could do at such short notice — and so far, I had not heard from any of them. I looked up at the wall clock. It was 10.50. The Investigation Board was listening to the shrink give his report, then it would be Simon's turn. I would not be back before the inquisition until after lunch. So that gave us a couple of hours to play with.

I had not heard from Flynn, so I had no idea how successful, or persuasive, he had been. Nor did I have any way of getting hold of him — he did not have a cellphone and would not think to call me to let me know if my theory had panned out. I told him he would need to show up by noon on Wednesday, and my guess is if he got to town at 11.30, he would stop for lunch.

Tucker would probably be back in his office by now. His reason for not contacting me with the info was because he was probably waiting for me to deliver my side of the bargain. I had walked into his office on Monday morning and said, 'You want him?'

Only his eyes moved from his paperwork to me. He remained motionless and silent.

'You want Flynn?'

After a long moment's continued silence, he set his pen down, leaned back in his chair and studied me carefully. 'Are you turning him in?' he finally asked.

'No. He's turning himself in.'

'To me?'

'Yeah.'

'When?'

'Wednesday.'

'Why?'

'Because I figure you'd be willing to hear me out first.'

He nodded towards a chair.

'And,' I added, 'because I think you might be willing to trade us a little investigative work for him.'

'Investigate who or what?'

'Ever hear of St Miltonville Estates?'

After I had filled him in on the details, he shrugged indifferently and said, 'I could make a few calls.'

I took that as an agreement. He had not been back to me either, so I was still running on theory — which would have been more of a concern had it not been for Freddie Moore being the next one to walk through my door.

'Tom,' he said in a well-rehearsed, conspiratorial whisper as he slipped into my office without knocking. He glanced behind him down the hall before he stepped inside and closed the door gently behind. 'How are you doing?'

'Very well, thank you. And you?'

'Yeah, yeah, fine. Listen, we just heard from the shrink. I shouldn't tell you this, but I think he and Amanda are setting you up for the big fall. I hate to see that happen.'

'Indeed.' That was a relief to hear because it just confirmed that he was getting overly anxious for me to sign the deed over on my soul. What he did not realise was that before he had even arrived that morning, I had tea with Amanda in her office — perhaps just one last cuppa for old time's sake, or maybe because my paranoia had been subsiding a bit in the last few days and I was starting to see Amanda as more of the ally she was. In any case, she showed me the psychiatric evaluation — she said I had every right to see it.

The guy had given me more or less a clean bill of health. Said that I might show indications of occasional delusions of persecution that were probably rooted in some childhood insecurity, but a strong dedication towards my job. He also said I suffered from the occasional bout of low-level depression. It was an accurate assessment of my personality.

Sane? Who would have thought? But there it was, in black and white; the bottom line — as we in the corporate world like to say — is that I was officially sane. They could not claim that I was out of my gourd at the time and had tried to see how close I could get two airplanes, or that I was suffering from a homicidal episode or delusions of 'godness' as Flynn called it.

Amanda seemed quite relaxed about the impending investigation — I had already given her my resignation and permission to heap all the blame on me if it would help her out, though I did not expect she would. Her only concern was that the psychiatrist had told her off-the-record that he thought I had my own agenda. She was right and I did not lie to her.

'I do. But what the hell — I'm leaving anyway. If you want you can fire me at the end of it — I won't resist,' I said and was about to add, 'I'll go limp,' but did not think she would get it.

She looked down at her teacup, gently stroked the handle and looked like she wanted to say something.

'Amanda, let me have my say — just this once before I go. It's not meant for you, it's for Freddie Moore.'

She smiled at me with that sultry allure she used to use back in the old days at Milton Gorge. 'Do you think it will do any good?'

'No. Probably not, but maybe it will be good for me.'

'Thomas,' she said, then paused and shook her head, 'just be careful. You still have something to lose.'

'I know,' I smiled. 'More than you think.'

'I'm telling you,' Freddie continued on pointlessly, 'the way this head doctor painted the picture — you're a lunatic. A regular mad man.'

'I'm feeling much better now.'

'I'm not joking, Tom.' Freddie moved around my desk and stood too close, hovering over me. 'This is serious. Look, I'm pretty sure I can get this to go away real fast, before you have to go in there again and start answering questions about your sanity and your drinking problem.'

'My drinking problem? I don't think that's an issue — you're confusing your incidents I think.' And just for dramatic effect, I slid open my bottom drawer, pulled out the bottle of Glenfiddich, unscrewed the top and took a long slug from it. 'Ahhh!' I said and held the bottle out to him. 'You see, technically, I'm not on duty today. Here, Freddie, have a belt.'

'I'm serious, Tom,' he ignored my offer. 'They're planning on bringing it up all right; and what are you holding out for? That guy Simon — I heard him talking to Amanda and he's planning on giving you up real fast.'

More bullshit. Simon was presently not even on speaking terms with Amanda. Besides, if anything, he was going to try to beat me to the punch at self-destructing his career. It was one of his faults that he looked up to me the way he did. He saw me trying to get fired and must have thought it was the cool thing to do. I thought Freddie Moore was better at bullshitting than this — maybe he was getting desperate, maybe he was starting to panic.

'Mr Moore, can I call you Freddie?' I asked, still leaning back in my chair — I refused to look intimidated. 'I'm afraid we cannot stop the proceedings just yet. Not until I am given the opportunity to offer my complete defence. There are complexities in this matter that need airing.'

'Oh, I see. That's what this is about. You're pissed off about the radar equipment. For Christ's sake!' He moved back a couple of steps and started pacing the floor in front of my desk. He was uncharacteristically irritated.

The radar equipment was the last thing on my mind.

'You controllers,' he shook his finger at me. 'You think holding me to ransom is the way to get the problem fixed? I'm telling you the techs are working on it!' He turned and paced back the other way. 'This is not the place for you to air your petty grievances.'

'I think it's the perfect place to air my grievances. Besides, it's not about the radar, which, by the way, is not a petty problem.'

'Then what is it about?' Freddie stopped his pacing and looked at me, and for the first time, I think he was really looking at me.

'It's about the truth, this time,' I said. 'It's about St Miltonville Estates.' I was taking a punt I knew was a bad idea even at the time, but I wanted to catch his reaction and in that briefest of moments when a flicker crossed Freddie Moore's face — his eyes narrowed — and then, in probably less than two seconds, his face relaxed and he was calm again. It was at that moment I knew my suspicions were correct.

'What are you talking about?' he asked, a grin tugged at his lips. He was moving into his crisis control mode: calm, cheerful and deadly. 'Saint — what was it?'

'You know, it used to be Milton Gorge Aerodrome.'

'Oh,' he nodded, then grinned at me as if he had just come to understand the heart of my problem — I was past my use-by date. 'Did they sell that property off? I think I did read something about that.' Freddie let out a quiet chuckle as he shook his head. I suspected he knew I was bluffing at this point — like he knew he had covered his tracks better. Maybe he did not sign anything. Maybe he did not even use his real name.

'Tom,' Freddie said quietly as he leaned onto my desk, 'don't make a fool of yourself in there. You are so out of your league. You don't have any idea what you're talking about, or who you're trying to implicate. But, you know, I can see that you're smarter than anybody has ever given you credit for, so I'm going to stop bullshitting you. With your intelligence and lateral thinking, you are exactly the kind of person we need in Head Office — the kind of man I need. Good God, you're miles ahead of Carlton Woodcock in imagination. And not only is it being wasted here, it's positively doing you a disservice. Sign up with me now, Tom, and come with us to Fiji tonight. We're having a team-building seminar, and you can take Woodcock's ticket.' He leaned closer and winked, still smiling. 'Drop today's little crusade — because whatever you think it is, it's only a windmill. Drop the Malahide incident. We will put all this behind us. Tomorrow you can wake up on the beach with a Bloody Mary in one hand and a little brown girl in the other. Over a lobster lunch, we will talk about how to fully utilise your talents, and I promise you, your next crusade will be huge — it'll be global. And I can put you in the major leagues. What do you say?'

I could almost see the flames of hell rising above him.

'I burn easily.'

His smile widened as he stood up, straightened his tie and smoothed back his hair. 'Think about it, Tommy boy. You have until lunch to consider the offer. Try something in there — ' he pointed in the direction of the boardroom, 'and you will be finished. Not only here, but anywhere you think you might be able to run to. You will be finished. We can fuck up your chances of getting back in, believe me we can. Or anywhere else. We can make it so you will never work in this business again. We will hang you by your balls.' He opened the door, then turned back and added cheerfully, 'Enjoy your lunch.'

I found Sarah waiting for me on the patio. She was sitting alone at one of the picnic benches with a green salad in a Tupperware container that she was stirring around with a fork, but she was obviously not interested in eating. I sat down across from her.

What interested me was what was under the table wrapped in brown paper. I pulled it from her side to my side.

'So?' I asked. 'Did your friends down at the med school lab find anything?'

She shook her head, 'I don't know. I didn't want to read it.' She held up a sealed envelope, but did not offer it to me. 'Tom, I'm getting so scared. This could be nothing, but could be serious. Think about what you've already been through over the last few days.'

'What I've been through was decades ago, Sarah. I only had to relive it a few days ago. And, you know, this time it seems much less important to me than the other things in my life right now.'

I paused and looked down at the table top — grey and cracked, weatherbeaten from only a few short seasons sitting outside. I ran a finger along one of the long splits in the wood. I opened my mouth and tried to tell her some of the stuff that was spinning around in my brain — the phone calls I made this morning, the complete uncertainty of my life. But I had already bared my soul to her and Flynn a few nights earlier. It was odd, but I still felt kind of embarrassed around her. I had already shown her all of me that ever was, and I knew now it was her decision. And I wish I knew what she thought of me now that she'd seen the ugliest side of me.

'We don't need to talk about this now, Tom.' She shook her head.

'I want to talk about it now. We may never have the chance to again, because whatever is in that report, whatever happened at that river a few nights ago, whatever happens or never happens again between us, I need to tell you.' I fixated on the cracked wood of the table. 'You ask me if I love you and, believe it or not, it would be easy for me to say, "I love you." I've said it to others in the past.' I looked up at her; tears were welling in her eyes. 'But then it would turn out I was wrong. I thought Janey loved me, I thought my dad loved me, and both of them left me alone. So maybe I just started wondering what the hell love was.'

I tried to look her in the face but found it too difficult, so I focused on the table.

'Shit,' I said. 'If I just knew the words. With you, it was always different. I wanted to say it a thousand times, but was afraid that I would screw it up. It was just never enough to express how much I needed you. With you, I don't know, you're like a homing beacon — it's like I was an airplane and all the needles on all my instruments keep pointing me to you.'

She choked back a sob.

'Excuse me, Mr Hardy.' It was Doris, the tea lady, approaching cautiously in her smock. She glanced between the two of us and obviously could feel the mood in the air. 'Sorry to intrude, but Ms Sheppard just rang down and said they were waiting for you in the boardroom.'

'Thank you, Doris, I'm on my way.'

Doris hastened back inside.

I took the brown paper-wrapped square from under the table, then gently pulled the toxicology report from Sarah's hands. I leaned over and kissed her several times on the face to dry her tears. 'I love you, Sarah,' I whispered. 'But you need to make a decision now, too.'

I left Sarah sitting there and walked away. When I opened the glass door, I caught sight of her reflection, bent over her Tupperware bowl, silently crying.

This could all go so seriously wrong. No sign of Flynn, no sign of Tucker. It was just possible my best option was to consider Freddie Moore's offer seriously. Hell, I didn't even know if the offer was real. I was pretty sure the threat was real. The only thing I knew for sure was that I was walking back into that boardroom and I had no idea what I was going to tell them.

I opened the toxicology report on my way up the stairs, but it was confusing to read and I was parlayed before I could make any sense out of it. As I rounded the corner I paused and stood at the end of the long corridor, looking at the solid wood doors at the far end. Freddie Moore and Carlton Woodcock were down there, talking and nodding. It was my turn again. It was almost one o'clock and in another minute they would start looking at their watches and wondering where I was if I was not in my chair in the centre of the room.

This is crazy. I was crazy. What was I thinking? I've already blamed Freddie Moore for one crime he couldn't logically have committed. I had no evidence to support my other claims. Where was Flynn? I started a slow walk toward the boardroom doors.

'Tom,' the voice said calmly as I passed the open door to my office. I paused and turned.

'Captain Tucker,' I said to the man leaning against my bookcase.

'So where's my man, Flynn?'

'I don't know — he was supposed to be here by noon.'

'We had a deal.'

'I know — I had a deal with him too.'

Tucker straightened up and took a couple of steps towards me until he was standing in the doorframe. He had a manila folder in his hand.

'Thomas!' Amanda raised her voice from the end of the corridor. She pointed at her watch. 'If you don't mind?'

'I'm coming,' I said, but was looking at Freddie Moore, who was looking at me, but saying something over his shoulder to Woodcock, who then turned his attention to me as well. I turned back to Tucker.

'What's that?' I asked.

'My end of the bargain. Where's yours?'

'I said I don't know — look, I'm sorry, I was sure he would be here.' I pushed past him and into my office. He closed the door behind us.

'The evidence suggests you were right about your suspicions,' Tucker said. 'Moore and Woodcock orchestrated the sale and development of Milton Gorge Aerodrome to a consortium of businessmen who call themselves M & G Properties — a group it appears of which Moore and Woodcock are the principals. That's illegal. The evidence, mind you, is circumstantial, but it's enough to warrant an investigation by the Serious Fraud Office, to whom I've already turned the case over. My guess is there'll be some prosecutions ranging from complicity to collusion. But Tom,' Tucker looked me in the eye, 'you can't bring this subject up in that boardroom today.'

'I can't? But you said I was right.'

'Yes, but it's not just your hunch any more. This is real police business now, and if you tip them off in there, you could find yourself in a lot of trouble.'

I sat against the edge of my desk. 'Then I'm screwed.'

'I'm sorry, Tom,' he said. 'Really, I am. You played out a hunch, which turned out to be true and now you can't use it against them to do whatever you had in mind in there.' He looked at the folder, then at me. 'Is it going to cost you your job?'

'Probably, but that's not the point. I was leaving anyway.' I walked over to the window and stared out at the tower.

'The point is, if I recall what you were saying to me just last week, that truth doesn't always lead to justice, and it's hard to fight big money.' He waved the manila file at me. 'And it's true there's some big money here.'

'Yeah, it's nice to be right,' I said unconvincingly.

'However, I still disagree with you,' he said stepping up behind me. 'You know, there are things I believe in too, and I promise you the justice system will do something about these guys. They'll pay for their crimes.'

'Maybe. Maybe not.'

'They will, I promise. Now, you understand, I'll have to go in there with you to make sure you don't say anything to tip them off?'

'Yeah, I understand.' I turned around and faced him. 'You may want to tell the Serious Fraud Office to act sooner rather than later. I think I may have already tipped my hand to Moore.'

'How much did you say?'

'Nothing, really. I just mentioned the name to see if I could get a reaction.'

'Okay, thanks for the heads up.' He nodded, then studied me in silence for a moment as if he was measuring me up. 'You really stuck your neck out, didn't you?'

'You could say that.'

'Well, I'm going to stick mine out now and show you a page of this.' He waved the manila folder. 'Completely off the record of course — but it may make it easier for you to take.'

He pulled out a sheet of paper and handed it to me.

I scanned down the page until I saw the name at the bottom. 'Shit,' I whispered.

'Yeah, I thought it might catch your eye.' He took the page back from me and slipped it back into the folder. 'If your friend Flynn still wants to come forward you tell him to come to me, and I'll do everything I can to help him out. Now I've got a hunch you might be right about him, too.'

'Thank you, Captain Tucker.'

He laughed and shook his head. 'What the hell, Tom, you may as well just call me Eddie. That's what my friends call me.' He held his hand out and I took it.

'Eddie.' I held the door open for him. 'If you'd care to join me, my final judgment awaits.'

THIRTY-TWO

Stay loose, Freddie reminded himself. Remember it is all a game.

Sure, Hardy was getting to be a bit of a worry, but the game was only really challenging when your opponent was worthy. The rest of these schmucks ... Freddie glanced around the boardroom as he entered. No challenge. Hardy was worthy only because he was completely unpredictable. Yeah, it was a worry to see him in a scrum with that cop — but really, what could he have?

'Carlton, something's come up,' Freddie whispered as he leaned in close to Woodcock's ear.

Woodcock glanced down the corridor and caught a brief glimpse of Captain Tucker talking to Hardy. Colson and Amanda were speaking in hushed tones just inside the door. Skidmore had been in the toilet for twenty minutes.

'Shit,' Woodcock said. 'What's he up to?'

'Hardy knows about M & G.'

'What!'

'Now, now, Carlton,' Freddie whispered. 'Keep cool, keep your head on — now is the moment that separates the men from the boys.'

'What do you mean, he knows?' Woodcock asked, trying to keep his voice down. 'How can he — '

'It doesn't matter how, right now. All that matters is that he knows and he's going to try to blackmail us with it.'

Woodcock squeezed his eyes shut. 'Fuck, fuck, fuck — I'm going to jail.'

'No you're not, Carlton,' Freddie said soothingly, 'not if you can just stay calm long enough for some damage control.'

'Damage control?'

'Yes. This is what you have to do. I think it would be judicious if you went down to the St Miltonville office and collected certain documents — certain incriminating documents that might be better off in a more undisclosed location.'

'Me? You want me to go and destroy evidence? Why don't you do it for once? Why don't you get your fingerprints all over this mess for a change?'

'Carlton, keep your voice down. Let's not attract attention. And let's not argue. You know I can't leave until this little circus is over. You, on the other hand, can claim to have another meeting to attend.'

'Bullshit, Freddie. I'm not — '

'Carlton, look,' Freddie reached in his pocket and pulled out his car keys, 'you know that BMW you always wanted? It's yours. Take the keys. Take the car down to the M & G office and do this. We don't have much time. Here's a new BMW for you. My gift to you to show my appreciation for all the little things you do for me.'

'For keeps?'

Freddie nodded.

Carlton stared at the keys in Freddie's hand and then, cautiously, as if expecting Freddie to snatch them away again, he reached for them. 'This doesn't mean I'm happy about — '

'I know, Carlton. I understand. You're a good man. Now go.'

Woodcock started down the corridor.

'Oh, Carlton, wait,' Freddie said as he ducked inside the boardroom and came back with his briefcase. 'Don't forget your briefcase.' He held it up and patted the briefcase.

'Of course,' Woodcock said nervously as he took it from Freddie, then hurriedly left the room.

With Tucker's arrival in the boardroom, Colson and Amanda

stopped their quiet discussion. Amanda raised her eyebrows and said, 'Captain Tucker, I'm sorry this is a closed meeting.'

I liked the way she referred to it as a 'meeting' — keeping the fact that it was a lynch mob on a 'need to know' basis only.

'I've been invited,' Tucker said with a nod to me.

'Oh?' Amanda turned to me.

'Ah, yeah …' I shrugged. 'He's my personal bodyguard. He's quite reasonable. Six bucks an hour, and he's got his own gun.'

'All right, enough, Thomas,' Amanda waved me away. 'Take a seat then, Captain Tucker.'

I caught a bit of Tucker's glare as he turned and walked towards the side of the room — people might think I'm crazy, but even Sergeant Joe Friday had a sense of humour and I think he would have smiled at my witticisms. He positioned himself against the wall next to the door and defiantly refused to sit down. I took my seat and set my brown paper square on the floor to the side of the chair.

'And what is that?' Colson asked.

'Visual aids,' I said, which seemed to satisfy everyone's curiosity.

Freddie Moore, meanwhile, seemed to be enjoying the scene immensely. He was smiling, letting out the occasional relaxed chuckle and had his eyes locked on me — possibly even in admiration. Or maybe it wasn't admiration — there was definitely a glow about him, but I was developing a new theory on the spot that the more threatened Fast Freddie Moore felt, the more relaxed and chummy he appeared. So maybe he was not so much admiring my quick wit as warning me to not try any funny business.

When Skidmore returned to the boardroom — looking well rested and with a level of contentment with life that only a good bowel movement can produce — Amanda and Colson took their seats, and Amanda announced it was time to recommence.

'Is Mr Woodcock coming back?' she asked.

'I'm afraid not,' Freddie explained without taking his eyes from me, 'he had some other, rather urgent business to attend to.'

'Very well, then we shall proceed.' She looked down at her notes and read them silently for a few moments before looking up at me. 'Thomas, we have now reviewed all the supporting documents, listened to the tapes, heard expert testimony and have questioned all the controllers involved. The only evidence that does not fit with the rest is your statement. Therefore, we can only conclude that your statement has been falsified. According to Civil Aviation Rule Number 12.63, you could be subject to prosecution and/or separation from service if the information you have provided us turns out to be false. None of us here wants to see that happen, so we have agreed to give you this opportunity to explain to us, in your own words, what happened. Are you willing to do that?'

I was only looking at Amanda as she was talking to me, but when she asked me if I was ready to spill my guts, I paused long enough to look around the room and I realised that everyone in the room was smiling at me. Tucker's was more of a grimace — waiting in tense anticipation of me divulging sensitive state evidence against Freddie Moore. Amanda was not so much smiling either, but looking very satisfied with herself for being in complete control of this meeting and offering me one last chance to save my future. Colson had been smiling ever since he heard the word 'prosecution' — really, did he think he was going to take me to trial over lying on my statement? Skidmore's smile was unadulterated warmth — the blind love of a grandfather who attends his grandson's trial thinking it is an award's ceremony. Freddie's smile had not changed — only my interpretation of it had. It was as if he too was experiencing the tense anticipation of a father whose kid is about to perform his first public solo — it was my performance that he was waiting for. Would I play the fiddle or sing for these people? If he was uncertain about what tune I had in mind, he didn't show it.

'Yes,' I said after a long silence.

'Proceed,' Amanda said.

Oh Amanda, would it have been different? Could it have been different?

She had spent her life trying to prove something to her father, trying to satisfy the expectations of a man whose expectations would never be satisfied, trying to live up to his reputation, trying to be as big as him. But when I saw Sir Richard Sheppard's name listed as one of Freddie's partners, I realised something that Amanda had yet to. She was already better than him, already a bigger person than her father. Her father would knowingly get involved with guys like Freddie Moore and their illicit business practices to gain a profit — they would portray their actions as the necessary means to gain the objective on the battlefield of business. Amanda, on the other hand, had one thing that would probably make her an early casualty in that war — she had integrity. I disagreed with many of her views, and her corporate spirit irritated the hell out of me. I was convinced she was wrong about so many things. However, the one thing I had never noticed about her was that she had never, and probably would never, sell her integrity to move ahead faster. She believed passionately that the corporate approach to this industry was the right way — and who was I to say it was not? After all, the civil bureaucracy way is not exactly ideal. In the end, Amanda stood for something — something that I disagreed with — but she did so honestly.

I looked at her and remembered the good old days back at Milton Gorge. She used to radiate then, she used to laugh more when she thought of what the future held. Suddenly, I felt sorry. Not sorry for her, but apologetic.

So it was only to Amanda I spoke.

'I have misled this investigation.'

Amanda's face relaxed slightly, as if she knew I was finally going to play the game on her team.

'I have falsified documents,' I continued, 'and withheld information. For this I am deeply regretful.' I glanced around the room. Okay, so the St Miltonville Estates scandal was out. It was not Freddie Moore I was afraid of, or Captain Tucker — I was just not going to humiliate Amanda publicly, which meant all I had left was to get my gripes off my chest. But I would not have any proof to offer that it was anything more than the whinging of a disgruntled employee.

'But my actions,' I continued slowly, 'although unprofessional, were not done out of malice or with a view to cover my own culpability or anyone else's. I felt compelled to do what I did to illustrate a point. I did it to illustrate the very real role I did play in that incident that night. It is true that I was not the controller responsible for the position. It is also true that I was not present in the tower cab during most of the events leading up to the incident. And, furthermore, it is true that I usurped that controller's authority by interceding in what I thought was a critical situation.

'My reasons were not to divert the truth, but to uncover it, because I was guilty of something. I am not talking about my temporary absence from the operation during which time the incident occurred, because it is typical for the supervisor to occasionally attend to duties elsewhere in the facility. I'm talking about my other role in which I failed that night.' I leaned forward in my chair and spoke only to Amanda. 'This job comes down to one man or woman in the chair, talking to the airplanes — that is who we look to as the person responsible — but that one man or woman only represents a single part of a big machine. They are the user interface, they are the voice of the system. In the end, though, the whole machine has to work properly for that person to provide the optimum service. And if things go wrong, we look to that one person to take responsibility for the failures of the system.

'I only took responsibility for the incident of last Thursday night as a controller because there was no place on the incident form for me to take responsibility as the system. But that was my role that night. I was the system.'

'Oh come now,' Colson interrupted, 'Now you want us to believe you were representing the entire air traffic system —'

'Mr Colson,' Amanda held up her hand. 'Mr Hardy has the floor. You may continue, Thomas.'

'Thank you, Amanda. And yes, Mr Colson, I do believe I was

indicative of the infrastructure that failed to provide adequate support for my controller to do his job. I was the one who told my crew that day it was now an important duty for them to spend time inputting data into the computer for the purposes of billing the user, even while they were logged onto a control position. I was the system that certified as usable radar equipment that was, in fact, unreliable. And I was the system that told an inexperienced controller to depart the aircraft in the opposite direction to the landing aircraft so that we, the system, can avoid the politically sensitive issue of noise abatement around the airport.

'And, finally, I failed to ensure that these new controllers understood what their most important role was — what their purpose was. I failed in that because I lost my sense of purpose. Making this business cost-efficient is not inherently wrong in itself, as long as we remain focused on our primary purpose — but what is our purpose? Providing a service to the citizens of this country and the air-travelling public worldwide that abides by the highest safety standards is what we do. Unfortunately, safety is a terribly unprofitable and ambiguous concept. It is something that requires us to spend a lot of money never knowing for sure if it is paying off or not. We will never know how many lives are saved if we maintain the highest standards, but we will know how many are lost as we whittle away at that great big vague area on our pie-chart called "the safety margin" — we will know. We almost found out last Thursday night.'

'Because one man screwed up,' Colson interjected.

'No, that's what I'm trying to say. It is not just one controller we should be putting under the microscope here — it is the system. We need to get clear, all of us, what is the system's primary purpose. Is it safety at all costs? Or is it the bottom line? A little safety traded off for a lot of profit? Is it exploring new commercial opportunities?' I turned and looked at Freddie Moore, who had let his smile droop. 'New investments that have nothing to do with fulfilling our true mission but only serve to distract the attention and resources of the organisation?'

'Bravo, Tom!' Freddie clapped his hands together three times loud enough to interrupt me. 'Did you rehearse that? Or is that something your union provides for you on an inspirational calendar?'

'Mr Moore, please,' Amanda said, but Freddie was not going to back down. I suspected he figured going on the offensive was the only way he was going to stave off a frontal attack. But I was quite through — I was not going to say anything more — that was it from me. Adios, amigos.

'Very dramatic,' Freddie continued. 'You could probably sell that to the BBC. I was the system!' He was doing a not bad Richard Burton impression — or perhaps an impression of Richard Burton doing Winston Churchill. 'We will know, by God, we will know! Tom, really, very good.' Once again he applauded — it was the first time I realised that one could clap sarcastically. 'However, I must disagree with you. Once again you go on the assumption that controllers alone have exclusive rights on wisdom and, once again, you fail to see what you like to call the "big picture". This business is not just about keeping the planes apart.'

'It's supposed to be.'

'Well, it's not. Not any more. Wake up, Tommy boy. What you don't know about the real world is as vast as the sky itself.'

'Mr Moore, please settle down,' Amanda stepped in. Her voice was resolute and did not invite argument. 'This is not the place to get into an argument. In fact, we invited Thomas to make his statement, and he did. That does not mean you are allowed to go on the offensive like that.'

'Fine.' Freddie glared at Amanda — obviously not appreciating her challenge to his authority, but also looking somewhat fearful of crossing her right now. 'We came to settle this matter. If ol' Tom wants to wear it, then I say let him. All I know is I'm going to Fiji.' He stood up.

'Sit down, Mr Moore, this meeting is not over,' Amanda commanded.

Freddie stared at her for a moment, then slowly lowered himself back into his chair without saying a word.

'Thank you, Thomas,' Amanda said, then lowered her eyes to her notes. She was not reading, she was thinking and the moment stretched into many until there was an uneasy silence blanketing the room. Skidmore was nodding and smiling, but I was pretty sure he was still thinking about fly-fishing. Colson was studying me closely with narrowed yet unblinking eyes.

'I think you're right,' Colson finally said, 'I think it was your fault.'

'Mr Colson, please,' Amanda said. She did not look up, but continued staring at her paperwork. Still, she said nothing. Colson backed down and we all waited for Amanda. Even I was starting to get nervous. I shot a glance at Tucker, who shrugged.

'As a matter of fact,' Amanda finally spoke, but paused as she looked up at me, then to Freddie, then back to me, 'I agree with you.'

I straightened up. 'Really?'

'Yes. But what do we do?' She raised her eyebrows. 'This is what I propose ...' she glanced at Colson. 'Number one, that Thomas, you will consider yourself as having been reprimanded; number two, that Simon Henare be placed on two weeks' remedial training and upon the successful completion of that he will begin his probationary period from the beginning.'

'In other words, everyone gets off Scot free?' Colson asked.

'Not at all,' Amanda continued. 'Number three, that we establish a new Investigation Panel to review the operational procedures that were involved in this incident. And we,' she turned to me and offered a playful smile I hadn't seen since we were last eating chicken stir-fry together, 'investigate the system.'

'I have no responsibility to participate in this,' Colson said, looking somewhat regretful that he was not going to get to prosecute me, but Amanda was not inviting argument and he could see it. Without her support, there was not much he could do.

Skidmore smiled, nudged Colson and just said, 'I say, she's a smart one, isn't she? She reminds me of Edna Bascom in her prime. I tell you, you wouldn't want to cross that woman, she could — '

'Oh, for God's sake, shut up,' Colson snapped at Skidmore.

Skidmore smiled warmly at Colson as he tilted his head and studied the young man. 'You know, I knew a guy just like you during the war. Sounded a lot like you when he talked. Dressed nicely, too, just like you.' Skidmore nodded, the glow in his eyes was following a long lost memory. 'They say the North Koreans got him.' He leaned closer to Colson and winked. 'That's what they say.'

Colson stared at Skidmore for a cautious moment, then turned back to Amanda. 'Do what you want, I don't care.' He was sounding disappointed that the day's hanging was called off, and started gathering his notes together.

'Fine by me,' Freddie said, slapping the table, 'as long as I don't have to be on that Investigation Panel. I'm sure Carlton will be available for you.'

Amanda looked at me.

'Sure,' I shrugged. Simon gets to keep his job and Amanda rejects the dark side of the force — not a bad day's work. I smiled at her and whispered, 'Thanks, Amanda.'

She winked back.

'So,' I turned to Freddie and smiled. 'National training manager, you say?'

'No, I don't think so,' he smiled back. 'You're not exactly what we're looking for.'

'I didn't think so.'

Freddie had a lot of damage control to get stuck into and stood up to leave, but, unfortunately for him, it was at that moment that Owen Flynn returned to the world of air traffic control.

Thirty-three

Other than a dog, I had mostly just had the TV to keep me company when I was growing up. As an offshoot of that, one of the more irrational fears of my childhood was finding out what character I would be cast as in a TV show, if in fact my life were a TV show. In a cop show, I think I would be a cop — not a Sergeant Joe Friday, mind you, not the lead; but also not the by-the-book captain who's always riding the hero's ass and completely missing the point. Realistically, I would probably be the hero's comic sidekick — not stupid; I'd offer clever witticisms and the occasional bright but utterly obvious insight, like 'He's dead, Jim.' Beyond the cop show, however, the fear gets more complicated. In a medical drama I would be the likeable guy that dies slowly and painfully, but still has a witty comment to the end. The Western is the one that had me the most worried. I would never have the physical stature or dramatic carriage to be a Matt Dillon. I would totally lack the killer eyes or murderous stubble to be a bad guy — they wouldn't call me anything that included 'the Kid' — which really only left the role of town drunk, or a reliable, but usually intoxicated, deputy named Festus, who somehow always ended up in the horse trough. It was an odd fear, I admit, but that is why it is referred to as irrational.

Why that flashed through my mind at that moment was because Owen Flynn had what I did not. He had dramatic presence. He had timing. They could have called him the Rangitikei Kid, and it would have stuck. The way he came through those boardroom doors, throwing both open as if he was a gunslinger entering a saloon — it was a great entrance. I never could have pulled it off myself. One of the doors would have been locked and I would have dislocated my shoulder.

'Sorry I'm late, Cowboy,' he said to me as he strode in. 'Hope I haven't missed too much.'

'Owen?' Amanda said in a stunned whisper.

'Hi, Amanda,' he said, turning to her.

'Who?' asked Colson.

'Well, I'll be a son of a bitch,' Freddie Moore said — once again, a cheery buoyancy returned to his expression. 'If it's not the mad bomber himself.'

Flynn smiled. 'Hello, Freddie. How's the new car?'

'Less cooked than the last one.'

Tucker stood up straight. 'Owen Flynn? I'm Captain Edwin Tucker of the — '

'Yeah, yeah,' Flynn waved him off. 'I know who you are, Eddie. How many years have we known each other? I'll be right with you. First, I want to introduce you to a friend of mine.' Flynn went to the door and nodded.

I probably should have stopped him then — I had already decided to drop the whole St Miltonville Estates issue — but, like everyone else at the moment, I was just a spectator.

A moment later the man entered. He looked the same as the last time I had seen him. He still stood tall and straight and walked in a slow, measured pace. His face was still deeply etched, but I expected him to look much older. The only difference I could notice was that he was not dressed in his old flight fatigues, but instead in a loose fitting and long since dated grey tweed suit.

'Everyone, I would like to introduce you to Mr Amos Scuffield, veteran pilot, gentleman farmer, and ...' Flynn turned and winked at Freddie, 'demolitions expert. Amos, everyone.'

Amos looked around the room, nodding, then paused on Skidmore. 'Well, Wynnie, this is a surprise,' he said in low, gravelly voice. 'Aren't you dead yet? I heard it had been taps for ol' Wynnie Skidmore years ago.'

'Not quite, Scuffs,' Skidmore shook his head. 'Yet, I was sure I had outlived you, you old fart.'

'This is an absolutely heart-warming reunion,' Freddie said, 'but I'm out of here.'

'You're staying,' Flynn said, 'if I have to tie you to that chair.'

Freddie locked eyes with Flynn for a moment, then let out a bored sigh and leaned back in his chair.

'Flynn,' I said, 'this may not be the right time.'

'But you were right, and it took a lot of convincing to get this old man up here, and now you and everyone else are going to listen to what he has to say.' Flynn turned back to Scuffield. 'Now, Scuffs, would you mind telling these people who removed the structure formally known as Milton Gorge Control Tower.'

I exchanged a glance with Tucker, who shrugged, keeping his manila file tucked safely under his arm.

'Of course,' Scuffield smiled and turned towards Amanda. 'I did. You see, I had a business arrangement with Mr Moore here.'

'For Christ's sake,' Freddie huffed, 'now I've heard everything. You think you're going to turn Hardy's hearing into my trial? Nice try, but this is preposterous. Do you think they'll believe a fugitive and this old bag of bones over me?'

'Oh, there is no need to take my word for it, Mr Moore.' Mr Scuffield smiled at Freddie, as he reached into his coat pocket. The room was silent. All eyes followed Scuffield's hand as he slowly brought out a microcassette recorder, set it on the table in front of Amanda and, with a trembling index finger, pushed the play button. 'We can listen to your own words.'

Although the voices on the tape were somewhat muffled, they were unmistakable — Scuffield's rough, life-hardened voice, Freddie's Canadian accent and, in the background, Woodcock was snorting his disapproval. The tape was cued to the juicy bits.

'I think ten grand is pretty bloody generous,' Freddie was saying, *'considering you would probably do it for free. Don't think I don't know about that little stunt trying to fly your airplane through the building a few months ago.'*

'It doesn't sound completely legal. I would normally have consent from

the council to do this work,' Scuffield said in response, *'I'm a tired old man and I'm dying. I can't afford to be put through the stress of being arrested at this stage in my life.'*

'You won't be, I've already got that covered. Now listen, I told you — this may seem a bit unorthodox to you, but it's a legit request. My partners and I own that airport. We want the tower gone. If we do it this way, no one will have a chance to file protests. There will be a beautiful new subdivision there and the airport will be long forgotten before anyone even notices.'

'Long forgotten — I know the feeling.'

'Spare us the memories, Grandpa,' Woodchuck interjected. *'We didn't see you shedding any tears for your old mate Rumbold.'*

Hearing Thornie's name jolted my mind.

Of course, it was logically impossible for Freddie to do it. I pulled out the toxicology report again and scanned it as fast as I could, while everyone else continued to listen to Scuffield's tape — his 'insurance policy' as he referred to it when a job's legitimacy was dubious.

'Look,' Freddie started again, *'we all know you're dying to do this because you've always held a grudge against the place.'*

'Yes, I am dying,' Scuffield's voice was almost inaudible.

'The job is simple: remove the building, no casualties, and then you're never heard from again.'

No more casualties, I thought.

'So it's taps for Ol' Milton Gorge then, eh?' Scuffield said, which brought a loud snort of approving laughter from Woodcock.

'Ha! Taps for ol' Milton Gorge,' Woodcock repeated, *'I like that.'*

And it was taps, for old Thornie.

At this point, Scuffield reached up and hit the stop button. 'There's more of interest on there,' he said. Then he turned to Freddie and added, 'You don't really think I'm such a daft old fool as to have that conversation and keep no record of it, do you?'

Freddie shrugged, rolled his eyes back and pretended to be bored.

When Flynn had contacted his ex-landlord, Garrett Scuffield

— Amos's son — he was surprised to learn that Amos Scuffield was still alive, though no longer flying because he had been grounded due to his illness, and was living down-country with a daughter. But it was when I had phoned Norwynne Skidmore I had learned much more. Although it took him over an hour to tell me the story, I didn't mind because, apparently, he'd known Amos for the better part of fifty years and I really didn't mind letting him get started on the long, uncut version of that story. For one thing, it made me feel kind of good just listening to someone who enjoyed telling a good story properly, but it also filled in a little background info on Amos Scuffield. Like, for instance, that from the end of the war until about fifteen years ago when he retired, he was widely considered one of the best demolitions men in the country. If anyone wanted a structure removed cleanly and efficiently, he was the man to call. Or they could just look in the phone book under *Taps Structure Removals*.

Amos addressed Wynnie Skidmore. 'Oh, I tell you, after doing Milton Gorge Tower I felt revived, young again. Before the blast, my doctors told me I'd be dead within four months. But it did something to me — it made me feel alive again, it rejuvenated the very cells of my being. At least I agreed to the treatment, and look at me now — still kicking.'

'Wonderful! You've invented terrorism therapy,' Freddie said. Except for a brief angry glare at Scuffield while the tape was playing, Freddie appeared quite passive, considering he was totally screwed.

'I call it being cleansed by fire,' Scuffield smiled back. 'And so, Mr Moore, from the sounds of it, your operation was not entirely as legitimate as you claimed.'

'I have nothing to say. I know my rights. I am a lawyer, or at least was a lawyer. However,' he turned to Tucker and pointed at Flynn, 'you still have the man who torched my car and I want you to arrest him.'

'Excuse me,' I interjected, 'but I might be able to help you on that one. Woodchuck — I mean, Mr Woodcock — is the man you want to talk to about that.'

'What are you talking about?' Freddie asked, but he shifted in his seat nervously.

I shrugged. 'Sorry, Mr Moore, he told me you told him to do it. He also kind of let it slip about your arrangement with Mr Scuffield. We were peeing at the time. To be honest, I think he has it in for you and was expecting me to pass the info on.'

'Bullshit,' Freddie said. 'I never gave such orders. He wouldn't take such orders and he certainly wouldn't tell you.'

Freddie was right. It was bullshit. Woodcock didn't really confess to me. Not in so many words at least, but I think that's what he was getting at. In any case, I was taking another punt, but it just seemed that, if it wasn't Flynn but only made to look like Flynn, Woodcock was the logical alternative. And I wanted to keep Freddie there one minute more.

'Where is Mr Woodcock anyway?' Tucker asked. He walked across the room towards Freddie. 'Where was he really going?'

'Well,' Freddie rubbed his chin and thought about it. 'I believe he's on his way to the St Miltonville offices to destroy important evidence. He seemed to be a bit worried about some possibly incriminating documents in his briefcase.' Freddie looked down at his feet. 'Of course, in his haste, he grabbed my briefcase by mistake. You see, we have the same briefcase and often confuse the two. So I just hope he doesn't get carried away and go off destroying my ham and cheese sandwich. I'm pretty sure this one, however,' he lifted the other briefcase onto the table, 'is actually Carlton's because it has his monogram. See?' He pointed to the initials CVW. 'Except I think they got the middle initial wrong.' Then he spun the briefcase around to face Tucker. 'Well?'

'Well, what?' Tucker narrowed his eyes at Freddie.

'Well, we are on airport property, aren't we? And you are aviation security, aren't you? And, if I'm not mistaken, that gives you the right to search any bags brought on to the premises.' He nudged the briefcase closer to Tucker.

Tucker stared at it for several seconds before he reached down and pressed the buttons to open it, then carefully lifted the lid.

'Don't open it!' I said.

Tucker turned to me.

'Why not?' Freddie asked innocently. 'Don't you want to see whose name is scrawled all over those incriminating documents? 'Cos I can assure you it ain't going to be mine.' He smiled at Amanda, who ignored him and stared straight ahead.

'It's like you said, Eddie,' I said to Tucker, 'this is evidence for another investigation.'

Tucker considered this for a minute, then lowered the lid and pointed a sharp finger at Freddie. 'You don't move.'

'Where would I go?' Freddie shrugged, leaned back, clasped his hands behind his head and smiled at me. 'What kind of idiot do you think I am, Tommy boy?'

Tucker went to the telephone and called in an arrest warrant for Woodcock and requested a security detail to the boardroom.

'He's probably driving a stolen black BMW!' Freddie shouted at Tucker. Then he turned to me and said, 'You sure you don't want to open it up and see what's inside?'

'No,' I said. 'I'd rather you open this up.' And I tossed the brown paper wrapped square on the table in front of him.

'What's this?'

'Open it, Freddie boy.'

Tucker was trying to take it all in while talking on the phone at the same time. All eyes turned to Freddie as he reached across and tore the brown paper back.

'Gee, Tom, how considerate, you gave me a blotter. Of course, I don't know how much thought you put into this. After all, it's two years old and has a pretty messy stain on it.'

'It was Thornie's blotter,' I said. 'The one he died on.' Then I tossed the other piece of paper on top of it. That's the toxicology report. Surprising the number of chemicals a dried stain can be broken down into, but if you look mid-page you'll see one I don't think normally occurs in tea — potassium cyanide — especially in such high doses.'

Tucker put the phone down and started towards Freddie — just in time, as it turned out, because when it dawned on Flynn what I was saying, he made a lunge at Freddie. 'You son of a bitch! You murdered Thornie!'

Tucker caught Flynn's left arm as I caught his right to stop him from ripping Freddie Moore to pieces.

Freddie jumped back and stood in the corner of the room. Like a chameleon, his face was going as pale as the tasteful cream pastel colour Amanda had selected for the walls. It was the first time I had seen him scared, even panicky. 'Jesus Christ!'

'It was in the tea, wasn't it? Or more probably the milk is my guess.' I took a step closer to Freddie. Skidmore stepped up and took my place to gently but firmly hold Flynn back with Tucker.

'I don't know,' Freddie said as he looked from face to face of those encircling him. Even Skidmore looked like he wanted some serious answers or he'd let Flynn go. 'I swear to God! I wasn't even there! Don't you remember? Tom,' he turned to me with pleading eyes. 'Don't you remember, you found him. I came *after* you found him!'

'But you could've been out earlier and spiked the milk.'

'No, it was Woodcock! Remember, he was there earlier that day. He did it!'

'But you ordered it.' I stepped right up to Freddie. For some reason he didn't seem as tall as he used to be.

'No, I swear to God I didn't. I've always suspected it, I admit that. But I only knew for sure right now. He's a nutcase, and he has a background in chemistry. I didn't do it. He told me all I needed to do that day was to make sure the cup was washed and the milk tipped out before anyone else who might drink the milk showed up.'

'And you took orders from him?'

'No, I didn't have any intention to. But when I got out there and found what I found, I realised he was crazier than I could ever have imagined.' He looked from me to Flynn, to Amanda, to Skidmore, and back to Flynn. 'I'm sorry, I swear to God I never would have condoned such an action.'

By this time, the airport security had arrived and the police would soon follow.

As they led Freddie Moore away in handcuffs and the crowd dissipated, Colson finally left, disappointed there would be no hanging, but satisfied enough with the action to warrant his trip up from Wellington.

Tucker paused in front of Flynn and Scuffield. 'Mr Flynn,' he said, 'it would appear you might be an innocent man and Mr Scuffield, you might have had a valid contract to do what you did. If you two don't mind hanging around Auckland for a couple of days — I think I can expedite this matter with the police.'

Flynn nodded.

Tucker left.

'Well, I say,' Skidmore murmured after a moment's silence. 'Can't say we've seen this much action around this airport since Thornie, me and Abercrombie were — ' he stopped and looked around at the faces in the room. 'Yes, of course. Scuffs? What do you say we go find a pub that's willing to serve drinks to a couple of old dinosaurs, and we can raise a glass to Ol' Thornie?'

'That old bastard?' Scuffield asked. 'I guess it's as good a reason as any to have a pint or two.'

All that remained in the boardroom were myself, Flynn and Amanda.

I looked at Amanda. She was quiet, just staring down at her notepad.

'I'm sorry, Amanda,' I said.

She looked up. 'It was my father's name scrawled, as they say, all over those papers, wasn't it?'

I nodded. 'I'm sorry.' I exchanged a quick glance with Flynn. 'I just found out he was part of this a half hour ago. I was hoping it wouldn't be brought up. Anyway, this is pretty much all my fault and I — '

'Thomas,' she stopped me, 'thank you. But you needn't apologise for him — this is nothing new. It's just standard operating practices. It won't even cost him one hour with his solicitors in the end.' She stood up and started gathering her papers.

'So you see then?'

'See what?' she paused.

'You have nothing to prove to him. You're willing to stand up ...' I raised a hand to the now near empty boardroom, 'to jeopardise your own career advancement for what you believe. You're already a better man — I mean a better person — than he is.'

She looked at me and smiled. 'Thanks, Thomas. And thank you, Flynn. It was good seeing you again.'

'Likewise,' he shrugged, 'and maybe you should call me Owen — don't want to have to deal with too much change.'

Amanda started to leave, then stopped at the door, turned around and walked back to me. 'You know, Thomas, I'm quite busy this week. I suspect it will take me a full week to get to my in-box. If you change your mind about leaving ...' She finished the sentence with a tilt of her head and added, 'If not, then good luck,' and she leaned over, kissed me on the cheek and left the room.

'So, Cowboy,' Flynn said as we walked down the corridor, 'just out of curiosity, what was that shrink's diagnosis in the end?'

I stopped and turned towards Flynn, looked both ways to make sure there was no one within earshot and leaned close to him.

'Completely sane,' I whispered. 'Completely and utterly and more or less sane.'

'You're shitting me?' Flynn looked truly surprised. 'How did you pull that off?'

I shrugged.

'You going to be okay then?'

'Yeah, I think so. Not a god, not a speck of dust.'

Carlton Woodcock cruised along in the BMW, savouring the blur of pastoral scenery and the seamless craftsmanship of his new car.

At last! My BMW.

There was no reason why it wouldn't continue to be either — Freddie Moore was history. Carlton would make sure of that. Sure, he could go back and shred documents and get Freddie off the hook. On the other hand, if he didn't — if he just removed the documents to a safer location — Freddie Moore was history. Such a simple question really: to shred or not to shred? It was all in Carlton Woodcock's hands — he had control.

'It's taps for you, Freddie,' Woodcock said aloud and laughed as he pushed his glasses back up the tiny bridge of his nose. 'Time to rock and roll!' He gave the volume knob on his stereo a quick twist and the thunderous onslaught of surround-sound completely drowned out the siren that was rapidly approaching from behind.

Woodcock could only hear the crashing beat of the drums and the anguished cry of an electric guitar when he saw the flashing lights in his rear-vision mirror. The smile dropped from his face. 'What the?'

Then, slowly, the smile reappeared. He let out a snort and a loud burst of laughter. 'Bye-bye, Freddie!' He punched the accelerator. 'Yeehaaa!'

THIRTY-FOUR

Airport lounges just have that effect on me. How can you not be introspective while waiting for a plane to leave? Whether you are coming or going, travelling into the unfamiliar or the knowingly mundane, flying to the next town down the main trunk, or reaching for what Maori call *te taha atu o te rangi*: the far side of the sky.

I believe the reason airport lounges have that effect is two-fold — there is the forced meditation aspect of travel, coupled with the fact that it takes place in an environment that completely exemplifies the transient nature of life itself. We think of ourselves as static beings, but we never are. We are born, we travel through life, we die. Motion is, paradoxically, our natural stasis. And the airport lounge is a reminder of that — the plane unloads, the people mill about in chaos, and then they are gone. Life is not about being born and it is not about dying — it is about the journey between those two main hubs, and the airport lounge is the place where everyone must act out the physical manifestation of their spiritual lives: *I move therefore I am: this one travels light, that one is heavily burdened; this one is frightened by the strangeness, that one is thrilled by the unknown; this one just wants to get to the end, that one enjoys the ride.*

They should have more churches in airports.

I was thinking about this when I was looking out to the tarmac at the great lumbering beast — the Boeing 747 — that promised to take me home. Home? Or just back? Or backwards?

It was dark outside, and my thoughts and vision drifted between the otherworldly events going on to prepare that machine to stumble its way across the ground until it broke free, and the ghostly reflections of the people waiting for their journey. When I saw his reflection, at first I thought it was certainly my mind playing tricks on my tired eyes. But then, it didn't surprise me to see him sitting at the bar, having a drink.

I approached him.

'Buy you a drink?' Freddie asked as he twirled the ice cubes around in his vodka and tonic. He didn't look surprised to see me, either.

The barman approached and put a cocktail napkin on the bar in front of me.

I looked at Freddie, then at the barman. 'Glenfiddich on the rocks.'

'Put it on my tab,' Freddie said to the barman and waved his own glass for another.

'Going somewhere?' I glanced at Freddie's suitcase on the floor.

'There's a whole world of opportunity out there, Tommy boy.' He took a sip of his vodka. 'I've had enough of this business anyway — it's too insane.' He glanced across at me and smiled.

'Yet I could have sworn the last time I saw you was about eight hours ago being hauled off in handcuffs.'

Freddie smiled. 'Not my finest hour, I admit. All rather embarrassing. I'd just as soon wish that little misunderstanding was forgotten. But,' he toasted me, 'a lot can change in eight hours with the right connections, the right lawyers, and the right amount of money slipped into the right hands.'

'Little misunderstanding?' I asked. 'Are you telling me that if I didn't just raise my voice and call for security, that you wouldn't be back in custody in minutes.'

'I'd imagine law enforcement tonight is more interested in catching Public Enemy Number One.'

'So Woodchuck takes the rap?'

'Don't worry about Carlton, Tom.' Freddie laughed. 'He'll be the next CEO of ControlCorp.' He lifted his drink to his lips, but paused to add, 'I mean, after they catch him, of course, and if he beats the murder rap.'

The drinks arrived and I sat down on the stool next to Freddie.

'So you're going home then?' Freddie asked into his glass. 'Back to the old job, back to the old wife, back to your good old days, eh?'

'Not quite.' I pulled my boarding card from my pocket and looked at it. 'I suppose LA at least, but I can't go back — the wife is gone for good, and the job ...' I dropped the boarding card on the bar. 'I declined the offer. I decided you can't ever really go back.'

'Yet, you're still leaving?'

I looked into my drink. 'So where are you off to?'

'Well, Fiji tonight. Nobody is going to ruin that for me — not Amanda, not Carlton.' He pulled his boarding card from his pocket, waved it, then dropped it on the bar too. 'Then, I'm thinking Borneo.'

'Borneo?'

'Borneo.'

'Why Borneo?'

'I've noticed an opportunity opening up there in the rubber industry.' He looked at me and studied me carefully for a moment. 'You know, Tom, you're a good man — and I still could use a good partner. They got diamonds in Borneo. And real estate.'

I looked at Freddie and said nothing.

'No,' Freddie answered himself. 'I didn't think so. Pity. We could have made a great team.' He paused to take a sip of his drink. 'You idealists. Your problem is that you want to blame me for the death of democracy, but I'm not the one who's making the world like this. I'm just trying to make a buck in it before I'm outsourced too.'

'Is that the ControlCorp Culture? Where the only real value you hold is the value of money?'

'That's the Corporate Culture, Tom. And you Americans started it and took it to its extreme when the government outsourced governing to the Corporation. The days of democracy are over — it's a corpocracy all the way to the top.'

'And in this new society you've created, the class system is back, freedom of speech is out, respect for the working man is set back a hundred years. I thought we were supposed to be evolving.'

'Survival of the fittest, Tom.' Freddie smiled and took a sip of his drink. 'I didn't write that rule. There's just a new social structure in town. The truth is, in the business world you sometimes have to lie a little, cheat a little, maybe even steal a little — it's called progress, and progress is painful for the idealist, my boy.'

'You ever have to kill a little?'

Freddie paused his drink midway to his mouth and smiled. 'No. I can't do that because at heart I'm just a petty schmuck. Just a small-time, petty schmuck. It's just hard to shake away your roots, Tom.'

'Did you give the order?'

'Did you?' He turned and looked me in the eye as if he knew what had happened out at that river. He turned his attention to his drink. 'Of course you didn't. Neither did I — you have to draw the line somewhere, right? Besides, to do something like that you'd have to be a pretty nasty piece of work — and what kind of guy do you think I am? I just like playing the game, Tom. No, you'd have to be a real nutcase with a real mean streak.' He drained the rest of his drink, got off his bar stool, slipped his ticket into his pocket and picked up his suitcase. 'It's been a pleasure to know you, Tom. It's been a good game.' He reached his free hand out. 'Just remember, in the end, that's all it is — a game.'

'It's not a game to me.'

'I know. That's why as long as there are people like me, there will always be people like you. Keeps the universe in balance that way. That's just the truth.'

I looked at Freddie's outstretched hand and, hesitantly, took it.

Freddie smiled. 'And don't take things so seriously, you'll give yourself an ulcer.' He turned and walked away.

'You taking care of this?' The barman asked as he slid Freddie's tab in front of me.

Yeah, that was his truth. I guess it's different for everyone. I hope it is.

If there are people like Freddie, there must be people like Janey to keep the universe in balance. Life must be kept in balance. I've had this thing about people and their causes. I'm attracted to them, and scared to death to participate. I was scared all right. Scared because it was some nameless, faceless guy like Freddie Moore who killed my dad. Or maybe not.

My dad was committed to his cause. He was dedicated to his students, to literature, to the ideals of academia. But the university was changing its attitude, and he was becoming a dinosaur in his department. They tried pushing him into early retirement and he was fighting back — fighting a losing battle. He began drinking more; his black spells got longer, blacker and more frequent. I didn't know what his struggle was all about, not back then at least. I didn't care — his primary role in life, his purpose, as he saw it, was to maintain a tradition of excellence in education, to protect a heritage, to protect the past. All I wanted was for him to be my dad — take me fishing, buy me a dog. I didn't care about his crusade; I just wanted a dad.

I guess that's where my delusions of godness started. My problem was not feeling like an insignificant speck of dust, it was being God. But Flynn put me in my place. Flynn and his structure of the universe philosophy — not a god, not a speck of dust, but an integral part of a continuum. He had a certain kind of gumboot wisdom.

The seeds of my god-problem were planted a long time ago, but did not blossom until Thornie Rumbold died. I didn't believe the Corporation killed Thornie in the beginning. I wanted to. I wanted to believe someone had killed him — someone else. I needed to because the alternative was too painful. The truth was, I killed him. Or to be more accurate, the fiction was, I killed Thornie. Truth, fiction. They are not mutually exclusive and sometimes the line between them is blurred. And sometimes I've had a little trouble distinguishing between the two, because sometimes one becomes the other.

The idea that Thornie died precisely the same death as my dad was no coincidence because it did not happen. My dad died his death and Thornie died the death I had scripted for him. And telling Flynn and Sarah about it in the hut that last night on the Rangitikei was the first time I had spoken of it ever.

'I thought you might need a friend.' I could hear my dad's voice. '*Your wily snares an' fechtin fierce.*'

I lifted the puppy from the box up to my face. 'Wiley,' I said and the puppy approved by slurping his smelly little tongue across my nose.

'Can we take him fishing with us, Dad?'

But we never went fishing again.

On Saturday morning it had rained. When my dad returned from his meeting with the dean, he went straight to his den and shut the door without saying anything.

'He's not feeling well,' my mom said. Her face was pale, the day was grey — it is like a black and white memory, but it is the shades of grey that have become hard to define. Not feeling well. One of his moods. Daddy's delicate condition.

But this one was not like the others. This time the blackness came in and never let him go.

Later in the afternoon, my mother called me into the house. She was going out to the store to pick up a few groceries and wanted me to come along, but I wanted to stay and play with Wiley — I was still trying to teach him to fetch, but he was proving to be a slow learner. She said it would be okay, but only if I stayed in my room and kept very quiet until she got back. She reminded me not to bother my father.

So I went to my room to work on the Robert Burns poem and play with my dog. I tossed the red rubber ball across the floor and whispered, 'Fetch, Wiley, fetch,' and the dog would run over, stumble over the ball, try to get his little teeth into it and then try to keep me from getting it back.

I was playing tug of war with him, trying to get the ball back, when I heard a thud downstairs, as if someone had bumped his head.

No, it was like a *pop*.

Wiley pricked up his ears, dropped the ball from his mouth, looked at the door and let out a short whimper.

I went to investigate. I opened my bedroom door and looked out. There was no movement in the house.

'Dad?' I called quietly, too quiet for anyone downstairs to hear.

I stepped into the hall — the house was silent and still. I walked to the top of the stairs.

'Dad?' I called out, louder, leaning over the banister to direct my voice towards the door to my dad's study. There was no response, no sound, no movement. I inched down the first couple of stairs, the wood creaking under my feet. As I slowly crept down the stairs, the study door came into view. Halfway down, I tried calling for him again, but still no response. If I could just hear Dad's muffled voice, arguing with someone on the phone, or the slam of a desk drawer, or even the crash of a lamp. But there was nothing — nothing but a heavy, eerie silence. I continued slowly down the stairs and into the hall.

It was always a quiet house. But this, this was different. Like feeling alone in a thick fog, where the brain knew that there was life out beyond the greyness, in the shapes and shadows, but it still felt so alone. I was alone and I felt alone — but I was not supposed to be alone. I stood in the hall across from the study door.

'Dad?' I called again. The stillness crept in around me and I swallowed hard.

Alone.

My heart beat faster. I looked down the hall towards the stairs — Wiley was still at the top of the stairs, whimpering quietly. The house looked dark and gloomy — it was raining again outside. I remember the pitter-pat of the rain on the roof.

'Dad!' I called loudly, but still no response.

My hand shook as I reached up, turned the knob and pushed the door open just a couple inches. 'Dad?' I whispered through the opening. 'Can I come in, Dad?'

I peeked around the door. It was dark, the light was off and only a dim grey glow seeped in through the shades.

'Dad, I'm learning some Mr Burns for you. Do you want to hear it?'

At the desk, I could see the dark figure with his head down on his blotter. The room had the bitter smell of firecrackers and the smoke that slowly laced its way through the grey light towards the ceiling.

'Do you want to hear it?' My voice cracked. I stepped inside. '*Great is thy pow'r and great thy fame*;' my voice trembled as I whispered words I did not know I knew. Tears welled up in my eyes. '*Far ken'd an' noted is thy name; An' tho' yon lowin' heuch's thy hame, Thou travels far; An' faith! thou's neither lag, nor lame, Nor blate, nor scaur*. Dad?'

I stood before the desk and could see the dark pool forming on the blotter. My dad was face-down on his blotter. The handgun was still held tightly in his hand, its barrel pointed awkwardly towards the ceiling. I reached up to touch him. When I put my hand in the blood puddling on his blotter, it felt warm — almost hot.

'*An' let poor damned bodies be*!' I whispered.

My dad shot himself through the head. When the two of us were alone in the house — not counting his demons of course — he put a .38 revolver to his head and decided at that moment to stop being a dad. Or maybe he had never started. All I ever wanted was a dad who would take me fishing every once in a while. I guess I thought it was my fault — it was hard to believe he would do that.

In the months that followed my dad's suicide, the child psychologist told me repeatedly that it was not my fault. I would sit in the big blue chair in his office, staring at the wall and listening to the clock — tick, tick, tick. I never cried in his office, I never spoke, I just stared at the wall and listened to the ticking while he told me how sick my dad was. He told me my dad had not known I was in the house. My mom had said I was going with her. He told me over and over again that my dad had lost his job and was not thinking normal, that the blackness had descended and smothered him. He did not know what he was doing. But I just stared at the wall and thought it must have been my fault. It was hard to believe my dad would choose to leave this world instead of hanging out with me. I didn't want to believe it. Then I couldn't believe it. Then I didn't.

So I rewrote the script. Gave him a slightly more noble death. Heart attack, at his desk, while drinking tea. It sounded more civilised, I guess. It sounded so … English.

I spent more than twenty years trying to believe in things that weren't true. I pushed it down deep — down between what I believed and what was true, between truth and fiction. So I made something up. Heart attack, at his desk, while drinking tea. It was all fiction.

Then the fiction became truth. I wrote it, and because I had, someone ended up having to act it out. Thornie acted out the fiction of my dad's death down to the last detail — the wooden desk scarred with age and experience, the smell of old books, the warm tea and the kindly old man who left this world not by his choice, but by the choice of God and a heart attack. Just God's fault and no one else's. The Corporation did not murder Thornie — I did. I was the author of his life. I was his God. At least, that was how I felt when I found Thornie had acted out my fatal fiction almost to the letter.

The first time I met Owen Flynn, he stuck a signal pistol in my face and threatened to turn my head into a roman candle — or an ill-fated Corolla — I guess that was a clue right there. I could have turned and walked away. I'm glad I didn't.

I do not know if I will ever see him again, but I owe him everything.

It was the smell of the gunpowder. When I fired Flynn's rifle across the Rangitikei River, it was the smell that opened a door and let go an avalanche of memories that had been buried so long and so deep, and came back to hit me with brutal vividness. Every ghost in the closet came charging out like an army of Cossacks thundering across the steppes. I tried to explain it to Flynn, but I think he figured it out.

He and Sarah took me back inside the hut and while she made

coffee he sat me down and made me relive every moment of my dad's death. When I was all talked out, exhausted from sobbing, when I expected him to pat me on the shoulder and say, 'There, there, it was not your fault,' he didn't. Sarah just held me and stayed silent, occasionally giving me a gentle squeeze. Flynn remained silent for a few moments, then let out an amused little chuckle and asked, 'Did Thornie ever tell you how he lied about his age and enlisted in the Air Force?'

'What?' I did not know if I heard him correctly. Here I had just relived the most traumatic event in my life and he suddenly wanted to tell me a funny story?

And he did. He laughed at the thought of it and told me the story Thornie had told him about how he joined the NZRAF when he was sixteen and learned to fly in a Tiger Moth. When he was done with that story, he told me another about Thornie's days as a top-dresser, and another of Thornie and Skidmore in the early days of Milton Gorge and the airborne pissing contest those two had with Amos Scuffield from as far back as the post-war years. He told me about Thornie's long-suffering wife and his two daughters. He told me about everything he knew of Thornie. And when the sun came up again and we were still sitting in that hut talking about Thornie and my dad, it dawned on me what Flynn had done. He gave Thornie's life back. He knew if I could have known Thornie for the man he was, I would have known the man had lived a lifetime full of experiences and love and friends and adventure that had nothing to do with my dad or the script I had written.

No. Not a god. Not a speck of dust, either. To hell with psychiatry, to hell with the Corporate Culture and the New Social Order — give me the Rangitikei River and a couple of canteens of mountain screwdrivers any day.

I did not tell the shrink the truth about my dad, of course. That would have been crazy.

But that's when I decided to make an issue out of the incident. I did not know if it was the right thing or the wrong thing, if it was important or not — but it was important to me. So I decided to do it. Thinking of Janey, I decided to get rid of the safety net. That's why I called up my old boss Ted Kazniak and thanked him for going to bat for me, thanked him for getting me my job back, thanked him for being the kind of guy who thinks enough of people to do something like that. And then I said, 'No thanks,' and declined his offer. No safety net. Not this time.

Now it's over, and I find myself at another airport, in the departure lounge, looking at the great lumbering beast that would take me home or just take me back. Or not at all. Again I think about the corporate structure of the universe. Not god and not dust, but a place in the continuum — whether it was interpreting and reinterpreting the works of long dead poets, or trying to keep airplanes from running into each other, or being a right pain in the arse of the corporate execs — one role equally as important as the next.

Recognising my place was part of the battle, but where that place was remained to be seen. After we left the boardroom that afternoon, I went looking for Sarah on the patio. She wasn't there and I haven't seen her since. To me, she was everything I needed; she was the part that had always been missing in me. But that had to work both ways and I had hoped that her not being there was not her answer. It just felt empty without her.

And that's why I needed to be here tonight, in the departure lounge, waiting with the rest of the people who were embarking on their journey, all for different reasons: going home, leaving home, running to, running from, eager to embrace the new, reluctant to let go of the known. I needed to know what she wanted and this is where I would find out.

I saw her standing there long before she saw me. She was talking to the gate agent, almost arguing. The plane had been pushed back and was getting ready to taxi. I couldn't hear what she was saying, but I imagined she was trying to convince the gate agent to bring the plane back to the gate.

I stood there for the longest time behind her before I said her name: 'Sarah.'

She turned around and stared at me without moving at first. The gate agent looked somewhat relieved and took the opportunity to move on to other duties. She approached me slowly. Her airport security ID dangling from her pocket, she had used it to gain access to the departure lounge. She was smart, resourceful.

'I didn't want you to leave ...'

I pulled her close and kissed her. Then I looked her in the eyes — I had found my 'where'. I do not know exactly what she saw in mine, but I prayed it was the same, prayed there was something there for her — that she could see in me a part of her as if we were part of a continuum.

'I thought you were going to be on that plane.'

'No, couldn't do it in the end,' I said. 'Besides, I lost my ticket on a bet.' I held up the other ticket. 'But I probably would have boarded that flight to Fiji in another hour.'

'I've been thinking.'

'So have I.'

'There's so much I'm not sure about,' she looked into my eyes. 'But I thought maybe we could —'

'Be synergistic?'

She stared at me, then shook her head and smiled. 'I was going to suggest we get something to eat.'

'It's a start,' I said. 'Anyway, no more in-flight meals for me.' I pulled her closer and kissed her again.

'So who's got your LA ticket?'

'Freddie Moore. He pulled the ol' "switcheroo" on me in the bar.'

'You think we should contact aviation security? At least they could nab him at the other end.'

I looked towards the gate, at the great beast as it lumbered away into the blackness of the night. So ungraceful, like a whale trying to walk — but, boy, when it lifted off, that was something else entirely. When it broke free from the earth, when it stretched its wings and climbed into its element to where it belonged, it could fly to the far side of the sky and beyond. *Te taha atu o te rangi*.

Orville and Wilbur, even Richard Pearse would be proud of us. It was beautiful, it was magic.

'Naah.' I shook my head. 'It's like I've been trying to tell you guys all along — you got to look at the big picture.'

'Which is?'

'Well — if I'm not mistaken, Kenny is on duty on the Oceanic Sector tonight, right?'

'Yeah?'

'Without his rat?' I shook my head slowly. 'That flight will be lucky to end up in Bangalore.'

Tami Lee Ward

Daniel Myers grew up in California and has lived in New Zealand since 1987. He has travelled extensively throughout North America, Europe and Asia and has worked as a pilot, a flight instructor, an air traffic controller, an English teacher in China and a television scriptwriter. His publications include the novel *The Second Favorite Son* (2004), the acclaimed short story *The Bridge* (1998), and numerous articles. Aside from writing, he is currently publishing Aviation-English textbooks, runs a literary agency and is still active in aviation.